VIRTUAL STRANGERS

Sam Canning is a Northern Irish writer based in Edinburgh. *Virtual Strangers* is her debut novel. In her spare time, she can be found roaming the city to find the weirdest things she can and desperately trying to keep her one and only plant Stanley alive.

VIRTUAL STRANGERS

SAM CANNING

ZAFFRE

First published in the UK in 2023 by
ZAFFRE
An imprint of Bonnier Books UK
4th Floor, Victoria House, Bloomsbury Square, London, WC1B 4DA
Owned by Bonnier Books
Sveavägen 56, Stockholm, Sweden

Copyright © Samantha Canning, 2023

All rights reserved.
No part of this publication may be reproduced,
stored or transmitted in any form by any means, electronic,
mechanical, photocopying or otherwise, without the
prior written permission of the publisher.

The right of Samantha Canning to be identified as Author of this
work has been asserted by her in accordance with the
Copyright, Designs and Patents Act, 1988.

This is a work of fiction. Names, places, events and
incidents are either the products of the author's
imagination or used fictitiously. Any resemblance to
actual persons, living or dead, or actual
events is purely coincidental.

A CIP catalogue record for this book is
available from the British Library.

ISBN: 978–1–83877–922–1

Also available as an ebook and an audiobook

1 3 5 7 9 10 8 6 4 2

Typeset by IDSUK (Data Connection) Ltd
Printed and bound in Great Britain by Clays Ltd, Elcograf S.p.A.

Zaffre is an imprint of Bonnier Books UK
www.bonnierbooks.co.uk

Prologue

Dumping my bag at my work desk sent a flurry of loose Post-it notes flying all over the place.

Every. Single. Time.

They really needed stickier backs. I gathered them together and set them back on the desk.

Cora, the office manager, appeared behind me. 'Morning, Ada,' she said brightly.

She was a goddess of a woman, tall and willowy with a laugh that could pull a smile out of a stone. Despite being six months pregnant with mad morning sickness, she still managed to look as though she'd just ambled out of the pages of *Vogue*. I in no way felt like a total scruffbag beside her.

'Do you know the thing I miss the most about being not-pregnant?' she groaned, flinging her coat onto the back of her chair and setting her bag down.

'All the weekend parkour?' I hazarded.

'Coffee,' she sighed. 'Followed closely by the parkour, of course.'

'Fair.' I side-eyed my fresh takeaway cup guiltily. 'Still feel like you've spent the night wrestling a bear in a hedge?'

1

'That is a frighteningly accurate description.'

'Aw, sorry you've got it so rough. If it makes you feel any better, you look as if you've just had a week at a spa with minimal bear encounters.' It was true – the woman was glowing. 'Although it can't be relaxing for you to wrestle your way onto the Tube these days.' It was one thing I'd never got over missing about Edinburgh – the place was eminently walkable if you needed it to be.

'It certainly isn't.' She lowered herself into her chair. 'I hear your event last night had a few hiccups.'

I let out a tiny howl. 'Would that be the food that was delivered to the wrong address or the author getting lost en route?' Shaking my head, I took a sip of coffee. Instant regret as it burned through the top layer of my tongue.

Our boss steamed into the room a mere second later, barking 'Team meeting at nine thirty!' as she made her way to her desk.

Yeesh.

Cora and I exchanged glances. Veronica wasn't one for the warm and fuzzies but she usually spent at least a few seconds asking after us of a morning. We also never usually had a meeting at the very start of the day – the woman was strict, but she wasn't a monster. She made her way over to me. 'Ada, can I have a word with you in the meeting room now?' She spoke so quietly that her words didn't make it past me.

I felt a lump of molten dread settle into my chest. 'Yes, of course!' I said, far too brightly.

'I'll see you in there in two minutes.' She left the room as abruptly as she'd entered it.

I dashed to Cora's desk, on the other side of mine. 'Veronica wants to speak to me,' I huffed in a panicked breath. 'She's heard about yesterday. She'll know about all the things that went wrong. Oh my God, she's going to fire me!'

'Ada, you say this all the time. She's not going to fire you at a team meeting,' Cora replied.

'This won't be *at* the team meeting – she wants to see me now!'

There was an awkward pause. Yep. I was definitely going to be sick.

Cora put her hand on my arm. 'Hon, the food was the caterer's mistake and the author didn't use your directions. None of it's on you and I'll tell Veronica that happily.' I stepped back, definitely not convinced. 'Plus, you sorted it all out anyway,' she continued.

Nope. The squeezing in my chest would not be appeased. 'What else could it be?'

'Throw a dart in any direction and see what it hits,' she sighed. 'Veronica could be mad about literally anything. This festival is running on fumes, the goodwill of its poorly paid employees and whatever spare change Dan throws our way.'

I felt a small shiver at the sound of Dan's name. Six months in and the mere thought of him still made everything in me riot: I couldn't wait to see him later.

'You should probably go – you don't want to keep Veronica waiting.'

Banishing Dan to the back of my mind, I felt the panic flood back in. I forced my legs to walk me out the office door and into the meeting room.

I settled into a plastic chair in the airless, glorified stationery cupboard that masqueraded as our meeting room and tried not to fidget as I waited for Veronica to start.

As I watched her creak around, getting comfortable in her own chair, I distracted myself by once again trying to winkle out what on earth possessed a woman like her to get involved in organising a romance literature festival. She seemed more the type to be busting balls in some faceless corporation's boardroom – I couldn't exactly picture her curling up with a Mills & Boon at the end of a difficult day. And yet she could answer any question you threw at her on the subject, a fact I learned three weeks ago when I watched her cut the legs out from under a woman at an info event for the festival who was insisting romance was for 'bored middle-aged housewives with nothing better to do'. Veronica had responded with a brisk run through of statistics on the broad range of readership, tartly pointing out that Mills & Boon sold a book every ten seconds before finishing up with a blunt query on how many bored housewives that might amount to? Suffice it to say, the woman would not be saying that again in a hurry – at least not without a careful recce of her surroundings first.

'I'm sure you're wondering why I've asked you here.' Veronica's voice cut through the silence, dragging me back into the room. She took a deep breath. Was she nervous? Surely not? 'This is an incredibly delicate matter and not something I would ever normally get involved with, but this is a small team and I don't want to put you or anyone else in a . . . a difficult position.'

'Uh, OK?' I didn't see the point in hiding my confusion.

She watched me for a moment and her eyes felt like laser beams cutting into my head. Shit, did she know about Dan?

Anxiety laced through my veins.

No, that was ridiculous, she couldn't possibly know. And even if she did, it wouldn't matter, would it? OK, so he was the festival's main – only benefactor, really – but it wasn't as if he was my boss. Plus, we were both single, consenting adults.

'How long have you been in a relationship with Dan Townsend?'

And there it was.

So much for keeping it to ourselves. I somehow managed to hold onto my poker face; not that it mattered, because those laser beam eyes weren't having any of it.

'I'll make this easy on both of us, Ada, and tell you that I already know you are. The two of you are not as subtle as you like to believe.'

I felt my face heat up and cursed my burning cheeks for giving the game away. Yet another downside to being so pale I was practically see-through. I was not, it would appear, built for subterfuge.

'So everyone knows?' I asked, willing my embarrassment away by telling myself sternly that there was nothing to be embarrassed about. Except the whole 'boss having to talk to me about my sex life' thing, of course. That was, perhaps, a smidge embarrassing.

'Actually, no, I don't think they do. As it stands, I believe yourself, Dan and I are the only people in this particular circle to know.'

'Oh, OK. Good.' I settled in for the inevitable lecture on the ethics of the situation and lined up the carefully worded rejoinder I'd been crafting for this very eventuality. If only I could remember a single word of it.

I looked up and found that Veronica's laser stare had softened, which was somehow worse. The whole thing had the vibe of being chased by a shark only to have it offer you a cigarette.

'Ada, I'm not here to judge anyone's actions. I don't care what you do in your spare time, it's none of my business.'

Erm, OK.

She paused a moment and I braced for impact.

'But his wife has decided she wants to get more involved in the festival, at least until the baby comes, and I don't want anything derailing the chance of us pulling this off. Do you understand?'

His *what*? The *baby*? What the fuck was going on? I somehow scrabbled words. 'S-sorry, I . . . what?'

Veronica repeated her sentence more slowly. It didn't help. There must be some kind of misunderstanding.

'Dan doesn't have a wife. He's not – they're separated.'

Veronica's face shut down completely. It was a look I'd only ever seen her do once before, on a day back when I'd first started and we heard we'd lost our council funding. I felt my stomach flip.

'No, no, they are,' I continued blindly. 'There were papers.'

Veronica sat back in her creaking seat, looking slightly cornered. 'Did you see any of these papers?' she asked, gently.

Did I? I tried to think back. 'No, b-but he . . . he said there were. Why would he lie about that?'

There *were*.

Veronica's shuttered look was gone now, replaced with a pained kind of sympathy that was somehow infinitely, *infinitely* worse. I didn't know much about her private life except that there had once been rumours of an affair with a TV breakfast show host. She leaned forward and put a hand on my arm.

'I'm sorry, Ada. I thought you knew.'

In a moment of blinding clarity, I understood that this meeting was her way of letting me off a hook I hadn't even known I was on.

Because of course there weren't papers. Dan was still married. And his wife was having a baby.

God. Oh God. Oh *fuck*.

Chapter One

The door hit the inner wall of the school office with a bang. In its wake, Amanda, the insanely glamorous school secretary strode through – not the usual type you'd expect to find working the reception of a Catholic secondary school in Edinburgh. On closer inspection, she was distinctly less majestic than usual, though.

'Hi, Ada, have you been into the gym hall?' she asked, in a tone that suggested that all might not be well in said gym hall.

'Not since lunch. Why?'

'Um . . . you're going to want to see this for yourself.'

God, I hated that hall. Every time I went in, I found myself catapulted screaming back to my own school days by the chipped wooden floors, gloss beige paint and the ghost of a thousand endless PE lessons. And I hadn't even gone to this school.

Gesturing to the dozens of name badges I was desperately trying to wrestle into plastic wallets before the event kicked off, I replied, 'I'll just finish these up and I'll be right in.'

She grimaced. 'OK, let me rephrase. You have to see this for yourself because the Headmistress is insisting that you do.'

8

I felt a flutter of panic. 'What? Why?'

Amanda was looking more concerned by the second, but there was something else in the background. If I didn't know any better, I'd have said she was trying not to laugh. 'There's been . . . let's call it a mix-up with the display for Steve's book talk.'

Of course there was. Since I'd started working as Steve Annick's publicist three months previously, I'd asked him to do one single thing because I had run out of time – send the cardboard display image to the printer for what was *technically* a promotional event for his TV show's upcoming anniversary, but I was also piggy-backing his soon-to-be-released autobiography onto. That was it. That was all he'd needed to do. How on earth had the man managed to screw that up?

I threw down the tag I'd been fiddling with and took a deep breath. 'OK. On a scale of one to clown massacre, how bad is this?'

'You're looking at a squeaky-shoed eleven, I'm afraid.' Amanda, a woman I'd never set eyes on before today but who was growing steadily in my estimation, gave me what would be a grimace on a less beautiful person. 'Sister Catherine is threatening to lodge a complaint with "whoever is overseeing this abomination". I won't lie, she's a step away from calling in the Swiss Guard.'

Jesus. I pulled myself out of the chair and made a dash for the door, swiftly followed by the clip-clop of Amanda's heels on the horrible seventies lino.

The assembly hall was no more than a hundred metres from the school office, but my stress levels had me huffing as though I'd run a marathon by the time I hit the double doors. Swinging my way into the room, I came face to face with a pursed-lipped nun wearing a frown so deep you could have buried bodies in it. Which was entirely fair, given that behind her stood three display stands and a giant cardboard cut-out of an almost-naked Steve, twenty years younger, seductively draped across a velvet couch in nothing but the tightiest of whities. The words INSERT TITLE HERE were also rather unfortunately positioned.

My palm hit my mouth without me even registering it moving.

'Good gracious! Lord in heaven!'

I spun to find two more nuns staring from the doorway and crossing themselves. Honestly, cheap event space was for the birds. This was the last time I was doing anything in a Catholic school.

'*What* do you call this?' the Headmistress demanded.

I couldn't think of a single thing to say. I was going to *murder* Steve.

Mind whirring, I cleared my throat. 'I'm so sorry about this; there's clearly been a mistake with our order and I will be writing a strongly worded email to the printer about it.'

'There are children seeing this – this filth!' She gestured to the windows that ran along the corridor to the left, where a gaggle of giggling schoolchildren were peering in. 'It's practically pornography!'

'Well, I mean, you're not seeing any actual . . . private bits,' I reasoned.

Her face suggested this was the wrong route to take. I held up my hands. 'No, of course, you're right. This is

10

unacceptable filth and I'll get it all covered up immediately.' To be fair to her, no one in the world needed this image in their lives. 'Would you happen to have something nearby we could throw over them?'

Without even blinking, she shook her head. 'No, I'm afraid we don't.'

'Nothing at all?' I nudged. 'Gym towels or, um, tarpaulin maybe?' Tarpaulin? What on earth would a bunch of nuns need tarpaulin for? Their rooftop swimming pool?

As I galloped through a list of ever less useful suggestions in my head, I heard Amanda quietly murmur, 'Perhaps you could erect some wood around it?'

Stifling a giggle, I sent a silent plea for help in her direction.

Mercifully wading in to save the day, she turned to the Headmistress. 'Sister, I'm sure we can find something in the building that will do the trick. I think there might be some dust coverings in the store cupboard?'

The nun gave her an ironclad glare. It was nice to have it redirected, albeit momentarily. 'I don't know that there is.' The glare reverted back to me. 'But if you don't get this covered right now, I'm going to have to ask that you move your event to a different venue.'

Oh, come *on*. 'No, no, there's no need for that – we'll get it sorted right now.' I sent Amanda another pleading look.

'Let me go and see what I can rustle up.' She went out through the double doors as I called out my thanks after her.

The Headmistress and I were left looking at each other in the now ringing silence, occasionally helpfully punctuated by passing teenage sniggers. I searched around for something to appease the increasingly truculent nun until Amanda's return. 'Um, how about I get these turned around in the meantime?'

Now that I thought about it, why hadn't it occurred to me to just do that before? Desperate to move myself out of her line of fire, I hurried across to the stands and pulled around the first one I reached. I stood back to admire my genius problem-solving skills.

The printer had put the image on both sides of the stand.

Well, wasn't that thorough of them.

Was there any point in turning the others?

On balance, I couldn't bring myself to move back into the Headmistress's sights so I decided I'd do it anyway. As I moved to turn the second one, Amanda re-entered the room, her arms full of dust sheets, her face barely hiding a grin. Thank Christ! Dashing over, I grabbed one from her. As I tried to toss it over the top of the first stand, I vowed to myself that if I ever needed display of any kind again, the damn things would be retractable – extra faff be damned.

And Steve was going to rue the absolute day when I got hold of him.

Chapter Two

Despite being so tired I could *feel* gravity, I decided to forgo the delights of sharing a noisy lift home with Steve and walked instead. The days were getting towards their longest point now and though the sun was well on its merry way to the Southern Hemisphere by the time I hit Princes Street, the sky was still a riot of hazy pinks and purples. The castle and gardens basked in front of it and even I could admit that this city had an obscene amount of scenery. Obscenery? At least that was one upside to schlepping back home to live with your mother with your tail between your legs at the grand old age of thirty.

By the time I got to Dalry, the ache in my feet was seeping its way up my legs, making me walk like a ninety-year-old. I slipped my key into the front door of the building and dragged my exhausted carcass up the dimly lit stairs to my mum's place. You could live in the fanciest of flats in Edinburgh and still feel like you might be mugged in the crack-den stairwells – although, admittedly, Dalry was not what you might deem a fancy area. The faint smell of scented candles and lemon cleaning spray greeted me as I made my way through the front door and heard Mum call out a cheery hello.

'Hey,' I called back, shucking my shoes off and hanging my coat on the too-high coat rail in the hall. It was hard to credit why Mum had placed it where she had – at five feet six, I still had to practically scale the wall to reach it. 'I thought you'd be in bed already.' I made my way into the cosy living room, noting the addition of yet another plant on the brightly tiled fireplace that would no doubt die in screaming dehydration three weeks hence. God bless the woman, she never lost hope that one of them would one day make it.

Mum smiled up at me from the sofa, still in her nurse's uniform, her hair pulled up in a messy bun. It was uncanny how alike we were – on more than one occasion we'd been mistaken for twins, which I didn't find quite as much fun as Mum did. But they weren't necessarily wrong. We had exactly the same blue eyes, we were both a size twelve and had the same size feet, which was handy back in the day when I would steal her shoes and sparkly tops and sneak to the pub with my best friend Amal and our fake IDs. Even our hair was almost identical in colour, if not style – dark brown with a hint of a wave – but she put red lowlights in hers and somehow managed to make it look cool in an effortless sort of way. I'd learned long ago that mine was best straightened, hung high in a slightly curly ponytail, or buried under hats all the way.

'Just catching up on *Heartbeat* – thought I'd wait up to see how your event went.'

Mum had recently discovered a glut of ancient Sunday afternoon TV on-demand and had been binge-watching a parade of pensioners solving the world's least credible crimes ever since. She was obsessed. I slumped down onto the other end of the sofa to the sounds of an old man trying to hide a chicken he'd clearly just stolen from a neighbour.

'You know they've made new TV since the nineties, right?'

'It will never hold a candle,' she replied, pausing the TV in case a vital clue was missed. 'How did Steve's talk at the school go? I still can't believe my daughter's wangled her way into being a PA for a real-live famous person.'

I fought the urge to remind her that I was a publicist, but, to be fair to her, I'd basically also turned into his PA at this point so the confusion wasn't unjustified. Just the other day I'd spent four hours moving furniture around his house for a photoshoot because he didn't like how it looked. I sure as hell didn't remember that being part of the deal when I took him on as my first-ever client. And that was before today's unmitigated shitshow. I stretched out my arms and yawned. 'Aye, right,' I snorted. 'Steve Annick: known to literally dozens of people in the Midlothian area.'

Mum waved her cup of tea indignantly at me. 'Hey! *Leith, Laugh, Love* was my favourite soap growing up – *EastEnders* be damned. That man is a national treasure.'

'He's a national something, all right,' I grumbled. 'You won't *believe* what happened today.' I regaled her with the tale of the display disaster, watching her crinkle up with laughter.

'You're not serious?'

Pulling out my phone, I showed her the pictures I'd taken. She crumpled up again.

'I thought the nun was going to have conniptions. If the receptionist hadn't found the dust sheets, I think I'd have had to resort to sticking on fig leaves.'

'Well, as a nun I'm sure she'd have appreciated the biblical subtext.'

It was my turn to snort. 'The best bit was that when I pulled him up on it, he tried to say it was a mistake. Aye, he just so happened to have accidentally mixed up a black-and-white headshot with an eighties glamour photo that I have *seen* him showing people, as if it's anything like what he looks like now!' I sucked in a frustrated breath.

'Ach, you love him, really. All grist to the mill for the show and his future book sales, isn't it? Plus, you'd be bored stiff if he wasn't a character.' She took a last gulp of her tea and set the mug down beside the sofa.

'Doubt that.' I glanced at my phone to check Steve hadn't somehow managed to offend any more nuns on his way home. Urgh. How was it nearly eleven already? 'How was your day?' I asked.

'Just the usual,' she shrugged. 'Here, you'll never guess who came into A & E today.'

'Ooh, was it a celebrity? Someone hot? Can I have their number?' Nothing ventured.

'You absolutely do not want this man's number.'

I wrinkled my nose. 'Who was it?'

'Dermot Clemont.'

Why was that name so familiar? I wracked my brain. 'Wait, that fascist millionaire guy?'

'The very one.'

'No way! What was he in for?'

'In an unsurprising twist, a punch to the face.'

'Hah. Did you treat him?'

Mum shrugged. 'It's not exactly optional. I did make a point of pulling harder on the stitching than may have been strictly necessary, though.'

'All this violent TV you've been watching is clearly rubbing off on you.'

I watched a smile pool across her face. She'd always seemed young for her age to me, probably because she'd been so much younger than all my friends' mums growing up. But she was looking more and more tired as the job got harder and harder and I felt a wave of guilt. She'd been a nurse for thirty years and it never ceased to amaze me how she still had any energy or enthusiasm for it because, by all accounts, it was a shitshow. She'd come home with all these mad stories or just the fact that she'd been on her feet for fourteen hours, for rubbish pay in horrible conditions, and then ask me what I'd done with my day. My response would usually be something ridiculous like, 'Oh, you know, just spent a couple of hours on the phone and then the rest of the day trying to hammer home to a middle-aged man that it's not in fact educational to tell a WI group that you once had sex with a Page 3 model in the back of a Honda Civic.'

'Who's Dan?' Mum asked now.

I surfaced from my mini-spiral. 'Huh?'

'You just got a message from someone called Dan.'

17

I looked down and, sure enough, there was a text flashing up with his name on it. I felt my stomach heave. Every goddamn time, despite my clear instruction to never contact me again. I'd left all his messages unread, to show him I didn't give a shit about what he had to say, but every one pulled harder at the threads of my willpower.

It took a second for the room to settle again. 'Nobody. Just a guy I know.'

'I knew a Dan once. He was a prick.'

I let out a laugh. 'I'll be sure to let the rest of the Dans know.' Although she certainly wasn't wrong about this one.

'I'm on the night shift tomorrow. In case you want to bring him over?' She gave me a shimmy.

Heat seeped into my cheeks. 'Mother!'

'I'm only saying, you never bring anyone home! I just wondered if this might be one I'd get to meet?' she grinned. 'Don't worry, I'll save the really good stuff for the wedding speech.'

Her words wrapped around me and squeezed. I forced myself to return her smile, as his unread message burned a hole in my brain. 'There's no one to meet. Really.'

Mum replied by making a kissy noise.

I waved her away. The kissy noises did not abate.

'You're the worst. I'm going to bed.'

'If you must.' She nodded to the TV. 'But you're missing out on a great episode. Some hippies have come through in a caravan and they've brought absolute anarchy with them. They're smoking and drinking and listening to all sorts of racy music. And don't even get me started on the poultry racket this guy has happening.'

'Oof, it's all go in Aidensfield.' I pulled myself up off the sofa, leaned over and kissed her on the head. 'Don't let Nick Berry get you too riled up before bed.'

'I mean, he's no Steve Annick.'

I stuck out my tongue.

'Night night, sweet pea,' she laughed. 'Don't let the bedbugs bite.'

The sounds of chicken-related criminality and rowdy hippies followed me down the hallway to my bedroom. Closing the door behind me, I leaned back onto it. Mum had a penchant for redecorating and my room hadn't escaped in the years I'd been gone. A feature wall of deep green pulled emphasis from the white side walls and wooden floors, giving the place a slightly foresty feel. Overall, I liked it. I was glad that my move home hadn't included being catapulted back to my childhood bedroom at least. No need to be reminded about my terrible boy band phase just now.

Pulling out my phone, I stared at Dan's name for what must have been a whole minute. He did this, sometimes. Sent messages, usually late at night. Late nights and lunchtimes had been his meet-up message *modus operandi* when we'd been together. Though I assumed the late nights were more baby-related these days.

And there was that bastard ache again, creeping into every single crease of me, wringing all of the oxygen out of my lungs. In that moment, the endless potential energy of all those unread words were like hot wires snaking around my chest. The idea that there could be something somewhere in those messages that might make what had happened between us less of a regret, less of a loss, less of an ongoing open wound . . . Oh, it was impossible to resist. Reading one wouldn't hurt. Just to see.

I closed my eyes and forced air back into my lungs.

Not today, Ada!

I swept the notification off my screen and felt the pull of it slacken slightly. I hadn't quite managed to bring myself to block his number yet. That was a problem for Future Ada. Future Ada was not a huge fan of present, or indeed past, Ada.

I moved across the room and threw my phone on the bed, properly tuning into my surroundings. It took a moment to put my finger on what was different.

Yep, the room had been tidied up. The bin was empty and the bedding was changed again. I peeked into my wash basket to find the rest of my suspicions confirmed – it too was empty. Irritation itched my teeth. I loved the woman, but how many times did I have to tell her that I'd been an independent entity for over a decade now and that I could clean my own room? I reminded myself once again that I was lucky to have a mother who welcomed me home with open arms as I pulled back the covers and crawled into bed. It smelled of soap powder and guilt.

After ten minutes of trying to get comfortable, I sat up to plump my pillow. As I turned, I spied something new but somehow familiar in the corner by the wardrobe. Clambering back out of bed, I knelt down to investigate.

It was an old shoebox, completely covered in band stickers and buttons and glitter and in massive black felt tip pen over the top read: ADA's – DO NOT OPEN.

No *way*.

I pulled open the lid. Inside was a litter of old writing pads, scribbled notes, badges, cinema and gig tickets, wristbands, and an endless parade of magazine cuttings. I pulled a few of them out and scattered them on the bed, feeling a swell of nostalgia. I'd thought these things were long gone – where had Mum found this?

Pulling apart the crackling paper, careful not to tear it, I read through the bright, scrawling handwriting. There was note after note, full of chatter from people I hadn't seen in years and names I'd completely wiped from my memory. Who on earth was Callum and why was past-me so obsessed with his backpack? It was a mystery.

God, and how many hours had I spent neatly cutting out articles on local emo bands, saving notes and mementoes, decorating the box itself? Though I had to admit, giant pearl-like sequins were a bold artistic choice. I could so clearly remember doing it, too, feeling like it was the most important thing in the world. At the bottom was a sheaf of printer paper folded in half. I opened it up and almost let out a whoop of laughter. *How* had I forgotten I used to write fan fiction?

Pages and pages tumbled out. But not just any old fanfic. Oh no, heaven forfend it should have been the run of the mill 'Team Edward or Jacob' stuff. Nope, I'd gone full tilt, all in for Agatha Christie.

As I fought through my terrible handwriting and endless spelling mistakes, I thanked the heavens that I'd kept this to myself. *Imagine* if this had found its way online.

And then I remembered that it actually had, via the medium of an ancient Agatha Christie fan fiction site – the kind that had been chock-full of colourful backgrounds and Comic Sans. I hadn't thought about it for years. It surely couldn't still be there? Feeling a wave of giddy embarrassment, I reached for my laptop.

I typed a few different options in and scrolled through. Sure enough, a website matching the name of the old one was there. Feeling a flutter, I entered.

If it was the same one, it'd definitely seen an upgrade or two, though it was still fairly basic. And it had none of the original stories, thank Christ. But I was surprised at how many stories there still were, and recently uploaded too. I clicked into some and actually found them pretty compelling. As I read through, I realised that the buzzing in my brain that had started when I'd seen Dan's name flash up on my phone had settled down. Not now I'd noticed it, of course. No, it was well and truly back, flashing through my head like a bike light in a blackout.

I picked up the handwritten pages – a short story I'd once submitted as part of a local library competition. Maybe a little jaunt back to the past might be a nice distraction from the present. I could rewrite it, maybe pop it up on the website. What harm was there? Mum and Amal were forever harping on at me to find new hobbies and make new friends, after all.

There was a sign-up page to create an account. Before I could change my mind, I clicked in to set up a basic profile. It immediately demanded both a username and a mandatory picture to go with it.

A careful run-through of everything that rhymed with my own personal Lordess and saviour, one Miss Jane Marple, gave me a brainwave. I typed out my chosen username. After a brief search, I found the picture to go with it, an admittedly very low-res photo of Brie Larson. Job done, I hit save and surveyed my new domain with pride. A message popped up in the corner.

Hello, Captain Marple,
*   Welcome to Agatha Christie Fan Fiction!*
*   Before you get started, please take a moment to go through the site to familiarise yourself with how it all works, including how to upload new stories, direct message, review and comment on other people's work, and the rules and regulations of the site. We look forward to seeing what your little grey cells come up with!*
*   Best wishes,*
*   ACFF.*

Chapter Three

It was my weekly dinner at Amal's. As I turned into her driveway, I took a second to wallow in the fact that she had a whole actual driveway to turn into, and in fancy old Morningside, no less. Growing up in an Edinburgh tenement and then spending eleven years moving from grotty London hovel to grotty London hovel really gave one an appreciation for a good solid driveway. Which didn't even make sense because I didn't own a car and couldn't drive, but there were probably worse things to aspire to in life.

I made my way through the inexplicably unlocked front door of her house to find chaos unfolding. As I shut it behind me, a naked toddler streaked past with what could only be described as a maniacal giggle, swiftly followed by a distinctly less amused Amal.

'Benji, I swear to God if you pee on this carpet again— Oh, hello, pet, how did you get in?'

'The door wasn't locked.'

'Shi . . . ugar – really?' Amal reached out and caught the escapee, in one fell swoop, scooping him up and hauling him back towards the bathroom. 'I must have forgot when I brought the shopping in. Aiden's in the kitchen.'

24

I saluted, following the smell of something delicious. Since I'd arrived back in Edinburgh, Amal had insisted on feeding me once a week. Thankfully, it was her husband doing the food prep though, because she was an abominable cook. We'd met in a Home Economics class when we were eleven years old and although many things about our lives had changed since then, her terrible cooking wasn't one of them. I found Aiden stirring a pot, crooning 'Three Blind Mice' in a Kermit voice to a baby in a high chair.

'Hey, Aiden, hey, Mo.' I leaned in and gave the baby a kiss and a tiny high five. 'I see Benji is as fond of bath time as ever.'

'Yep. Amal drew the short straw this evening.'

'Well, I've brought the usual bottle of wine to ease the process,' I announced, producing it from my bag and setting it on the table.

'She'll be glad of it tonight.' As if on cue, a squeal pierced the air. 'That'll be Benji in the bath now.'

'Or Amal.'

'Hah, probably.' Aiden moved to the counter and poured me a glass of wine from an already opened bottle. 'How are you doing, pal?'

I settled into the chair beside Mo and assumed the standard baby entertainment stance of cooing and shaking his teething rattle for a moment. 'Oh, just wading through an unbelievable amount of work admin shite. Ach, sorry, Mo.' Not swearing was by far the hardest part of hanging out with other people's babies.

Aiden laughed. 'He's seven months old – I'd say you're fine.'

This was one of the things I loved most about the A-Team. For such a disgustingly successful couple, they were very laid-back parents. Not in a negligent 'future documentary' sort of way, they just had a surprising knack for not getting wound up about a situation that, to me at least, looked as if it could get you pretty tightly wound.

'How about you?' I asked. 'Still enjoying your pat leave?' Aiden had stepped back from his software engineering job a couple of weeks ago to take over baby-wrangling duties when Amal went back to work.

'Aye, the jump from one to two's been interesting,' he replied. 'But we seem to be managing all right, don't we, Mo?' Mo seemed largely indifferent which, on balance, probably meant they were managing just fine.

'What's for dinner?' I asked. 'It smells incredible.'

'Tonight we're having roast gnocchi with blue cheese and wild garlic pesto and sticky toffee pudding for dessert.'

'God, I knew I was right to tell Amal to shag you.'

'And you charged such reasonable bribery rates.'

'What can I say? I'm a giver. Can I do anything to help?'

'You're doing it by keeping him entertained.' Aiden turned his attention back to the pan of amazing food.

The kitchen door opened and Amal strode in with a calmer, now be-nappied Benji in her arms.

I moved across to greet them, taking Benji into a huge hug before he demanded I be introduced to his new dinosaur.

'Absolutely not,' Amal interrupted. 'Dino is in bed, which is exactly where you're going, mister.' This went down like a lead balloon.

Somehow, between the three of us, we managed to get the kids safely in bed and out for the count with food on the table at a reasonable hour, which meant we were getting to eat in peace and quiet. Not always the way the cookie crumbled.

'Well, this is as delicious as I'd hoped,' I mumbled, shoving another forkful of gnocchi goodness into my face. 'Nailed it again, Aiden.'

He leaned forward in a small, seated bow and then took a sip of his wine. 'I do my best.'

'I feel bad that you're always cooking, though. Maybe you could come to mine for dinner one night?'

Amal did a comedy spit-take with her wine. 'Do you *remember* how we met? I ended up having to help you clean potato off a classroom ceiling!'

'Hey. That was not all me!' I reminded her. 'And anyway, it's been at least six months since I've got potato on a ceiling.'

She nimbly changed the subject. 'So how is the flexible workspace going? It's still that café on Lothian Road, right?'

I nodded as I chewed.

'Not as disruptive as you'd worried it might be?' She swept her hair over her shoulder and out of her way.

It never ceased to amaze me how, even though she was back at work full-time – as a lawyer at a huge investment company, no less – and raising two tiny wrecking balls, she still looked incredible. I'd been keeping a weather eye open for a hidden picture of her somewhere in the attic but had yet to find it.

'Yeah, I think so. The café owners have a back room they set aside for people paying for the workspace and it's pretty nice. Bright and quiet, although they could do with a few more sockets.'

'And how's Ol' Soapy Steve doing?' Aiden refilled my wine glass as he spoke.

'Please don't call him that – I've only just managed to get local media off it.'

He laughed. 'Sorry. Bad week, eh?'

I sighed. 'No, actually it's been pretty quiet on the Western Front – by his usual standards at any rate. He did seem to feel pretty scundered on this one.'

'I still can't believe you took him on as your first proper client,' Amal said. 'Talk about biting off more than you can chew.'

'Gah, don't,' I groaned. 'He's totally harmless – he just hasn't quite caught up with how technology works these days.'

'It was quite the eye-opening video for him to "accidentally" tweet. I didn't even know you could do that with a bar of soap.' We all paused to ruminate on an image we'd probably never be able to scrub from our minds. 'Are you sure it wasn't some kind of publicity stunt?' Amal continued.

28

'I don't *think* it was intentional; he seemed genuinely taken aback when I pointed out that it was up there for all to see. Although "Soapy Steve" could now be his epitaph and I think he might be loving it.'

'Well,' offered Aiden, 'worse things happen at sea.'

I sighed. 'Try telling the producers of *Leith, Laugh, Love* that.' Their geriatric demographic had had more than a few things to say on the subject, which was surprising because I'd assumed they'd be as technologically illiterate as he was. The show's sponsors weren't thrilled either. 'On the plus side, I've finally got him to give up the passwords to all his social media accounts so at least I can limit the damage if he decides to do it again.'

Aiden stood up. 'Dessert?'

'Yes please, you absolute king,' I replied.

As Aiden pottered about sorting the sticky toffee pudding, I turned the tables. 'So what about you? How's work been?'

Amal gave me a tired smile. 'It's been a bit of an adjustment. But they put a profile of me on the website and I've been asked to do an interview in *Lawyer Monthly*, which is nice.'

'Ooh, that's fantastic! Let's see the profile.'

She found it on her phone and held it up.

I let out a squeak as I gave it a scan through. 'This is so cool – you're so fancy! That's a great picture, too. You look like you're about to go and shout at Tom Cruise in a courtroom.'

'Hah, yeah. Except that they had to crop the bottom half because my boobs leaked on the way there so there were giant wet patches of milk. A triumph of a day.'

Aiden set bowls of the steaming dessert in front of us and the sweet spiced smell made my mouth water. God, that man knew his way around a sticky toffee pudding.

'Leaky boobs or no, you look great.' I picked up a spoon and dug in. 'When is the interview? Want to go through some prep beforehand? I can give you some points and prompts I put together for Steve?'

'I wouldn't say no. I'll send you the date and we can go through it maybe the day before?'

'Works for me.' I took a mouthful of delicious dessert. 'Compliments to the chef, this is incredible. Really got to find myself a man who can cook.'

I caught a look pass between the two of them. It wasn't the first one this evening either. 'What?'

'What?' Amal echoed, giving me a faux innocent look that had never once worked on me in all the years we'd been friends. They'd been rumbled and she knew it.

I waved my spoon accusatorily between them. 'I know a meaningful glance when I see one. This is it, isn't it? You're about to break up with me.'

'Correct,' piped up Aiden. 'Sick of the sight of you. Get out.'

'All right. But I'm taking my sticky toffee with me and you're not getting your bowl back.'

'Ach, hush,' grinned Amal. 'We're not breaking up with you.'

'Buuut you do have something you want to say so come on, spit it out.'

She sighed. 'OK, fine. But hear me out this time.'

It was my turn to eyeball. 'This better not be the dating thing again.'

'Oh, it totally is,' laughed Aiden, nodding to his wife. 'I told you she'd not have changed her mind.'

'That's because she *hasn't heard me out yet.*'

'Noooo, I don't want to. We've been through this. I've barely got back and I've too much on—'

'You said you'd hear me out!' she cried.

'No, *you* said hear me out. I agreed to nothing.'

'You've been back for six months now and you've not been out with anyone since . . . well, when? The last person I heard you mention was that Dan guy, whoever he was, and that was ages ago.'

I swallowed another mouthful, feeling it turn to lead in my throat. Dan. Definitely not a topic for this evening. Or any other evening if I could help it. 'I've – I've had a lot on.'

'Everyone has a lot on, that's an excuse and you know it.'

'And on that note, I'm going to go and check on the bairns and let you two catch up properly.' Aiden stood up. 'Another refill before I go?'

I made an inch sign with my fingers and he refilled both of our glasses to the top before making a tactical exit. I took a gulp to avoid Amal's increasingly blunt stare. Sheesh, more of a third degree than I'd been expecting. We sat in the silence for several long moments.

She set her glass down with a sigh. 'I'm not going to force you to tell me anything you don't want to but I'm a bit worried about you, pet. These last few months . . . I don't know, you're not yourself. Coming home and announcing you're starting your own business out of the blue like that? Don't get me wrong, I love *so much* that you're back . . .' She paused, leaned over and set her free hand on top of mine. 'I know I've been busy with the babies and being back at work and everything, but I hope you know that I'm always here for you. No matter what it is. If something's happened, you can tell me. And if it's really bad, I'm a lawyer. I can probably get you out of it.'

I let out a laugh that sounded hollow even to me, as guilt stirred a burning circle in my stomach. We'd not had time to delve into the big stuff since I'd been back, but even if we had, I wasn't sure I'd have been able to. I didn't have it in me to hash out how big an idiot I was to anyone else, no matter how much they loved me. And if I was being completely honest, it bothered me how much it all still hurt. I'd thought that once I was back and set up and settled in, it might somehow at least begin papering over the cracks. That time would do as advertised and kick-start some kind of healing process. But so far said cracks seemed to be staying resolutely paper-free. And the idea of Amal feeling bad about the fact I hadn't shared my feelings with her only made me feel worse. I forced myself to meet her eye and gave her a smile. 'I'm not keeping anything, I promise. I just needed a change.'

She held my gaze, searching. Clearly not convinced by any length at all. Drastic times called for drastic measures. I pulled the pin out of the grenade. 'So, I'm assuming you

32

have someone in mind to set me up with or we wouldn't be having this conversation.'

She blinked. '*What*? You'll do it?'

The idea of dating again filled me with a nameless sort of dread. It had been something I'd enjoyed back in my fancy-free younger years. Now when I thought about it, all I could see was a world of new and interesting ways to be lied to, heartbroken and just generally fucked around. But it was that or talk about Dan, so . . . 'Sure. You're right: what have I got to lose?'

'And you're not just doing this to change the subject?'

I absolutely was. 'Of course not!'

Amal let out a little squeal. 'You will not regret this! OK, so I actually do have someone in mind. His name is Neil – he's a friend of Aiden's from work. He's' – she leaned in conspiratorially – '*magnificent*. Don't tell Aiden I said that. But really. Top-notch.'

'I could live with that,' I laughed.

'It might take a bit of time for me to set it up but I promise I'll arrange everything. All you'll have to do is tip up where I tell you and you'll be guaranteed an evening of delicious food and a very handsome man.'

'Wait – am I not meant to . . . like . . . talk to him first or something?'

'Where's the romance in that?'

It was my turn to blink. I didn't have an answer for that question but only because it was so ridiculous. 'I don't want to go in cold. I hate that!'

'Well, I did have another thought that kind of connects to that.' She took on a slightly cautious tone.

'Go on then.'

'To warm up and get back into the swing of things, I was thinking you should do a bit of online dating.'

I snorted. Was she serious? 'Absolutely not.'

'No, no, listen!'

'I've been listening and so far I've yet to hear a good idea!' I cried. There was no way in hell, heaven or high water I was diving back into the carnival of fuckery that was online dating just now. Or ever. But especially just now. The idea made every bit of me want to curl up and fall down a hole.

'Listen,' Amal insisted, 'I know you hated it before but this time would be different because I could choose people for you!'

I stared at her. 'What part of that is meant to be a selling point? Do you not remember Stuart Cormrie?'

'Stuart who?' She wrinkled her nose in concentration. 'Oh, for— I set you up with him when we were *thirteen!*'

'He was the worst! Some things don't have a statute of limitations.'

To my surprise, she became pensive. 'Ada, love, you can't keep shutting yourself away like this. I've never known you to be so . . . so risk averse.' She searched my face and I felt a sudden heat behind my eyes. I'd never thought of it that way before but she was right. I'd spent so much time and energy trying to close off all the leaking parts of myself that the thought of opening them up again filled me with genuine panic. All because of Dan. Fucking Dan.

Except I couldn't put it all on him, could I? It wasn't like he was here, now, forcing me to turn down every

34

single opportunity of meeting somebody at least semi-decent. And there was an argument to be made for the sheer fact of putting bodies between us. A part of me hated that he was the last man to touch me.

I wasn't sure if it was the alcohol, the atmosphere or Amal, but I found my resolve weakening. She could tell that I was creaking at the corners. I took another sip of wine to brace myself for what I was about to agree to. 'OK, maybe.'

Amal clapped her hands gleefully.

'But can we at least close a few doors?' I begged. 'Like, what are your criteria? Because I don't want another Stuart Cormrie situation on my hands. Everything about him was . . . moist.'

'Oh my God, of course! Yes! You will not regret this.'

I was very much sure that I would. 'I suppose I should have a think about what I want the profile to say.'

'Well, it's funny you should say that because I've actually put together some pictures and a bit of a blurb for it.'

'That is psychotic,' I laughed. 'Am I allowed to see it before you start catfishing random men on my behalf?'

She seemed to need a minute to think about this. 'I suppose, if you insist.'

'Oh, I very much do.'

We spent the rest of the evening going through what she'd written, picking pictures and setting up a profile. It's always an interesting exercise, realising just how your friends see you. And the whopping great lies otherwise honest people will happily tell on your behalf.

Chapter Four

Idly scrolling through a story on the *Agatha Christie Fan Fiction* site, a box flashed up on my screen informing me I'd received a message. It was the first one I'd got from the site since I'd signed up and I was catapulted back to my teen MSN Messenger days. The thrill of unexpected contact, inevitably followed by Mum picking up the phone and crashing the internet.

I opened it.

> *Hi, there, Captain Marple,*
> *Congratulations! Your story,* A Pocket Full of Pie, *has been nominated for the Story of the Month award by Myster-E.*
> *We'll be in touch to let you know if you've won but in the meantime, feel free to attach the button below to let other readers know about your success.*
> *Good luck and happy writing!*
> *ACFF*

I felt a little buzz run through me at the thought of a total stranger reading my story and not only liking it, but actively nominating it for something. I'd only put it up two days ago. Who was this excellent judge of literature?

Their profile name was hyperlinked in the email, so I looked at their page. The screen name had a picture of a mouse with a magnifying glass. Cute, but not helpful by way of identification. Moving through their page I was surprised to find they had a prolific number of Poirot short stories.

Pshaw! Everyone knew Marple was the better detective.

I checked out their intro to discover it was a he, based in Edinburgh and . . . not much else, info-wise. Finding his most recent offering, I clicked in and gave it a quick skim. This stuff wasn't half bad; I could see why he'd won a bunch of the internal comps. He'd kept fairly close to Agatha's style so it surprised me that he'd liked mine enough to nominate it, given it was a set in a futuristic dystopia and I'd made Marple a robot. I opened the DMs feeling the slightly anxious bubble that always preceded contacting someone I didn't know. But no, I would thank him, if only to encourage future nominations. I could use more wins right now.

Just wanted to say thanks for the nomination – not a bad way to finish my day! That's a pretty great bunch of stories you've got going yourself.

I hit send and then stared at the screen for a bit. Hmm. No instant reply. All right, Myster-E man, have a life then, if you must.

I mooched around doing other things but kept finding myself drawn back to the chat. Which was nonsense. I decided to make like Marple and get a cup of tea. Should

I take up knitting again? No, too far. God, I used to have a life in London. Now I was waiting for a random stranger to reply to me on the internet. So much for *thirty and flirty and thriving*.

Mid-stirring of tea, my laptop let out an unfamiliar bing. Pulling it towards me, I was faced with a little envelope emoji doing a dance. God, I loved this site. I opened up a response from the fabled Myster-E.

It was a great story – looking forward to reading more! I loved how even though it's way in the future and Marple's a kick-ass robot who can do anything, she still forces Rooney to do all the trekking about fields and such while she drinks tea and gossips with the locals. Classic Marple.

I felt a little frizzle of pride. That'd been my favourite part to write.

I like to think so! Although if I didn't know any better, I'd say that sounds a bit like shade you're throwing at the world's greatest literary detective (Arthur Conan Doyle can suck it. There. I said what I said), not to mention my own personal hero and who I plan to become when they inevitably recycle me as a robot.

I hit send and took a sip of tea, once again forgetting to let it cool down. Would I ever learn? It was a miracle I had any taste buds left.

The chat informed me Myster-E was typing and my taste buds took a back seat.

No shade here (although you should know there'll be an army of Sherlock Holmes' fans burning your house down any minute now. But fear not! I promise to provide the investigating officer with all of my side-kicking skills.

You will be avenged). But admit it, Captain M, if your elderly uncle had just kicked the old proverbial under suspicious circumstances, leaving everything to your creepy cousin Archibald, who would you want to have on the case? Gotta be Poirot! No question.

Well, that was emphatically wrong. This man was clearly an idiot. But I was nothing if not a diplomat.

I mean, absolutely not. Marple every time.

Not necessarily a *good* diplomat, mind.

However, I will allow Poirot to be an excellent substitute were Marple to be incapacitated. Or better yet, a dream-team combo of the two. There could be a Marple/ Poirot crossover where they could solve crime together. Maybe even get to some smooching. What an absolute scene that'd be!

I hit send and then immediately wished for an unsend button. Or better yet, an 'undo the last thirty seconds of your life' button. What a game changer to have. Why on earth had I chosen this moment to introduce smooching, a word I hadn't used since I was old enough to find it the correct amount of horrifying, to our conversation? I was pretty sure this person hadn't come here for the image of two octogenarians macking on each other while occasionally solving crime. Oh God!

The typing resumed.

Ask and ye shall receive.

Sorry, what now?

The typing continued.

If it's old person hanky-panky you're after, I have the story for you BUT it comes with an ardent content

39

warning and the guarantee that you will not be able to unknow any of this. I'm all for oldies having their fun and fervently hope to one day be one of them, but I will confess that had I known what I was getting into, I would have prepared myself more thoroughly.

And there was me thinking the word smooch was a bridge too far.

What is this madness? Send the link immediately!

There was a pause.

OK – but you have been warned.

A link appeared beneath, a story called *Something Wicked This Way Comes*. I mean, it was no *A Pocket Full of Pie*, but anyway . . . I started reading.

A few minutes in, the bing clanged out again.

How are you coping? I'm here if you need to talk.

I let out a chuckle then realised I was alone in the flat and sounded like a crazy person.

I have to say, it's highly educational. I just learned what a silent duck is. Def should have gone incognito for that one.

The conversation continued down an increasingly hysterical route as the story unfolded.

How have they managed to do this? They're so old! Their muscles, one would have to assume, would have the structural integrity of a wet tissue!

Myster-E took a moment to reply.

I've not had much experience with rope play, more of a furry handcuffs kind of a guy, but I guess the knot does a lot of the heavy lifting – and in this case, presumably the chandelier? Kudos to Marple, though – she's clearly not been skipping arm day if she can hoist him up so high. Must be all that knitting.

I laughed out loud again. Dark horse, was he?

Furry handcuffs, you say. I imagine that would cushion it a bit. Satin all the way for me – doesn't chafe nearly so much.

Jesus, had I really typed that? What was this story doing to me?

I don't do nearly so much knitting though, I continued, *so I suspect I'd not have as easy a time of all the hauling about.*

We were in the midst of figuring out the mechanics of exactly how the chandelier was holding up when the sound of keys scraped in the front door and Mum sailed into the room.

'Oh, Jesus!' she exclaimed. 'Sorry, pet, you startled me. I didn't think you'd still be up.'

'Hello!' I snapped the computer shut, feeling oddly rumbled. The woman could read me like a book – it would be a hard sell to explain the roads I'd been roaming down tonight. 'Did you get off shift early?' I asked, leaning up to give her a brief hug.

She looked slightly baffled. 'No, love, it's 3.00 a.m.'

I glanced at the clock – shit, she wasn't wrong. How on earth had it got so late?

'Hope I'm not keeping you from anything, though.' Her bafflement had morphed into a grin.

I clambered up, offering to put the kettle on and asking about her day to try and hide my ludicrously obvious embarrassment. I almost wished it had been porn – that at least would have been easy to explain. The laptop let out another bing and I decided to wait until I was in my room to say goodnight to Myster-E.

Our conversation continued in fits and starts across the next few days. In between work and seeing Amal and the kids, I found myself reading more – not only his stuff, but across the site. It inspired me to dig through my teen scribbles again and cobble them into something new. All in all, not the worst way to spend my time.

Myster-E's chat mingled in with random asides and hypotheses, pointing me in the direction of some good stories he knew. He even helped me solve a conundrum that had been stalking me for days, re: that my coffee shop – or coffice as I liked to call it – had a door to nowhere.

Seriously, it's right in the middle of the room but when I've tried to figure out what'd behind it I keep hitting quite literal dead ends. Only metaphorically, of course. I'm not mad enough to actually try to look inside because we both know that there is a solid chance that it's a portal to the Bad Place. Also I don't want the barista to shout at me. Café Tière may be a friendly place, but I don't think they'd tolerate snooping, mainly because, as I previously mentioned, they are the guardians of the portal to hell.

His reply took longer than his previous one – he had the audacity to leave me alone with my conundrum for a whole day. I opened his reply when it finally arrived, eager to hear how right my concerns were.

That was not what his reply said.

While these are all very reasonable fears – I have, on more than one occasion, accidentally opened a portal to hell – I'm going to suggest it's probably an Edinburgh press that they never took the door off. Café Tière is part of all those old tenement buildings, right? They'll have more Edinburgh presses than they know what to do with (literally, if they stuck a door on one, ha ha). However, it's probably best not to open it. Just in case.

No. I was having none of this 'sensible response' palaver. I replied to inform him that that was clearly nonsense because no one would be insane enough to leave a door on and thus hide a perfectly good Edinburgh Press. No, it was a portal to hell or it was nothing at all.

Out of the blue, one day, Myster-E sent me a single DM.

When did you discover how much you loved Aggie?

Normally an almost-stranger referring to my personal hero and one of the greatest crime writers in history as Aggie would be enough to send me into a lengthy rant, but I was surprised to find it didn't bother me. Maybe it was because he was on a fan site, so clearly adored her work, despite his ludicrous protestations that Poirot was the better of the two detectives. Or maybe it was because, in a way, it kind of suited her. Either way, Aggie it now was.

Hmm, but when had I discovered my love for her? I found myself typing, without really knowing what I'd say.

Don't judge me but it was The Murder of Roger Ackroyd. *I know, I know, pick a less obscure option, right? It was for English class – we had a teacher who was obsessed with crime fiction (one of multiple red flags on that guy, I can't lie . . .) and I was furious about being forced to read some dusty old whodunnit from a thousand years ago. But then it turned out to be so sassy and fun and intriguing and then I got to the twist. I have such a clear memory of getting to that ending. I was reading in the bath and I was so buzzed that I had to get out and find my mum to tell her about it. She was running late for work and, God bless her, I made her listen for a solid ten minutes before she could escape. She acted as though it was the most interesting thing she'd ever heard, even though it must have been so stressful trying not to look at her watch – I would have 100 per cent have told me to jib off. Anyway, I went straight to the library the next day and borrowed every single Aggie I could find, thus becoming the world's most suspicious teenager.*

I felt a crinkly little ache in my abdomen at the nostalgia of it all; I hadn't thought about any of this in so long. The shock of that ending, the overwhelming need to discuss it immediately with somebody. It was hard to believe I shared any kind of DNA with the excitable, curious, ginormously nerdy teen who'd started that journey. I glanced at the web logo peeping over the chat screen. Well, maybe some of the nerdy bit was still kicking around.

What about you? When did you stumble across her?

I hit send and made my way to the kitchen to start dinner. When Mum came home later, she found me reading on the sofa.

'You've dusted off your old Agatha Christies,' she said, shrugging off her coat. 'This better not lead to a new lease of life for your whole "I want to be a private detective" thing.'

'I have indeed. But you'll be thrilled to hear there are no current plans to change career.' Again. 'There's some cottage pie in the fridge. I'll heat it up for you.'

She gave me a tired smile. 'Thanks.'

I pulled myself out of my chair and gathered her into a massive hug. 'Love you, Ma.'

She hugged me back, clearly taken by surprise. 'Love you too, pet.'

A day passed with no reply from Myster-E and I was surprised to find that I was waiting with, if not baited breath, then at least some hiccupping.

In the meantime, though, I would soldier on because I had bigger fish to fry – namely the fish that had sat itself at my usual table in Café Tière.

I went through the main customer area bit as usual, winding my way through the little Parisian-style tables. Was I imagining things or were there more than before? It seemed like they squeezed a new one in every week. Surely it was becoming some kind of fire safety hazard at this point? A lot of wicker to burn through. I waved my pass to Lauren, one of the newer baristas, to indicate that I was heading through to the office part at the back, thankfully marginally less packed. She gave me a smile and a wave, moving firmly up my 'favourite barista list'. Bertie had some strong competition these days.

The 'office' itself was a similar style to the main café, although perhaps a smidge more tired-looking. But the windows at the back were stained glass, huge and bright. When it rained, which was unsurprisingly frequently, the sound was almost hypnotic. It was my absolute favourite thing about the place. There was a broad mix of people working and always busy with not a lot of talking outside of their online meetings. I nodded hello to a few of the other regulars as I went past. They nodded back, which made me happier than it had any right to. Part of me missed having colleagues, but that wasn't the most inconvenient part. No, that would be that everyone sat at the same desk each time, which seemed to leave me a grand total of three sockets to choose from.

I'd spent my first week there playing the electrical equivalent of Goldilocks. One socket had been broken, one had been under the brightest neon light I'd ever come across and then, glory be, the final socket was at a table close to the window, albeit only with the view of a fried chicken shop on the other side of the road, but it worked. Just right.

Halfway to my usual table, I realised it was inconceivably occupied. By a man, to be exact. Early thirties, slightly messy dark hair framing his face, wearing some kind of obscure band T-shirt and staring intently at his laptop, occasionally surfacing to check out his phone or his surroundings. He was, if I was being objective, quite a handsome fellow. Possibly more handsome if he'd not been sitting at my goddamn table.

Unsure of how to deal with the situation, I sat down at the nearest empty one.

This newbie couldn't just come in here and take whatever seat he wanted! I'd spent a week trying to find the perfect spot. It was a jungle out there, and if I had to learn that the hard way then, by God, so did this guy.

I forced myself to take a few deep calming breaths to gear up for our smackdown. Making my way over, I did the usual 'about to talk to a stranger' hand dance to grab his attention. 'S'cuse me? Hi!' I said. It came out oddly screechy but hey ho, it was out now.

The man looked up with a jovial hello in return. I was surprised by his disarmingly friendly brown eyes. Too friendly, really. 'Sorry, this is going to sound a bit strange but . . . um . . . you're sort of sitting at my table.' I probably should have planned this out better. Out loud, I sounded, to be frank, like a bit of an arsehole.

His smile morphed into immediate concern. 'Oh God, I'm so sorry. It's my first time here – I didn't realise these were pre-assigned.' He scrabbled around, trying to gather his things.

I held out my hands, feeling suddenly guilty. 'No, I guess, it's not so much a rule as a guideline.'

He paused, clearly confused, and then set his laptop back down. 'What do you mean?'

'Well, they aren't officially preassigned but there's an . . . an understanding?' My voice went up at the end – goddammit, why had I suddenly made that a question? Now I looked as if I didn't know what I was talking about.

He was looking at me strangely. 'So, this isn't your desk?'

'It is and it isn't,' I replied, helpfully.

'Um . . . right.' He pulled his hand through his salt-and-pepper flecked hair, which I had previously thought to be dark brown.

I decided to attempt further clarification. 'Basically, everyone here uses the same table every day.' I gestured around me. 'It took me a while to figure it out too. There's a guy, Clive, over in the corner . . .' I side-eyed a middle-aged man in a suit as surreptitiously as possible 'who bitched me out because I didn't realise and took his spot on my second day here. Some people get really shirty about it.'

'Oh. Does that make you my Clive?' he asked innocently.

'What? No!' I snapped. Rude. Although in a way, I guess I kind of *was* his Clive, wasn't I? Well, maybe now that I was older and wiser, I could see that Clive had a point. I said as much.

'Look, this is the only free table that seems to have a working socket.' He gestured to where his laptop was plugged in. 'So if you can get the owners to fix the others, I'll happily move but until then, I'm afraid I'm paying the same amount as you are and I need this space. Possession is nine-tenths of the law and all that.' He gave a 'what can you do?' kind of shrug.

But . . . but the unwritten rules! I briefly imagined grabbing his laptop and running away with it – let's see what he thought nine-tenths looked like then. But he struck me as the athletic type and I emphatically was not. Goddammit, Clive wouldn't have put up with this shit.

There was nothing else for it. I either had to use the shit table or go home. And I'd be damned if I was letting this no-beard hipster win. No, I would sit at the rubbish table and make a point to be in early enough to stake my claim on my real desk in future. I'd carve my name into the wood if I had to. That'd show him.

Then I remembered how scared I was of being shouted at or worse, of having Lauren or Bertie think badly of me. Probably no table carving, then. But I'd be getting my table back, that was for sure.

Chapter Five

As a result of my unexpected desk woes, I decided to make my way home earlier than usual. This had the unintended benefit of giving me more time to get ready for the first of my Amal-mandated dates. The extra time in no way made me feel less nervous.

I made my way into the bar we'd arranged to meet at – a swanky establishment attached to an even swankier hotel – and immediately found myself staring at a thousand Adas staring back. The whole wall was covered in bits of shattered mirror, throwing distorted versions of different bits of me all over the room. Jeez, somebody was going to be getting a lot of bad luck for that monstrosity.

I forced myself to not keep staring at the multiple-mes and made my way to the table I'd been directed to by the maître d'. Amal had told me to wear a frilly red top she'd once insisted I buy and I'd paired it with some nice jeans. I'd been pretty happy with the outcome but hadn't bargained on the horror mirror wall, or indeed, the fancy surroundings. Out of the corner of my eye, it looked as if I was bleeding profusely.

I'd arrived a few minutes early, thinking it'd give me an advantage. I'd be able to sit myself down and make sure I wasn't sweaty or covered in lipstick or toilet roll or something. It turned out I'd massively overestimated the amount of time it takes to check these things and wound up twiddling my thumbs while wondering, on a scale of one to ten, how angry Amal would be if I made a screaming exit and went home.

God, I hated this. *Hated* it. How did I let her talk me into doing it? She was a sneaky one, with her reason and sense and 'it's just a drink, you'll live'. How did she know? The stress of it risked early aging at the very least. When you broke it down, leaving would be a favour to both of us really – at least that way Amal'd not have to listen to me whine about it after. Because as I sat waiting for Connor to arrive, I realised there really was not a single part of me that wanted to be here. The bar for what would interest me in dating right now was so high that if *Roman Holiday*-era Gregory Peck walked in, I'd still . . . well, no. Of course I would marry him on the spot. But that was how high the bar was. The anxiety engine that powered 99 per cent of my activities these days thrummed through me, louder than ever.

The waitress arrived to ask if I wanted to order. Fuck it. Yeah. I did want to order. Because it really was that or leave.

'I'll have a large glass of house white, please,' I replied, barely managing to stop myself repeating the word large and miming something roughly the size and shape of a bathtub.

She disappeared and I found myself once again twiddling my thumbs as I stared at the door. I'd promised myself I wouldn't take out my phone because I hadn't wanted the first thing my date saw to be me staring at it – especially not to check on Myster-E – but it was practically pulsing in my pocket.

No. It couldn't be helped. I pulled it out to find a reply from Amal to the selfie I'd sent her before I'd left the flat:

Smokin'! I've heard the bar is gorgeous – send pics so I can live vicariously through you xx

I eyed up my surroundings. I mean, it was very beautiful, in a 'we are a no-shoes household, peasant. Tread lightly' sort of way. The kind of place designed specifically to be a backdrop for pictures, which conversely made me not want to take them. But an Amal request was not one to be brooked. I held my phone low and proceeded to paparazzi my way in a circle around me, paying special attention to the horror mirror at the end. As I was weighing up sneaking into what would undoubtedly be a glorious bathroom to take some more pictures, the door opened and a man entered, taking off his coat and handing it and a large fancy golf umbrella to the maître d'. I was suddenly uncomfortably aware of the fact that I'd haphazardly chucked my coat on the back of my chair. Was that wrong?

He scouted the room, found me and gave a small nod and wave as the maître d' showed him over.

I had to admit, he was not quite as advertised. A solid few years older than the pictures he'd been using on the app, with a receding hairline that he'd tried to cover with strategic strand placement. Ah well. Everyone knew the dating game was a whole heap of smoke and mirrors –

quite literally in this case, as a thousand versions of him made their way towards me. Weirdly, the only thing I could think as he reached the table was that it was a mighty big umbrella he'd carted in on this dry, mild day.

No! Focus.

I stood to say hello and then immediately regretted it. What was I, a Victorian gentleman?

Oh well, I was up now. I gave him a bright smile, said my hello and he leaned in to give me a kiss on the cheek, introducing himself as Connor.

I had to hand it to the man, he smelled amazing. He was wearing an expensive cologne. The kind that, like all really classy things, only really announced itself upon closer interaction.

As I moved to sit back down, I noticed his eyes slide over me and for a jarring second I was absolutely sure that he hadn't necessarily been thrilled with what he saw either. I couldn't quite put my finger on what it was that made me think it but there was . . . something. I mean, I may not have been in the running for a modelling con-tract anytime soon, but it wasn't like I'd wandered out of a bog. And even if I had, that was fairly rude.

No. I was being paranoid and going off at the deep end. The nerves were stressing me out – he was a nice, normal guy. I thanked Christ people couldn't read minds.

Just as we'd settled in, the waitress arrived out of the ether with my glass of wine. She must have some-how picked up on my secret exhortation to bring me all the wine in the land because the glass was the size of a Belfast sink.

'You've ordered?' Connor said, surprise etched into his face.

Shit. Was that bad? Oh God, it was. 'Um, sorry, yes. I was early and a bit nervous so I thought I'd ease myself into it.' I thanked the waitress as she set the glass down. It was a miracle I could see over it. 'Didn't realise it'd come in a bucket, though.'

For a second, he looked kind of mortified. But I'd seen the waitress give an amused smirk so I didn't feel too bad. Not a cracking start, mind.

'Sorry. Do you want to order?' I asked, magnanimously.

'I'll have a sparkling water with a squeeze of lime, please,' he said to the waitress.

Shit. 'Are you not drinking?' I hadn't meant to say it out loud but it was out now. I was pretty sure our first date probably wouldn't survive me trying to push a recovering alcoholic off the wagon. *This* was why people harped on about talking online for longer than ten minutes before meeting!

'I'm driving,' he replied.

Phew. But wait. If he was driving, why did he have the world's biggest umbrella with him? So many questions.

The waitress went to get him his party water and we were left to our own devices.

'So, Connor, it's lovely to meet you. How's your day been?'

'It's been fine,' he replied.

I waited for elaboration. None was forthcoming. OK, then. I took a sip of my wine.

'Was the traffic bad?' Jeez, how had I literally steered us into traffic talk so soon in the date? Like some kind of awkward uncle at a garden party. Not quite the kind of witty repartee I'd been aiming for two minutes in. Man, I was rusty.

'It was fine. The usual for the time of day.'

'Ah, good.' Cool story, bro. 'So, your profile said you're a lawyer, is that right? Sounds like a pretty cool job.'

'Property law.' He shrugged. 'It pays the bills.'

'I'll know who to come to when I finally get around to buying my mansion,' I replied brightly.

He let out a small concessionary 'ha ha'.

The waitress arrived with the water and it was all I could do not to beg her to stay. For a brief, wild moment, I contemplated accidentally knocking my glass over, just to feel alive again. In lieu of this, I took a huge gulp from it.

He must have picked up on this, because he shifted slightly in his seat and offered up a question on my own job. I chatted briefly about Steve. How he'd somehow managed to spin a role in an obscure Scottish soap into a lifelong career, invitations to open local fairs, off-season pantomimes and, in an unbelievable twist, an actual book, which he had categorically insisted on calling *Leith, Laugh, Lothario*. But everything I said felt as though it was disappearing into some massive void between us. He didn't seem to react at all to anything. Finally I ran out of different ways of saying 'I beg Steve not to do stuff and clean it up when he inevitably does.'

He nodded. Once he realised I'd run out of steam, he finally spoke. 'I know of Steve Annick. My firm represented a local business he broke a contract with once. He was . . . quite the character.' He said 'quite the character' in the same way I might say 'Fred West'.

'Uh, yeah, that he is. It's been a handful, for sure. But I like a challenge.'

He quirked an eyebrow as he took a sip of his water and I was in the process of trying to decipher if it was a good quirk or a bad quirk when his face crumpled up.

'No, sorry.' He raised his voice. 'Excuse me.' He clicked his fingers in the waitress's direction.

Clicked his fingers.

If I could have burst into flames of shame I would have.

She made her way over. 'Can I help you, sir?'

'I asked for a squeeze of fresh lime. This is neither fresh nor a squeeze.' He abruptly handed it to her as I tried to fervently signal with my eyes that I was in no way party to this action. She took it without reacting, making her way back to the bar.

My poker face wasn't quite as refined as hers. Connor turned back before I'd had to time to fully rectify my abject horror.

'Is something wrong?' he asked, in a surprisingly haughty tone for a man who'd so recently been the absolute worst.

'Just worried they might spit in your drink,' I offered diplomatically, trying to inject my tone with some jovial nonchalance. It didn't take.

For a second, he looked surprised but he wasn't down for long. 'You have a problem with me returning my drink?' Ah. Our old friend 'clipped tone' was back.

Two could play at that game. I dug in and found my 'telling Steve off for nefarious things' voice, modifying it slightly for my audience. 'Not at all. Just not sure all the finger clicking was strictly necessary.'

I had to hand it to him, he looked genuinely confused. 'Sorry, is it not her job to take my order? And if she gets it wrong, which she did, is it not also her job to fix it?'

'She misjudged the amount of lime in your drink, she didn't key your car.' I'd reverted to trying to up the levity in my voice but we both knew we were beyond that now. God. Had I ever been on a date that had gone this downhill this fast before? There was the man who'd commented on me getting a starter on account of 'my BMI', but we'd at least got to the stage of ordering food before it hit the deck.

We settled into silence as she returned with the drink. 'I'm very sorry, sir. It's on the house.'

He took it and said thank you, throwing a pointed look my way.

Jesus.

I thanked her too for good measure, taking a long draw on my wine. Vat though it may have been, I was determined to make my way through it as fast as possible, if for no other reason than it would ease the passing of this terrible, terrible night. Amal and I would be having serious words about her taste in my men.

He took a sip of his own drink, clearly deciding the lime was fine this time round. Thank God. If he'd clicked his fingers again they'd have to declare an international incident on account of me losing my goddamn mind.

A part of me wondered why I didn't leave. Even if I was being generous and putting it down to a simple clash of personalities, there was still nowhere for this to go. We'd been in each other's company a whole ten minutes and had managed to say approximately a few hundred words to each other, eighty of which had been an argument, with the odd nod bestowed for good measure. But I couldn't bring myself to do it. And for a man who clearly didn't massively care about being rude to people, he seemed to be resolutely avoiding doing the same. Maybe he was hoping for another waitress to berate.

Then I had a brainwave. It was time to check out the toilets.

I was right – they were magnificent. Peacock wallpaper, gilded mirrors, soft music piping in and a giant plush chaise longue to one side, in case one needed to swoon at the sight of such elegance. There was something mildly depressing about the toilets being the highlight of my date but a win was a win in any weather. I clicked a thousand pictures and sent them to Amal.

Glancing in the mirror, I realised my lipstick was almost gone and there was mascara peppered under my eyes. Fantastic. I swiped it away and reapplied the red liberally, watching it pull colour back into my face – without it I very much ran the risk of looking like a Victorian ghost child. Dark blue eyes, pale skin and a hint of freckles that never really managed to turn into the cool ones I'd been desperate for as a kid. I finished up by helping myself to some fancy hand lotion and then begrudgingly made my way back into the bar.

To my disappointment, Connor was still there. I made my way to my seat and gave him a bright smile. I'd made a decision in the bathroom. I was going to enjoy my evening and he was largely incidental to that. I was in a nice bar, I'd spent time in a bathroom so fancy I'd briefly contemplated moving into it, and the wine really was going down a treat.

'Can I ask you something?'

Connor looked wary – the most emotion he'd exhibited all night. 'OK.'

I'd wondered if I'd actually allow myself to say it but in the end, the Marple in me simply had to know. 'Why did you bring a golf umbrella?'

Suffice it to say, the night didn't improve: some back and forth about the umbrella – 'it looked as though it might rain'; some stony silence and one half-hearted attempt at décor chat. We wished each other a swift goodbye after I'd paid for my wine, leaving a heftier tip than usual. The woman had earned it.

I trudged home through loud tourists ambling twelve abreast and pausing every seventeen seconds to take pictures. When I finally got in, I texted Amal to let her know that it hadn't been the love match she'd hoped and waited for the inevitable Spanish Inquisition. It wasn't incoming, suggesting she was in the middle of child-wrangling. Fair enough.

Mum was out tonight. It was normally nice to have a bit of space, but the flat felt kind of lonely. I decided to have a bath. Sinking into the lavender-scented bubbles, I tried to figure out why I felt like the emotional equivalent of a smacked arse. It wasn't as though I'd expected the date to be a winner – I hadn't even wanted to go.

But I knew what the problem was, really, because it was the same problem as it had always been: Dan. I hadn't been on a date since him and, as I sat opposite Connor tonight, I'd been reminded of all the other terrible dates I'd been on in my life. And I finally understood exactly what it was that bothered me about that. It was that meeting Dan had felt like such a game changer. Stupid and short though it was, I'd started to let myself think that maybe I wouldn't have to date again for . . . well, ever. Or at least a very long time. And now here I was, right back at square one. The odds were a hundred to one that I'd find anyone I'd even be remotely interested in because it had taken so long just to find Dan and I was acutely aware I was hitting an age where the decent ones were taken and all that was left were the clicky-finger brigade. How had Amal managed to have all this on track so early and so easily? It blew my mind.

I felt a tear splodge down my face. Every time I thought I'd got to the end of my Dan-related misery, there was another reveal to give a whole new layer to my sadness and rage. Fucking *fucking* Dan.

I took a deep breath and wiped my face.

No. This was unacceptable. I was absolutely not going further down this nightmare alley. I made myself get out of the bath and dry my hair, briefly checking to see if there'd been any word from Amal.

Not yet.

I threw my phone onto my bed and, as it landed, a bing rang through the air. It took me a second to realise that it had come from my laptop, which I apparently hadn't fully switched off last night.

I opened the screen to find a reply from Myster-E. It was a longer one too.

It was as if someone lifted a dustsheet off me. All the heaviness from the date and my impromptu pity party cleared away. I nipped downstairs and made myself a cup of tea, and then settled in to read what he'd sent.

Chapter Six

So, I knew this would happen – that you'd ask me the same question back and of course, as soon as I'd sent it, I realised I actually couldn't remember. Ridiculous, isn't it? Aggie was the doorway into my love of reading and books and even, in a weird and very roundabout way, my job. But I can't remember the first book of hers that I read. I know when I started but the memory is a bit of a wash. I wish I had what you had – that clear eureka moment. I envy you it. But in a way I like that I can't pinpoint exactly when it began because it makes me feel like she's just always been there.

Wow. Written down, that looks even more losery than I'd thought it would, doesn't it? You should brace yourself for more though, I'm afraid!

The reason that I first got into Aggie was because I lost my mum when I was twelve and went to live with my aunt and uncle. My uncle loved crime fiction and he introduced me to her – she was such an incredible escape. A world of logic and facts and mysteries to be solved. And maybe getting to know characters – particularly your good lady, Marple – who had experienced grief and come out the other side of it. That it didn't define who they were as people or how they interacted with the world.

Sorry, don't know why I felt the need to bring down your day with such unnecessarily depressing information – the gist of it all being that I can't really remember exactly when I first read her but I'm very glad I did.

Anyway, to better things!

Namely: who would win in a battle of the sidekicks: Hastings or Raymond?

Jeez. Kind of wish I'd put a bit more thought into my answer now. It took me a while to formulate a reply. I decided to start with his question, if only because it'd be hard to circle back to whimsy if I dived into the dead parent thing right off the bat.

Who would win in a fight between Hastings and Raymond? Has to be Hastings all the way, right? Was in the war, steadfast sidekick dispatched to do all the proper legwork and running around and actual physical catching of criminals. (You could argue that the true takeaway from Aggie's work is, wherever possible, get a minion to do all the heavy lifting. Can't fault the logic.) He'd beat Raymond no bother.

Now for the tricky part.

I'm so sorry about your mum – that's an awful age to lose a parent (not that any age is good, obviously, but so young seems really terrible). Do you miss her? Urgh! God, sorry – what a ludicrous question. You're not going to be like 'a bit at the time, but all squared away now, thanks!' I'd never thought about it that way before but you're right, there is a thread of loss running through a lot her work, especially Marple. So many of the stories we read focus on the point of impact – someone loses a loved one and then you see how they deal with its aftermath, etc. – but there is something comforting about having it in the periphery of a story. As you say, it shows that life goes on. People survive and, even if it changes them, it's almost as if it makes them more human, more relatable. And it sounds that it's a nice thing you have in common with your uncle. You should get him on the site! Or is he more of a purist?

The little typing emoji flashed to confirm that more typing was occurring and I felt a frisson of anticipation. It was so strange to think that I couldn't pick this man out of a line-up, yet with more and more time passing, feeling kind of like I knew him. I mean, objectively, he was probably some seventy-year-old with false teeth and a bum hip but I made the executive decision to not believe that. He felt young.

Said everyone who's ever been cat-fished.

Regardless. I was going to enjoy this for what it was. Look at Dan – I thought I'd known him and where had it got me? When you broke it down, it was a risk getting to know anyone, ever, really. This at least was low risk. Total anonymity and a shared interest? Yes, please. Plus now I'd get to know what it might feel like to have an old-fashioned pen-pal situation from the days of yore. It'd be great!

Although how anyone managed to live with the suspense of waiting on a letter arriving was beyond me – I was struggling with the mere time it was taking for him to finish typing.

The bing alerted me to his reply.

Yeah, but Raymond has money and connections – why not pay people to kill for him and make it look like an accident? He could easily do it that way.

Fair and accurate.

He was typing again.

No, my uncle isn't on the site – he passed away last year.

Christ on a bike. How did I manage to walk around so easily with one foot lodged permanently in my mouth? I was typing a reply before I registered my fingers even moving.

Jesus, I'm so sorry. God, I swear I'm not usually so bad at conversation! Are there any other traumatic memories I can dredge up for you while we're here? Learning Santa was a lie? The time your dog ran away? The first person to rip your heart out and jump on it?

I hit send and then read it back which, in hindsight, I really should have done immediately. I'd forgotten that typing something stripped all the tone out of it so I'd missed the witty self-effacement mark and appeared to have landed in the long grass of general psychopathy. Shit. Should I follow up with an emoji? I opened the options, frantically scanning for something that said 'hah, japes!' while also projecting deep sympathy for the terrible time he'd been having. Upside-down smiley face, perhaps? Before I could find anything remotely suitable, the icon showed me he was typing again.

And as it happened, what he was typing was a hysterical laughter emoji. Maybe there was a God.

Words followed soon after.

Nah, it's my fault for ostensibly having the origin story of a Dickensian orphan despite having an actual childhood firmly entrenched in the nineties, ha ha, but now we're getting into the good stuff!

Let's see, well, first off, Santa is real – what on earth are you talking about?

I never had a dog run away but I did have a hamster basically resurrect itself – how's that for a story? He was my first pet. His name was Goldie (because he was straw-coloured – what an imaginative child I was!). I got him when I was five and he lived an insanely long time for a hamster. One day, I thought he'd died but Mum insisted on wrapping him up and keeping him by the fire and, sure enough, he came back to life. I remember genuinely believing she was magic. Imagine if we'd buried him! But it did mean that when he actually died, she had a tough time persuading me he was really dead – I kept insisting he just needed to be warmed up. All very Wes Anderson.

First heartbreak has to be Cara McCafferty. I was eleven, she was twelve. Asked her out at the school disco but she said no because Dean Kearns had got there first. Never fully recovered, if I'm honest.

What about you?

I took a sip of tea and was surprised to find that even after my horrible date and bathtub wallowing, I was feeling reasonably at peace with the world again. Who knew tea could work such wonders? I began to type.

I never had a dog run away or anything resurrect itself, sadly. We weren't really allowed pets in the flat so it was basically a parade of goldfish. I remember my first one so clearly. His name was Flipper. I won him at a fair in Leith – he and I became firm friends during our short acquaintance. Although I loved them all dearly, I'll admit it's hard to be too cut up when they swam off to the giant goldfish bowl in the sky.

Heartbreak from boys, however, now that's where I have you beat, I'm afraid. I was fourteen years old and Ben Mackie from across the way asked me to be his girlfriend. I was beside *myself – I'd fancied him for ages. Anyway, went to latchkey club with him only to discover that he was really into Annie Ford and I was but a smokescreen to make her jealous. I cried for a week. And in hindsight, am starting to think that might have been the start of a pattern there . . .*

Jeez, it was good to see I was consistent in my taste for heartbreakers.

Anyway, you seem pretty sound to me – I'm sure you'll have had plenty of people say yes to you since Cara McCafferty! I heard she was a terrible person anyway.

I hit send and realised I needed to pee. Throwing the laptop aside, I nipped to the loo. By the time I'd returned, there was still no reply. Before I knew it, my eyelids were getting heavy but I couldn't help myself, I kept checking back for a reply. Ten minutes passed and I realised he must have gone to bed. I once again cursed how basic the site was – surely it wouldn't have killed them to add 'last online'? I reluctantly shut up shop for the night and dozed off.

Chapter Seven

Amal and I had arranged to meet up to have a date debrief and general catch-up in Bruntsfield. Now she'd mostly finished breastfeeding we were actually able to venture to a real live restaurant instead of her kitchen. When I arrived, she was already there, glass of wine in hand. The place she'd chosen was chock-full of chesterfield chairs, wood-burning fires and the kind of ambiance that suggested you were sharing the space with whisky-sipping, cigar-smoking titans of industry. Past-Ada and Amal would have absolutely lost their minds at coming here. If I was being completely honest, present-Ada wasn't far from it. No cheap cider in Dalry Cemetery for us these days, that was for sure.

'Hello, my love,' she said, greeting me with a hug.

'Hey! You look incredible as always,' I cooed, sitting down opposite.

'Thanks, pet. I feel like a foot.'

'How so? You OK?' I asked. It wasn't like her to admit a weakness.

She waved it away. 'Ach, nothing. Just Mo hasn't been sleeping basically since the day and hour he was born. Benji was bad the first few months but he settled. Mo . . . not so much.'

'Still? That sucks. Sorry, pal, I thought he was getting better with that – what was it, that self-soothing thing you were talking about a while back?'

She looked slightly surprised at the mention of it. 'God, that was so long ago! Nah, we tried it for a few nights but he got into such a state it ended up being worse.'

'Hopefully he'll get the hang of it soon. Somebody needs to invent some kind of baby-safe knockout pills. Why hasn't that happened yet?'

I realised as I spoke that a waiter had appeared by my side. Awks – let's hope he didn't hear the bit about the baby sleeping pills. I'd hate for someone else to cadge my amazing idea.

'What are you drinking?' I asked Amal. She informed me it was a wild Sémillon. Far too fancy for my taste. 'I'll have a house white, please,' I said to the waiter. 'Unless you want to get a bottle?'

She shook her head. 'No thanks, can only really have one. On the night shift with Mo tonight.'

I nodded and ordered a glass and some water for the table, feeling a tiny tinge of . . . something. We never got to go out and do stuff anymore. Which was fair enough, she had tiny humans depending on her for their every need. And it wasn't that I didn't worship Mo and Benji and dinners at their house and getting to be a part of that life. But sometimes I really missed just getting shitfaced with my pal.

Which was ridiculous. We were grown-ups now. At least, one of us was . . . being jealous of babies was not hugely grown-up.

I watched her sip her wine and felt instantly guilty. The woman wasn't just a rock, she was the friggin' keystone. I was being a dick.

'So, tell me about this date,' she said. 'Not a goer?'

I cringed at the memory of it. 'Hard no, I'm afraid.'

'What happened? You seemed such a good match!' she cried.

'Were we, though? All you were really going on is that he mentioned being a lawyer and that he loves Thai food. Honestly? I don't think I've ever had anything less in common with someone.'

She shrugged. 'Well, the odds of you meeting a viable match on your first date was always slim to none.'

'You did with Aiden. Wasn't he your first date after Stuart?'

'That doesn't count – we were twenty-one! Nothing counts at twenty-one.'

'Maybe.' I decided against pointing out how easy that was to say when you'd easy to say when you'd met the love of your life at twenty-one.

The waiter arrived with my wine, which I took gratefully. I needed all the Dutch courage to tell her what I was going to do next. 'OK, don't get mad but . . . I think I'm binning the app.'

Amal gave me *The Look*. I hated *The Look*. It had been the beginning of every argument I'd ever lost to the woman.

'Don't!' I insisted.

'You've been on one date,' she admonished. 'You absolutely cannot bail on this after one date. I will not allow it. Just think, the next one could be amazing!'

'That's easy for you to say – you weren't on it. Remember my text? He *clicked his finger at the waitress?*'

'Oh yes, thanks for the reminder – I really must call the police about that,' she replied.

'Come on, I guarantee you that if you'd been there, you would have told me to never see or speak to this guy again.'

'And I'll say that to you now. What we won't agree on is that you should abandon the male species entirely. Why would you let one shit man dictate your life like that?'

Excellent question. I forced myself not to fall down the Dan-shaped hole again.

'Ada, it's been months since you've dated anyone at all. The last one you mentioned was . . . who? That Dan guy? And all that happened there was you "drifted apart". That's hardly something you need time to bounce back from.'

Ah, fuck. Sometimes I forgot that all Dan's secrecy had seeped its way into everything. I couldn't bear telling her the truth when it all fell apart so I'd hedged and just told her it had fizzled out. Regretting that now.

I'd clearly been silent for slightly too long because Amal leaned forward and said, 'What aren't you telling me?'

'Nothing.' I took a long sip of my wine.

She watched me silently for a moment. 'Is it something I've done?'

'What? Of course that's not it!'

'Aha! But there *is* something,' she said triumphantly. 'I knew it!'

Goddammit.

She leaned forward, all trace of humour gone. 'Ada, love. I meant what I said before: if you don't want to tell me, you don't have to. I just want to know you're OK.'

I looked into her big, beautiful, tired eyes and felt suddenly, inexplicably emotional. I'd wanted to tell her what had happened with Dan so badly. Since the gut-punch plane-wreck of an ending, all I'd wanted to do was to talk to her. But anytime I'd tried, I just couldn't bring myself to say the words. To explain it without feeling like the world's biggest idiot one minute, the world's biggest bitch the next.

'It's really nothing,' I replied, sounding more croaky than I'd meant to.

Amal didn't dignify that with a response. Maybe if she'd spoken, or moved or the waiter had walked past, or a series of inexplicable but hilarious comedy skits had resulted in a pile-up of broken crockery nearby, I might have managed to hold on to the silence. But nothing occurred to block me and I found myself telling her everything about Dan. How we'd met, how he'd told me he was separated, how it'd turned out he was a massive fucking liar. How broken I'd felt after. How broken I still felt all these months later. It all came flooding out of me.

It took longer than I'd meant to, and before I knew it, I was a weeping mess at the table. Amal – Mary Poppins that she was – produced tissues out of apparently nowhere but didn't interrupt until I was done.

I drew in a stuttered, uneven breath. 'I'm so sorry. Look at the state of me.' Pulling out another tissue, I dabbed under my eyes. 'Is my mascara everywhere?'

72

'Probably better you don't know,' she replied.

I let out a snotty, tear-filled laugh. 'Are you mad I didn't tell you?'

She paused for a moment. 'No. I'm sure you had your reasons.'

'But I didn't! I don't know why I didn't tell you. It just . . . it got away from me.'

She watched me with steady eyes and didn't say anything. For a moment I felt oddly off-kilter, wanting her to say something – anything – else.

The waiter, who'd been wisely keeping his distance during my histrionics, was back with some menus. We each took one and spent some time poring over them before deciding what to order.

'Do you ever speak to him?'

The question surprised me. 'Who, Dan?'

'No, the waiter. *Of course* Dan.'

'God, no. He messages sometimes but I never reply.' Why had I felt such a strong need to caveat that last part?

We were silent again for a moment.

She reached over and squeezed my hand. 'I'm so sorry, pet. I had no idea.'

I felt my eyes heat up again. 'Don't – the waiter will never come back if I cry again.'

'You're right – get it together, McKenzie. I'm starving and this is the first meal I've had in months that hasn't involved doing an airplane landing into someone's mouth.'

'Jeez, I thought Aiden was getting better with feeding himself?'

'He just can't get a handle on it.'

73

We both sat in contemplative silence for a moment. 'I'm sorry he did that to you, hon – what a prick,' Amal exclaimed. 'Urgh, and his poor wife.'

My insides squirmed. 'I know, right?'

I caught the waiter warily approaching the table again from the corner of my eye to take our orders and was surprised at how relieved I was by the intervention.

Amal watched me for a long second and I was sure she wasn't going to let me away with moving past it so quickly. But then she turned to the waiter with a smile and gave her order.

I followed suit with mine. As I watched him leave, I heard Amal's throat clear.

'So, I do understand why you might be feeling a little bit gun shy on the dating front. But please, *please* don't give up on the app yet. Closing yourself off to new experiences will only make it harder to forget the old ones.'

So we were done talking about Dan, it seemed. And right back onto the dating. Great. 'I don't care, I'm not doing it,' I declared resolutely. 'It's so miserable.'

'But you have to,' she continued. 'You need to practise for when I introduce you to Neil! Aiden's invited him over for dinner next week so my plan is slowly coming together.' She thrummed her fingers together like a straight-up Bond villain. 'You promised, remember?'

'I most certainly did not! In fact, I'm fairly sure I never fully agreed to the Neil thing, you know.' *The Look* was back. I didn't even bother to wait for her to berate or correct me. 'OK, fine. Yes. Maybe I did.' Sigh. 'But I still don't understand why I need to continue with the app if you're setting me up with him. Can't I just practise my dating moves on, I dunno, you?'

Amal put her hand over the top of mine. 'Darling, Sweetie-Pie, other love of my life, must I really remind you that I have two children under the age of three? I live vicariously through you. Please do this for me? I need this. *You* need this. Everybody in the whole world needs this.'

I scowled at her. God bless her, I knew she just wanted to help, to give me the kind of happiness she had. Which was nice of her. But also a little . . . interfering aunt-ish at times. Anyway, she'd clearly made it her mission to couple me up and the only way out appeared to be through.

'OK, OK,' she relented. 'I'll make you a deal. One more practice date on the site and one date with Neil if I can wangle it and then I absolutely pinkie-promise that I will never, ever badger you about dating ever again. I will let you die an old, sad, lonely crone in a hedge at the bottom of my garden.' She crossed her heart.

Pants on fire. But at least this would get me a ticket out of the dating for a little while.

I let out a theatrical sigh. 'OK, *fine*. But I want at the very least a shed in your hedge.'

She cheered victoriously. 'You won't regret this!'

The food arrived and was set in front of us but my appetite had apparently abandoned me. I'd kind of assumed that telling Amal about Dan might help clear some of the wreckage he'd left, but as I listened to her wax lyrical on what they planned to serve Neil for dinner, my stomach felt as if it was being drip-fed pebbles. I took a bite of pasta and forced myself to swallow it with a smile.

Chapter Eight

I got home feeling slightly sad and so sleepy that I could have nodded off on a mechanical bull. Pulling off my clothes, I climbed into bed but I couldn't help myself. Sitting back up, I pulled my laptop onto my knees and checked to see if there was any reply from Myster-E.

Sure enough, there was.

My heart gave a little kick as I opened the message. When had these become such a highlight in my day? Or night, to be more precise. The checking of the messages had become a ritual, because most days since we'd started chatting, there would be something. A GIF or a link to a cool story he'd found and then our conversations. A small part of me might have been becoming a teensy bit reliant on it. Which was fine and not at all a risky move for me emotionally, just now. Nope. No siree. Creating an emotional tie to this utter stranger couldn't possibly backfire in any way.

I opened the message.

I think Cara ended up marrying Dean so probably best that I didn't get in the way of fate there. Although not sure I've ever been fully on board with people marrying the person they've been with since they were basically in the womb. I was an idiot as a kid, absolutely not to be trusted with more complex decision-making than which pair of trainers to wear. But maybe I'm just a dead-hearted cynic. Although this is where you tell me you actually worked it out with Ben and you're in the midst of wedding planning, isn't it? Although I rather suspect the suggestion of a pattern means you're not? That does sound ominous, though . . . dare I ask for follow-up information?

Follow-up information. Hmm. How much did I want to talk about Dan to this random stranger on the internet? I picked up the glass of water by my bed and drank the whole thing down, feeling the cool liquid focus my thoughts. On balance, I was surprised to find that I actually kind of did want to talk about Dan to this random stranger. Who knew?

The question was, to what extent? I got my typing fingers ready.

Oh, the usual. Girl meets boy. Girl falls for boy. Boy turns out to be married with a kid on the way, which girl only discovers when her boss brings it up in a meeting. Fun times.

And there it was, blinking out at me in black and white. It was peculiar seeing it phrased like that – like I was talking about someone else. Gave me a bit of distance. Not the worst thing in the world, perhaps.

The typing emoji blinked to life and I realised that Myster-E was actually online right now. My heart did a tiny wheelie and I ordered it back into place. Absolutely no need for that sort of behaviour.

His reply arrived surprisingly swiftly.

Jeezo. That's grim. Maybe getting with Ben might have been better for you after all!

77

More typing.

God, that was a really dickish response written down, sorry! I wasn't trying to make light of what happened – and sorry you had such a shit time of it. I'd like to be able to say that all men aren't as bad but that skims dangerously close to #notallmen and I'd rather eat shit and die than suggest that, so please do feel free to ignore any and all of my ramblings.

I found myself laughing out loud. I decided to put his mind at ease.

Meh, it's fine. I'll allow that perhaps many men probably wouldn't actively deceive on that level – for the most part I've been lucky. The shit I've encountered has mostly been of a very banal nature. You know, the whole 'it's not you, it's me' or, on one memorable occasion, 'it's not me, it actually is you.' To be fair to the man who said it, I had just been sick in his bin.

God, I'd forgotten that particular interlude. Worst one-night stand ever. For him, of course. I'd been having a grand old time until the bincident.

Yourself? Any tales of woe?

Apart from, you know, losing pretty much everyone the man had ever loved? I, at least, had managed to refrain from writing that to him.

I was engaged, actually. Until last year. That was not a good year, now I think about it.

Holy shit. How did I manage to hit the mark every single goddamn time?

Oh God, I'm so sorry, that's pretty rough. Do you want to talk about it? You don't have to if it'll bring it

*all screaming back to you? I know I've really hit the nail
on the head on that front a few times now ...*

I waited for a reply – it was slower coming this time. I was beginning to wonder if this might have been the straw that broke the camel's back when his reply pinged up.

It's no problem to talk about it, but I have to go as I'm falling asleep on my keyboard (you know what they say, always keep 'em wanting more!). Talk later, though. Night!

Fair enough, it was getting late. Even though every single atom of my being wanted to hear his story. But no, patience was a virtue and all that.

I replied, wishing him a good night. So he'd been engaged. Past tense. Which probably meant that he was currently single – although not a guarantee, of course. For a moment I let myself try to picture what he might look like, where he might be sleeping. Did he live alone or have flatmates? Were there day-old water glasses by his bed too?

I pictured asking him any or all of these questions and then immediately pushed the image aside. There was something nice about not knowing. Knowing was a problem for Future Ada. Present Ada had more than enough random men to attempt to date just now anyway.

I dreamed I was in bed with someone I couldn't see properly. We were kissing and fumbling and pulling off clothes, warm hands everywhere in the darkness. His felt soft and firm and sure on my body and he smelled of coffee and

79

heat. As I moulded myself to him, feeling him move on top of me, the cover fell back and I found myself looking into the eyes of . . .

Poirot!

I woke with a start.

Jesus. Amal was right. I really needed to get back out there.

I'd continued messaging a few guys on the dating site. All but one basically fizzled out, which by default left a single solitary option to fulfil my promise to Amal. The dream was looming over me so I pushed the boat out and asked if he was free the following night for a drink.

By the rules of any benevolent universe, it should have been a roaring success. Me and this last-chance-saloon – or Matt as his friends and loved ones liked to call him – should have spent an evening filled with sparkling conversation, smouldering looks, a hot night of super-sexy fun times, swiftly followed by a lifetime of mooning at each other.

Alas, I was very much stuck with the universe I currently lived in, so what actually happened was a lukewarm drink at a terribly lit bar full of awkward silences and a kiss on the cheek to say goodnight – a clear sign that neither of us was madly on board for a continuation of our evening.

To my endless surprise, Amal was thrilled when I regaled her about it the next morning in her living room.

'I'm so relieved!' she crowed.

I paused giving baby Mo mini air-throws and leaned back on her sofa to give her better access to my bemused expression. 'One more date was your idea!' Mo gave a burble that I liked to think was seconding my point.

Amal waved it away. 'Yeah, but that was before. Because I have excellent news! Remember I was telling you about Aiden's colleague, Neil?'

'You mean the man you've been actively trying to talk me into marrying every single time I clap eyes on you?'

'Aye, that's the fella. Well, good news. He came over for dinner and, when I told him all about you, is very much keen to meet up.'

Mo and I exchanged suspicious glances. Well, mine was suspicious. Mo's was a wee bit skew. 'What exactly did you tell him about me?'

'Oh, all the good stuff. I can't wait for you to meet him, he's so nice! He's free tomorrow, which I know is short notice but I figure, why not just get it over with so you can realise that I'm right about everything and that you've finally met a decent guy! You're welcome. Also, it's a Friday night, which is win-win should you wish to – you know . . .' She did a little shimmy.

I detangled Mo from my necklace and planted a barrage of kisses all over his face. He let out an adorable baby giggle. I held him up. 'Your mummy thinks we missed the fact that that she's swerved giving us any actual details on this man but we didn't, did we? No, we didn't!' I cradled him again and raised an eyebrow at Amal. 'Nice try though.'

She waved a finger at me. 'You promised, remember? One more go. Trust me. I've a good feeling about this one.'

Loathe though I was to admit it, it wasn't as though I had any other scorching plans for my Friday. And she did say he was super-hot.

'Plus, if I left it to you, you'd never meet anyone at all.'

'Excuse you – I meet loads of men.'

'Yeah? Name me one man you've met in the last six months outside of the dates I've made you go on?'

As she spoke, Myster-E popped up into my head. Did that count? He was a man. We chatted daily – I spent more time than I could ever admit to anyone checking for his replies and I found myself more and more thinking of things I'd see or hear that I'd want to tell him about. He was funny and charming and . . . probably my age. Definitely – or most likely – single. And I'd met him all by myself.

See? I could meet men! In Amal's face!

Except for the part where I hadn't really met him. I couldn't actually pick the man out of a line-up – if he walked into the room right now I literally wouldn't know it was him. I couldn't even guess at his real name. So that would make the crowing about him quite hard to do, really.

On balance, probably best left unmentioned, just now at any rate.

But was it odd that I didn't know his name? Should I ask him? I'd thought about it but . . . it felt kind of too late. We'd built a little bubble and the thought of doing anything to burst that felt like the worst thing I could do in the circumstances. I just had to trust that there would come a time when it would work to ask him all these things.

Chapter Nine

I was anxious about my impending date with whoever Neil turned out to be. Tossing and turning in my bed was doing me no favours. I decided to go into my café-office early, which would have the added benefit of surely giving me enough time to cadge my usual table in case the random table-stealer decided to make a reappearance. I was just finishing up some toast when I heard Mum come in the door. She looked knackered so I made her a tea and sent her on her way to bed before I left.

My table was mercifully unmanned so I settled in with a coffee, starting up my laptop and diving into sprucing up Steve's brand-new website. It had taken me an *age* to persuade him he should have one. It had clearly been too much to hope he'd hire a professional so I dusted off my WordPress skills and built him one myself. It wasn't the shiniest, but it was a damn sight better than the rag-tag mile-long list of – usually embarrassing – media stories that showed up when you typed his name. With a bit of positive promotion, I could only hope that eventually this would outrank at least some of the more excruciating ones. I knew it was just sheer stubbornness on my part but I'd committed to raising the profile of Edinburgh's answer to Dirty Den and, goddamn it, I was going to do it if it killed me. I forwarded the newest version to him for confirmation of a new colour scheme and pictures. A ping informed me that he had looked at it pretty much straight away. His reply was replete with crowing admiration, triggering an immediate suspicion that something was afoot. An hour and several coaxing emails later, I'd managed to get the story from him – a feat I wasn't sure even Miss Marple could have pulled off with ease. It basically amounted to telling a bunch of old people who'd won a radio competition to meet a local 'celebrity' a story I'd expressly, at great length, forbade him from telling.

I got so wrapped up in figuring out exactly what he'd done so I could specify the grovelling apology to the radio station and the oldies, that it was gone six before I knew it and I was officially going to be late for my date with Neil. How on earth had that happened?

I dashed home to do what I could with concealer and some lipstick, texting a quick apology to say I was en route.

I'd said it before and I'd say it again forever until I was dead: blind dates were the actual worst. The feeling of walking into a bar with absolutely no idea what you'd be up against for the next two hours of your life was up there with hearing the words 'tax form' uttered in casual conversation. The memory of Connor and Matt and all that awful awkwardness was far too fresh in my mind.

No. This would be fine. I trusted Amal. She'd not match me up with someone I wouldn't have at least something in common with.

Neil had booked a restaurant in Leith that I'd never been to before, mainly because, growing up, Leith had felt four thousand miles away and I'd hated getting the bus. Suffice it to say, living in London had radically altered my perception of distance and I found myself marvelling that it had taken me a paltry forty minutes on the bus to get here. It was a beautiful night and, as I crossed Bernard Street Bridge, I paused to gaze down at the Water of Leith, lazily sparkling in the evening sun. I'd forgotten how beautiful this part of the city was. A narrow escape from being taken out by a kamikaze seagull put paid to my reflections, but it was nice while it lasted.

I made my way towards the restaurant, swung open its door and stepped into the cool, dark room. The nerves, temporarily allayed by my walk, were at peak fizz now. I forced in a breath and made myself focus on my surroundings. It was small and intimate in an understated, expensive way, with wild flowers and candles on the rustic little tables. Quite the venue for a first date; I half expected a proposal to break out somewhere in the vicinity at any minute. Hopefully not from whoever Neil was, though.

A man at the corner table looked up and his face broke into a broad smile as he stood to greet me. Tall and lean with blond hair cut short and cheekbones you could crack a nut on. Well *done*, Amal. Thank God I'd gone home and spruced myself up a bit.

'Neil, hi. I'm so sorry I'm late!' I reached the table and moved in for a kiss on the cheek only to find his hand held out for a shake.

Whyyyy?

I managed to keep my squeal of humiliation inside, thank Christ. We both burst out laughing and instead he pulled out my chair for me. What a gent. Things were looking up.

I sat and we settled in.

'I hope you don't mind but I ordered us a bottle of red wine?' he said, sitting back down opposite. 'A rioja.'

I didn't love red but it could have been worse, I supposed. He could have ordered Chardonnay. 'No – that's perfect,' I chirruped. God, was my voice always this high-pitched?

The waiter materialised by my side with a pair of menus, and I did the usual first date thing of reading it as though it was the most interesting thing I'd ever seen. By the time we'd decided what to order the wine had arrived and I'd managed to calm myself down enough to be able to face Neil's glorious cheekbones without automatically looking away.

'It's lovely to meet you – Amal has such great things to say about you!'

'Pshaw,' I waved him away. 'She's very biased.'

He smiled. 'With good reason, I'm sure.'

'Well, we go way back so she's contractually obliged at this point, I think. You work with Aiden, right?'

He nodded enthusiastically. 'Yes, I started there last year. We work in different teams but we met at an away-day thing and he invited me to the pub a few times.'

I smiled as if this was brand-new information.

'I moved to Edinburgh for the job and it's hard to meet people so it's been really nice to make a friend,' he continued.

'Oh, that's nice. Where were you before?'

Neil briefly filled me on his comings and goings from a childhood in the Sussex countryside to his most recent job, in Crewe, of all places. Somebody had to live there, I supposed.

'You've recently moved from London, right?' he asked. 'What brought you back?'

Oof, right in with the big question. 'Oh, you know, thought it would be nice to come back for a bit.'

He took a sip of his own wine and I made a mental note to slow down. I was halfway through my glass already. Jeez.

'Amal said you've started up your own business too? A publicist? That sounds exciting!'

Did she happen to mention anything about the fact that I have a grand total of one aging, liability soap actor client, a handful of tiny events and a whole heap of nothing else? In hindsight, I should probably have asked her to tell me expressly what information she'd given about me beforehand. 'It's nothing – still very early days.' Another gulp of the surprisingly good wine took me closer to the bottom of my glass. 'It's nice to be back in Edinburgh, though, so I can't complain. What about you? How's software engineering treating you?'

Neil poured some more wine as he walked me through the highs and lows of his job. It wasn't the most thrilling of topics and I had to remind myself that not everyone got to spend their days wrangling errant actors with butterfly nets and herding them away from trending Twitter topics. Neil really seemed to enjoy what he did, though, and as I got through more of the wine I warmed to the subject myself. We waded knee-deep into the intricacies of something called git version control and for a brief second I even vaguely understood what that meant. Before I knew it, we were onto a second bottle of wine, the food was mostly eaten and the conversation had moved onto, of all the inexplicable things, Munros and the bagging of them.

'Wait, Munros are just, like, Scottish mountains, right?' I wondered aloud.

'Yep. If it's over 3000 feet in Scotland, it's a Munro.'

Phew. I hadn't totally embarrassed myself. Although I still wasn't fully clear on why the word mountain wasn't sufficient as a descriptor, but that was neither here nor there. 'Is that . . . do they really call it Munro bagging?' I tried not to snigger.

'They really do.'

'And that's . . . you do that? You bag Munros? Is there . . . like an actual . . . bag for it?'

Neil laughed heartily. I had to hand it to him, the man had been laughing at pretty much everything I'd said so far. A girl could get used to that. 'No, it's just the name for it. I thought Amal said you liked that sort of thing?' He dabbed his mouth with a napkin and dropped it on his empty place.

I found myself spending longer than was strictly acceptable staring at his lips. It took me a moment to realise I'd totally missed what he'd asked me. Shit. 'She did?'

'Yeah, she said you liked hillwalking? You've never wanted to get into the Munros?'

Wait, what? Amal knew I'd never met a hill I didn't hate – what was she thinking? Neil was looking at me expectantly, glorious green eyes sparkling in the candlelight. Hmm. Maybe the reason I'd not met a decent hill yet was that I hadn't given it the chance . . . How bad could a tiny white lie be? 'Oh, yeah. Um, yeah I've done one or two.' Or none. I'd done none.

'Which ones?'

Argh. Instant regret. 'I-I can't think of the names right now. It was a wee while ago.' In an actual other life. What on earth was I doing? Time to stop digging this hole and try to find a way to climb out of it. 'What about you? How many Munros have you . . . bagged?'

'To date, ninety-two.'

I narrowly avoided a comedy-style spit-take. 'Ninety what? That's insane!'

Neil shook his head, looking inexplicably ashamed. 'I know, I know. I'm so far behind the game but I only got into it a couple of years ago and only properly since I moved. Ninety-two down, 190 to go.'

Wait, there were 282 Munros? *Who* was climbing these? Why was this a thing? Oh God, I was meant to know that, wasn't I? He was going to ask me and if I didn't answer it right he'd know I was a filthy liar but I couldn't think of a single thing to say. 'That seems like a reasonable number to have got through,' I hazarded.

'It passes the time and it's so beautiful. But you'll know that yourself.'

'Of course!' And I would, the second I could find my way to the foothills of a Google image search.

We settled into silence. I could feel the wine zipping around my veins. The candlelight was bathing everything in a soft, warm glow and Neil was looking at me intently. I couldn't help noticing that the Munro-bagging had done a fair amount of sculpting, if the contours under his crisp white shirt were to be believed. For a brief second I let myself imagine running my fingers lightly along them and felt a little ripple reverberate through me. God, it'd been so long since I'd been with anyone – it felt like years since Dan. My weird Poirot dream came floating back to me. Up until the terrible reveal it had been . . . hmm . . . I found myself refocusing on Neil's crisp white shirt.

'What would you say to getting another glass of wine?' he asked, tentative now.

Mum was on night shift tonight again. I had the house to myself.

Yeesh, it'd been a while since I'd had to worry about something like that.

Focus.

I caught his eye. Saw his glance move from my eyes to my lips and back again. For a moment I let myself mirror him, then lifted my glass and drained the last of it.

'I've a better idea,' I replied. 'How about a drink back at mine?'

I watched the light slowly filter through the gap in my bedroom curtains. Was it time to get up yet? I'd barely slept, and time had slowed to a crawl. It could be 3.00 a.m. or 3.00 p.m. four days hence, I could no longer tell. I was desperate for a wee but Neil's arm was slung across me and I couldn't move. I was boiling hot, hungover and fervently wishing he'd decided not to stay the night. He was curled around me like a ginormous cat, doing a thing that wasn't snoring but also wasn't *not* snoring. I twisted slightly to test if there was a way for me to somehow manoeuvre my way out without waking him but the movement stirred him and he somehow pulled me into an even deeper hug.

'Morning, babe.' He kissed the top of my head.

Were we at 'babe' already? Was anyone in the world? 'Uh, hey . . . you.'

'Last night was amazing.'

The sex hadn't actually been bad. 'Yeah, it was great.'

He smiled down at me. He did have a great smile.

'So, I was thinking we could grab some breakfast. There's this great keto café not far from here – it does these brunches where—'

My bedroom door swung open and my mum paraded in with an armful of clean laundry. I let out a screech, pulling the blanket up to my neck, turning towards the door. 'Jesus!' I shouted.

'No, just me,' she declared jovially. 'Sorry, pet, I didn't know you were in.'

I stared at her. She was looking only slightly embarrassed. She was, however, fully clothed and not in bed with a strange man. 'Why don't you ever *knock*?'

'I'm sorry, I didn't hear you come in so I wasn't sure you were back. Hi, there, Ada's guest. It's a pleasure to meet you – I'm Fiona.'

I pulled myself up on my elbow. As I did, I realised there was something nudging my lower back. Sweet Mother of God! My mother was standing in my bedroom, I was fully naked and the man I was with was in the middle of some serious morning glory. I felt all the blood in my body race to get to my face. She leaned forward as if she might go to shake his hand.

'Get out! Get out of my room!' I cried.

She set the washing down and held up her hands. 'OK, OK, I'm going, I'm going. Although, you know, I *am* a nurse – nothing here I'll not have seen before. At least I hope not at any rate.' She gave me a small wink.

'MUM!'

'I'm going!' She went back out the door, shutting it behind her.

I sat up, throwing my head into my hands. 'Christ, I'm so, so sorry!'

Neil chuckled. 'It's fine – she seems nice. You're the spitting image of her.'

Not quite what I was hoping to hear at that moment. Fuck my life.

'So, about that brunch? Unless of course . . .' He leaned in and pulled me into a deep kiss.

My mother's brief intrusion didn't seem to have fazed him in the least – he still appeared to be full-mast. Meanwhile, I was, if anything, minus mast. And about to literally wet myself.

I pulled away from him. 'Ah, sorry, I actually can't. I . . . have some work to do.'

'But it's Saturday?'

Shit. Think fast, McKenzie. 'It's a press release thing. Steve's gearing up for a local book tour for the new release. Deadline was technically yesterday so I really do need to get it done.'

He put on a pouty face. It was a look that didn't in any way suit him. 'That's a real shame.' He kissed me, moving slowly down to my neck. 'Because,' kiss, 'there are so many,' kiss, 'things I want to do,' kiss, 'to,' kiss, 'you.'

So much for brunch. 'Maybe another time.' Did I want there to be another time?

'I was thinking about that. The weather's meant to be nice all next week. As you're free next Saturday, why don't we take a walk up the Pentlands?'

The memory of me informing him how little I had to do with my weekends in general at the moment came screaming back to me. God *why* could I never keep my big fat mouth shut? And why was this man's memory a steel friggin' trap? So now I'd have to spend my weekend hauling ass up giant hills.

'It can be practice for your next Munro,' he said, smiling down at me.

Honestly, had anyone ever had such immediate punishment for lying before?

Chapter Ten

Coming out of the bathroom, I heard Mum banging about in the kitchen. Sneaking in so Neil wouldn't hear that I hadn't gone straight back to him, I closed the door behind me.

'Hello, darling. Do you and your man friend want some coffee?' Mum asked, grin splashed all over her face. Her voice sounded so loud it could have woken the dead.

'No, thank you,' I ground out, keeping my voice low in the hope she'd mirror my example. 'Mum, we've talked about this – you can't just barge into my room without knocking! And for the love of God, stop doing my laundry!'

She waved me away. 'Ach, don't be ridiculous – like I said, it's nothing I haven't seen before.'

'This isn't about that!' I forced myself back down to a loud whisper. 'I just . . . I need my room to be private, OK? I need to do my own cleaning and change my own bedding and wash my own clothes. I'm not fourteen anymore – you don't need to do this stuff for me!'

Her face fell and my insides curdled with shame. Which was in no way helping the hangover.

'Sorry, love,' she said quietly. 'I just thought it'd be nice for you to be looked after for a bit.'

Oh God, I was the worst daughter in the world. Even if a part of me wasn't 100 per cent convinced that she didn't know full well she was guilting me.

I stepped forward and put my arm on her shoulder. 'I appreciate it all – you know I do. But I like to do these things, OK? I like looking after myself and knowing where everything is and . . . and being able to not have to worry that you'll accidentally walk in on me doing something that will literally kill me with embarrassment. Not figuratively. Literally. I know you've seen it all before but that doesn't necessarily mean I want you to see mine.'

She held up a hand. 'OK, consider me told.'

I shook my head, feeling irritation spike again. 'Don't do that. Don't do the guilt thing. It's not unreasonable of me to want some boundaries – I would never do that to you, just walk in, willy-nilly.'

I realised what I'd said before the grin had even reached her cheeks.

'Don't! You know what I mean,' I said, as sternly as possible.

'OK, fine. I promise I'll stop walking in *willy-nilly*.'

'Stop it! I mean it.' But it was too late now. The moment had passed and I knew I wasn't getting any more mileage out of this conversation.

She nevertheless gave me a *scout's honour*-style salute.

'What are you doing up anyway? I thought you were on the night shift?' I wondered aloud.

She shrugged. 'You know it always takes me time to wind down.'

That was true. I rubbed my eyes, which probably only looked marginally less exhausted than hers.

'Why don't you go back to bed and I'll make you and your . . . friend . . . some breakfast?'

I gave her a look.

'I'll set it at the door,' she insisted innocently. I may as well have been talking to the microwave, for all our conversation had landed with her. Letting out a sigh, I informed her that my guest would be leaving and that breakfast was definitely not required.

After my decidedly unsuccessful tête-à-tête with Mum, I'd hoped to be able to usher Neil out of the house and then collapse back into bed, maybe via some kind of toastie if I could be arsed. Unfortunately for me, he was about as big on the uptake as Mum had been. So instead of a bed-bound toastie, I found myself being shepherded out the door at his insistence that he 'walk me to work', as he marvelled at the blue sky and remarked on the freshness of the day.

How was this happening?

As a fairly suspicious person, it crossed my mind that he might somehow have been punishing me for my massively transparent lie. But making our way under the random little footbridge and onto the bottom of Lothian Road, it dawned on me that he was in fact being entirely genuine. I couldn't decide if that was better or worse.

As we walked, he leaned over and took my hand, continuing to chatter about an article he'd read on the positive impact of hillwalking on mental health. Glancing up, I was once again reminded that he was a very attractive man and decided there were worse ways to spend a brief wander on a Saturday morning. Plus we now had the added benefit of being no longer naked in the company of my mother.

My stomach gave an embarrassed lurch at the memory of it, helpfully reminding me that I was still feeling pretty rough. Jeez, a hangover really went out of its way to inform you that all alcohol was just a form of poison. My liver was practically whirring, it was working so hard. I made the mistake of peeking in a shop window as we passed. My hair, which I'd scraped into a bun, was making a concerted break for freedom and, despite my best efforts, I still had slight panda eye from the night before. To really hit the grunge look home, I'd thrown on an old flannel shirt with jeans, giving the overall impression that I'd been recently dug up. Next time, I would definitely run a brush through my hair before tying it up. Maybe even add a bobby pin or two.

It took me a minute to realise that Neil had stopped talking and was watching me expectantly. I'd totally missed the last minute at least of what he'd been saying. Something about . . . about . . . oh God. There was nothing for it.

'So sorry, Neil – I didn't catch the last part. The traffic's so loud here.'

For the first time possibly ever, the universe came through for me – a bus wailed past, drowning out his response. He gave me a dashing smile as I pointed out that we'd arrived at the café.

'That's a shame – we could still grab breakfast?'

'Ah, sorry, I really need to get a move on with this press release.'

'Maybe next time.' I found myself being pulled in by those tractor-beam eyes. Leaning in, he kissed me a long goodbye and I found myself watching him walk away, wondering if maybe Munro-climbing might not be the absolute worst thing in the world.

As I was now in work anyway, I decided that I might as well just write the damn press release. It wasn't actually needed for another week, but it wouldn't hurt to at least get a head start. As it was a Saturday, I'd assumed it would be easy pickings, table-wise, but when I got there, it looked busier than ever. Jeez, who were these losers working on a Saturday? I, a loser working on a Saturday, wondered.

To my utter enragement, the table thief was well and truly back, sitting there with all his plug points and natural light. My ability to snaffle it the last few days without incident had obviously made me complacent. The other, infinitely inferior, table was, surprise surprise, available and I slumped my hungover carcass into it.

God, I despised this seat as much as I had the last time – if not more – and not only because my whole body felt like a half-eaten, day-old sandwich and I currently hated everything. It was too near the migraine-inducing lamp on one side, too near the toilet on the other and miles away from the window, to boot.

I continued my almost-silent grumbling as I loaded up the most recent version of Steve's press release before remembering that what I truly needed in life was a coffee. I decided to live on the edge and abandoned my laptop momentarily to nip to the main counter and order one. There was a coffee machine in here but I decided I'd earned a fancy one. Maybe even a cake for good measure. No decent press release was ever written off the back of a hangover, a lack of cake and the entirely wrong table.

Slumping back into my seat, I sucked down the coffee in between mouthfuls of delicious chocolatey goodness before pulling the laptop back in front of me.

Much better.

It suddenly occurred to me that I'd gone a whole twelve hours without checking to see if there was anything new from Myster-E. He'd promised me an update on what had gone down with his ex and that'd be way better than a boring old press release! I logged in and, sure enough, there was a reply. I almost cheered at the temporary reprieve from having to do actual work. He had – as promised – filled me in on the details. I settled in to soak up his story.

We'd been together for four years and it seemed to be the next natural step. It wasn't that we were unhappy, just kind of ticking by. And then my uncle died. He'd been ill for a while and I moved in with them for a month or so to help my aunt look after him. It was kind of a watershed thing. They'd been really happy together and watching her nurse him and seeing how absolutely gut-ted she was when he passed was a bit of an eye-opener. They'd been together thirty years and I didn't find out until after he died that they'd never spent more than a night apart in all that time. Isn't that wild? It made me re-evaluate what I wanted from life. Not that I want that or expect it or anything. I'm very aware that this whole thing is making me look like some kind of crazed romantic – I swear, I'm really not! I'm mostly quite sane. (Although that's what a crazy person would say, isn't it?)

Losing him and seeing my aunt lose him was a bit of lightning strike, though. I realised that it wasn't fair to me or the person I was with to go through with some-thing I wasn't really sure I wanted. God, that sounds really cold, written down. But she didn't disagree which was how I think we both knew it was the right thing. We're not exactly friends but we keep in touch from time to time and I feel that I couldn't really ask for more than that. I'd certainly like to think that there was an under-standing, that she wasn't hurt by it in the long run. But maybe I think that because it's what I want to believe? I don't know. I guess we all want to write our own version of history, right?

Jesus, but he wasn't wrong about wanting to write our own version of history. Maybe it was the hangover, but I found myself feeling oddly emotional. I wanted so much to reply with something meaningful and in keeping with his message but I found myself coming up blank. I tried a couple of different versions before settling on:

It's definitely better to have done it before rather than after getting married – it's a brave move too, and to do it at such a difficult time is extra impressive.

I hit send, not completely happy. He'd replied something so considered and clear-eyed and all I'd gone back to him with was platitudes. But his story made me sad for some reason. Maybe it was because it felt as though it was reinforcing something I was starting to really think – that very few people got to find and hold on to someone they properly truly loved. That it was, more often than not, one giant compromise. And here I was, off the back of yet another date that would, for all Neil was very nice, end up either in nothing and go nowhere or, more likely, draw me closer to the compromise. The deepest connection I'd had since Dan was this random guy on the internet.

I couldn't quite get my brain to force out more words than that. I exited the site, vowing that by the time I wrote to him again, I'd have pulled up my metaphorical socks.

Now that that was done, I was aware that I'd basically run out of excuses for getting out of doing actual work. I just about managed to keep my sigh internal and dug out the press release, managing a grand total of three lines before the screen started to darken.

What?

A flashing icon drew my eye to the bottom corner of the screen to find that the battery light was flashing. Which was nonsense – I'd plugged it in overnight! Hadn't I? Fuck! I scanned the room in the hope that someone near a socket might have miraculously vacated. It was, after all, a Saturday.

No joy.

I found myself staring longingly at my old – no, my *usual* – table. Thought of all the good times we'd had together. The laughs, the tantrums, the close plug-proximity. Looking at it from a distance made me realise how spacious it was. A four-seater, albeit a tight squeeze for that many.

Two would fit in a breeze, though.

Goddammit, why had I got off on such a bad foot with the table-stealer?

I could always go home and work there. But the thought of facing Mum after this morning's almost peep show and awkward after-chat was too much to bear. Plus, I'd dragged myself the whole way here.

What to do?

My computer let out another panicked bleep.

It was go big or go home time.

I drew in a deep breath, which only made the hang-over nausea worse, waited for the room to stop vibrating slightly and made my approach.

'Um, hello again,' I said.

The man looked up at me and I saw the gears click into place as he recognised who I was.

'Hello, nice to see you again,' he said cheerfully.

Was that sarcasm? 'Sorry to interrupt – I think we maybe got off on the wrong foot before. Back when I, um, Clived you a bit.' God, did I just use Clive as a verb? Why did that sound so creepy?

'Ah, yes. Clive was the guy who stopped you sitting at a random public table that time?'

I bit down a response – my laptop needed me. I could roast him with a sick burn later. 'Yep, that's the one.'

'No hard feelings,' he replied magnanimously. 'What can I do for you?'

'So, as you already know from . . .' I gestured behind me as if to say *before* '. . . this is the only working socket nearby and I know you were here first and I totally respect that. Normally it wouldn't be an issue because my laptop is usually fully charged but I must have forgotten to plug it in last night and now it's out of juice.' Urgh, apparently 'out of juice' was a phrase I used now. I soldiered on regardless. 'It's about to die completely and there's something I need to get done.' I gave him my most imploring look.

He didn't reply straight away, continuing to smile at me. Under normal circumstances, I'd find it a bit unnerving but there was something direct and inoffensive about him doing it – maybe it was the friendly eyes. He really did seem to be thinking it through. Finally he spoke. 'I'm sorry I took your table. Your battery needs are clearly bigger than mine.' He nodded to my currently frantically bleeping laptop across the way. 'Give me a sec and I'll clear my stuff.'

Time for me to blow this diplomacy thing out of the water – Amal was always harping on at me to hone it as a skill and I'd make her proud of me yet. 'What I was going to suggest was that we could maybe share? That way we both get the socket, non-neon lighting, plus maybe even be a good example to Clive.' Poor Clive. I glanced across to where he usually sat. He really was never going to live down our unbelievably minor skirmish.

My potential new desk pal prevaricated for the briefest of seconds and then held out his free hand. 'Deal.'

I shook it as firmly as I could manage and then dashed across and picked up my panicking laptop, diving for the plug in time to stop it dying completely. I settled into the chair diagonally opposite and he sat down too.

'I'm Ada McKenzie.' Why did I say my *full name?* I wasn't on a goddamn game show.

'Fraser Evans,' he said, with what appeared to be very little judgement.

'Pleasure to meet you, Fraser Evans. What brings you to Café Tière on a Saturday?'

'I work mostly remotely and I was going a bit mad in my living room. A friend mentioned this place let you use the back as an office set-up/café and I thought I'd check it out.' He glanced around. 'So far I like it.'

'Yeah, it's not a bad spot, is it? When I first started coming here, I thought it would only be for a couple of days to get out of the house but it's been a few months and here I am still. I kind of love it now. Have you had the grand tour?'

'I have not! What does that involve?'

'Oh, it's very grand. Would you like me to take you on it?'

'I would be delighted.'

Now that my computer was happily sucking in charge, and we were on the path to being firm friends after our ropey beginning, I decided work could wait a little longer. It was, after all, a Saturday. I stood up and beckoned him. He followed me past the jigsaw of rustic wooden tables full of people typing furiously to the coffee stand in the corner. 'So, this is the coffee and tea point – you can help yourself to whatever you want.' I turned and pointed to the bright yellow door with WC stamped across it at the back of the room. 'That's the toilet.' Finally, I turned and pointed the way he'd come in. 'And that, as you may recall from your recent journey through it, is the way back out into the main café.'

'That does ring a bell.' He looked at me expectantly.

'And . . . that is grand tour over, I'm afraid. May have oversold it a bit. Tip not included in entry price.'

He laughed. It was a surprising laugh, deep and warm. 'Can I pay you in a free tea or coffee? Or perhaps,' he gestured to the individually wrapped packets of shortbread, 'a delicious Brodie's biscuit?'

'I would but I've had so many of them that I'm worried the owners might call the police.'

'Ah, there you go. I can smuggle them over to you.'

'I could live with that arrangement.'

He started pouring himself a coffee. 'Thank you for the tour – *highly* informative.'

'Yes, I'm sure you would never have figured any of it out on your own.'

'Nope, would have been totally at sea. The toilet would have been particularly tricky to guess.'

We made our way back to the table and settled back down, me with my fancy – albeit slightly cold now – coffee, he with his boring generic one.

'I like how brightly coloured it is. Very French. It makes me want to smoke cigarettes and drink breakfast wine.'

Fraser raised an eyebrow. 'Yeah, the décor doesn't overly scream "tourist trap", which is surprising, seeing we're right in the centre.'

'Lothian Road's not really the centre, is it?'

'We're a fifteen-minute walk from the castle!' he pointed out.

'It's Scotland. Everything's a fifteen-minute walk from a castle.'

'Fair enough.'

'So what do you do that doesn't involve an office?' I asked, pouring a sugar into my cup.

He followed suit. 'Me? I'm a journalist.'

'That's cool! What kind of stuff do you write?'

'You know, the usual Pulitzer Prize-winning fare. "Local finds image of Maradona in slice of bread", that sort of thing.'

'Do you mean the Madonna?' I wondered aloud.

'No, I mean Maradona, the footballer. Actual story I covered.'

I laughed. 'What a coup!'

'Yeah, it was bready stuff, let me tell you.'

'And a great way to bring in the dough.' I wasn't sorry. 'That sounds fun though. Do you enjoy it?'

He nodded his head and took a sip of his coffee. 'Actually, I do. I've done bigger things before. Don't get me wrong, I loved it, and I'll probably want to go back to it at some point. But I'm kind of enjoying doing local stories for the moment. I have a segment that reviews culture and events and all that kind of thing, so I get free tickets to stuff, which is pretty cool.'

'Ooh, nice. What sort of stuff? Let me guess, you get to swan around the likes of the Peacock Ball, hobnobbing with all the fancy folk?'

He laughed. 'No, nothing nearly as highbrow as that. Tends to be local shows and gigs and the odd opening of an exhibition.'

'Better than a kick in the teeth, I suppose. What's the weirdest thing you've ever reviewed?'

'Oof, that's a tough one.' He took another drink as he thought about it. 'I can't really think of anything too mad. Tends to be gigs, shows, fringe stuff – the usual suspects. I did once interview a woman who made ceramic model interpretations of dead people she came across in her local obituary.'

'That's not too shabby,' I laughed. 'Were they accurate?'

'Apparently she had a hit ratio of about one in fifteen being similar.'

I almost snorted my coffee. 'How many did she make?'

'Rooms full of the stuff. It was far and away the weirdest assignment they ever gave me.'

'That sounds *amazing*. You should do more segments on weird local stuff – that'd be fun.'

'I should, shouldn't I? What kind of thing would you recommend I put in it?'

It was my turn to consider. 'My mum once met a woman who made little dolls out of her friends' hair and gave them as gifts.'

He'd been running his fingers through his hair and actively paused. 'She what? That's so gross! Why would anyone ever do that?'

I shrugged – same reason as the woman making the ceramic dead people, presumably. 'Mum wasn't overly forthcoming on the details. I think she said they were some kind of talisman. She made one for my mum but she didn't have any of Mum's hair so she used her own.'

He wrinkled his nose. 'Jesus. Why does that creep me out so much?'

'I'd say it's cos it's pretty creepy.'

'Did your mum keep it?' he asked.

'Yeah, I think she did. She thought it was quite sweet.'

'I suppose it is, in a way. What about you? What brings you here?'

'Much like you, I needed a place to work that wasn't my house. I started up my own business recently and it was too hard to concentrate in my living room.'

'Fair. What's your business?'

I always felt awkward trying to explain what it was I was doing with my life these days. Saying it out loud always made it sound so ridiculous to my own ears. But he'd get it. If anyone understood the world of PR, it was a journalist, right? I toughed it out before my silence got too ambiguous and he'd start thinking I was an arms dealer or something. 'I'm a publicist.'

'Publicist, eh? That sounds fun. For anyone I might know?'

Oddly, not the usual follow-up question. 'It's still early days so I've only got one client so far.'

'Cool. Who's the client?'

The room was usually split into people who'd heard of Steve Annick and thought he was a charming chancer – a pool that was getting smaller by the hour, these days – people who thought he was a tool who shouldn't be given the oxygen of publicity, and those who had never even heard his name. I couldn't decide which camp I wanted Fraser to fall into. 'Steve Annick,' I hazarded.

He frowned and I could almost see his brain figuring out how he knew the name.

'Steve Ann . . . wait, you mean the guy from *Leith, Laugh, Love*?'

'The very one.'

He grinned. 'I met him once at a party – he's a funny guy. Told an unrepeatable story about a—'

I held up a hand with a groan. 'Please don't ruin my day.'

'Aye, that's a solid baptism of fire as your first client. I'd say you've got your work cut out for you.'

'It's like herding blind giraffes. On meth. You can't take your eyes off him for a second. Just staggering about the place, running into trees and falling over.' I paused. 'Metaphorically speaking, of course. I'm fairly sure he's not on meth.' Fairly.

'Is it true he once tried to break into the meerkat enclosure at an event *Leith, Laugh, Love* were putting on at the zoo?'

Christ, who even knew at this point? I decided to err on the side of denial, just in case. 'I haven't heard that one from him, so I'd say on balance, probably not true.' I was about to regale him with the inappropriate cardboard cut-out story when movement from the doorway caught my eye. My brain had registered who it was without my eyes really getting a look in and I had to forestall a groan.

What was Neil doing in here? Why on earth had he come back? Had I forgotten something? 'Um, can you excuse me one second?'

I jumped up and made my way across to him. He saw me coming and gave me a bright smile.

'Hey!' he said happily, and before I could react he'd leaned in and kissed me.

'Hi, Neil,' I replied, trying not to seize up completely with embarrassment at such a public display of his affection. Although I had to admit, he smelled really good, while I still very much looked like I'd slept in a hedge. How was that possible? Did he bathe in a stream on his way back? 'What are you doing here?'

'I know you were struggling a bit with the hangover so I thought I'd get you some pick-me-ups to help you work.' He held up a bag triumphantly. He looked so pleased that I couldn't quite bring myself to be annoyed at the fact that my one-night stand had boomeranged back unannounced.

'Um, thanks. You shouldn't have.'

He shrugged modestly. 'It was no problem.' He nodded over to where I'd been and where Fraser was sitting typing. 'Sorry, I didn't mean to interrupt anything.'

'You're not interrupting anything – we're sharing a table cos it's nearest the socket and has the best lighting.' Wait, why was I explaining this?

He nodded affably. 'Cool. It's a nice wee place here. I hadn't heard of it before.'

God, please don't let him suggest working here too.

'I was thinking, would you be keen to do that walk in the Pentlands next weekend? I know we talked about it but I thought we could pencil it in?'

What on earth had possessed me to imply at any point that I liked hillwalking? Oh wait, because Amal had inexplicably told him I liked it and I drunkenly didn't correct him. Bloody Amal. Bloody wine. Bloody me. The Pentlands were lovely, of course, but more for a quick spin and a picnic, not a whole-ass hike.

But he was looking so keen at the prospect and he'd brought me stuff for my hangover and he was hot and pretty good in bed and what did I have to lose? It wasn't like I had a lot else waiting for me next weekend. What harm?

I smiled up at him. 'Sure, that sounds good.'

A grin lit up his face. 'Great, I can drive us there too. I'll text you during the week and we can set up a time.'

'Yep, that works.'

He leaned down and planted another stubbly kiss. As he was about to leave, a horrible thought occurred to me.

'Erm, I don't need anything . . . specialist, right?'

He frowned. 'What do you mean?'

'Like, kit-wise?'

'No, don't think so. Except the walking sticks. And the camping stools. And maybe a generator?'

I could feel the horror etch its way onto my face before I could stop it. 'A-a generator?'

111

He chuckled. 'I'm kidding. You'll need some decent walking shoes and water. I'll sort us lunch.'

I laughed, despite myself. He'd got me good.

'I'll see you next week.' And off he went.

I made my way back to the table and Fraser. 'Sorry about that.'

'No worries – everything OK?'

'Yeah. Bit hungover so he was dropping in some stuff to help it.'

'Sounds like a keeper.'

Definitely best not to think about that. I took a peek into the bag he'd given me and my dreams of dough-nuts and coke withered and died. Inside, there was a bottle of Powerade, some protein bars and a bunch of bananas. Sigh.

'I don't know about that,' I said, pulling the stuff out of the bag. 'I'd have given a kidney for a donut.'

'I'd say those are probably better for a hangover, though,' he remarked, mildly.

'Note how I'm very purposefully not throwing any of these things at you.' Gosh, we'd palled up pretty quickly if I was directly insulting this man already.

He leaned in and picked up one of the bars, reading the back. 'These ones are actually pretty good. Can I have this?'

'Sure can. I probably won't eat all six of them.'

We chatted a bit more and then gradually settled into working, broken up briefly by the crinkle of him opening and devouring the protein bar in two bites. After a while I tried one. He was right, it wasn't too bad. I felt slightly guilty for giving Neil so much shit for it, albeit mentally. Maybe a jaunt in the Pentlands wouldn't be the worst.

A bleep alerted me to a message from Amal. I realised it was the third one she'd sent, insisting that if I didn't debrief her on the date, she'd arrive at my house and harangue it out of me in person. I replied a grovelling apology, claiming hangover and house guest. It was harder than it should have been to hit send because I absolutely knew the reaction it would unleash. Opening the message, I was in no way proven wrong. It consisted of approximately 9000 party popper emojis and the announcement that she was off to buy a hat.

Chapter Eleven

The hangover eased as the day wore on and, once I'd managed to fob Amal off with cries of work, I was surprised at how much work I actually managed to get done. I finished the press release for the book tour, put together a draft of a speech Steve needed for the *Leith, Laugh, Love* anniversary celebration next month that I absolutely knew he wouldn't stick to, and managed to delete not one but two vaguely inappropriate tweets he'd sent before they gained any kind of traction. Jeez, maybe I should work on more Saturdays.

I was still feeling ropey enough to decide on an early night, though, so I made my way home and to bed at the embarrassing hour of 8.00 p.m.

Even though I'd only emailed him earlier in the day, I decided to check if there was a reply from Myster-E. I wasn't overly comfortable with the weak platitude I'd sent – what kind or a response was it to tell someone who'd ended an engagement that it was better to have decided on it before marriage? I fervently wished I'd sent something less impersonal so I decided that I would try again. Logging in, though, I was surprised to find I wouldn't have to – he'd replied.

I don't know, I kind of feel like stuff like that is almost easier to do when the shit's hitting the fan everywhere else. If your life's burning down, you're as well doing it with a flamethrower as a match, no? But then it was my choice so that's also a fairly easy thing for me to say – it wasn't somebody else doing the burning. Must be harder to take the philosophical view with your situation, though.

Well, that was certainly on the money. I started to type a vague brush-off, as I'd done before, but something stopped me. Maybe it was his comment about doing something all-in. I opted for an honest reply. If anyone wasn't going to judge, I had a feeling it would be him.

Nowadays I look back and feel embarrassed. All of these memories and experiences and feelings that I had and then finding out that none of it was real. I mean, he said it was. That he hadn't meant for it to happen like that etc., etc. – sentiments you may recognise from every cliché that's ever existed in the history of the universe. I mean, I like to think he wasn't just laughing at my rampant stupidity the whole time, but there's always this thought in the back of my mind that he was. I don't know, I guess when you've been dating a while, you start to think that maybe you won't ever meet someone you click with and then when you do and it seems to be working out and you lose it . . . instinct told me the other shoe was going to drop and I didn't listen. Lesson well and truly learned.

I thought about bringing Neil home, about our plan to meet for our Pentlands walk at the weekend, and how I wasn't massively looking forward to it and felt a prickle of guilt. Neil was kind and nice and pretty easy on the eye, not to mention knowing his way about a bedroom. There were way worse ways to pass the time and it wasn't as if we had to marry each other. Why did I always have to be so intense about this?

Mid-spiral, I realised that Myster-E was online and typing and I felt the increasingly familiar little dizzy tingle through my stomach. His reply arrived moments later.

I think there's something to be said for taking lessons from things but that seems to be a pretty hardcore one. I'd hate to think you'd let one arsehole cut you off from future good things. Look at me, being all crazed romantic again, ha ha. I've been out of the dating game for a while and from what I hear from friends, it's a bit of a nightmare, so do feel free to tell me to piss off.

No, but seriously, I guess what I mean is . . . it would be a shame for you to cut yourself off from something good because of the bad actions of someone else. But then, trust is the hardest part of a relationship, isn't it? To put total faith in another human knowing how unbelievably fallible we are as a species is mind-blowing when you sit and think about it. How does anyone actually manage it?!

The idea of being able to do that again felt about as distant as anything could be at this point. But I decided to humour his most recent romantic delusions in my reply.

One thing I will say is that it taught me that, for a fleeting moment at least, I was capable of trusting someone and really loving them – I suppose, for argument's sake, that means I can again. Statistically speaking, of course, I'll be about a thousand years old when I do, but who's counting?

What about you – have you found it difficult to date? It must be kind of weird after being with someone such a long time? Although there's also something to be said for that – you certainly don't seem jaded. A unicorn of the dating market here, ladies and gentlemen! I wonder what kind of wishes you could grant, ha ha.

I hit send and was surprised at how awkward and teenagery I felt – had I really called him a unicorn? Jesus. Turns out there was more than one benefit to us not knowing each other's identity. He'd never be able to put a face to the world's biggest nerd.

I decided it was better for my sanity not to wait for a response. I closed the laptop, quickly checking my phone to make sure Amal hadn't texted to say she'd done something insane, like book a wedding venue for me and Neil. Or at the very least, explain herself for landing me in it with a Munro-bragger of all things. She hadn't yet, at any rate. But the week was young.

Chapter Twelve

A buzzing from my mobile dragged me out of my sleepy depths. How was it morning already? I peeled my eyes open and tried to make sense of my surroundings. Why was it still dark?

Pulling apart my tangle of thoughts, I realised it was because it wasn't my alarm. My phone was ringing. I dragged it towards me, wondering when my arms got so heavy and tried to make sense of the words.

Steve was calling.

It was . . . 4.00 a.m!

This couldn't be good.

'Hello? Steve?' I croaked, heart pounding.

'Ada, oh, thank God. I'm so sorry. Have I . . . have I woken you?' His words were so slurred he could barely get them out.

Was he kidding me? 'It's 4.00 a.m., Steve. Of course you've woken me. Has something happened? Are you OK?'

'I can't find Christopher,' he wailed.

'What?'

'Christopher. He's gone and I don't know where.' I realised the slurring was from tears, not drink. On second thoughts, probably both. But Steve lived alone. Who the fuck was Christopher? I don't think he'd ever even mentioned the name to me. Shit, had he? I couldn't think straight.

'OK, um. Don't panic, he'll not have gone far. When was the last time you saw him?'

'Yesterday morning when I left for work.'

'Right.' Now for how to work out who or what Christopher was. 'Did he . . . seem OK when you left him?'

'He was absolutely fine!' he wailed.

I couldn't get my sleep-pocked brain to figure out the kind of question that would get me the answer I needed. There was nothing else for it. 'Steve, is Christopher a person or an animal?'

'He's a dog,' he hiccupped.

'What? When did you get a dog?' Who would ever allow this man a dog?

'He's not mine.'

'He's not yours?'

'No.'

'Tell me the truth. Did you steal Christopher?' I could just see the headlines now:

Steve AnNicks Local Canine.

'Of course not!' He sounded mortally offended.

This was like playing twenty questions with a chimp. I forced myself to take a deep, calming breath. 'Right, well, good. But if you want my help, you need to give me more information. Who does Christopher belong to? Why do you have him?'

119

'My neighbour's mum got sick and she needed to go and see her so I said I'd look after her dog until she got back.'

I took a shot in the dark. 'This wouldn't be Sara Kohli, would it?'

'That's the ticket.' He was back to slurring cheerfully again.

Stunningly beautiful sports TV presenter from across the way. The world made sense again. I pulled my free hand across my eyes to try and scrub them open. 'Are you absolutely sure he's not in the house? There's a lot of rooms. Have you checked them all?'

'Yes!'

'Steve, let me be clear. If I come over to your house and find this dog in one of the rooms, I will quit. On the spot. Do you understand?'

'Y-ees.'

'So I'm going to ask you one more time. Have you searched every room in the house? The dog is definitely not there?'

There was a long pause.

'Hello? Steve?'

'I'll go and have a quick . . . just a liiiittle scootch around . . . let me put you on hold for one wee minute.'

'No, hang up, don't put me on—'

He put me on hold. The man had set up 'Bat Out of Hell' as his hold music.

Unbelievable.

Meat Loaf was hitting highways like battering rams when Steve picked up the phone again.

'Ada! Ada, I found him! He was upstairs this whole time! Say hello, Christopher, say hello to Ada, yeeees, you're the best boy! Good boy, Christopher!'

I looked at my phone – 4.15.

'Goodnight, Steve.' Without waiting on an answer, I hung up.

This was my fault. I should have learned long ago to put my phone on flight mode. Also, to stop enabling grown men with ridiculous habits.

I'd been so pleased when I'd signed Steve. It'd felt like such a boon, the beginning of bigger and better things. But then he's started sucking up all my time, with the added bonus of constantly being on the verge of being fired by *Leith, Laugh, Love*. Which meant I was constantly on the verge of being let go by my sole source of income. The gnawing anxiety I always got when I let myself think about that started sawing at my bones again.

God, I really needed to get new clients on board. Ones with actual strategies and upward trajectories and guaranteed income. Preferably also with better impulse control. I thought back to a conversation I'd had with Amanda the receptionist the day Steve offended the nuns. She'd mentioned her friend's dance studio were looking to expand and had been thinking of publicity. What were they called? Dance something . . . with a colour. Pink? Purple? I wracked my brains.

Indigo. That was the one. Indigo Dance.

Yes. First thing tomorrow, I was going to email them and introduce myself. Properly start to have a look around for other local potential clients. Offer up my services, maybe at a reduced rate to begin with if they were a small company. If, for no other reason than the chances of them needing me to mount a search party for a dog they didn't own who wasn't even missing at 4.00 a.m. were probably negligible.

I stuck my phone on silent and flung it back onto the bedside cabinet. Lying down again, I tried to get some sleep but it swiftly became clear that wasn't on the cards. I watched the morning light slowly drag itself across my bedroom floor until my alarm went off for real.

Hauling it across to switch it off, my dry exhausted eyes registered that I had a message from Steve. Opening it, there was a picture of him holding a little fluffy dog proudly up to the camera with a big smile and a thumbs up. I found myself smiling back at it and promptly shut the phone off.

Goddamn Steve.

Chapter Thirteen

The rest of the week flew by at a frankly ludicrous pace. Wee Mo got a cold, meaning a postponement of our weekly dinner, so I was given a temporary reprieve from a proper Amal inquisition over my date with Neil.

In the meantime, Fraser and I fell into a kind of routine at the café. We would text each other a rough approximation of when we would be arriving. Whoever was in first would grab the table and get a coffee in for the both of us – if it was Fraser, he'd also smuggle some of the biscuits. I hadn't quite managed to brave taking more just yet. The café was starting to introduce a new cheaper brand and I was pretty sure it was because I'd almost bankrupted them on account of eating my bodyweight in shortbread.

Once we were settled, we'd run through our plans for the day so we could hold each other accountable. It was a thing I really missed about working with other people – having someone, even this slightly random newbie, to keep me on track and bounce ideas off really helped to get the creative juices going. He had a strong eye for minor details. Had he not intervened, Steve would have been actively referred to as 'an animal loser' courtesy of my attempt at a blurb for the programme of a panto he was about to star in. Which, given Steve's most recent adventure, was surprisingly on the nose. It also maybe didn't hurt that Fraser smelled really good. Some kind of faint aftershave that I hadn't come across before – slightly woody with a hint of citrus – and it suited him down to the ground. Why didn't more men wear aftershave?

This, my temporary Amal reprieve and some top GIF game from Myster-E, meant I reached Friday feeling that I was firing on all cylinders. Fraser also seemed to be hitting his stride, work-wise, and Steve had somehow made it five whole days without accidentally starting any kind of fracas, which was nigh-on miraculous. I'd managed to book the final venues for his tour, got him some local radio spots to discuss it and got him to actually put the dates in his diary. The man had the attention span of a ferret so three months down the line may as well have been one hundred years – I was contemplating tattooing the dates on his forehead.

To cap it all, I'd got a reply from not one but two of the businesses I'd approached to discuss potential rep-resentation. Indigo Dance had come back with interest, but wanted a pitch, which was fair enough – we were in the process of setting up a date. And a local small film company on the rise had also replied and invited me to meet them for coffee. It was positively all go.

I saw Fraser scrunch up his face and mutter what looked a lot like the word 'Shit.' It was a look I'd only seen him pull a few times. It made him look slightly munchkin-ish and quite adorable.

I pulled one of my headphones out of my ear. 'What's up?'

He cast an eye to the back of the room where the toilets were, back to his computer and then to his phone.

'I'm waiting on a contact coming back to me but they were meant to call ten minutes ago and they still haven't.'

Maybe Steve had lowered my bar for unacceptable waiting times but ten minutes didn't seem *too* egregious. 'Are you on a deadline for it?'

'No, but there's a solid chance I'll wet myself if I don't pee now.'

It was a deadline of sorts. 'Were you never taught that holding it in will give you a UTI? Go and pee!'

He glanced at the toilet door again. I hadn't noticed before but he was rapidly tapping his foot, like some kind of cartoon character. 'I really can't miss this call.'

I shook my head. 'It's not like you'll be ages. And the longer you wait, the more chance they'll call.' He still wasn't convinced. 'Look, if your phone goes, I'll pretend to be your PA and ask them to hold.'

He laughed. 'Really? That would be amazing.' He was practically vibrating now.

'Man, you're stressing me out,' I laughed. 'Pee! Now!'

He nudged his phone in my direction, gave a grateful smile and was gone like a shot. I stuck one headphone back in and continued typing.

As is the law with these things, he'd barely cleared the door when his phone started buzzing. I pulled the headphone out of my ear, picked it up and swiped to answer someone called Lana.

'Fraser . . .' Wait, what was his surname again? Shit! ''s phone,' I finished lamely. *Good job, Ada.*

125

There was a slight pause. 'Hi, is Fraser there?' a woman with an English accent said uncertainly.

I put on my very best PA-style to make up for the very un-PA way I'd answered the call. 'Sorry, he's popped out for a second. He'll be back any moment now though – are you OK to hold?'

'It's OK, I can call him later.'

Eek. He'd expressly said that he needed to take this call. If he missed it because I'd insisted he pee, the man might never pee again. These were high stakes. 'Honestly, he'll be just a minute.'

'Can I ask who you are?'

How important was this call? Should I lie and say I was Fraser's PA? No, that would be weird. But then why was I answering his phone?

Out of the corner of my eye, the bathroom door swung open and Fraser strode back across the room.

Thank Christ for that.

'That's him coming back now. I'll pass you over.' I covered the receiver and handed the phone to him. 'It's for you,' I told him helpfully.

'Are you sure?'

Ah, a comedian in our midst. I scowled.

He laughed and took the phone. 'Mr Renfrew?'

Wait . . . Mr? Oh. Oh no.

Confusion flitted across his face. He looked at his phone. Which in hindsight was probably something he should have done before taking it. 'Lana? Hey! Sorry, I thought you were my contact at the Pitt.' He moved away from the table and I decided now would be a

126

good time to get back to work. After a few minutes, he returned.

'So, you're fired as my PA.'

'I'm so sorry – it rang and I just assumed—'

He settled back into his chair looking amused and waved me away. 'It's fine, a perfectly reasonable mistake to make.'

'Who's Lana?' I asked and then realised I already knew. 'Shit, wait, is she your girlfriend?' He had a girlfriend? Of course he did. Why didn't he mention that? Why *would* he mention that? Why was I even wondering why he'd mention that? I batted that thought straight out of my head.

A horrible thought occurred to me. 'And I didn't answer her when she asked who it was – oh God, Fraser, I'm so sorry! I was just trying to figure out if I should say I was your PA to make you sound fancy and then you came back and—'

He laughed and waved me away again. 'Ada, it's fine. Really, don't worry about it. Thanks for taking the call.'

I settled my feathers. He took a drink of coffee and then made a face. 'Yuck, cold.' He jiggled his cup in my direction. 'Refill?'

I nodded and handed him my empty mug and he made his way to the tea point to make us fresh cups. I watched him manoeuvre his way around the table.

It was weird because, initially, Fraser wasn't the kind of person I would describe, if asked, as confident. Even sitting with him, he'd been quiet at first and I'd assumed it was because he was a bit awkward or shy. And then he'd open his mouth and chat and be the easiest company in the world. It took me a day or two to realise that it was because he *was* at ease. With everything, apparently. I'd seen him take more than one fractious call, the kind that would twist me up no end. Not that I couldn't deal with it, more that dealing with it came at a cost afterwards.

But not so for my new work pal. He was frank and open when he wanted to be but careful about how he phrased things. He'd mull through his responses and after a while I put my finger on what it was that let him do it – he wasn't afraid of silence.

The bastard!

What kind of a maniac wasn't afraid of silence? Nothing good ever came of silence, everyone knew that. But I had to hand it to him, his ease was easy to be around.

'I've a proposition for you.' Suddenly he was back at the table and I realised I'd been miles away. It took a second to process what he'd said.

'You . . . do?'

'Yeah.' He leaned forward and put his elbows on the table, all very businesslike. 'So I need to nip out for a dentist appointment next week but it'd be a pain in the arse to take all my stuff and I don't want to mention it to my boss so I was thinking, I could leave it here and you could watch it and keep my laptop logged in and stuff? And if any calls come through you could answer them? And then I can do the same for you. You could go to that HIIT cardio class you were talking about. Just leave your stuff here.'

That wasn't the worst idea I'd ever heard, even if I *had* been joking about the HIIT class. 'That sounds suspiciously like a plan.'

'Great! But only if you're sure it's OK?' he affirmed.

'It's not like you're asking me to go all *Strangers on a Train* with you.' I lifted my coffee and paused. 'Wait – this isn't that, right? Like, dentist isn't some kind of bizarre euphemism?'

'Foiled again.'

I laughed and took a sip. 'Although, you know, your boss shouldn't be telling you that you can't go to a dentist, right?'

He looked sheepish. 'I may or may not have lied very recently about a dental appointment that never was. She'll be suspicious if I suddenly have another one.'

'Ah, I do enjoy a web of lies,' I replied. 'Where were you instead?' I realised after it'd come out that it might be a rude question, but he didn't seem to mind.

'My aunt needed help dropping something off.'

'That was very noble of you – I assumed it was a hangover.'

He shook his head. 'Nah. Although I will confess there may have been a tiny hangover too. But it's never stopped me before. Nor you, if I recall.'

I gave him a stiff middle finger.

'Let's do this! Shake on it?' He held out his hand.

'All right, *Mad Men*. Shall we light a cigar and get some whisky on the go while we're at it?'

'What? What's wrong with shaking on a deal?'

'Who shakes on a deal in this day and age? I say we make it interesting. How about a pinkie promise? Oh, or I could spit on my hand? No, wait! A blood pact?'

He shook his head, smiling. 'I'm taking this desk back. No more socket for you.'

'I'll stop. But only because I've run out of acceptable bodily fluid alternatives to suggest.'

He raised an eyebrow.

I felt an inexorable flood of heat rush to my cheeks.

My phone buzzed on the table and I grabbed it as if it was a lifebelt.

Jeremy.

Wait. Who was Jeremy?

Oh yeah, one of the guys I'd been chatting to on the app before it'd fizzled. Jeez, that felt like ages ago now. I opened the message. 'Oh for . . .! Why are men?' I wailed, dropping the phone back onto the table.

'What's up?' Fraser asked.

'This guy I was chatting to a while back just sent me a dick pic out of absolutely nowhere.'

His eyebrows almost reached the ceiling. 'Seriously?'

I picked up the phone and waved it at him. 'Look at that – he did. What the actual fuck, Fraser?'

He held up his hands. 'I can say, hand on heart, that this was nothing to do with me.'

'Explain this to me,' I persevered. 'I need a male perspective.'

'I'm afraid, having never been of a mind to send dick pics to a random women, I can't shed much light here. It's – if you'll forgive the pun – a bit of a dick move.'

'God, it just makes me so angry. You wouldn't do it in real life! Would you? But it's fine here?' I picked up the phone and started typing a tirade, only to see Fraser's fingers curl around the sides of it.

'As your newly appointed PA, allow me.'

Hmm. I let go of the phone. 'OK. What did you have in mind?' I asked.

He didn't answer. Silent for a solid minute, I watched him work and then he set the phone back in front of me.

'What did you do?' I asked.

'What every good PA does. I managed expectations.'

I picked up my phone and opened the message. 'Oh my *God!*' My shout echoed back at me and I slapped a hand over my mouth. 'Please tell me you used incognito mode for this.'

'I deleted the cookies so you shouldn't have any actual porn in your history – unless you do, of course.' He grinned. 'No judgement here.'

I couldn't stop laughing. Before I knew it, there were tears streaming down my face. 'It's so big!' I gasped.

'Only compared to his.'

Hah. 'Is this where you tell me this is actually from your phone?'

'Oh, I don't think I can claim anything quite that impressive. But I'm not quite as far off as young Jeremy here, though.'

'That's quite the review.'

'Well, again: it's important to manage expectations.' He seemed to clock what he'd said because he took a huge mouthful of his drink. Was my face actively on fire again? 'This ought to calm him down, though. Give him a sense of where he stands in the scheme of things.'

There was silence for a moment as I struggled to find a response that wasn't asking him to clarify his penis size or spontaneously combust from embarrassment. 'OK, but if he ends up being into this, I'm sending you on the date.'

Needless to say, I didn't get a reply from Jeremy.

After the dick pic excitement, we chittered our way through another few hours of work, deciding to call it a day at four. It was, after all, a Friday and we'd had quite the adventure.

'Have you ever been to the Pentlands?' I asked, as I piled my stuff into my backpack.

Fraser paused, mid-packing his own things. 'Of course. Haven't you?'

'What do you mean "of course"? Let me guess, you also spend all your free time yomping up mountains. Am I the only person alive that didn't get that memo? Was there some kind of rite of passage that I missed? A decree stating that every human over the age of eighteen must now be into scaling massive piles of rock in their free time?'

He stared for a moment then burst out laughing. 'Sorry, did you refer to the Pentlands as mountains? They're a bunch of hills.'

'A hill is a hill is a hill. You can still stab a person with a butter knife, you know,' I reasoned. 'If anything being blunter makes it worse.'

I watched him try to work through what I'd said and then ultimately shake it off. 'OK, so I'm getting the impression that one of us might be going to the Pentlands sometime soon? Perhaps a little bit against our will?'

I finished packing and zipped up my bag with a sigh. 'What gave it away?'

He finished zipping up his own bag and leaned forward onto it. 'If you don't want to go, why are you going?'

'Because I said I would. And I know I'm being a dick because it's so beautiful and not actually a mountain and I do quite like walking and stuff. But I prefer city walking, you know? With pavements and flat surfaces and indoor plumbing available when needed.' I let out another plaintive sigh.

'When are you going? Maybe it'll rain and you can cry off.'

'Tomorrow.'

Fraser pulled out his phone and checked the weather, pulling a face as he did. 'Eighteen degrees, cloudy with some sun and very little wind. What you have there, I'm afraid, is perfect hillwalking weather.' He slipped his phone back into his pocket. 'If you're going with the guy who brought you the protein bars, I reckon you'll be in pretty good hands. He struck me as the type who'd know his way around a compass. Big socks and sandals vibe.'

I hadn't even realised he'd seen enough of Neil to know anything like that. But he wasn't wrong.

'Look, it's set to be a nice day and the Pentlands are really beautiful at this time of year. You'll have a great time,' he reassured me.

'Promise?' I asked.

There was a slight pause. 'You'll have a great time.'

Chapter Fourteen

Neil dropped me off outside the flat after our Pentlands trip with an unfathomably cheerful goodbye. 'I had the best time. Thanks for coming!'

I forced a smile, wondering how you could tell if someone was delusional. For all the world he looked like a sane man but no sane person could look me dead in the eyes as genuinely as he was and say what a fun time he'd just had with me. I said goodnight, and somehow made it to my bedroom without my legs falling off. They were practically twanging, my muscles were so tired. The Pentlands may not be actual mountains or, indeed, Munros, but as far as I was concerned, they might as well have been. Munro-bagging was for the birds – I was having nothing more to do with it. Yet another life lesson learned.

I knew a bath would help my aching legs but I didn't have the energy. I crawled into bed and pulled the covers over me, but there was one thing I'd not forgo – Myster-E. We'd had some back and forth over the week but we both seemed to have been busy so it had been more banter and GIFs than anything else. My phone had had a hard time getting reception in the hills, so I hadn't been able to check for messages and the day had felt even longer for it. Opening the site, I was pleased to find that there was a reply from him and that it was longer than it had been in a while. I felt the little buzz start up.

I'll be honest, I haven't done much in the way of dating – bits and pieces here and there but I'll confess I'm not massively looking forward to it. I kind of have a fear that I'll fall back on all the old habits that I promised myself I'd move away from when I broke up with my ex. There's something very tempting about wanting to run face-first into intimacy with somebody, to have that closeness back, you know? I think we both know what a certain Mr Poirot would have to say about that.

A unicorn you say?

Groan. I'd thought I'd got away with the unicorn thing, seeing as I'd said it approximately a thousand years ago. Apparently not.

Shucks, Captain Marple, you do me a great honour. However I'm about as much of a unicorn as a horse with a horn glued to its head. I will, however, accept your compliment on the proviso that you accept one in return: I very much doubt that someone as winning as you are will have to wait 970-odd years (you're what, early thirties at a guess?) before you find something worthwhile with someone again. (Who knows, maybe I could grant you that as your unicorn wish ;))

Wait! Was that a winky face? I felt a flush of pleasure. Which was ludicrous, of course. All he'd done was group some punctuation together and return a compliment. And yet the pleasure was still very much there.

Because at least I knew it wasn't 100 per cent only in my head or only on my side.

But now I was struggling how to reply. Had all that fresh Pentland air somehow scrambled my brain? I scanned through, deliberately skipping the compliment so that it couldn't throw me again, and decided to start with the very important job of disabusing him of any romantic notions, Poirot-wise. Which, given the fact he had so recently starred in the most horrifying sex dream I'd ever had seemed more than a little hypocritical, but that was neither here nor there.

Monsieur Poirot can suck it when it comes to romantic advice. The only woman he was ever in love with was a former Russian aristocrat-turned-thief – hardly a man to trust in that arena (although I can't fault his taste – if one is going to fall in love, one should do so with aplomb, right? As the romantic, here, you'd be best placed to answer this, ha ha).

Marple, on the other hand – she'd probably look at you over her glasses and say something sage, like 'habits are the blanket fort we build to keep the world at bay'– only not that, obviously, and then presumably announce that the butler was murdered by your oldest, dearest friend.

But seriously. Obviously I can see the appeal of wanting the closeness back. One thing I will say for everything that happened with my ex, being with him opened up parts of me that being alone had closed off. Does that make sense? You get so used to a certain way of living and being, so used to not sharing certain pieces of yourself, that when you do start to, it becomes kind of addictive.

Romantic relationships are such a specific kind of inti-macy, and when you go for a while without them I think you almost become numb. You forget all that wonder and possibility: it's like a muscle that wastes away because it isn't being used. All that potential, all those hidden parts of yourself are still there, just ... dormant, I suppose. Even being touched – something as simple as holding hands. And knowing that (even though it turned out to not really be true for me), there is one person in the world who you come first for, and who you prioritise as well. Probably the only positive takeaway from what happened was that I was reminded how good that can feel.

In other news, you guessed my age fairly near the mark, you wizard, you. I'm thirty. And as for your whole 'horn glued on' thing, you know what they say about horses dressed as unicorns, right? A horn's a horn.

Chapter Fifteen

I limped my way into the café, wincing as I went. Every part of me hurt. I could have easily just worked from home but after an hour of faffing about on nothing at all, I realised I missed being in my little coffice and having somebody who would force me to actually knuckle down. Plus who'd harangue Fraser for biting his nails if I wasn't there? And who would feed me biscuits if I sat in the flat alone?

He was already there when I arrived and, when he caught sight of me, the polite smile became a not-so-polite laugh-out-loud.

'What happened to you?' he sang out as I made my way to the table, inching carefully down into the seat opposite.

'Don't.'

I could feel him surveying me. 'So this is an educated guess, but I'm assuming the Pentlands weren't all you'd hoped?'

'You said it would be fine!' I wailed, accusatorily. 'That it was just a bunch of hills.'

'Only because you called it a mountain! Also, technically speaking, they are, in fact, a bunch of hills.' Leaning forward, he closed his laptop and put his elbows on either side of it. 'So let me guess, you fell down it. Rolling all the way, like that bit in *The Princess Bride*. Am I close?'

'Man, I wish. I love *The Princess Bride*.'

'The poor attempt at a swerve around my question has been noted.' He grinned.

'Urgh, it's not even a swerve. There is literally no story to tell. We walked. *For hours*. Don't get me wrong, I like a bit of scenery. The outdoors is nice this time of year. But he'd said he was bringing lunch so I left him to it. Do you know what he brought?'

'If by "he" you mean protein-bar man, I'm going to go out on a limb and say . . . packet of crisps and a massive Cadbury's Dairy Milk?'

'Yes. That is *exactly* what he brought.'

He frowned. 'Seriously?'

'Don't pretend you don't know he made a salad!' The memory of it almost brought tears to my eyes. 'I mean, I have to hand it to the man, it was a good salad. There was some meat and fancy leaves and quinoa and stuff. And he'd bought some bread and hummus and in any other circumstance that would have been fine. But we were there for *seven hours*.' I put my head in my hands at the injustice of it all. 'By the end of it, my feet were blistered, I picked up what I'm almost sure was sunstroke and he was approximately fifteen seconds away from me straight-up eating him.'

Fraser chuckled. 'Sounds like a fun day was had by everybody.'

'See now, that's the worst part. When Neil left me back home, he said he had, and I quote, "the best time." He actively wants to do it again!' I leaned forward to give Fraser a closer view of my bafflement. 'What kind of monster is he?'

He shrugged. 'Take it as a compliment. You were obviously good company. Albeit a terrible hillwalker.'

I shook my head vehemently. I was many things in life, deluded wasn't one of them. 'I was terrible company, Fraser. The *worst*. We ran out of things to talk about before we'd even hit lunch so I spent the rest of it walking three metres behind him bitching about how sore my feet were. There are murderers who wouldn't deserve the punishment of having to haul me up hills all day.'

'Neil clearly doesn't agree.' He sat back. 'When's your next outing?'

I groaned. 'We haven't made a plan yet. But I live in hope that that it'll be indoors.' Or, if I was being totally honest with myself, maybe even . . . nothing at all? And then I imagined Amal's reaction when I tried to explain that I wasn't seeing him again and bottled the thought.

'Everyone needs a dream, I suppose.'

'Like, what's wrong with a nice trip to the cinema? Bit of Marvel, some popcorn, maybe a cheeky smooch in the back row? Ideal, no?'

'Maybe. All except the Marvel bit.'

'Don't tell me you hate Marvel movies?'

'They're just not my scene,' he said, shrugging.

'Why? Because you hate fun, whimsical, popular films?'

'Yep. Can't stand any of those things,' he deadpanned. 'And not just in films. All aspects of my life. No thank you, Madam, take your joy elsewhere.'

I laughed. 'Fair enough. What about you? How was your weekend?' I asked, now that I'd got both my salad rant and apparently also my Marvel rant out of my system.

'It's funny you should enquire because I wound up doing a really weird article that my editor loved and I have you to thank for it.'

I blinked. 'You do? How?'

'Remember you mentioned the thing about the hair doll? I ended up going down this spooky doll rabbit hole after you left. I threw together a thousand words and sent it on. My editor read it and loved it. It's the fastest I've ever had her agree to something.'

'Well, look at you! That's great. What did you learn?'

'Did you know there's a bunch of haunted dolls in Greyfriars Kirkyard?'

'I most certainly did not!'

He opened up his laptop and dug out the article, running me through it.

'Are you serious? What, are they just, like, strewn about the place?' It'd been a while since I'd swung by to say hello to wee Bobby, the adorable dog statue, and scowl at passers-by for touching his nose but I was pretty sure I'd have remembered a bunch of haunted dolls knocking about the place.

'No, no, they're locked up,' Fraser replied. 'You can't leave haunted dolls lying about, you know. That would be irresponsible.'

'True. 'That's great! When will the article be out?'

'Next week at some point. What's even better though is she wants more where that came from. So I now get to spend my time researching the weirdest things to do in Edinburgh. How cool is that?'

If I could have turned green with envy, I might have. 'I hate you. This is literally my dream.'

'That's a . . . fairly unconventional dream you have there,' he chuckled.

'This is so unfair. How did you manage to get such a fun job?' I huffed. 'I, meanwhile, will be spending the majority of my week using all of my faculties to talk a middle-aged man into reading a one-page memo. I shit you not, it will take me *all week*.'

'It's not that bad. You're meeting those production company people for a coffee too – all sorts of business plans!'

'That's next week.' Though until he'd mentioned it, it had fallen clean out of my head. I had to hand it to the man, he was an excellent PA.

'Why don't you help me out with some research? There's a talk on some kind of psychic architecture with a reading after at the Arthur Conan Doyle Centre.'

'What in the name of Sherlock Holmes is psychic architecture?'

He shrugged. 'You'll have to come along and find out. Although it's short notice.'

'How short notice?'

'Tonight at seven thirty.'

'Ah, that is short notice. Happily for you, I cleared a chunk of my terribly busy schedule after my walk on Saturday on the assumption it'd take at least a week for my muscles to untangle.'

'Happily for *you*, you mean. It's not every day you get to find out what psychic architecture is.'

'I already know what it is: nonsense.'

'Well, yes, but that's hardly the spirit, is it? If you'll excuse the pun. Also, full disclosure, I made up the term psychic architecture. I can't actually remember what it was called.' He held up his hands. 'But there'll be free drinks.'

'Then by all means, book me a ticket, Jeeves, and don't spare the horses.' I eased myself back in my chair, ignoring every screaming tendon in my body. 'How much will I owe you?'

He waved me away. 'It's like eight quid. I'll claim them back on expenses.'

And there was me thinking this deal couldn't get any sweeter.

'Excuse me?' a voice from above me rang out.

I looked up to find myself staring at my old nemesis, Clive. He was holding up a packet of shortbread with a vaguely combative expression.

'Oh, hello, Clive.'

He gave me a brief nod. 'I couldn't help but notice the banoffee biscuits you have there.'

I didn't dare catch Fraser's eye, instead making a point of picking up the biscuit packet to look at it. 'Ah, yes, so they are.'

'They run at rather a premium,' he continued, 'so would you mind terribly swapping me that packet for these?' He waved his boring normal shortbread at me. 'It does seem only fair, as there are such a limited number and you've had,' he looked at me pointedly, 'quite a few.'

I knew this day would come.

Before I could think of a response, Fraser had acquiesced, handing him the packet that was sitting on the table and politely refusing the proffered plain ones. He wished

Clive a lovely day and I could practically see the old coot melt. The frosty expression he'd worn on approach was replaced with a wrinkly smile, all but slapping Fraser on the back as he left.

None of which was directed at me, I couldn't help but note. 'Ah, Clive. What would I do without my nemesis?'

Fraser shook his head, amused. 'He's not your nemesis, he's just a slightly cranky old man.'

'Who turfed me out of his chair and stole my biscuits. That's prime nemesis-ing, right there.'

'I'd hate to see what you'd do about somebody who really fucked you over.'

Oh, just quit my job and move away so they'd never have to deal with the consequences of their actions was what I thankfully didn't say. What I did say was, 'I was really looking forward to that biscuit.'

'Can you keep a secret?'

I sure could. 'Yes.'

Fraser looked furtively side to side, stuck his head under the table and came back up with . . . another packet of banoffee biscuits.

'You beautiful bastard! Do you have a stash?' I exclaimed, managing to pull my voice down to a whisper so the biscuit police wouldn't return.

Fraser replied with a wink and a smile, reopened his laptop and went back to work.

Chapter Sixteen

The West End area around and about the Arthur Conan Doyle Centre was as familiar to me as breathing. I'd grown up in Dalry. Me, Amal and a cadre of friends had spent countless hours messing around down by the Water of Leith, around the fancy Georgian townhouses towards Charlotte Square and in the grounds of St Mary's Cathedral. It had all seemed so unbearably banal – all of us wiling away the hours until we could actually get to do the things we really wanted to do. I was running slightly late but I found myself pausing to stare up at the gothic splendour of the cathedral. I'd not really gone wandering around here since I'd come back and I was genuinely surprised by how beautiful it looked in the early evening light. The day had been cloudy but there was some sun breaking through, bathing the sandstone in a warm golden light. Was it nicer now or had it always looked like this and I just hadn't noticed?

I got to the lights by the Centre at 7.36 to find Fraser waiting outside the steps for me – that man sure was a stickler for timekeeping. Good thing I'd texted him to say I was running slightly late. He held up his hand in a wave and I felt a little frisson of excitement. This was the first time we'd actually done something outside work. We were friend-friends now, not just café colleagues.

I greeted him and we made our way past the black iron railings, up the steps and through the grand front door of the centre, which was in a gorgeous old Victorian townhouse that made me feel a bit like I was entering some kind of period drama.

I looked back at Fraser with an excited grin. 'I've been wanting to come in here for ages!' I crowed quietly.

'Me too, actually. It's pretty swish, hey?'

We each grabbed a glass of prosecco from a table as we entered the foyer. In front of me, a wide spiral staircase curled upwards to a domed skylight. It was plush red carpet and dark wooden panelling as far as the eye could see. I took a sip of my prosecco as we followed a stream of people making their way up the first flight of stairs. Soft music played – was that a *harp*? – and there was a swirl of incense perfuming the air.

A gal could get used to this.

Just as I was warming up to my new surroundings, my foot caught in the carpet, in a handy reminder that the universe giveth and she immediately taketh away. I flung out my arm and grabbed the banister to rebalance. Every muscle in my body screamed bloody murder, thanks to my recent ludicrous yomp through the Pentlands, and it took every iota of strength I had not to yell something deeply offensive. Thankfully, Fraser had gone ahead of me and missed my almost-foray into comedy pratfalls.

The astonishingly glamorous older lady behind me, however, didn't miss it, and leaned forward to ask if I was OK in the poshest English accent I'd ever heard. I gave her an embarrassed, if slightly winded, assurance that I was. Although it probably wouldn't have mattered if I'd hit the ground, anyway. The carpet was so soft and deep I'd most likely have bounced.

As we reached the first-floor landing, we immediately got tangled up in the queue of people filtering into the room where the psychic shenanigans were happening. Fraser turned back to me with a smile: 'Pretty cool building.'

'I mean, it'll do, I suppose.' I moved across to peek up to the skylight and then back down to the entrance hall. It really was ridiculously lovely.

The glamorous woman who'd been behind me appeared at my side and leaned over, following my gaze down. 'Careful of the vortex, though.'

It took me a minute to process what she'd said. 'The . . . what now?'

Fraser dodged between some people and arrived at my side. 'Did you say vortex?'

She smiled, enjoying her rapt audience. 'I did indeed.'

'I'm going to have to insist you elaborate,' I cried, delighted at such an immediate intro into lunacy.

She smiled at what, in hindsight, could have sounded like quite a rude thing to say. 'We've had numerous psychics stay in the building who have all reported seeing a vortex running from the floor all the way up to the ceiling and through the skylight. One hypothesis is that it is a portal that the spirits can move freely through. It's why the building has such a strong history of paranormal activity.'

This evening had officially upped the ante on my already high expectations. As had this woman. She was the last person in the world I would have expected to believe in that kind of thing.

'Do you own the building?' I asked. She certainly looked as though she could afford it.

She laughed and shook her head, her matching earrings and necklace catching the light and scattering it around her. I felt unbelievably scraggily in comparison, despite having made an effort this evening. I'd straightened my hair, donned a jade-green summer dress with bronze fireflies patterned all over it and even put on my good cream wedges. In this crowd, it didn't even come close to cutting the mustard. 'If only. No, I'm a psychic historian – I'll be giving the talk on the history of the building tonight.'

Fraser glanced down at the leaflet we'd each been given as we entered. 'You must be Helena Spencer, is that right?'

She nodded, regally. 'I am indeed.'

'And you're a psychic historian? What does that involve?' Fraser asked. I could see him mentally click his pen.

'Like any historian, it's dependent on era and subject area but I personally specialise in the psychic phenomena of old buildings that have a particular connection to the cultural history of Edinburgh, specifically.'

How convenient – Edinburgh was a city you couldn't swing a Ouija board in without hitting cultural capital. I caught Fraser's eye. I had to hand it to the man, his poker face was cast-iron.

'That's an interesting way into it,' he said affably. 'Can I ask what took you that direction?'

She looked slightly confused. 'What do you mean?'

He paused, trying to find a clearer way of phrasing what he was asking. 'I'm just wondering what made you particularly interested in the paranormal side of things? Was it a case of learning the history of the area and that being a gateway into . . . that side of it all?'

'Oh, I see! No, no, very much the other way round. You'll know yourself as a fellow Scot . . .'

I inhaled a bubble of prosecco and had to fight the coughing fit it brought on.

'. . . there's endless history here. My family seat was particularly steeped in it and I've known from direct experience, and from a very early age, that that history can open doors that you just can't find elsewhere.'

Presumably because most people's doors weren't part of ancient estates handed down over generations. There was a pause and I fought not to catch Fraser's eye again.

'Cool,' he replied. 'How?'

For a second I thought the woman might think he was taking the piss, but if she did, she didn't show it. And to be fair to him, he didn't seem to be.

'Have you ever been in a building that feels wrong?' She looked expectantly between the two of us before landing firmly on me.

'Um . . . I've been in buildings I didn't like,' I replied. 'But it was mainly a décor thing.' This went down like a rock in a birthday cake. I could *feel* the woman move the spotlight of her attention firmly back to Fraser. Which was probably for the best. I was definitively not the audience for her on this one.

'I'm not sure,' he hedged.

She smiled indulgently at him. 'I've always had an affinity – a sensitivity, you might say – to the psychic imprints in a building. The older the building, the stronger the imprint so you can imagine what a treasure trove somewhere like Edinburgh is. Any time I felt a connection to a place, I'd delve into the history of it and every time – *every single time*, would you believe – there was a link to something of historic importance.'

I did not believe. And unless I was very much mistaken, neither did Fraser. I glanced over but he was still wearing his poker face. I couldn't tell if he was giving this woman any credence. *Did* he believe this stuff? Now that I thought about it, I couldn't be 100 per cent sure. He'd been clear that coming tonight was for a lark as part of his job and I was almost certain that he was humouring the psychic historian lady out of politeness. Almost.

I'd been so busy puzzling him out that I missed what he replied to her. Before I could tune fully back in, a voice called out that we would be starting in five minutes. The woman excused herself, mostly to Fraser, and went to get ready for her talk.

I turned to him. 'So . . . vortex, eh?'

He laughed, taking a sip of his drink.

'God, how lucky is that woman. It just so happens that the places she most strongly psychically connects with also happen to be cultural goldmines. Have vortexes to other realms and everything.' I took a sip of my own drink. 'How positively fortuitous.'

'Shush, she'll hear you,' he whispered, seeming, I had to say, a tiny bit panicked. It was a surprising look on him.

I dialled it back. 'Sorry.'

We went to go into the room but I couldn't help myself. Drawing him to a corner away from the others to avoid embarrassing him again, I leaned in. 'Can I check something? Do you believe in this stuff? The ghosts and the psychic imprints and all that?'

He frowned and shook his head. 'Of course not – why on earth would you think I did?'

Thank God. 'No reason.'

He nodded and moved towards the room again.

But I couldn't help myself. 'It's just, you seemed kind of into what she was saying.'

He turned back to face me and I was relieved to see he was looking amused. 'What, because I didn't tell her she was a fake to her face?'

'But she is!' I reasoned, reasonably.

He chuckled. 'Yeah, maybe. But I'm not going to choose to go to someone's house and take a shit on their sofa, am I?'

'I sincerely hope not,' I replied. 'Or you're never getting an invite to mine.' For a brief moment I imagined trying to explain Fraser to my mother and shuddered at the thought of all the embarrassing assumptions she'd make – or worse – stories she'd tell. 'Though I'm not sure how shitting on someone's sofa is relevant here,' I pointed out.

'What I mean is . . .' He searched for the words. 'We didn't have to come here, we willingly bought tickets, right? Or at least we would have if I hadn't got them through work. If she or any of the other people here choose to believe in all this, for whatever reason, it's not as though it's harming anyone. They're not parading through the streets demanding everyone get involved. It's a private matter.'

'I guess that's true, but I don't know that I agree that it's harmless. Because we did buy tickets – it wasn't free. We paid money to be here – all right, I know, we didn't because of your work – but the principle remains the same. They charge people money to spin fantasy that those people are literally buying into. That's a bit . . . sketch.'

'Look at it another way,' he reasoned. 'Do you watch plays or films? Read books? They spin fantasy and charge for it.'

I shook my head. 'Nice try, pal. If I see a film or read a book, the parameters are clear. These guys prey on fears and tragedy. They profit on grief and the understanding that if you lose someone, you'd do pretty much anything to see or speak to them again. It's pretty terrible when you think about it.'

Jeez. We appeared to have hit a nerve I hadn't known was there. I half expected Fraser to look annoyed but he didn't. It was weird, though, I couldn't quite put my finger on what he was thinking right then. He was watching me in a way I could only describe as speculative. I was starting to understand that, for all our fun and banter, he very much kept his deeper self to himself.

After a moment, he spoke and I was surprised at how relieved I was to find he didn't sound irritated. But it wasn't his normal tone either. It seemed deeper, slightly more uneven than usual. 'I'll not argue against that. But there's a place for everything and some people really believe in this stuff. It helps them. And I'm not going to judge how anyone gets through their grief.' He nodded in the general direction of the psychic historian. 'You might be right. Maybe she doesn't believe it, maybe she's a charlatan. But maybe she does. Maybe this is her interest, her way of connecting with the world. Maybe even her way of trying to help people through hard times. If nothing else, she's opening the cultural market up to a new audience. It's just a different lens to look at things through, is all.'

Well, goddammit. How could a person argue with that and not end up looking like a dick?

But I couldn't allow it to pass completely unchallenged. 'OK, fine, maybe. But I draw the line at police psychics. Or anyone who profits directly off people's pain.'

'Oh, for sure. Those people are arseholes.'

Phew. I'd hate to have to end our friendship before it'd really grown legs. 'And can we at least agree on one thing?'

He looked at me sideways. 'What?'

'There's no friggin' vortex in this stairwell.'

His laugh bounced off the walls. Several people turned to look at us. 'I think we can definitely agree on that.'

We started making our way back towards the room.

'Am I allowed to ask questions?' I wondered aloud.

Fraser looked at me suspiciously. 'As in will they let you?'

'As in will you?'

His face crinkled into a smile and he gave a wry shake of his head. 'As if I could stop you,' he replied. 'Why, what's your question?'

'Right, so, I've been thinking a lot about this. If ghosts can come back and talk to us, why are they always so vague – it's always stuff like "remember that time when you were five and I read you a book"? And why do they never tell you what it's like on the other side? And why is it never someone fun, like Elv—'

A voice interrupted, announcing that the talk was starting in one minute and that we should all take our seats.

Fraser started to slide his way into a chair. 'I wonder if the ghosts have warned them about you?'

I nudged into him. 'I'm serious!'

'So am I.'

I lowered my voice to a whisper. 'It's just so . . . dull. If I were faking psychic powers I'd at least make it interesting. Mix it up a bit. Tell them the family fortune's buried under a tree in Stoke-on-Trent, that sort of thing. Inject a bit of adventure into people's lives.' I suddenly realised I was seated at the end of the row. 'Ah, wait, no. You need to switch seats with me.'

He'd settled into his and gave me a look. 'Why?'

'Because this is the end seat. They'll 100 per cent choose me to speak to.'

'I thought you wanted to ask questions?' he teased.

'Unless you want me to actually ask them my questions, you need to swap with me.'

'I absolutely do not want that.' He stood up. As I manoeuvred past him, my foot caught in the chair leg in front of me. I steadied myself and it took a second to realise I'd used him to do it by putting both my hands pretty much all over his torso. 'Shit, sorry!'

He looked down. 'If you wanted to grope me, you only had to ask.'

An unexpected rush of embarrassment railroaded through me. I unpeeled myself from his surprisingly taut abdomen, and finished shuffling past, making a much bigger deal of sitting down than could ever be warranted.

'Are you quite comfortable?' he asked, lips quirking. 'I could ask for a pillow.'

Just as I was about to tell him what he could do with his pillow, a voice was cleared at the front and a middle-aged man stood up and introduced himself as our psychic for the evening. As luck would have it, today he was wearing two hats: one as the psychic and the other as the emcee of the event. Plus, for no discernible reason, a literal flat cap.

He introduced himself as Max Carruthers, renowned psychic and purveyor of messages from the beyond.

'That's a good solid psychic name,' I murmured to Fraser. He shushed me but I could see the muscles in his cheeks fighting a smile.

Max ran through the programme for the event, which would involve a talk on a lighthouse where three of the lighthouse keepers mysteriously vanished at the beginning of the nineteenth century; followed by a talk on the psychic history of some of Edinburgh's most famous buildings. At this our new friend Helena from the stairwell popped up her hand and gave a jingly wave. Max then informed us that the evening would be finished up with a demonstration of his own abilities. I honestly wasn't sure which one I was looking forward to more.

The woman giving the lighthouse talk stood up and started her PowerPoint presentation. There was a surprising number of hypotheses on the go for this particular mystery and I found myself really getting into the swing of things.

Fraser leaned in. 'My money's on the aliens.'

I shook my head. 'Nah, one of them ate the other two and then threw himself off the top.'

He gave it at least three seconds' thought. 'They'd have found bits of them, wouldn't they?'

As it turned out, we were both wrong. In an unbelievably banal turn of events, the prevailing theory was that a giant wave had swept them away.

'I want my money back,' I whispered.

'We didn't pay, remember?'

'Fine. I want your work's money back. A giant wave? I was promised spooky shit – where are my ghosts?'

As if on cue, Helena Spencer got up and introduced herself. Her talk kicked off with her aforementioned belief that buildings could absorb emotion, using Edinburgh Castle as her jumping-off point, which I had to admit was pretty baller. If you were going to invent psychic history, there were few places more lucrative in the city. Despite this, I was drawn in – I had to hand it to her, the woman could weave a narrative. Before I knew it, the talk was over.

'That may be the quietest you've ever been,' Fraser remarked.

'It was pretty interesting in the end. Did you not enjoy it?'

'I did. Surprised you did, is all.'

'Hey, I like history as much as the next guy, you know. I'm not a total barbarian.'

'How are you feeling about that vortex now?' he asked in a butter-wouldn't-melt voice.

Before I could reply, Max the flat-cap psychic was back and introducing himself for the final talk of the evening so I could only stick out my tongue in reply.

To say that this man was a bad psychic was a discredit to anyone who'd ever been bad at anything. I was aware I wasn't an expert on the subject but before this evening I'd been under the general impression that, with enough practice, anyone could cold-read. This man was proving me totally wrong. He got a hit rate of about one in every six guesses and literally everybody he mentioned was a grandparent. I'd enjoyed it at first but after a while it just became painful, like watching a goldfish trying to kick a ball. By the time he'd honed in on Fraser, as I'd guessed he would, it was too much even for me. God bless Fraser, the man was throwing Max every bone he could, elaborating on stories to try to politely smooth over the fact that he didn't have a grandmother who could speak German, there was no dog called Ruffles and he'd never

157

had a swing in his garden. As the exchange wore on, you could have cut the tension in the audience with a knife. I spared a brief glance around me – a woman in the back looked genuinely pained. In the end, even Fraser's patience wore out.

'Sorry, pal, I don't know what to tell you. There's definitely never been a Westie called Ruffles in my family.'

Max blinked at him. 'Well, I'm – that's the picture that I'm getting.'

I could *feel* Fraser trying not to laugh. 'You might want to adjust the antenna a bit.'

Turned out all that meant was that he moved his attention onto me and then the rest of the row until the pained woman at the back piped up with 'My uncle had a Westie called Marbles – could that be it?'

Max watched her for a moment and then shook his head. 'No, sorry. Definitely Ruffles.'

I caught Fraser's eye and we both creased up into piles of silent laughter.

After the talk we decided to get a drink, finally settling on a fancy-looking bar that had recently opened just off Queensferry Street. After a brief but robust argument about who would buy the drinks versus who would get the cushy job of reserving the seat by the wood-burning fire – which Fraser won only by dint of having longer arms and getting the bartender's attention first – I sank into the seat, feeling kind of anxious. I was always anxious about something or other but I could usually at the very least put my finger on why. Watching Fraser chat affably to the bartender, I hit on what seemed to be causing it. I felt guilty. About him.

Before I could figure out exactly why it was I was feeling that way, Fraser had arrived at our table, setting a large glass of white wine in front of me, before moving round to sit down in the seat opposite.

I found myself fiddling with the stem of my wine glass. I'd realised what the problem was. 'Sorry if I was a dick earlier.'

Fraser settled into the seat opposite me. 'What do you mean?'

'With all the psychic stuff. In what will no doubt come as shocking news to you, I can be a bit forthright in my opinions.' I took a gulp and then set the glass away from me so I wouldn't fiddle with it anymore. 'I know you said you don't believe in it and all but I suspect you may be slightly more . . . open-minded than me.'

'You weren't a dick.' He took a sip of his own wine and we settled into a silence. I found myself noticing again how warm his eyes were. 'Did I say something to make you think I thought you were?' he queried.

'No, not at all. I was just thinking about it as you were getting the drinks and it occurred to me that if you did believe in it even a little bit, that I might have been a bit . . . on the nose.'

He smiled. 'I really don't, no need to worry on my account.' He took a drink of his wine and leaned back into his chair. We were silent again. I could see he was mulling something over. Finally he spoke. 'I guess I can see how it could happen – how people might want to believe in it.'

Fraser seemed more cloistered than usual. Not quite himself. 'Sure,' I said.

He didn't seem to have anything else to say on the subject and suddenly I wanted to know what he'd been thinking. I had so much fun with him but it was once again occurring to me how little of himself he gave away. For all the time we'd spent together, I wasn't sure I really knew much about him. I mean, I knew that he was a journalist and he had a girlfriend and that his favourite kind of crisp was pickled onion Monster Munch and that he bit his nails and that he thought sweetener in anything was a war crime. But I didn't know where he'd been born or if he had siblings or who his parents were. All I had was a brief mention that they weren't around anymore, which was presumably why he didn't talk about them much.

The thought hit me like an unexpectedly opened door.

'Fuck, Fraser, I'm such a prick. I'm so sorry.'

His eyebrows knitted together. 'What? Why?'

'You mentioned your parents were gone and here's me chatting shit about there not being anything else after and – oh God,' I put my head in my hands. 'It was so insensitive, I'm sorry.' I forced myself to look up at him.

He was laughing. 'For somebody so mouthy, you sure do panic when you think you've caused offence.'

'Only to people I like,' I replied, matter-of-factly. Wait, did that make me sound like more or less of a prick?

'That's nice to hear.' He shook his head, still chuck-ling a bit. 'Let me assure you, in no uncertain terms, that I don't believe in ghosts or psychics. I admittedly might have a slightly more complicated relationship with what comes next, but I also know that's just a basic human desire to see your loved ones again. You really don't have anything to apologise for. Though I appreciate the thought.' He nodded a thanks. 'And you really aren't wrong. There *is* something sinister about earning money out of grief.'

I felt instantly better. 'You should write a story about it.'

'Maybe I will.'

'I'm sorry about your parents. I don't think I said that before.'

'Thanks. It was a while ago now.' He took another sip and I realised he'd finished his glass. 'Another?'

I wasn't quite at the bottom of mine but there was something about how he said it. A change of subject seemed to be required – the vault had closed again. 'Sounds good.'

He went to stand and I held up my hand. 'Ah, don't think so, pal. This is my round.'

Before he could object, I was up and out. For some reason it was important to me that I bought the next drink but I'd clean forgotten that every muscle in me had recently been pulled so I ended up walking to the bar like I was John friggin' Wayne. When I eventually got there, I realised I had no idea what he'd ordered us. Ah well. These muscles weren't making that journey twice. 'Two large glasses of house white, please.' I glanced back at the table and remembered I hadn't finished my last drink. 'Actually, make that one large and a small, thanks.'

I carried them slowly back and painstakingly sat down again. Fraser had been checking his phone and set it back down when I arrived.

'Thanks.' He held up his fresh glass. 'And cheers. To psychic architecture!'

I returned his toast, feeling that the evening had allowed me more of a glimpse into my work pal's inner workings. It felt surprisingly good.

Chapter Seventeen

After all my psychic socialising, I ended up falling straight to sleep so I didn't get to see Myster-E's latest response until the next morning. I opened it, feeling odd tendrils of guilt that last night's events had, albeit briefly, pushed it from my mind.

'Habits are the blanket fort we build to keep the world at bay' might be my next (re: first) tattoo. What a great line. But I'm afraid we are once again at odds because I believe Poirot has the most to teach us about love. The only woman he ever loved was an absolute badass – that's a 'go big or go home' vibe if ever I saw one and I hope to channel that in my new romantic adventures. If my next girlfriend isn't a mad Russian con artist, I don't want to know. (You don't happen to be a mad Russian con artist, do you? I'm on the lookout.)

My heart gave my chest a high-five. I could be a Russian con artist. I'd be lying about being Russian but that counted as a kind of con, right? My eyes searched hungrily for more.

I will agree, though, with everything else you said. In the grand scheme of things I know I've not been single that long but now that I think about it, there are parts of myself that I have had to kind of shut down. One of the things I miss most is what you describe – the intimacy of sharing so much of yourself with someone else and of knowing so much about them. And touch. I read somewhere that touch can release oxytocin, which in turn releases dopamine and serotonin. It literally induces a kind of chemical high – how crazy is that? I think it totally makes sense that ignoring that need might lead to a kind of numbness, a shutting down. Self-preservation really. But as you said, if you had it once, you can have it again. After all, the heart's a muscle and muscle has memory, right?

I stared at the last line, reading and rereading it, and felt something tightly wound unravel. I'd never thought about it that way before. Or maybe it was that I'd been thinking about it in the wrong direction – focusing on how hard it was to forget the pain of Dan and his lies. Maybe a better use of my time would be remembering all the good things that I'd experienced up to that point. If I'd had it before, surely I could have it again.

And I found myself once again wondering about Myster-E. Who he was. What he looked like. The fact that he'd had a long-term girlfriend was presumably a good sign. And the man didn't half know his way around a romantic analogy. Hmm.

He'd given me a lot to think about.

A buzzing alerted me to my phone. Shit – I'd meant to confirm the time I was meeting Amal this morning for a picnic with the kids. I picked it up, fervent apology at the ready, only to find it was actually a message from Neil.

Hey, Ada. Hope you've recovered from our walk on Saturday and that work wasn't too stressful! I had such a lovely time – it's so nice to have company for these things. If you're up for catching up again, I was thinking we could maybe go for another drink? N xx

Jeez, our walk in the Pentlands felt like a thousand years ago now. Neil was one of the most decent guys I'd met in a long time. In so many ways he fitted the bill and Amal and Aiden were clearly Team Him. And yet . . . and yet. I just wasn't feeling it. That frisson. That itch to spend more and more time with him. We weren't even really text chatting.

But I couldn't put my finger on what it was that was missing. And, let's face it, I'd had *it* with Dan so maybe *it* wasn't all it was cracked up to be.

I stared at the text again. As I did, another message arrived, this time from Amal, confirming where we were meeting.

I imagined telling her my thoughts and her reaction to the idea that I was considering *maybe* not meeting Neil again. Particularly seeing as how I couldn't really verbalise why without sounding like a total prick. Hmm. Maybe I'd play it by ear. I texted to confirm our meeting point with her, carefully avoiding Neil's message. Yet another problem for future me.

As I arrived at the Meadows, I realised I'd caught the tail end of cherry blossom season and almost let out an actual whoop of joy. It was one of my favourite sights

165

in Edinburgh but I'd missed the window pretty much every year since I'd left. The petals blazed a zigzag trail of pink and white across the green, springing up like confetti. I stood for a moment at the traffic lights leading onto Jawbone Walk and took in the sight. A bright blue surprise of a sky and Arthur's Seat peeping over the proceedings framed my view perfectly. How had I forgotten how beautiful this was?

I made my way to meet Amal, feeling practically brand new by the time I got there. This lasted approximately the length of time it took for me to spot her and realise she wasn't alone. She'd picked out a spot on the grass and was sitting with Benji and Mo. There were four other mothers, all with their kids, patchworked in a square around her. The dreaded NCT group. This was not quite as advertised.

Amal glanced up and spotted me, giving me a wave in case I hadn't seen her. I waved back, fighting down the weird anxiety bubbling up in my stomach. I was unexpectedly about to spend a morning of my life being simultaneously put off having children and actively encouraged to have them. What fun.

'Hey, Ada,' Amal called as I finished my approach. Her greeting was followed by Benji launching himself at me. I pulled him into a massive hug, carting him back over as I leaned in and gave Amal a kiss on the cheek, swiftly followed by a forehead kiss for a grumpy-looking Mo.

'Hi,' I replied, plonking me and Benji down on the edge of the blanket. He immediately stood up and toddled over to where some of the other kids were playing on the grass.

166

Amal gave me a smile. 'Ada, you remember some of the women from my NCT classes?'

I gave a bright smile and affirmed that we had indeed met. 'Sorry, I'm terrible with names.' It was kind of true. I did actually remember two of them – Meera and Annie I was almost sure – but the others were a total blank. And I couldn't even guess at the kids.

'This is Mia and her wee girl Catherine,' Amal continued. 'This is Christina and her boy Tilney.' She gestured between them and I nodded hello, relieved that she'd started with the ones I couldn't remember. She ran through the rest and I said hello again, bobbing my head like I was on a car dashboard. What felt like a slightly awkward silence bloomed around us all. For something to do, I pulled open my bag and announced that I'd brought some snacks, laying them out carefully. It turned out they were unnecessary though, as the women had brought a frankly staggering spread between them, absolutely chock-full of the best platter foods Waitrose had to offer. I almost repacked mine. The mini-Babybels looked particularly ashamed of themselves next to their glitzier picnic pals.

'Thanks, pet,' Amal said brightly.

Everyone chittered amongst themselves, regaling each other with stories of doctors' trips and domestic woes. As I heard them talk, it struck me once again how busy their lives were. I felt like a lazy bastard by comparison, just bumming around, living my best life. It was times like these I genuinely questioned whether marriage and children were a life choice I actually wanted to make.

'So how did it go with . . . Neil?' asked Amal, suddenly.

'I . . . oh.' The unexpectedness of the question blew right through me. Besides a few quick texts the next morning, I'd not had the chance for a debrief with her – that was what today was meant to be. But I hadn't banked on the question right then, or indeed the audience. Why on earth would she bring it up in front of all these people?

'Oooh, who's Neil?' asked about three of the women in tandem.

Amal was more than ready for the question. 'Oh, it's this guy I've set Ada up with – he's a friend of Aiden's from work.' Urgh, handy reminder that this whole endeavour may not have been stake-free. 'He's an absolute dreamboat.'

I blinked into my blini. Dreamboat? Had Amal ever used that word in her life before? I looked up to find all eyes eagerly on me. What the tap-dancing fuck was I supposed to do now? I'd struggled with how I might articulate my feelings about Neil when it was just Amal in the mix. How on earth was I meant to do it with all her pals looking on as well?

'It was . . . um . . . good, yeah,' I mumbled, stuffing the blini in my mouth as a distraction.

'It was better than good!' Amal turned to her pals. 'He stayed the night.'

The women were riotous in their approval and I had the uncanny feeling that I was suddenly part of a nineties sitcom, sans laugh track. They threw a number of follow-up questions and saucy innuendos my way, none of which I was in any way inclined to answer. I stuffed two more blinis in my mouth, and did the whole 'chewing, pointing at my mouth, eye-roll' thing to demonstrate that I couldn't quite talk just now. It worked. After a moment, they fell back into other conversation.

Catherine leaned over to Amal. 'Is Aiden still annoyed about cancelling date night again? You really should check out that therapist I mentioned – she did wonders for me.'

If my ears could have physically pricked up, they would have. I caught Amal's eyes as she looked away, panic spilling out of her. She waved the comment away and completely changed the subject.

What the fuck? Therapist? She hadn't said a word about there being any issues with Aiden to me. I thought we talked about everything. And yet here we were, apparently not talking about whatever it was Catherine meant. Why would Amal not tell me this?

I tried to catch her eye again but she resolutely wouldn't let me. For possibly the first time in our nearly twenty-year friendship, I was sure she was deliberately keeping something from me. The feeling stung like a bitch. OK, so I'd kept some things from her, of course, but that was different. She didn't know Dan. Aiden was like a brother to me.

Meera offered me a fruit kebab and I took it, forcing a smile and trying to look as though the rug hadn't been pulled out from under my day. She leaned in conspiratorially and asked more about Neil. God, someone really needed to build an ejector seat for unwanted social interactions. I made a mental note to suggest it to Fraser. Maybe he could write an article about it.

Before I had to dig too deep in the conversational bin though, she remembered something and was tapping Amal on the shoulder. 'Oh, I almost forgot, I have something for you.' She reached into her bag and pulled out some kind of cream. 'Works wonders for the scarring.'

'Oh, thanks, pet.' Amal put what looked like some kind of balm into her bag.

I'd assumed this would have been enough to move the spotlight away from the whole Neil shebang but once again I was proven very wrong. Meera was back with more questions and soon joined by Catherine. And then the brainwave hit – Fraser! He was my way out of the interminable Neil chat! In a way. I took a bite of my fancy fruit kebab and announced to the group that I'd spent the evening in the company of a haunted vortex. It worked a treat – the rest was, albeit briefly, psychic history.

I'd hoped to be able to wangle it so that I could walk back at least part of the way with Amal so that we could talk properly. Before I could suggest it, though, Catherine swooped in with the suggestion that the two of them grab a coffee with the kids at hers so they could 'catch up properly'. She barely had the sentence out before Amal had eagerly agreed.

I tried to tamp down how much it irritated me. Who on earth was this Catherine woman? Why did Amal feel that she could talk to her and not me? For a moment, I imagined inviting myself along – just to see what Catherine would do with it. What Amal would do with it.

Instead, I gave Benji and Mo a kiss goodbye and made my exit, waving goodbye to the others as I went. Maybe if I was lucky, next time I'd get to hang out with the Amal I used to know, not this secret-keeping stranger with a penchant for the use of the word 'dreamboat' in an actual real-life conversation.

And then she gave a smile and squeezed my hand and I felt tears prick the corners of my eyes. This was ridiculous! I forced them back down and strode back across the Meadows, the pinks and purples barely registering as I went.

Chapter Eighteen

I made my way into Café Tière in a fairly terrible mood. A part of me knew how ridiculous I was being but all I could picture was Amal's face when Catherine had mentioned Aiden and therapy. They've always been such a solid couple and Amal such a lynchpin in general and now it was as if the ground under my feet had shifted. I felt kind of nauseous.

Fraser gave me a wave as I approached and I settled into my seat with a sigh.

'That sounds ominous.'

I shook my head. 'I don't want to talk about it.'

'Weren't you at some kind of brunch thing? It's not something I spend a lot of my time doing but I've been told it's generally thought to be a pleasant thing to do?'

'I thought it was just with Amal but then a bunch of her mum friends were there and it just . . .' I shook my head again. 'I don't want to talk about it.'

Fraser watched me for a moment, as if deliberating whether to pry further and then, thankfully, decided against it. 'I have something that might cheer you up.'

'Is it a time machine that can take me back to being twenty and not having a care in the world?'

'It's *way* better than that.' He leaned under the table and produced a banoffee biscuit.

I let out a gasp. 'I thought they'd stopped getting these!'

He shrugged. 'I know a guy. Just don't let Clive see.'

'You're right! This is better than a time machine,' I laughed. I had to hand it to Fraser, he always seemed to know how to cheer me up when I needed it.

I hit send on Steve's daily reminder of his schedule, triple underlining the profile interview I'd set up for him with a local magazine and, after some deliberation, a meeting with the producers of *Leith, Laugh, Love*. I may not have actively been his PA but there'd not be much to publicise if the man lost his job.

Once it was sent, I started a spin through some of the alerts I'd set up attached to his name. Always best to do that before the coffee had fully kicked in. It didn't take me long to remember why. I paused my scrolling and let out a swearword.

Fraser's head popped up from behind his laptop, pen hanging out the side of his mouth. 'What's up?'

'It's another story. That's the third one this month,' I huffed, spinning my laptop around to show him. 'All in your paper, no less. Have you guys run out of actual news to write about?'

'You're talking to a man who recently wrote a thousand words on haunted dolls, so yeah, maybe.' He scanned the article. 'Ah, yes, the inappropriate storytelling to the schoolchildren. Another Steve classic.'

'*Leith, Laugh, Love* are going to kill him – every time one of these shows up I get a furious email from the producers. But what can I do? The only way to stop Steve would be to put him on a boat, sail it out to sea and sink it,' I groaned. 'What I can't figure out is how they hear about it. It's not like he's properly famous. Could you ask –' I glanced at the article – 'Mark Selby where he's getting his leads?'

'I know Mark – nice guy.'

I scowled.

'What?' he asked, in a tone that very much suggested he knew what. 'Is the story untrue? I'm pretty sure I remember you mentioning it happening?'

'No, it's true,' I grumped.

He looked at me with what I could only describe as a directness. 'What then?'

I was finding it difficult to find a way to say *because while it did happen, it's relatively small fry and it makes my job infinitely harder than it needs to be.* Instead I once again channelled diplomacy. Couldn't risk my biscuit supply. 'I just can't see how it could be of interest to anyone and every time a story comes out, he gets into more and more trouble. It's not like he's causing any real harm.'

Fraser shrugged. 'True. But I don't know what to tell you, we write what we write because people are interested in reading it. Someone must have an interest or the articles wouldn't be published.'

'Yeah, I know,' I sighed.

'Plus, without it, you would have much too easy a job.' He gave me a cheesy grin, highlighting the fact that his pen had leaked.

'You have ink all over your face,' I pointed out.

He slapped a hand to his mouth and rubbed. 'Did I get it?'

All he'd done was smear it further afield so it looked like he had half a blue beard. 'Yeah, that did it.'

'Here, can I get your opinion on something quickly?' he asked.

I made a point of not looking directly at the ink stains all over his mouth. 'Sure.'

'I need to ask one of my contacts for a favour and I want to run it past somebody to make sure it doesn't come off weird. She's a bit stand-offish.'

'Sure, pass it over.'

'Thanks.' He handed me his laptop and I scanned the email.

'Jeez, you've really got that stiff upper-lip thing going on, haven't you?' I laughed.

'What do you mean?' he asked, sounding slightly indignant.

I parroted the first few lines of the email back at him. 'You'd think you were writing to the Queen!'

'Is that bad?'

'It's not bad, I guess, just different. Doesn't sound like you. Not to mention quite unexpected, from a man who spent an entire day mocking me for using the word surreptitious.'

175

'Surreptitious is a ridiculous word and I stand by my mockery.'

'Well, buckle up, baby, because you're in for at least a week's worth of shit from me for this.'

'Is it really bad?' He looked pained. 'I don't know what it is but I've never got the knack for writing casual emails. Must be the scholar in me.'

'Hello, humble brag,' I snorted. 'Can I fix this?'

He frowned and thought about it for a moment. 'OK. But don't hit send, I want to read what you wrote first.'

'Fine.'

'While you're doing that, I'm going to grab a coffee. Want another?'

I nodded and off he went. I wondered idly how long it would take for someone to point out all the ink on his face.

Hah. Scholar indeed.

Despite all the stories – or more likely because of them – Steve had continued to be on surprisingly good behaviour, leaving me with more time than usual in my day to help Fraser on his 'finding weird things' quest, mostly by way of internet searches and one impromptu field trip to some allegedly haunted public toilets.

We'd continued working through our own to-do lists when a gasp drew my eye to Fraser's side of the table. 'What's up?'

He glanced up, a look of amusement playing across his face. 'What are you doing right this second?'

'Working on a Twitter campaign for Steve's book – why?'

'My pal's just texted to say that Skeleton Si is back at the meadows putting on one of his shows and I've been wanting to do an interview with him for my column. Want to come? We'll be gone an hour, tops.'

'Who and/or what is Skeleton Si?' I asked.

Fraser raised an eyebrow at me. 'Only one way for you to find out.'

There was objectively a lot more than one way for me to find out, but in person would definitely be the most fun. 'OK, if we make it quick. But don't tell Steve – he gets jealous when I talk to other weird entertainers.'

Suffice it to say, I was unprepared for Skeleton Si. I'd expected him to be some kind of street performer with a skeleton painted on. What I got was a man strapping what looked like the bones of an actual human skeleton to a tree in the middle of the Meadows, before painting them bright colours, throwing what looked like dust over them and performing a short but intense dance.

So far, so Edinburgh.

The part I was unprepared for was that his name was actually Simon Alderley, he was a well-respected professor of anthropology and when not dancing about dressed like an extra from *Oliver Twist*, he was the most nondescript-looking person I'd ever seen in real life. Having agreed to talk to Fraser when he was done packing up, we settled onto a nearby bench to wait for him.

'What was that?' I whispered. 'Some kind of ancient mystical dance?'

Fraser paused writing some notes. 'Nope.'

'Then I'm at a loss.'

'It's all part of his . . . I guess, outreach programme, you might call it?' He unclicked his pen and swivelled to almost face me. 'Kind of like what fireworks are for a show. He lures people in with the mad dance and then sneaks lessons on stuff like confirmation bias into the conversation. A bit of knowledge exchange with your entertainment. The dust bit is new, though.'

'I mean, I sort of get it, I suppose. Not quite as weird as I'd hoped, I'll be honest.'

Fraser chuckled. 'Yeah, may have got you here under false pretences. What I was actually after was a gourmet sausage roll from that guy.' He pointed to a stand by the exit onto Buccleuch Place. 'Want one?'

'I wouldn't say no.'

Just as we stood to get some, my phone rang. A little part of me panicked, as it always did when Steve's name came up on my screen. 'Hey, how's it going?' I answered brightly.

'Sorry to bother you, Ada, dear, but I thought I should run something by you for this newspaper interview next week.'

'The *Edinburgh Scene* one?' Jesus Christ. 'Steve, that's tomorrow, not next week.'

'Yes, yes, that one.'

I suppressed a groan. Fraser wasn't bothering to suppress a smile, because of course he could hear Steve. People in Haddington could hear Steve on the phone.

'No, no, it's tomorrow. Let's be absolutely clear on that. Tomorrow, three on the dot. I'm going to resend you the address.' Note to self: staple this appointment to his actual person.

'OK, you do that. I was thinking I could wear my purple velvet suit but it needs to be dry cleaned and I probably couldn't get that sorted by tomorrow. What should I wear instead?'

I held in another sigh. 'Are you really calling me for fashion advice?'

The nudge pushed him back on course. 'No. Well, I mean, a bit, yes. But I wanted to run a story by you as well, just in case you don't think it would be appropriate.'

He was running a story by me before telling it? Had the man been lobotomised? I put on my most encouraging voice. 'Sure, go for it.'

'So, back in the nineties I got involved quite heavily in what they were calling the "club scene" – have you heard of it?'

Oh *God*. 'I'm familiar with the concept, yes.'

'Well, I made friends with some pretty high-profile people and there was this one time, I got invited back to this orgy at one of their houses. I think there was some kind of video somewhere at one point – the nineties, eh? It was *wild*. There was mountains of—'

'No!' I cried. I could feel Fraser shaking with laughter on the bench beside me. 'Absolutely *not*. You are, under no circumstances, allowed to bring up anything about a drug-fuelled orgy at this or any other interview. Do you hear me? Steve? You can't. You're on your last legs with *Leith, Laugh. Love.* I have had actual emails from the producers. Please promise me you won't do this.'

'But—'

'*No buts*. Steve, I mean it. Promise me you won't, I'm being deadly serious.' I put on my most deadly serious voice, which was made harder to do by Fraser's now borderline hysterical silent laughter beside me.

There was a pause on the end of the line and then a slightly truculent voice agreed that *fine, he promised he wouldn't*.

I let out a sigh. 'OK. Good.' I decided to at least attempt to incentivise his good behaviour. 'Want to send me some wardrobe ideas and I can help you choose for your interview *tomorrow at three on the dot?*'

It did the trick, moving Steve firmly away from any talk of orgies. He wittered on for a minute about options before informing me he'd send me pictures and then hanging up the phone before I'd managed to get another word in edgeways.

I slipped my phone in my pocket. 'Don't say a word,' I warned Fraser.

He was grinning from ear to ear. 'Didn't say a word.'

I nudged him. 'Here comes Skeleton Si.'

As Simon came towards us, Fraser stood up and waved before sliding his hands into his pockets, a movement I found oddly endearing. I followed suit with a small wave and leaned in to Fraser.

'Don't forget our sausage rolls.'

After the sausage rolls, we made our way back to the coffee and settled into work again. For all of ten minutes. A question on Skeleton Si degenerated into an increasingly random set of google queries.

'Is that a work laptop?' I mused. 'Because if it is they're going to have some serious questions about your search history.'

Fraser raised an eyebrow at me. '*My* search history? You just spent twenty minutes looking up the world's oldest sex toys.'

'I'll admit I went down a bit of a . . . *rabbit hole*,' I hur-hurred.

'I quit,' he replied. If I didn't know any better, I'd say he'd gone a little bit pink. Aww.

'Anyway, I have Steve as a client – if anything, he'd probably assume I was doing some kind of research for him.'

Even Fraser couldn't argue that point.

'I forgot to tell you, my editor actually made a request for a weird article! Have you ever done pottery?' he asked.

I looked up from what had turned out to be a very graphic article – on balance maybe *too* graphic to be reading in a public arena. I minimised the page and returned my attention to Fraser. 'Pottery?'

'Yes,' he replied.

'As in the thing with the clay and the wheel and stuff?'

'That is the general definition, I believe.'

'Yeah, actually, I got quite into it at uni.' I felt my nose crinkle up in confusion. 'Wait . . . pottery's not weird. Are we about to have our first fight?'

He held his hands up in mock surrender. 'I have nothing but respect for the noble art of clay wrangling. But I can only assume there must be something about it or she'd not have told me to go.'

'Hmm, sure. What's your article angle going to be?'

'Dunno, yet. I've always wanted to try it out though.'

'That is suitably reasonable. We can try pottery.' I hadn't meant that to sound quite so . . . *we*-ish. I decided to bury it. 'If you like, I can do something to make it weird and you can write about that. Recite rubbish poetry and pretend I'm reliving my own birth or something.'

'Perfect.'

'When is it?'

'Tomorrow night. Are you free?'

I was free as a bird. Mainly because I hadn't actually got around to replying to Neil's text yet. The thought and its associations made me feel heavy inside. I informed Fraser I was indeed free.

'Great!' he grinned. 'It's in,' he paused to check the website again, 'the basement of that church with the red door at the bottom of Broughton Street.'

'Oooh, I've always wanted to have a nosy in there,' I cooed. Jeez, when did I start talking like I was in an English country village in the fifties? I could only assume all

182

the Aggie chat with Myster-E and the re-reading of her books was clearly messing with my vocab. Before I knew it I'd be 'hey what'-ing and 'I say'-ing all over the show. And then presumably committing some kind of terrible murder to see if I could get away with it. I imagined telling Myster-E that and hearing what he'd have to say. Maybe even mentioning my day with Amal to him.

'You know you can just go in and look around, right? They let you do that in churches,' Fraser pointed out.

I zoned back in and reminded myself what we were talking about. Churches – that was it! 'Can't.' I replied. 'I'd burst into flames, doncha know.' I gave him a theatrical wink for good measure.

Nope. No more Marple for me.

I reread my reply to Myster-E, debating whether to hit send or not on what I'd written.

Sure, I'll be your mad Russian con artist, but only if you'll be my internationally renowned pernickety detective. I should warn you, though, the moustache is non-negotiable. (I don't know if I mentioned this before but I had a Poirot-themed sex dream (!!!) Must be all your lobbying for him. And of course the octogenarian hanky-panky. I will say it is something I hope never to repeat . . .)

Can I also say, more seriously, that your last message really struck a chord with me? The heart is a muscle and muscle has memory . . . you kind of put words around something I'd been struggling with for a while. It's true. It has so much memory and I love that you meant that in a positive way. I've been thinking about it this whole time as a negative thing – that the memories mine had were bad and it had learned and held onto those bad things. But that was a choice in a way. And I don't mean that it is for everyone, of course. I do think there are some things that are much harder – maybe too hard – to unlearn. But for me, and for now, that I can choose the memories that mine holds onto is a pretty cool thing. So thanks for that! I've had a bit of a day today so it's been nice to ruminate on something positive.

That was as close as I could let myself get to unpacking what had happened with Amal this morning.

I stared at the blinker and out of nowhere felt a wave of . . . something . . . crash over me. A recklessness. A slightly mad rush of go big or go home. Like an itch that suddenly, desperately needed to be scratched. Yes, I hadn't replied to Neil and yes, everything with Amal maybe wasn't what it seemed and yes, I was still getting random text messages from Dan in the middle of the night, no matter how much I ignored him. Why not add one more stone to the pile for Future Ada? She already hated me anyway. I started typing.

And to that end, (deep breath!) . . . I was wondering if maybe you might want to meet up? Have a drink and say hello in person? I promise you don't have to grow a moustache to do it . . . I just figured it would be nice to finally put a face to the (screen)name. No worries if you'd rather keep it online, though! Always worth an ask.

Hah, had I really just basically written 'no worries if not'? So much for going big.

And yet it felt so big. Myster-E had become such an enjoyable part of my life – how much of that was tangled up in the anonymity of all of this? If we met, would it break that spell? What if he didn't find me attractive? What if I didn't find him attractive? What if I *did*?

It felt like a lot to lose.

But then what was the alternative? We kept writing forever? That seemed insane given that we lived in the same city, were roughly the same age, and were both single.

I pushed down the niggling little reminder of Neil's text.

No, we *were* both single. And at least this would mean we would know for sure. I knew from previous forays into online dating that all the banter in the world didn't mean you'd have a connection. It was best to ask and to meet and to know.

But what if he said no?

At least then I would know for sure in either direction. And there was no reason we couldn't be friends in real life.

I pulled in a real-life deep breath and hit send.

My phone buzzed and for a mad disorienting second, I thought it might be Myster-E.

It, of course, was not. Amal had sent a picture of Benji wearing one of her sanitary pads as a hat. Underneath, she'd typed *He takes bloody-minded to a whole new level. Lovely as always to see you, pet. Hope you had a fun day. We need to have a proper catch-up re: Neil asap – Benji and Mo send kisses and another drawing for your collection xxx*

I scanned the message for anything that might seem different or off but it played pretty much the same as all our usual interactions. Had I imagined what had happened? Was I blowing a non-issue out of proportion? I didn't love being around some of her NCT pals – was there a chance I'd let my discomfort with them lend weight to everything else? It wasn't completely beyond the realms of possibility.

I sent back some hearts and laughter emojis and the assurance that I couldn't wait for a catch-up.

Chapter Nineteen

Fraser was out interviewing all the next day so for the first time in a while I had the café table to myself. It was very boring. I decided on a fancy coffee to amuse myself in his absence, greeting Barista Bertie as I entered. He was a favourite of mine on account of his incredible name and even more incredible moustache, which curled up and out and heavily suggested the ownership of a monocle. Poirot would be proud. Bertie caught me up on the latest coffee update – a cheeky little Brazilian single origin number with hints of dark chocolate, red apple and molasses. I, a heathen, smiled and nodded and poured in sugar when I was sure he wasn't looking.

Settling down, I shot a message to Steve: Edinburgh Scene *Profile Interview. 3.00 p.m. DO NOT MISS AND DO NOT BE LATE* and started work on the finishing touches to his website. With a bit of engineering, it would soon be the first thing you saw when you googled him. Which admittedly Steve would probably not give two shits about, but at least *Leith, Laugh, Love* would appreciate it, with the extra bonus that I could mention it in my meeting with Contrast Creative. I felt a frizzle of nerves – how was that tomorrow already? A part of me couldn't believe I'd set it up. It felt so . . . official.

But I had done it and I would nail it. They may not have anything going just now but I was going to network the absolute shit out of this. And was in no way going to throw up as I did.

At midday, I got a reply from Steve.

Aye Aye, Captain. Pinkie promise I'll be there.

He followed it up with a picture of him holding his pinkie finger aloft. Was he wearing a sailor's hat? The man could be fairly adorable when he wanted to be. I replied with a thumbs up and a pirate emoji and settled back into the website.

The afternoon brought a surprising follow-up from Amal.

Hey, Lovely – Aiden's work friend has given us four tickets to see some kind of cabaret show at the weekend and I was thinking you, me, Aiden and Neil could go – what do you think? We could grab a drink and catch up beforehand and meet the boys there? I'll get a babysitter and everything, it'll be just like the old days xxx

The idea of a proper adult hang with Aiden and Amal filled me with delight. A double date with them and Neil filled me with indigestion. God, I *still* hadn't replied to his message. I could hear Amal's voice in my head asking me why and I didn't have an answer. What was the harm in spending a little more time with him? It wasn't as if I didn't like the man and it didn't have to go anywhere if I didn't want it to. Plus, this way, I could see what he was like with other people, with the added benefit that there'd be other people to keep the conversation going if it didn't go well. Hmm. I set my phone down and went in search of a biscuit.

Before I knew it, the rest of the day had slipped past and I was running late if I was going to meet Fraser on time for pottery. I still hadn't replied to Neil or Amal but I'd finished the site, done a deep dive on Contracts Creative, and had only checked for a reply from Myster-E, maximum, four billion times. What can I say? I take my wins where I find them.

Fraser and I had arranged to meet outside the church for the pottery session and I thanked the sweet baby bejesus for getting me away from the refresh button on my laptop. I'd basically worn the damn thing down checking to hear from Myster-E.

Wait – was there a way he could tell that? Oh God.

I forced myself to go home and change, deciding to err on the side of caution and put on my painting dungarees. They were dragged out any time Mum took the head staggers and decided to change random bits of the flat on a whim, which was approximately every ten minutes. Tying my hair in a top knot and not bothering with my contact lenses meant that I basically looked a little bit like a cool hipster. Should I dress like this more often? It was the most comfortable I'd been in weeks.

I was interested to see what Fraser might look like slumming it, as it were. It wasn't that he ever was particularly dressed-up – he was very much a T-shirt and jeans kind of a guy. But they weren't idly thrown on. He seemed to put thought into what he wore – the man was clearly a hardcore ironer – so I was looking forward to seeing what passed for his version of paint clothes.

I arrived at the church ten minutes early. The big red door beamed out at passers-by, luring them towards it so it could show off the leafy garden nestled a level below. It was a beautiful evening. I leaned myself against the railing to get a better look at the incomparable view of the roundabout adjacent to the church, once again wondering as I often had when passing, how such a striking building came to be in such an ordinary part of town. And then I remembered I was in Edinburgh and she liked to show off whenever possible. A trait I very much respected in the old girl.

Before leaving the house, I'd made the executive decision to not check for Myster-E replies on my phone tonight. The site wasn't hugely suited to mobile interfaces and I didn't want clay clogging up my phone. Plus it felt important to have a separation for at least a while. Every time I'd refreshed to an empty inbox, the disappointment had become harder to take and I didn't want it to ruin my evening. Plus, I was genuinely worried he'd be able to tell and take out some kind of injunction against me. Which, yeah. Fair enough.

I was wallowing deep in the thought when Fraser managed to scare the shit out of me by appearing out of the ether from Canonmills direction. It turned out he was extremely light of foot and didn't announce his presence until he was right on me.

'Jesus! Where did you come from?' I cried, hand on stuttering heart.

He looked at me like I'd suggested the moon might be on stilts. 'That way.' He pointed the direction he'd just come.

'Thank you, Captain Obvious. I thought you lived in Bruntsfield?'

'I do.' He was looking amused. 'I managed to cut off the tag they give residents of the area limiting me to its confines. I can roam wherever I please now, a true man of the city.'

'All right, point taken.' I'd noticed he did that sometimes. Make a joke as a way to avoid giving actual information. And then it occurred to me why he was coming from there – Lara must live there. Or was it Lana? Oh God. Was it too late to ask what his girlfriend was called again?

'I didn't realise you wore glasses.' He pointed at my face, in case I didn't know where they were. 'You look really different.'

I felt suddenly slightly self-conscious. Did he mean that in a good way?

Do not ask that.

'It's cos I'm Superman,' I said instead. Phew.

'Really?'

'Aye. Watch this.' I slipped them off my face and struck the time-honoured Superman pose.

He laughed. 'Superman! But what have you done with my friend Ada?'

'I know, right?' I put my glasses back on. 'But you can't tell anyone, obviously.'

'BT removing all the phone boxes must have really put a crimp in your world-saving,' he observed lightly.

'Yeah. Hedges are not nearly so accommodating.' I pointed at his garb. 'You look like you always do. Are you not worried you'll ruin your nice neat clothes? What if they get covered in clay?'

He frowned. 'They'll give us aprons, though?'

'Yeah, but they'll be used. You'll probably get more crap all over you wearing one than not. You really haven't done pottery before, have you?'

He looked slightly alarmed. 'Aw, man, these are my good jeans!'

'It's OK,' I soothed. 'It'll give them a rustic look. People pay good money for that these days. Especially in Bruntsfield.'

'I can't believe I didn't think of that,' he laughed ruefully.

'I can't believe you didn't – you're supposed to be the brains of this operation.' He looked genuinely a bit gutted. I decided to cut him some slack. 'On the plus side, you wear them well. It'll be a nice little treat for everyone inside.' I only really registered what I'd said once it was fully out there, flapping in the wind. Wow! What a creepy thing to say.

If Fraser found it creepy, he didn't let on though. Which was more than I deserved really, given the circumstances.

192

'Why, thank you.' He pointed to a particularly large splodge on the front of my dungarees. 'Is that paint?'

I glanced down. 'Ah, yes. But this is not just any paint. This is called Dead Salmon and was, for a glorious day and a half last month, the colour of our bathroom.'

'It is *not* called Dead Salmon.'

I took out my phone and googled it, brandishing the screen at him.

'Oh God, it is! Is that pink and beige all at the same time?'

'Yeah, a delightful shade of peige. Bit of brown in there for good measure. I don't know what possessed Mum. Though, credit to the manufacturer, it looks exactly like the colour you would expect a dead salmon to be.' What sane person would look at all the millions of colours available and say 'yes, this horrible pinkish grey-brown is the one for me'? The woman would never make sense to me. 'I can only assume she did the test swatch after a long shift at the hospital, and was presumably delirious at the time. She insisted I help her finish it and then we changed it two days later.'

'What does your mum do at the hospital?' he asked.

'She's a charge nurse at the Royal. Been there going on thirty years now, which is insane.' Imagine having the same job for thirty years. Mad.

'That's cool. I've spent a fair amount of time there, visiting family and the like. The nurses were great. I wonder if I've met her?'

The idea of my mum having met Fraser in the past was a slightly jarring one. 'She works in the A & E.'

193

'Ah, probably not then. Although I've been there a few times myself over the years.' He gave a wry little chuckle and I found myself once again itching to know more but not quite able to bring myself to ask. Why was that? We hung out every day and it wasn't like I wasn't completely comfortable with him. Some people just had that vibe, I supposed.

'You have the tickets?' I asked.

He nodded, gesturing towards his phone and I waved him in ahead of me.

We made our way to the room we'd been directed to. I had to admit, I was pretty excited now. I'd really enjoyed pottery when I was younger. There'd always been something about it that I found soothing, and maybe even a bit sexy. The feel of the wet clay and the mess it made . . . in hindsight, I'd perhaps seen *Ghost* at *too* formative an age.

We made our way into the room and an astonishingly beautiful middle-aged woman greeted us, introducing herself as Thea. She was tall with wild curly hair and cheekbones you could slice bread with. Her dark purple skirt billowed out behind her as she beckoned us in. The strings of brightly coloured beads around her neck clacked about like castanets as she walked.

'A pleasure to meet you both,' she said, briefly checking a sheet she had in her hand. 'You must be Fraser,' she nodded to him, 'and you must be Ada?'

We both agreed that yes, we were.

'Excellent, if you could take your seats in your spot over there.' She pointed to a pottery wheel in the corner.

Wait. Just the one? I gave Fraser a querying glance and he shrugged. All right, then.

We made our way to the corner as Thea briefly pointed out the other people in the class. Everyone was in groups of two people to one wheel so at least it wasn't because we were the last in.

We smiled and nodded at the women nearest us, picking up the aprons that had been set on our chairs. Out of the corner of my eye I could see Fraser trying to inspect his before sliding it carefully over his head and tried not to openly snigger. Sitting down, I wondered how on earth this was going to work. There was very definitely only one wheel and one lump of clay on the wheel. Were we going to take it in turns? It made sense, I supposed. It must be fairly expensive equipment and it'd take an age to set up each week if you had loads.

'Hello, everyone.'

I cast my eyes back onto Thea, who was now standing at the front of the room.

'Thank you all for coming. It's a pleasure to see some new faces and to meet with old friends again.' She beamed at us. What a nice woman. 'Tonight is the beginning of our summer term but it is also part of a series of standalone sessions. So for the new ones amongst us,' she gestured to me and Fraser and a man and woman closer to the front, 'I'll come around to each of you and we'll take a few minutes to go through the basics of how to use the wheel and shape the clay and talk through your intentions for your work tonight. Those of you who have been here before are welcome to get started but if you have any questions, do please raise your hand and I'll come to you. Does anyone have any questions before we begin?'

I did not and nor did anyone else it seemed.

Thea looked pleased. 'Wonderful! Welcome to Erotic Pottery.'

Oh no, wait.

I *did* have a question.

There are moments in life when something so gloriously, hysterically unexpected happens that you don't really know what to do with yourself when it arrives. This was just such a moment. It took a few seconds for the words that she'd said to land and when they did, I literally didn't know what to do with myself. I somehow managed to unglue my brain and turned to Fraser. He was still in the glued section, face frozen in half-baked surprise.

'Sorry,' I whispered, 'did she say erotic pottery? What . . . is that?'

No response.

I looked around to see if there was anyone else as spectacularly unprepared for this revelation as we were. Everyone was really taking it in their stride. A thought occurred to me and I couldn't keep it in.

'They really missed a trick not calling it erottery.'

Fraser didn't react to it. He still seemed to be very much in the coming-to-terms stage.

He finally turned to me, blinking in confusion. 'What the fuck is erotic pottery?' he whispered.

'I was rather hoping you'd tell me, seeing as how you booked this,' I replied, feeling not entirely unrattled myself. This had taken quite the turn.

Fraser, for his part, seemed to have permanently panic-stalled. 'I don't . . . it didn't . . . my boss just said to come! She couldn't possibly have known or she would have warned me.' He paused. 'Wait – we're not going to have to recreate our . . . bits or anything, are we?'

'Who knows?' I glanced around, fighting the giggle pushing its way up my throat. 'We should prepare ourselves just in case.'

If his face could have rolled in on itself it would have. I decided to put him out of his misery. 'If you want to leave, we can.' Although I had to admit that now we were here, I did have a bit of a hankering to know what erotic pottery was. Was everyone aware this existed? How had I never heard of it before? What exactly did it entail? 'I doubt you'll have to do or model anything you don't want to though.'

'I'm so sorry – I really didn't know it would be this.' He looked positively plaintive.

I couldn't help laughing now. He just looked so concerned. 'Well, I will say, you wanted something different – this is definitely that!' I pointed out. 'Look, what harm? We'll probably just have to make some weird shapes and it'll turn out a fun article. Who knows? Maybe you'll even learn a thing or two.'

He looked vaguely affronted. 'What's that supposed to mean?'

'Just that there's nothing wrong with touching base with that side of yourself. As it were.'

'I'm perfectly in touch with it, thank you very much.'

'I bet you are,' I grinned at him. A part of me couldn't quite believe I was saying it. For all our banter, this was an area we didn't really go near. *When Harry Met Sally* we were not.

He turned pink but I could practically see his muscles relax. Before he could say anything in reply, Thea arrived by our side.

'Hello, Fraser. Hello, Ada. How are you both?'

I smiled at her, returning her greeting, and was surprised to find Fraser greeting her equally warmly. You wouldn't have known the man had been having conniptions mere moments before.

'It's a pleasure to have you both here today.'

We echoed the sentence back at her, me perhaps a touch more fervently than Fraser. 'As you've signed up for a single workshop rather than a series of classes, it will make your experience here slightly different, but by no means any less of a journey.' She smiled warmly at both of us and, honestly, I wasn't sure I wasn't falling a tiny bit in love with her. The woman radiated benevolence. 'I'm going to give you a quick demonstration of how to use the wheel. Have either of you done this before?'

I mentioned that I had and then we ran through the process.

'You're in good hands there, I think, Fraser,' Thea smiled. I gave him the *honk honk* hands signal behind her and watched him struggle not to smile.

'OK, the next step is intention setting for the session. A lot of people hear the words "erotic pottery" and assume it's all about fashioning phalluses and so on.'

'It did, uh, cross my mind,' Fraser confessed gruffly.

Thea shook her head earnestly. 'No, no, not at all. Though don't worry, you're not the first to think that. Some do choose that path, of course, and it can be a very tactile experience for those who prefer to express themselves that way, but this is driven entirely by yourselves. It's about connecting with each other through the sensuousness of the clay; working together to create pieces that symbolise your relationship and what you mean to each other.'

Our what now?

'How long have you been together?' she continued.

Oh. Oh dear.

'Excuse me, so sorry to interrupt.' It was one of the women nearest us. She smiled apologetically. 'Thea, our pedal's jammed.'

'Yes, that one is terribly sticky.' She turned to us. 'Sorry, I'll just be one moment. While I'm sorting this out, have a think about the kind of thing you'd want to make together as a symbol of your relationship.'

She was up from crouching in one graceful move. I glanced around me properly for the first time and genuinely couldn't believe how I hadn't noticed. The room was full of couples. That was why we were sharing a wheel.

I turned to Fraser. 'Oh my God!'

It was his turn to look amused. His shoulders were shaking with laughter. 'How has this *happened*?' he gasped out.

'Shh, she'll hear,' I hissed.

He seemed to gather himself a little but his eyes were swimming with mirth. 'What kind of object would best define our relationship, do you think? What if we made a little pottery laptop? Or maybe a Brodie's biscuit to commemorate the ten billion of them we've eaten from the café?'

I elbowed him but his laughter was infectious. It was too hard not to get sucked in by how ludicrous this whole thing was.

'What are we going to say?' I was deeply aware that a pedal would surely not take that long to fix. 'We need a plan. We can't tell her you're writing an article – she'll think this is a set-up and that we're bad people! Look at her – she's too wonderful to disappoint.'

And sure enough, there she was, somehow managing to both fix the pedal and chatter away in a soothing yet joyful tone. The people she was talking to were clearly also fans.

Fraser was watching her too and I suddenly had the fear that he was going to blow our spot on this. I knew what I had to do.

When Thea returned, hunkering down in front of us again, she briefly apologised for the interruption and asked where we'd left off. Before Fraser could open his trap and make this woman hate me forever, I jumped in. 'We've been together a couple of months.'

I could *feel* his eyes burning a hole into the side of my head. A part of me couldn't quite believe I'd done it. Why had I? I honestly didn't know. As soon as the words were out, I could feel the lie weighing on me, though. I forced myself to glance his way. The man was unreadable. God, I was practically sweating. How the fuck had Dan managed this for six whole months? I froze the thought. This was absolutely not the same thing.

'Ah, new love. The first flush of a relationship is such a wonderful time,' she smiled. 'So full of connection and discovery. How is it that you two first met?'

Instant regret.

She looked between me and Fraser expectantly waiting for one of us to reply.

'Oh, I'll let you take this one, darling,' Fraser replied, pulling me into a half-hug under his arm, which I had to admit, fitted me quite nicely. 'You tell it so well.'

Fair enough, fully deserved.

Fuck. What was it they said about lying convincingly? Keep it as close to the truth as possible? 'Um, we met . . . in a café.' Technically true. 'And he'd stolen my table from me so I suggested we share. And the rest is history.' Yep. I tell it well.

'*Would* we say stolen?' Fraser asked brightly.

'Absolutely,' I replied.

'Isn't that lovely!' Thea replied.

I suppose she couldn't really reply 'snooze, what a boring story'.

'And what would you like to make in today's session?' she continued.

Shit. We hadn't got around to discussing that properly. I tried to think of something but the only idea running round and round my head was 'Brodie's biscuits'. Stupid Fraser.

'We thought we could make a mug for each other,' Fraser replied.

Oh. Not stupid Fraser.

Thea beamed. 'An excellent choice and a beautiful symbol of how you met.'

She wasn't wrong. I was impressed.

'OK, as you have previous experience, Ada, I'll let you both get on. This first session will obviously be about creation and then your final session will be after the clay has been fired, when you can decorate it. A wonderful way to channel your appreciation for each other into the pieces you create here today.'

Ah. A second session. I should have remembered that the clay had to be baked before you could glaze. Fantastic.

'But please do call out to me if you need anything. There are no rules here. As I said, all I ask for is connection and communication. Ada, the mug you make for Fraser should be a representation of how you see him and how you feel he interacts with the world. Fraser, I ask the same of you.'

We both nodded and thanked her and she floated off to the next table. We realised at the same time that his arm was still around my shoulder and he stepped back, taking his glorious aftershave with him.

'That is . . . a lot to ask of a mug,' Fraser murmured.

'At least it's not a cast of our genitals, I guess,' I replied. 'Good idea on the mug thing though – some fast thinking.'

'I like a mug.' He shrugged, looking almost bashful. 'So what's yours going to look like?'

'I think you mean what's *yours* going to look like?' I replied. 'You heard the woman – we have to make one for each other.'

He groaned. 'You're going to put a penis on mine, aren't you?'

'Just a small one.'

'Well, as we have previously discussed, that wouldn't be accurate.' He winked and it was my turn to go a little bit pink.

For an unexpected erottery session, it was a lot of fun, in the main down to the surprising difficulty Fraser had with keeping the wheel turning and the clay upright.

'You want me to be able to drink out of this thing, right?' I teased.

'Hey, we can't all be artistes,' Fraser replied, nudging the clay upright again. His tongue was sticking out of the corner of his mouth as he concentrated, like an honest-to-God cartoon character. 'It's the keeping the pedal thing going that's the problem. Plus . . . there's a lot . . . going on.'

An understatement if ever there was one. We'd been working hard to keep our attention on the task at hand but it turned out there'd been a very specific reason for sharing the wheel. Some of the couples in the class were really embracing the connection elements Thea had been encouraging and there was more . . . *Ghost*-style clay-shaping than either of us were strictly comfortable being this close to.

'What's the weirdest date you've ever been on?' Fraser asked, out of the blue.

'Good question.' What had my weirdest date been? 'Scary weird or normal weird?'

He looked momentarily horrified. 'Normal weird!'

I mulled it over. 'An ex of mine used to have a giant ear-ring hole in his earlobe that he'd use as a cigarette holder sometimes. Even when they were lit, he'd pop them in there. As someone who constantly despairs of the lack of pockets in women's clothing, I respected his hustle.'

'And scary weird?' he asked, almost tentatively.

'Oof, not sure we have enough time to go through all those.' I thought about it for a moment. 'I did once have a man ask if he could peel off my nail polish. Then he put my finger in his mouth and tried to bite my nail.'

His momentary horror was becoming semi-permanent. 'He did not! Why?'

'Unclear.' I shrugged. 'His insistence that we meet at the zoo should have been a red flag, though. So that one's on me, really.'

'Don't forget dick pic guy.'

I wrinkled my nose. 'Which one?' And then I remembered – the guy from the dating site. 'Jeez, I'd forgotten all about him.'

'Jesus!' He looked forlornly down at his mug. 'Men really are the worst.'

'Ach, some of them are all right.' I nodded to him. 'You, for example, can stay.'

He put his hand against his cheek and attempted an *aw, shucks* pose.

'You've covered yourself in clay.'

'Shit!' He instinctively brought his hand to his face again, making the whole thing worse. What was it with this man forever smearing stuff all over his face? And there was me thinking all those cutesy moments in films where they bake and end up covered in flour were ridiculous. He still hadn't forgiven me for not telling him about the ink all over his face the other day. In my defence, I actually did tell him. Eventually.

'What about you?' I asked. 'Weirdest date?'

'No one's ever tried to unexpectedly bite my nails.'

I waggled my eyebrows. 'The night is young.'

He blushed again. For such a cool guy, he was becoming surprisingly easy to make uncomfortable. I managed to just about hold in an evil cackle.

'I did once have a date carve up my food and try to spoon-feed it to me.'

'Like, in a sexy way?'

'It was more in an "I was doing it wrong" kind of way . . . yeah, it was an odd evening.'

I thought back on my recent forays into the dating world. I might not know what to do about Neil but at least he'd never done that. Shit. It really wasn't OK that I hadn't replied to his text. I redirected my thought train. 'Did you ever see her again?'

'Nah. Well, except for sex a few times.'

I was fairly sure my eyes bulged out of my head. 'You didn't!'

He let out a laugh. 'Of course I didn't – the woman carved up the food on my plate and tried to spoon-feed it to me!'

'Gosh, maybe you *are* a keeper.'

'Maybe I am.'

Between our date chat, Fraser's attempts to fix his mug and me creating my own masterpiece, Thea announcing that we needed to finish up came as a genuine shock. We pulled off our aprons and looked at each other. Sure enough, both of us were covered head to toe in clay, although Fraser was way more.

'Aw, man! Your good jeans,' I wailed, shaking my fists at the sky.

Fraser mock-scowled at me. 'You joke, but you didn't fare much better.'

'Hence the dungarees, my good man.' I snapped the straps. 'These babies will outlive us all.'

'I don't doubt it.'

'But here, at least your skin will look amazing.'

He looked baffled. I pulled a tissue from a box on the table and moved across, leaning up to brush it across his cheek. It had dried in but enough came off to show him.

'Thanks.'

'Hey, you have freckles!'

'Nope,' he replied, matter-of-factly.

'Oh, in that case, I'm doing a terrible job of this.' I handed him the tissue and pointed to where he needed to remove more clay from.

'You have some on your face too,' he replied. Leaning in, he brushed a thumb along my cheek. The unexpected touch sent a shiver through me. That was . . . new. His hands were surprisingly soft. It took me a second to realise I'd observed it out loud.

He gave a chuckle. 'Must be all that clay.'

I laughed, the warm trail of his thumb on my skin still ringing through me. What was it Myster-E said about touch and oxytocin? That was it – just a plain old chemical reaction. Still, it was definitely time to go.

We filed our way out, thanking Thea as we passed.

'It's my pleasure – you truly do make a lovely couple. I saw how much fun you were having tonight. The key to any good relationship is humour and you have that in spades.'

'Erm, yeah. Yes. Thank you again,' I replied awkwardly, pushing away the thought of Fraser's thumb on my face. Stupid erotic pottery.

'I'll be away next week but I'll see you in a fortnight for you to paint your mugs.'

We shuffled outside. It was growing dark, throwing the church and its bright red door into cool, slightly spooky shadow.

'Well, what a lot of twists and turns tonight had,' I said. 'Can't wait to read your article on it.'

'Yeah.'

I glanced up at him. 'Aren't you going to do an article? It'd be so funny.'

'Yeah, I guess.' He rubbed the back of his neck and I suddenly realised he was feeling awkward.

God, of *course* he was. Imagine if his girlfriend read it. The reminder of her was like an unexpected ice-cube down the back of my neck. *Uh, sorry, tell me again who this random woman was that you went to an erotic pottery class with?* How had that not occurred to me? It was all I could do not to slap myself across the head.

A part of me imagined trying to explain it to Myster-E. Or Amal, God forbid. Not that there was anything to explain or that I owed either of them an explanation. But it would certainly make for an interesting conversation. Particularly with Myster-E, if I was being honest. Hanging out with Fraser had never come up between us, for no real reason other than it just . . . hadn't. We'd dived straight into the big stuff and it had been all systems go since then. But I couldn't help but wonder that if it hadn't been that way – if I'd told him more about my day-to-day life – would I voluntarily mention all of this? People were funny and you never knew how they'd take stuff. Best all round not to go there.

I'd made myself go the whole evening without checking if he'd replied to my message yet but I had a sudden overwhelming urge to check again, only just managing to stop myself. What if he said no to meeting? Or there was no message at all? That was definitely something I needed to be alone in my room for.

I bade Fraser good night. He seemed cheerful and normal as ever. I was clearly just being an idiot and reading into things – something that seemed to be becoming a bit of a habit these days. Watching him walk away as I waited for a bus to at least take me marginally closer to home, I found myself musing on the difference between my interactions with him and Myster-E. What made someone like Myster-E so able to openly talk about the big things, given that we literally didn't even know each other's names – while Fraser, honest almost to a fault in many ways, was on lockdown on so many others? Horses for courses, I supposed. But a part of me did itch for even a brief glimpse into Fraser's internal workings.

And in the meantime, what of it if I found myself rushing home at a far faster clip than usual to check my messages?

Flinging myself into my room, I grabbed for my computer and switched it on, heart chittering away in the background. The whirr as the laptop started up felt deeply fitting. After what felt like eons, I logged into my account to find . . . nothing. All that lay before me was the last message I'd sent. I closed the laptop, trying to fight the sickly, sinking feeling that I'd made a terrible mistake. Of course he didn't want to meet. Had he ever even hinted at it? Why on earth did I bring it up?

Scrolling down, I caught sight of Neil's message. The guilt was amassing weight at an astonishing rate now but at least that was something I had control over. Myster-E may be a mystery, but on balance there was no harm in taking Amal up on her offer of a double date with Neil. Because really who did know? Maybe we'd all have a great time. Maybe what I needed was to spend more of my life around uncomplicated, decent men. I typed out a fervent apology for taking so long to come back to him and repeated Amal's offer of the tickets for a double date.

I sat on the bed. Mum was, in a non-surprise, at work – she was on so many nights at the moment that I'd almost forgotten what the woman looked like. The house felt deathly silent and, for a moment, I felt sad. Over the last year, my life had somehow turned into a snow globe someone kept picking up and shaking. Every time I thought the snow had settled, something else popped along to stir it up. Dan. Amal. Work. Neil. Myster-E. Even Fraser was causing some flurries these days, if tonight had been anything to go by. I slumped into bed and then remembered the shit ton of stuff I had to get ready for my presentation in the morning. With a groan, I hauled myself up and dug out my list.

Chapter Twenty

The Contrast Creative meeting day arrived grey and breezy. Had I slept a wink? Nope. Was there a fair to middling chance I was going to barf? Yep. But I had my fancy portfolio binder and even fancier coffee – albeit not from Bertie this morning – and I was actually wearing heels. When I arrived at our table, Fraser gave a whistle.

'Hello, Fancy-Suited Lady. I'm afraid this seat is taken by my pal Ada.'

I pushed down the nausea and gave him some jazz hands. 'Do I look OK? Would you hire me to do your PR?'

'Oh God no. I'd never hire a woman for anything.'

The jazz hands morphed into a middle finger and he chuckled.

'You look great. If I had anything in the way of a need for PR, you would absolutely be my first port of call.'

I let out a deep breath.

'What time is the meeting?'

I looked at my watch. 'Eleven. I need to do some follow-up on the *Edinburgh Scene* interview that Steve did yesterday. Make sure he didn't say anything *too* inappropriate – ' Like casually mention a drug-fuelled orgy '– but I think I'm going to push it to this afternoon and just focus on this.' In as much as I was currently able to focus on anything. Were my hands actually shaking? Maybe the fancy coffee was a bad idea . . .

I took another deep, sucking breath and sat down, opening my laptop.

I was knee-deep in reminding myself of Contrast Creative's company history when my phone started buzzing. The vibrations rippled through the café table, startling both me and clearly Fraser, by the jump he gave.

'Sorry, need to put this on silent,' I muttered.

'I enjoy an unexpected drill, from time to time.'

'Bet you do,' I sniggered, answering the call.

'Hi, would it be possible to speak to Ada McKenzie?' an oddly familiar female voice asked.

'Speaking – how can I help you?'

'Hi, Ada, it's Danielle from *Edinburgh Scene*.'

'Of course, hello, Danielle – lovely to hear from you again. How are you?'

'I'm very well, thank you. I'm sorry to bother you but I wanted to let you know that we won't be able to reschedule our interview with Steve after all. I'd hoped it might be possible to squeeze him in this afternoon but my boss has confirmed that our copy needs to be ready today.'

I blinked at my screen. 'I don't understand. Why did you need to reschedule him?'

There was a pause at the other end of the line. 'I'm sorry, I assumed he'd run it by you. He didn't show for his interview.' Her voice went up at the end, as if she was asking a question. 'We tried to get hold of him but by the time we did, it was too late.'

What? I could *scream*. Why didn't they call me before now?

'I'm so sorry, Danielle – I actually didn't know. He assured me in the strongest of terms that he'd be there.' I managed not to wail anything about his pinkie promise or the fact that I'd reminded him twelve million times. 'Is there any chance at all you could reschedule? I can bring him to your offices or . . . or anywhere that works for you? I'll personally take him so I know he'll definitely be there?' I scrubbed my hands over my eyes. It was work to keep the stress out of my voice.

Without this interview, Steve wouldn't have done a single piece of promo for his book *or* the upcoming panto *or* the anniversary of the show – and every single organiser was moments away from pitching absolute fits. Why did the man have to be *such* a walking liability?

'I'm so sorry, the window is closed. We do have a slot for next month that I could pencil him in for?'

It would help the book, but the panto would be half-way done and the anniversary would have passed. I sucked the groan back into my lungs. It was better than nothing at all though. 'Sure, that would be great. Thanks for doing that and for letting me know. I'm so sorry again for him not showing.'

'No problem. Have a nice day, Ada,' she sing-songed.

'Yes, you too, bye.' I hung up the phone and threw it onto the table.

'What's up?'

I looked up to see Fraser watching me.

213

'Fucking Steve again!' I snarled. 'I don't know what to do with him. All he had to do was get in a taxi and do a quick thirty-minute interview. It's not like he doesn't love talking about himself!'

'He missed an interview? Who with?'

'That *Edinburgh Scene* profile I was telling you about.' I saw him wrinkle his nose. 'Don't. They are literally the only place I could persuade to give him any kind of coverage and the bastard didn't bother to tip up. I literally don't have time for this today!' I sat back in my chair and fought the urge to scream into a pillow. 'Also, not that this is the most pressing issue, but who does a fucking pantomime in *May*?'

'You took the words right out of my mouth.'

I picked up my phone and dialled Steve's number. Surprise, surprise, he didn't answer. His voice message boomed out at me. I didn't even bother to try and regulate my tone. 'Steve, call me back as soon as you get this and explain exactly why you didn't bother to go to the *Scene* interview. And it better be good because I need to tell many *many* people why you didn't.'

I ended the call and forced myself to take deep, calming breaths.

'No answer, huh?' Fraser asked.

'Nope. I'm going to have to cancel my meeting. I have to find him something else right now or they'll fire him. God knows what, though. Maybe I could channel the Hearts fan thing and see if they could add it to their newsletter?' God, what had my life become?

'It's a possibility.' Fraser leaned forward and shut my laptop.

'Hey, I was using that!'

'Don't cancel Contrast Creative. It's a coffee and a couple of hours. It'll make no difference to this.'

'I can't, Fraser. I have to sort this. If for no other reason than if he doesn't pull his weight for the anniversary festivities, he's one step closer to being binned by *Leith, Laugh, Love*.' I really needed to come up with some kind of acronym for that show. 'Which will leave him with roughly zero need for a publicist.'

'I get that but it's after ten now – that's too short notice to cancel and still have Contrast Creative want to meet with you,' he said. 'If ever you needed other irons in the fire, it's now. Steve brought this problem on himself. The solution can wait a bit.'

I looked truculently at him. He stared right back, daring me to contradict anything he'd said. Which I couldn't, of course. He was entirely right.

'God, right, yes, fine. I'll go and meet them.'

'Good. Leave your laptop and stuff here. PA mode is activated.'

'What? No, you don't have to do that,' I insisted.

'It's our deal.'

'Yeah, but today there's a higher than average chance of you actually having to do something.'

'Good. I like to flex every now and then.' He jokingly flexed an arm. 'If you take your laptop, you'll get distracted by it. Tell me I'm wrong.'

'You're wrong.' Except, of course, he wasn't.

He gave me a giant, victorious smile. 'Right, now that's settled, coffee for the road?'

Jeez, if I drank another coffee right now, my heart would literally explode. 'Don't happen to have any Valium on you, do you?'

I made my way back into the café to find Fraser still sitting where I'd left him three hours ago.

'Hello,' I beamed at him.

He glanced up and returned my smile. 'You're back! How'd it go?'

'Really well!' I settled in opposite. 'They were so lovely and keen to chat about future options. They're not quite at the "needing a publicist" stage yet but I gave them a mini pitch and threw in that I have some events and comms experience. We went over their plan for the next six months – they have honest-to-God real-life plans, Fraser! It was like returning to the mothership.'

'That's great! Did they give you an ETA of when they'll let you know?'

'They said it'll be a few months at least but they want to keep in touch. We've a meeting set up for two months from now to see where they're at.'

'See? Told you it was worth going,' he said.

'You did. And in payment for that, and your no doubt incomparable PAing, I come bearing gifts.' I pulled a packet of chocolate Hobnobs out of my bag and set them in the middle of the table.

'My favourite!' he crowed, reaching over and grabbing the packet.

'You've earned it.' Fraser handed me back my laptop. 'And now, back to the coalface. Did I miss anything?'

'Nothing much.'

'Grateful for small mercies, I suppose,' I sighed, flipping it open. 'Still nothing from Steve. No surprise there. He's probably gone into hiding. God. What am I going to do?'

'About what?' Fraser asked.

'About advertising this bloody panto and the anniversary stuff,' I sighed, feeling my good mood evaporate. 'I had a thought while I was out. You know how I'm planning his mini book-and-blog tour? Do you think we could do one for his panto as well? Get them off his back that way?'

Fraser laughed. 'No.'

'Booooo.'

'But I wouldn't worry, you'll not need it.'

I paused my googling and glanced up. Fraser was watching me with an excited grin and I was only now realising he'd basically been wearing said grin since my return. 'What do you mean?'

'While you were out and about I made some calls. My editor agreed to let us do a wee segment with Steve. I borrowed your laptop to email him, we had a quick back and forth and it'll be in sometime next week.'

'You . . . what?' I couldn't wrap my head around his words.

'I had to tweak a little bit of what he said but I can show you and you can veto if you don't like it. He just has a bit of a tendency to ramble sometimes.'

I felt my throat get tight. 'Fraser, I can't believe you did that! Thank you – that's above and beyond. I . . . I don't know what to say.'

'It was nothing.' He shrugged modestly. 'I don't know why you didn't just ask me. I mean, I do work for a local paper.'

'I didn't want you to think I was pulling favours because I knew you,' I confessed. 'Plus I really didn't think you'd run it.'

'As you so recently pointed out, we didn't seem to have a problem publishing the other stories about him. I'm all about fair and balanced journalism.' He pulled a biscuit out of the packet. 'And Hobnobs.' He shoved it into his mouth in one bite.

'Oh my God! How did that fit?' I cried.

'My mouth is like the TARDIS. Lot of room.' He gave me a biscuit-filled smirk. 'Women can get lost for days in there.'

'How does that even . . .' I laughed, leaning forward and grabbing a biscuit for myself. It felt like an honest-to-God weight had been lifted.

He cringed. 'Yeah, it wasn't nearly as fun out loud as it was in my head.' He jammed another biscuit in his mouth, taking the time to bite into this one.

'But seriously,' I continued, 'thank you. You've saved my arse. On multiple fronts. And Steve's, of course. Although he's not what you would call a deserving man.'

'You are most welcome. He's good craic. I was surprised at how funny his replies were.'

I scowled. 'Aye, he's hilarious. When he bothers to show up.'

Chapter Twenty-One

As I wandered home along Lothian Road, a message pinged up. I clicked it open to find a picture of Steve holding a piece of paper that he'd scrawled the word 'Sorry' on in big block capitals, with an exaggerated sad-face expression.

No. I was not falling for this today. I hit reply.

Nice try but you're not getting away with it that easily. I worked so hard to get you that spot and you could have lost your job over this, Steve. I know you like a mess-around but there are some things you need to take seriously. I made it so clear that you had to go to that interview!

His reply was swift for a man whose average reply window was a week to ten days.

I know, I know. I'm really sorry – I promise I meant to go but I was in Newcastle and the train was late back. I did try to reschedule and they wouldn't let me! I swear it won't happen again. And that article Fraser did is way better than anything Edinburgh Scene *would have done, so you could argue I did us both a favour.*

No. I was not rising to the bait. And what the fuck was he doing in Newcastle anyway? I started to ask and then decided I didn't want to know.

You promised you'd be there on the day of the interview. If you'd told me you were stuck, I could have rearranged! It's unprofessional and unacceptable and you being saved by Fraser only makes it worse because it was yet another person having to go out of their way to help you. You have to be better than this, Steve. It isn't just your livelihood on the line, you know.

Another message arrived from him.

I know it doesn't mean much just now but I promise I will def be better in future. I'm truly sorry, Ada.

Aye, right.

You're the best publicist and I've sent a little thank you to Fraser that I think you'll both like. I cc'd you into the email I sent him – check it out.

Well, this was a turn-up for the books. An apparently genuine apology and a thank-you present at the same time? Maybe he really did mean it. I went into my email. Sure enough there was something from him at the top.

Fraser, a small token of my gratitude for your interview today. I hope you and Ada have a wonderful time. S

I opened the attachment and actually gasped.

It was two tickets to the Peacock Ball at the Signet Library next weekend. Jesus! They went for hundreds and sold out months in advance. How on earth had he wangled this? I grabbed my phone.

Steve, this is too much! How did you get these?

He replied again surprisingly fast. *I called in a few favours. You've earned a decent night out – enjoy!*

Eek! I'd never been to a real-life ball before. And at the Signet Library to boot!

Thank you – that's incredibly generous.

I hit send and then had a thought.

But if you miss another interview I'll kill you, ball or no ball.

He replied with a salute emoji. It'd have to do.

When I got home, I put my big girl pants on and made myself check for a reply from Myster-E again. It had become a kind of dread looming over me now.

Still nothing.

I once again cursed myself for lobbing it at him. It was clearly something he hadn't wanted. I started to type a message, though I wasn't sure what to say. Perhaps something along the lines of *Lol! Didn't mean to send that invite to meet to you – that was actually for another Myster-E that I know . . .*

And then I remembered I was a grown woman and it had only been a few days. And hadn't I done something very similar to poor Neil? Hmm on reflection, not a great example to use. I was still a bit surprised that he'd agreed to come along to Amal's suggested double date, given the length of time it'd taken me to reply to him.

I clicked out of the screen. It'd look more insane to rescind my invitation. If Myster-E wanted to say no or disappear without a trace, that was his prerogative.

Chapter Twenty-Two

I spent the walk into the café the next morning musing on Steve's surprise tickets to the Peacock Ball, and the instruction to Fraser to take me which was, admittedly, a touch weird. I briefly contemplated reneging on mine so he could take his girlfriend. This fit of altruism lasted the approximation of a google search of pictures of previous balls.

Nope. His girlfriend could prise this ticket from my cold, dead, hands.

Despite this decision, by the time I arrived at the café, my nervous system was acting as if I'd just shoved a fork in a toaster. So it was something of a surprise to find Fraser as excited at the prospect of attending such a fancy shindig as I was. For some reason I'd expected him to feel as awkward, but it was clearly all only in my head.

We were mid-ball discussion when my phone buzzed to tell me I had a message from Amal.

'Oh for fu—' I stopped myself and slid my phone back on the table.

'What's up?'

'Ach, nothing.' I picked up the phone again and stared at the message, trying not to sigh out loud. 'I was meant to be going to something with Amal but she's texted to say the babysitter's cancelled.' The uneasy feeling I'd had the day of our picnic reared its ugly head again. 'I mean, I know she can't help the babysitter cancelling but—' I stopped myself. 'God, sorry. I'm being a dick.'

Fraser shrugged. 'Always disappointing when plans are cancelled last-minute. But I guess you're not allowed to just leave kids knocking about by themselves anymore.'

'Were you ever allowed to do that?'

'I think it was pretty much the law in the eighties.'

I found myself humming a bar of 'It was acceptable in the 80s' and then remembered I had to reply to Amal because she knew I'd seen the message and she'd probably worry I was upset. Which was tricky because I was upset. But I couldn't very well tell her I was pissed she had to look after her kids – still, it felt like we never did anything anymore.

The second the thought was out, I could feel it gnawing at me. God, had I always been this selfish? For fear she could somehow sense this arseholery, I opted for a swift *That's fine, maybe next time,* followed by a smiley face and some kisses. Who says technology killed the written word?

'What'd been on the agenda?'

I set my phone back down. 'Oh, it's some kind of cabaret performer called Bubbles Dell'arte – one of Aiden's friends recommended it, apparently.'

'Oh, that name rings a bell – I think someone at the paper was talking about her. I could come along – maybe do some kind of review if there's a ticket going spare?'

'That's a great idea!'

Fraser beamed at me. 'Cool. Is it tonight?'

I opened my phone to check the details and the thought hit me like a brick. Amal was only cancelling for her and Aiden – Neil was still very much a fixture of the evening. *How the fuck had I forgotten Neil?*

'Sooo . . . tonight, yeah?' Fraser replied in a way that suggested he'd said it more than once.

I blinked up at him. 'Um, yeah, eight thirty at the Liquid Rooms.' Shit. Was there a way to google 'the dos and don'ts of an unintended thruple'? Hmm. No, that would definitely lead to porn. OK. It was fine. I could handle this. I scrambled for a plan. 'But you don't have to if you don't fancy it – honestly, it's no trouble.'

'Don't be silly – it'll be fun!'

Great plan.

OK. Options. I could just tell him. Just say it. 'I'm sorry but you'd be third wheeling my date'. Nothing wrong with that – it was technically true. So why couldn't I say it? Fuck.

'We could grab food beforehand if you fancy? Unless you're the kind of monster who doesn't factor dinner into your nights out?' He eyeballed me, looking genuinely wary.

This was it! My moment had arrived. 'Absolutely not,' I said, louder than intended. I recalibrated the levels to an indoor voice. 'I *will* have to remind Neil though. It would appear he is the exact kind of monster who doesn't.'

There was a pause. 'Oh . . . Neil's coming?'

Did he seem disappointed? And did that bother me? 'Yeah – sorry, I thought you knew that. Which is ridiculous in hindsight because I realise now I didn't actually mention it.' It almost came out smoothly.

'I mean, it's fine by me,' he replied, looking now for all the world as if he meant it. 'Not sure how Neil's going to take me third wheeling, mind.'

Oh, Christ on a bike – how *was* I going to explain this to Neil? All because Amal couldn't get a friggin' babysitter to tip-up? It took all the willpower I had left not to throw my head in my hands and wail.

No. This was entirely fixable. Deep breath time.

'No, no – he'll be grand. It was a group of us going anyway.' I narrowly avoided the phrase 'double date'. No need to up the awks levels any higher at this point. There'd be plenty of opportunity for that when I had to tell Neil about our threesome.

'OK, great. Do you want to book somewhere?' Fraser was looking at me a bit funny. Which was fair enough – this must have felt like the conversational equivalent of explaining the space-time continuum to a ballpoint pen.

'Oh, uh, nah, we can see if somewhere has tables.'

'OK, great.'

My phone let out another buzz and I wasn't overly gutted to have my attention moved elsewhere. It was Amal.

OK, well, have fun.

Fun. Sure.

To make a bad day worse, I realised that if I didn't tell Neil to come to dinner before the show, I'd be having dinner with Fraser then taking him to *meet* Neil and there wasn't enough alcohol in the world to make that a thing I could cope with just now. The only upside was it meant that I could tell him Fraser was joining us via text, so at least I didn't have to watch his reaction unfold in front of me.

By the time I was watching the door to see if Neil had arrived, I was stressed to the absolute hilt. I'd effectively spent the day working myself into a kind of mad anxiety bubble over Bubbles and wondering why I'd ever let any of this happen. Steve and Amal and Myster-E had barely got a look-in.

Neil arrived just as Fraser had nipped to the loo – finally the universe was cutting me a break.

'Hey, Ada,' he called and made his way to the table. I stood up to greet him; he was taller than I remembered. And I'd genuinely forgotten how attractive he was.

I smiled back and, ever the gent, he leaned in for a kiss on the cheek.

'I'm so sorry about all the changes to the plans. Amal couldn't get a babysitter and Fraser'd heard of Bubbles and wanted to check her out and I figured there was no point in wasting the ticket so I said it was fine.' I realised I hadn't breathed in about twenty minutes and stopped to suck in air.

'It's – it's really fine. Just a bit unexpected,' he replied brightly. 'Is he bringing a partner or anything for the spare ticket?'

Shit, I hadn't even thought to ask that! Why hadn't I? Why hadn't Fraser? Oh yeah, because I hadn't told him there was another ticket spare. What was wrong with me tonight? I looked up to find Neil's polite smile becoming rictus and realised I hadn't actually replied. 'Um, no, it was . . . too short notice to ask his girlfriend to come.' Not strictly a lie and at least it shoehorned in the fact he had a girlfriend. I could swear I saw Neil physically relax.

'Well, that's a shame. I look forward to meeting him.'

As if summoned, Fraser reappeared.

'Hey, Fraser – this is Neil,' I said, stepping aside to give them unfettered views of each other.

Fraser leaned forward with a smile and shook Neil's hand. 'Nice to meet you, pal.'

'Shall we eat?' I piped up. Best to get this show on the road before I somehow managed to add a fourth wheel to the proceedings.

To my endless surprise, dinner was substantially less awkward than I could have hoped, for which I would happily have handed over multiple organs. Fraser and Neil hit common ground on a shared love of – of all things – curling. I'd initially thought Fraser might be taking the piss – I'd even shot him a warning glance when it first came up, which he returned with a querying look before ignoring me and continuing on. By the time the drinks had arrived, they were knee-deep in sweeping and sliders and spares and I was knee-deep in boredom.

By the time we arrived at the venue for Bubbles, the drinks had chilled me out, though, and I was finally ready to be entertained.

'I grabbed a flyer but I won't lie, it hasn't given much away,' said Fraser, handing me it. I held it out so that Neil could see too but before we got anywhere, the lights dimmed and Bubbles arrived on stage in an incredible bright pink diamanté skinsuit.

'Doesn't leave much to the imagination,' Neil whispered, doing a remarkable impression of a Sunday school teacher. But the part-cabaret, part-mystery, part-surprise anatomy lesson had, in fact, left much to the imagination – just not for long.

'Is that . . . oh my God! Did she pull a string of handkerchiefs out of her hoohah?' I screeched. And it was a screech – there was so much cheering around us that I could have yelled it through a megaphone and it wouldn't have made a difference.

'It's still going!' Fraser cried back. 'Is this a thing women do that I didn't know about?'

'What, use our vaginas as handbags? Of course! Where do you think I put all those biscuits I steal?' As if on cue, a little ping-pong ball arrived, ending the handkerchief extravaganza.

'I'm going to get another drink – do you want one?' Neil shouted over the din.

'Sure – um, a vodka and coke?' I replied.

He nodded. 'Fraser?'

'No thanks, Neil – I'm good.'

'Here, let me get you some cash.' I went to dive down and pick up my handbag.

Neil looked mortally offended. 'No! You got the last round, this is on me.'

I shouted my thanks and he disappeared off down the aisle.

After a moment, Fraser nudged me. 'Not sure Neil is enjoying this quite as much as we are.'

I glanced back at where Neil had been standing, feeling a tiny bit bad. It wasn't that I'd been trying to talk to Fraser more, it was just that Neil didn't seem to be seeing the funny side. 'It's perhaps not quite what he had in mind for his evening.' As if on cue, Bubbles produced a skipping rope and began an eye-wateringly X-rated nursery rhyme. 'I have to say, this isn't something I'd have imagined any of Aiden's pals being on board for.'

Fraser shrugged. 'Takes all sorts to make a world.'

'This must be an absolute coup for you, at least,' I pointed out. 'You're bound to get an article out of this.'

'I plan to demand a whole series.'

I caught a glimpse of Neil returning with the drinks, looking deeply uncomfortable, and tugged on Fraser's sleeve.

'I feel a bit bad about Neil, though. Would you have enough for an article now because I might say to him we can go and get a drink somewhere else? The poor man's clearly in his own private version of hell.'

'Bet he didn't expect it to have quite so many nipple tassels,' Fraser mused. 'Yeah, that's grand. I had enough to be getting on with article-wise about five minutes in anyway.'

That bit at least was true.

Neil arrived beside me and handed me my drink.

'Hey, listen,' I leaned up to his ear so he could hear me properly, 'I know this isn't your scene – shall we go grab a drink somewhere else once these are done?'

For a second he looked as if there was nothing more he'd want in life. 'No, no, it's fine. It's . . . I'm enjoying it.'

I put my hand on his arm, feeling my heart squeeze at how bad a liar he was. He clearly wanted the ground to swallow him up. 'Honestly, it's not a problem to leave.' Although a part of me did desperately want to see what else ol' Bubbles had in her vagina purse.

He shook his head and plastered on a smile. 'No. No, it's really fine. It's . . . fun.' He glanced up at the stage and then back at me.

'OK, well, if you're sure?'

'Yep! Totally sure.' He continued to beam at me with all the energy of a hostage in a bank vault. The man really was the worst liar.

I turned back to the stage and Fraser leaned in.

'Stay or go?' he asked.

'Stay,' I replied.

He nodded, looking pleased. 'Tin hats on.'

Chapter Twenty-Three

'Hey, love,' Mum called out as I came into the flat.

I made my way into the living room to find her watching TV – it was *Midsomer Murders* tonight. I gave her a cheery hello. We'd barely had time for anything more than that in ages. She was curled up on the end of the sofa with her hair in a messy bun, finishing up the last of the lasagne I'd made the day before. It occurred to me once again how beautiful she was.

'Earth to Ada – are you OK, love?'

'Huh? Oh, yeah. Grand.'

'Great! Then can you move? You make a terrible window and Barnaby's about to hand this clown his arse.'

I glanced at the screen to find Barnaby was, as reported, arresting an actual clown.

Mum turned down the sound and patted the sofa. 'Catch me up – I feel like I haven't seen you in eons.'

I slumped down beside her. 'Mum, you wouldn't believe the night I had. Aiden's pal gave him tickets to something but then they had to cancel at the last minute because they couldn't get a babysitter.' Amal would have loved tonight. I was starting to wonder if we'd ever get

231

to do anything fun just the two – or three – of us again. I felt that guilty little twist of disappointment and shoved the thought aside.

'I hope Amal's OK,' Mum said. 'Two kids and being back at work will be hard going.'

I waved it away. 'She's fine – Mo's been a bit of a handful, though. It's a shame they missed it because it turned out an absolute riot.'

'Ooh, how so?' Mum set her plate on the side table by her chair and readied herself for the tale.

I regaled her with the highs, lows and general insanity that had been Bubbles Dell'arte.

'Wait – she took a fake shit on stage?' She howled.

'I mean, I'm almost sure it was fake. It couldn't have been real, could it?'

'I'm a nurse, love. Someone taking a shit in public and turning it into performance art is about a six on my scale.'

'Jesus. What's a ten?'

She held up her hand. 'You're not ready for that.'

'I believe you.' I shook my head. 'It was quite the ride.'

'Who'd you go with in the end? Your fancy man?'

What? Where had that come from? I felt myself flush red. 'Fraser's just a friend,' I replied.

'Oooh, who's Fraser?' she crowed. 'What happened to Neil? Have you two men on the go?'

Fuck, of course she meant Neil! I'd somehow managed to bury her brief meeting of him, on account of it being one of the most embarrassing moments of my life to date.

232

'No! No, Fraser is just a friend from the café. Neil is . . .' How to explain Neil? Jeez, it was a good thing I'd never brought up Myster-E to her, she'd be beside herself if there were a third man in the equation. A veritable tricycle. 'We've been out on a few dates. He's . . . very sweet. I don't think it's a long-term thing, though.'

'No reason for it to be anything you don't want it to be. But you were with Fraser tonight?'

Ah. This was also going to be quite hard to explain. 'No, Neil was there too.'

Mum raised her eyebrows. 'So you were on a date with Neil with your "just a pal" Fraser third-wheeling? How'd that pan out?'

'It was fine. There were tickets to spare and it seemed a waste not to use them. Fraser's a journalist so he's going to write about it.'

'Will they print all the gory details, do you think?'

I laughed. 'That's a good question. I imagine he might have to soften it a bit.'

'Did Neil and just-a-friend Fraser thank you for this journey of the senses?'

'Weeeellll, that's where it's a bit awkward. Fraser did – we had grand old time of it.'

'But . . . ?' Mum pressed.

'Neil did not feel the same way.'

'He was not amused?'

'He was *minus* amused. He tried to play along, bless him, but he clearly hated it. I offered for us to leave early because he looked so uncomfortable but he said no. So, of course, Bubbles honed in on him.'

Mum put her hands over her face. 'What did she do?'

I squirmed at the memory of it. 'She did this bit at the end where she kind of tied herself to a chair and was begging for someone to release her. Nobody would so she got more and more insistent and then she caught sight of Neil, who to be fair, was dressed exactly like an accountant and clearly wanting to be anywhere but there, so she called him out and kept begging him specifically to do it.'

'Lucky Neil.'

It was my turn to hide behind my hands. 'I thought when he refused at first that she'd let it go but Bubbles Dell'arte does not know how to read a room. She kept going until he broke.'

'Wait – so he did it?'

I nodded. 'At a run.' Literally. He'd jogged up, untied her and then jogged back down. 'He was so annoyed. Which was fair enough, she really didn't need to go on about it the way she did.' I shook my head. 'Anyway, we went for a drink after and he only had an orange juice and then went home. I feel a bit bad now. Maybe I should have just insisted we leave when I saw how uncomfortable he was?'

Mum looked pensive for a moment. 'Not everyone's going to agree on everything all the time. So he didn't like it. If he really wanted to leave he would have. Although it sounds a *little bit* like you might have more in common with this Fraser guy.' She elbowed me. 'Been keeping that one under your hat, haven't you?'

How was she so unbelievably good at making me blush over things that were in no way blushworthy?

'There is no hat – Fraser is *a pal*. He's got a girlfriend!' I replied, wishing I was wearing a real hat that I could pull down my face and hide behind.

'All right, then,' she said in the tone she always used when she didn't believe me.

'What about you?' I asked, deciding the safest shore was a new shore entirely.

'I've not been to any sex shows with multiple paramours of late, no.'

The imaginary hat was pulled further down. 'Any men on the go?' I pressed on. 'Or women? No judgement here.'

'How very magnanimous of you,' she laughed.

'You raised a benevolent child,' I agreed. 'But not a stupid one. Change of subject denied.'

She snorted. 'I'm off the back of a sixty-hour week – what do you think?'

'I think there's a lot of beds in a hospital.' It was my turn to nudge her. She shrugged and I gasped. 'Oh my *God*, I was kidding! Have you actually *done* that?'

'Couldn't possibly say,' she replied, winking like some kind of panto dame.

'Mum!'

'What? You think I've been celibate since your dad left? That was twenty-eight years ago!'

'Well, no. But you never mention anybody.'

'Like you mentioned Fraser and Neil?' she replied innocently.

Fair point. I'd got into rather a habit of not mentioning the men in my life to people. 'Anyone interesting at the moment? I mean, you're not half bad if we brush your hair a bit and scrape you out of those scrubs. There's got to be somebody on the radar?'

'Jesus, you make me sound like Old Mother Hubbard!' she cried. 'You're my daughter, this is entirely inappropriate!'

'Says the woman who barged into my room and introduced herself to the naked man in my bed!' I cried.

She rolled her eyes exaggeratedly. 'Ach, that was one time.'

'That's too many times!'

She laughed.

'But seriously . . .' I tried to find a way to explain what I wanted to say. 'I know me coming home is *probably* not what you had in mind for either of us at this point. I hope I'm not, I dunno, cramping your style.' I managed to unhook my fingers from my palms and picked awkwardly at a nail, feeling unbelievably self-conscious. Mum had never asked me a single question when I asked if I could move back in with her – she'd welcomed me home with open arms. All this time I'd been thinking about how hard it had been sloping in with my tail between my legs but what must it have been like for her? Finally able to get her life back after raising a baby alone from the age of twenty-three and all of a sudden, there I was again with my big stupid head, taking up all the room in the flat and – let's face it – her life.

She leaned forward and took my face in her hands. 'You are my baby. You will always be my baby. There will never be a second you won't be welcome here. I would fight a bear for you.'

I felt heat roll up behind my eyes and tried to blink it away.

'Seriously, an actual real-life bear. I'd rip his face right off.' She made to demonstrate the act of ripping the face off a bear.

'Aw, poor bear,' I laughed. 'Minding his bear business, in the middle of Edinburgh, for some unfathomable reason. Just out getting himself some whisky, maybe a haggis. Just living his life.'

'Right. Off.' Mum reiterated the face pulling.

'Is there any reason you're needing to fight this bear for me?'

She shrugged. 'Just to prove I would. I'm a woman of my word.'

'I love you, Mum.'

'I love you too. And I'm so glad to have you home.'

My eyes wobbled again. I put my head on her shoulder.

'Even if it does mean I have to hide all the men I'm seeing in the cupboard when you come back unexpectedly.'

'Shut up!'

'Under the bed. Behind the curtains. It's amazing the places you can hide a man in such a small flat.'

'Look, it wasn't an unreasonable question. It'd be a shame for such a fine specimen to go to waste.'

She let out a peal of laughter. It went on so long I wasn't sure she wasn't going to hyperventilate and die.

'Mum!'

'Sorry, oh God, sorry.'

'What's so funny?'

'The idea that you think I've somehow been celibate – I mean, I made a point of keeping it from you when you were younger but I'm clearly better at espionage than I thought I was. Maybe I should consider a career change.'

'But you were just done telling me you worked a sixty-hour week!'

'Like you said, lot of beds in a hospital.' She gave me a Cheshire Cat grin. 'Sweetheart, I could tell you stories that would make your legs fall off.'

'Why would my legs—'

'You'd shrivel up and die of embarrassment.'

'As if!'

We settled into silence for a moment, as I absorbed the news that my mum was some kind of mad sex fiend – that'd keep my future therapist in fancy shoes for a while at least. 'Have you ever dated anyone you wanted me to meet?' I wondered aloud.

She thought about it for a moment. 'Not really. To be honest, I'm happiest alone. I have you. And there's enough attention for my . . . other requirements. Don't really need anything else.'

I looked up at her. She seemed entirely serious now. I'd never spent much time thinking about it before but my mum really was an absolute fucking legend. Sitting here now, she seemed completely content with her lot. I couldn't begin to imagine what that must feel like.

'What's your secret?' I asked.

She nodded to the TV. 'Nineties crime shows,' she replied. 'And a really good vibrator.'

'*Mum!*'

'I see Neil's not the only prude in the wood,' she cackled.
'I'm going to bed!'

Mum continued cackling until I reached the stairs. 'Night, my darling.'

'Night, Mum.'

'And don't forget, if you ever come across a bear, send him my way.'

Chapter Twenty-Four

I made my way into my bedroom and decided to check for a reply from Myster-E one last time. I'd found myself looking so frequently that it was bordering on psychotic so if there was nothing there tonight, I would force myself to take a break. There was a solid chance I'd also have to dig a hole and bury myself in it, but I'd cross that bridge when I came to it.

The message waiting symbol buzzed through me like a physical shock. I'd honestly just assumed he was never going to reply at this point. Out of nowhere, I felt sick. It was definitely going to be a no – it had to be. Why else would it have taken him this long to get back to me? And even though I knew that in the grand scheme of things it didn't really matter, that in five years' time, I'd barely remember this, it was going to be a pretty tough gig to come back from in the moment. I briefly considered not opening it. Leaving it a day or two, to show that I could. But only briefly. Did I mention this whole incident had made me borderline psychotic? I didn't have to reply straight away but I was pretty sure the suspense of not reading it instantly would straight up kill me, even if it was a no.

Sorry for taking so long to get back to you – it's been a hectic few days! But to answer your most important question, I would love to meet up! I'd been debating asking but I wasn't sure if it was something you'd want, or if you'd rather keep it all online so I'm very glad you brought it up. Let's grab a drink somewhere – any suggestions? I live in the south of the city but am happy to travel if that's easier for you? I've another busy few days ahead of me, but I could do beginning of next week? Maybe Monday? Not a great day for drinks, I know, but it'd be a nice way to start a new week!

Thank you for your very kind words about my muscle memory comment – I hadn't intended for it to be so close to the bone but always glad to be of help if I can! I think you're definitely right about there being a downside to it though. It's a fickle old organ – it'd be nice if we could somehow have more of a handle on it, wouldn't it? In the meantime, as you say, let's try and pick and choose the things we want it to remember.

But please don't think this has in any way got you out of talking about the fact that you had a sex dream about a certain Monsieur Poirot! Be honest, was it the bowler hat? Because I've been considering getting one and this may be the clincher.

The about-turn in my emotional landscape was almost dizzying – I felt suddenly light as a feather. It was embarrassing how big it felt. If I'd been in an eighties movie I would have punched the air in slow motion.

I wanted to play it cool. God help me, I did. Even as I typed, I could hear Amal's voice in my head, telling me to slow it down and think about what I wanted to say. He'd taken days to respond and I should at least leave it a little longer. But I'd never been one to take sound advice. What was the worst that could happen?

I replied with the name of a fancy cocktail bar on Queen's Street, with the suggestion that we wear certain things so we could recognise each other. What can I say? In for a penny, in for a pound. I would wear a green dress and he could bring his bowler hat if he decided on purchasing it. Or failing that, some kind of tweed jacket, perhaps. Because I was fairly sure every man over the age of twenty-five in Edinburgh owned a tweed jacket. I hit send. To my surprise, he happened to be online and replied almost instantly – immediate vindication of my decision to reply. To my non-surprise, he did in fact own a tweed jacket – though sadly not a bowler hat. We set the date to finally meet.

I closed my laptop and took a deep, steadying breath. I had a date with Myster-E! The thought hurled swirls of panic and excitement through me. Was this insane? To be meeting someone I knew so little about? But I'd gone on plenty of online dates in my time and hadn't thought anything of it. And it felt like I *did* know him. Wait . . . was that better or worse?

I guessed I'd know for sure next Monday.

Chapter Twenty-Five

And now I had two things to get super-nervous about: meeting Myster-E and the Peacock Ball. I'd thought the anticipation of both would slow time down, but Fraser's piece on Steve brought interest from a few other local outlets, which meant upping the ante on making sure Steve didn't go rogue. Sometimes I wondered if a publicist boosting Steve's profile was in fact a terrible idea – he was a man who in many ways should probably not be encouraged. Either way, the days flew by. In what felt like no time at all, the ball had arrived.

With everything else going on, I hadn't even had the chance to panic about the fact that I had nothing suitable to wear, the upside of which was that I needed Amal's sartorial assistance. We were the same height and mostly the same size, and she had gussied me up on more than one occasion. I'd arranged to swing by hers to try out some options. She'd been pretty quiet since the cancelled double date and we'd not seen each other since the picnic. To cap it all, the cancellation had been followed by another rain check of our weekly dinner because Mo still wasn't well. By the time I was approaching her house, I'd convinced myself she was mad at me and it felt like my whole body was full of bees. I took a deep breath and rang her doorbell.

This was nonsense; I wasn't worried about seeing Amal! It was just nerves about the ball. Everyone got nerves before a fancy ball, right?

Amal answered. For a split second all I could think was how tired she looked but then she gave a massive smile and pulled me into a massive hug and the bees dispersed. As I leaned into the hug, I had to swallow the lump in my throat. I'd missed her. How silly. But I had.

'I hope you're prepared for me trying on everything you own.'

B-day arrived and I swished my way into Amal's living room in the dress we'd decided on.

'Oh my God, you look amazing!' she cried. 'Give us a spin.'

I smoothed down the dress and twirled around. The knee-length skirt flared out in a cobalt halo around me and I found myself giggling.

'I love this dress so much!' I crowed. 'Thanks for letting me borrow it.'

'You're most welcome. It'll be a while before I'm into a size twelve again so at least the old girl's getting some attention.' She looked at me wistfully. 'I can't believe you're getting to go to the Peacock Ball. Do you know who I would have killed back in the day to go to that? You. I would have killed you.'

'I know – I can't believe Steve gave Fraser these tickets.' I suddenly wished Amal was coming too. We'd always had so much fun at parties. 'It's a shame he couldn't have wangled more or I'd have taken you guys.'

She waved me away. 'Ach, something would probably have got in the way of us going anyway. And just because my days of dancing the night away with handsome men are over doesn't mean yours should be.'

'At least part of you will get to go.' I shoogled the dress in her general direction.

Amal stood up. 'There's one more finishing touch.' She disappeared out of the room. I took the opportunity to check out the makeup she'd plastered on me. I had to hand it to her, the woman knew her way around a glow-up. She'd curled my hair properly and pinned it up on one side so it spilled down over the other shoulder. A subtle smoky look made my eyes look bigger and somehow bluer, and she'd finished it all off with a pop of ruby red lipstick. It surprised me how sophisticated I looked – why didn't I make an effort more often? Oh yeah, because I was far too lazy. As a result of said laziness, there was a fair-to-middling chance that Fraser might not actually recognise me when I arrived. I felt a swirl of something I couldn't fully pick out. Anticipation? Hmm. That was new.

Amal came back into the room and I hopped back from the mirror.

'OK, last bit.' She held out what I thought was a necklace until she tried to put it on my head.

'Wait, what? No, that's too much!'

Amal slapped my hand away. 'It's not too much, it's perfect and you are not to take it off.'

She fiddled with it a bit more and then turned me back towards the mirror.

It looked so goddamn cool. It sat in my hair like a hairband, with delicate silver spirals winding into a floral shape all across one side of my head, glittering like little fireflies in the light. It was the fanciest thing I'd ever seen. Why on earth was I only learning how much I loved hairpieces now? Years of my life wasted.

'I'm never taking this off.'

'Please don't. You don't even want to know how expensive that was.'

I felt panic rise. 'Nope. No. Don't trust me with it.'

I turned to find Amal openly laughing at me. 'Sweetie, it's fine. You won't lose it. And even if you do, at least I can tell people it was lost at a fancy ball at the Signet Library.'

Aiden came into the room. 'Taxi's here in five. Oh, hey. You look great, Ada!'

'Good enough to fit in at the Peacock Ball?'

'Oh, God no. But you'll do.'

I gave him the middle finger.

'You'll be the belle of the ball,' he laughed.

'God, I'm so nervous. Why are rich people so scary?'

A look crossed betwixt the A-Team.

'You know, if you're going to keep insisting on throwing meaningful glances at each other, you really need to get better at hiding it,' I unceremoniously informed them.

246

Amal moved across, handing me my handbag. 'We were wondering if it's the rich people making you nervous or if it's the person you're going with.'

'No. Don't start that again. He's got a girlfriend and I've got—'

'Neil? Highly unlikely as you've barely said a word about him.'

Wait, was Amal annoyed about that? Her tone had been light but the words felt heavy.

Urgh, who was I kidding? It wasn't good. And Neil was Aiden's pal! Were they mad at me for how I was treating him? I mentally set that rock back down. Nothing good was coming out from under there just now.

'Neil's a lovely guy,' I replied lamely.

'But he's not Fraser?' Amal asked, a sudden gleam in her eye.

'No!' I spluttered. Where was this coming from?

'Or that stranger on the internet you've never clapped eyes on?' Aiden asked innocently.

I *knew* I shouldn't have told them about Myster-E. It'd been barely a mention at all but clearly enough for them to have latched onto the idea and I was regretting it immensely just now. Amongst other things. 'That taxi here yet?'

Aiden checked his phone. 'Still two minutes. No getting saved by the bell on this one, I'm afraid.'

I decided to steer the conversation firmly away from Neil and Fraser, crashing it on the safest shore of my available options. 'I'm meeting Myster-E next week so he won't be a stranger much longer,' I informed them.

Amal's eyes widened. 'You've arranged a meet-up? Why didn't you tell me?'

'I just did!'

'Poor Neil. Poor Fraser. All these men on the go,' she replied with a smirk. Was I imagining that it didn't go all the way to her eyes?

I let out a melodramatic sigh to hide the unease I was sure was rolling off me now. 'Fraser's a pal and I'm not into him. And as I've said a bajillion times, he's still very much with someone.' Neil was probably best left unmentioned in Amal's company just now.

'Aye, a girlfriend you've never met who he doesn't seem to ever do anything with. A romance for the ages, that one,' she remarked baldly.

Aiden's phone bleeped. 'OK, taxi's here.'

Thank Christ for that. I swooped in and gave Amal a hug, finding myself holding onto her a little longer than I normally would. 'Thank you for helping me get ready, I love your face.'

She returned the hug for as long as I did. 'You're most welcome, my love. You look amazing. Have the best night.' I let go, feeling slightly tearful. 'And you are into Fraser, by the way,' she piped up. 'Or you wouldn't have said the girlfriend thing last.'

I forced a laugh. 'That's weak, even by your standards.' Blowing her a kiss, I walked out the door.

In the grand tradition of everyone who'd ever got in a taxi, I jovially insisted that 'anywhere around here is great', culminating in me being dropped off further down George IV Bridge than I appreciated in my heels. I carefully negotiated my way back along to the Lawn-market. The Mile rolled down in front of me, all cobbles and cultural landmarks. St Giles Cathedral was still cut-ting about in the middle of it all, lounging over the pubs and pedestrians like the grand old dame she was. The place had the buzz of early summer about it with tourists milling down from the castle and up from Arthur's Seat and I felt slightly incongruous in my fancy dress.

I'd been worried I'd struggle to remember which of the buildings the Signet Library was, and I didn't want to google it and end up looking like a tourist but the red car-pet spilling out and kilted gents on the door announced it nicely. I took a deep, steadying breath.

My fancy hairpiece and dress – not to mention the tickets hopefully sitting in Fraser's pocket – gave me courage now, though, and I strode forward as assertively as the cobblestones would allow. I'd arranged to meet him inside. Nodding to the man at the door with a con-fident smile, I made my way through as he held it open.

Fraser had already arrived and stood waiting at the other side of the grand staircase running up and down to who knew where. He was staring up at the portraits on the landing above.

I realised that I'd never really paid attention to him from any kind of distance before – the man had incred-ible posture. Although admittedly it was hard to tell if, much like me, his surroundings were bringing out the best in him. He was wearing a blue jacket with a red kilt lined through with blue to match. When he turned towards me, I noticed that, in a baller move, there were braces peeking out from underneath the jacket, where a waistcoat should have been. His hair had been wrestled into line, sitting almost neatly – the cowlick still stubbornly sticking its tongue out in a wave over his left eye. I moved towards him.

'Hello!' I said brightly, feeling suddenly, unaccountably shy.

He focused in and gave a huge smile. 'Hey – sorry I didn't see you there.' I felt his eyes sweep over me from top to bottom. 'You look fantastic!'

I looked down to cover the embarrassment that had reared its head and gave an exaggerated shrug. 'What, this old thing? Just threw it on.'

He laughed. 'Aye, same here.'

'You look great too,' I offered. He really did. Not that he ever looked bad, but he looked so dapper.

'I love these.' I leaned forward and ran a finger along his suspenders, only realising at the last second that that was a fucking weird thing to do. What had got *into* me? Stupid Amal's stupid comments before I left – that was what had got into me.

'Thanks. I'm always looking for an excuse to wear them.' He seemed amused, at least, which was definitely better than weirded out. 'I like this.' He gestured to my hairpiece, almost but not quite touching it in return. 'It looks a bit like a crown.'

'Yeah, I'm always looking for a reason to wear my crowns. Thank God Steve gave us these tickets, eh?' I said lamely.

It was definitely time for a drink.

Someone asked us to show our tickets, which Fraser did with alacrity. In return, we were handed a whisky each by a passing server, which seemed a pretty sweet deal.

'What a way to start a party,' I muttered, as they walked away with the tray. We weren't even in the room yet. Fraser cheersed me and I returned it, the two of us knocking back our whisky in a oner.

It was an Islay whisky, full of smoke and sting. I held in a cough, feeling my eyes water as it burned its way down my throat, leaving a pleasantly warm feeling in its wake. It hit my stomach and I realised that in my nervousness, I hadn't really eaten much today. That would be fun tomorrow.

Fraser gestured towards the direction of the main library. 'I've heard rumours of more where that came from – shall we head in?' I nodded and he held out his arm. 'M'lady?'

I slipped my arm through the crook of his. 'Thank you, kind sir.' His jacket was surprisingly soft to the touch. I nodded to it. 'We match! Sort of.'

'You said you were going to wear blue so I thought I'd give it a go. This is the only blue jacket I own though, so we do seem to have struck it lucky.'

Indeed.

We entered the main room and paused to take it in. There was something about opulent places that always made me want to touch stuff. Feel the textures and imagine all the work that went into making them – I was an absolute liability in a museum. Gazing around,

I somehow managed to keep the urge to run my hands over everything in the room at bay, but only just.

The place was *stunning* – as chock-full of fancy cornicing, fresh flowers and Grecian-style pillars as I'd hoped. Behind the pillars were little book-lined alcoves lit with whatever the posh equivalent of fairy lights were, giving a dream-like quality to the whole room. This was only enhanced by the entertainment dotted about the place, performing the poi dance with flame-coloured ribbons that floated around them in hypnotic undulations. At the back, a stained-glass window was set-off by the Art Deco-style ceiling and win-dowed dome. The whole thing was utterly breathtaking. I thanked my lucky stars I had Amal. Without her input, I'd have looked like the little match girl here.

Fraser caught my eye and we both burst into a fit of laughter, managing to keep it down in the nick of time.

'I think we may be a bit under-dressed,' he croaked.

'You think? I swear that woman over there has actual diamonds in her dress. You're not even wearing a tie!'

A waiter sailed past us with a tray of drinks, then paused and turned back. 'Champagne, madam?'

Had anyone ever said no? And then a thought occurred to me – was there a polite way of asking if it was free? The whisky had been but you never knew. Before I could think of a way to check, Fraser had cadged us two glasses and the waiter was on his merry way again, with no hint of a charge.

Phew.

He handed me the glass and we cheersed again and drank.

'Is it bad that I feel like this would be improved with some orange juice?' I wondered aloud.

'Wheesht, they'll kick us out for sure if they hear you say that.' He took another sip. 'You're not necessarily wrong, though.'

I took a mouthful and found myself looking at Fraser surveying the room. He had a slight five o'clock shadow and I'd never noticed how long his eyelashes were before. It took a moment for me to realise that he was now watching me watch him with a curious expression on his face. 'What?' he asked.

An excellent question. What was wrong with me tonight? Fraser was Fraser, for Christ's sake. And as I had informed Amal, I had Myster-E to look forward to. And, probably, kind of, Neil. Erk.

Wait, what was his question again? I scrambled around for a response. 'I was just noticing how criminally long your eyelashes are. Do you know what I would give to have mine look like that naturally?'

'Thanks.' He gave me a cocky grin. 'I grew them myself.'

I deliberately forced myself to look away and noticed for the first time that a band had been setting up in the far corner and were getting ready to play. A terrible thought occurred to me. 'Wait, are we expected to actually dance?'

Fraser snorted into his champagne glass. 'I'd hazard there's a reasonable chance, what with it being a ball and all.'

'Yeah, but I assumed it would be a ceilidh sort of deal, not a fancy Jane Austen thing!'

Fraser looked around. 'It doesn't look like a ceilidh set-up so probably some regular dance dancing, I think?'

I found myself fiddling with the stem of my glass. 'It's just that . . . I'm not an amazing dancer.'

He was clearly amused. 'I'm sure you're fine.'

I'd been so caught up in the excitement of going to the ball without actually getting to the part where I was at the ball and what that might entail. I swear my palms were starting to sweat. 'I mean, I can throw some shapes in a discotheque if I need to, but that's usually solo or pissing around with friends or too drunk for it to matter.'

'Sorry, did you just use the phrase "throw some shapes in a discotheque"?' Fraser asked.

'If that's your threshold for embarrassment, you're in for a very long night.'

'Then I guess it's my turn to confess something.' He set his glass down and his face took on a deeply earnest look. In the background, like some kind of bar-genie, the server was back handing us more champagne. 'I took dance classes as a teenager. A couple of different styles. I was pretty good – even won some trophies.'

'How is that – that's not embarrassing! If anything it's the opposite.'

'I never said it was embarrassing,' he said, very reasonably.

I found myself feeling slightly flushed. Less champagne would probably be helpful at this point. I downed the glass and set it on a nearby table. Hey presto! Less champagne.

'Me, I hate a man who can dance. Yeuch. Gross. Nothing at all attractive about that.'

He laughed and a crease that was almost a dimple appeared along his cheek, but only on one side. How had I not seen that before? For a brief, mad moment, I imagined running my finger along it. Or my tongue.

Jesus! Right, seriously. No more champagne for me for a while. A solid ten minutes at least.

'Would you like me to teach you some steps?'

I made myself focus. I absolutely did not want that. But also I absolutely did. Decisions, decisions. 'Oh, I suppose if you must.' I held up a finger in warning. 'But you should know, I'm a terrible student.'

'Luckily for you, I'm an excellent teacher.' He held out his hand out and gave me a playful bow.

'Wait, now?' I panicked. 'The band hasn't started yet.'

'Yeah but there's music playing in the background and this way, you'll be ready to go when the band does come on.'

I couldn't fault his logic. 'All right, then.'

I tentatively took his hand, fervently hoping mine had stopped sweating, and received a supportive squeeze for my trouble. He led me further into the corner, which had the dual benefit of slightly louder music and being further away from people seeing me make a tit of myself.

Turning towards me, Fraser laid my right hand gently over his shoulder, holding the other out to the side. He was about five feet ten, which still gave him four inches on me, and when we were out and about in day-to-day life it seemed a lot. But now that I was facing him in heels, we were almost the same height and there was something inescapably frank about being this evenly matched with someone. He held my gaze with an ease and air of confidence: it rolled off him in waves.

I'd forgotten that my dress fell in a wide V down my back to my waist so when he pulled me to him, his hand met bare skin. The warmth of his skin on mine sent an unexpected shiver through me. He smiled, kind eyes crinkling at the sides, and I found myself smiling back.

'So we shouldn't need much to muddle through.' He was speaking more quietly now, and I could feel his breath tickling my ear. 'I'm assuming you're not planning on challenging anyone here to a dance-off or anything?'

I popped the strange bubble I'd fallen into and tried to get my head back in the game. 'Not initially but if I turn out to be a natural then I can't make any promises.'

He laughed and we were so close that I felt it rumble from him to me. 'Fair enough.' He somehow straightened his posture more. 'OK, the basic box step is really easy and once you have it mastered, we can throw in a couple of turns. That should be enough to see us through at least a couple of the fancy dances.'

I nodded studiously, though concentrating was getting harder as the champagne and our proximity bumbled their way about my system.

'Right. So what you need to do is this: right foot back, left foot side, right foot closed.' Despite there being barely any pressure from any part of him, Fraser somehow seemed to be guiding me so that I followed his instructions almost intuitively. 'Great, nailing it. OK, next bit is the same but back towards me, so left foot forward, right food side, left foot closed. Just like that in a count of three – see how it makes a box?'

'I do!' I exclaimed, feeling altogether too proud of myself, given that it was the most basic of basic steps. We did a few repeats until it felt more natural.

'Want to try a turn?'

'I'd like to see you try and stop me!'

'Wouldn't dare,' he chuckled.

It was slightly more complicated but Fraser ably guided me and before I knew it, we were cutting about our corner in a satisfactorily box-like fashion. The music and beautiful surroundings felt as though they were weaving a kind of glamour around us. The faint scent of his aftershave and the feel of his hand on my back and his voice in my ear flitting between instruction and silly asides made him feel so familiar and unfamiliar all at the same time. Fraser, my friendly neighbourhood work pal who I sometimes did random stuff with had, at some point this evening, become Fraser, a funny, confident, nice-smelling, cool dancer man.

A small voice in the back of my head reminded me that, regardless, he had his girlfriend and I had my Myster-E man. But they were both starting to feel about as distant as the moon.

Not that any of it mattered, really. In the cold light of coffee shop day, I would wake and remember that *Cinderella* is actually more of a warning than a fairy tale. The magic always wears off at midnight, leaving you stumbling around in one deeply uncomfortable stiletto. All of this nonsense was the ball talking.

Fraser lifted his arm and spun me under it unexpectedly, pulling me back into the present and, deeply unhelpfully, his arms, as he cradled me from behind.

'You're a natural,' he murmured into my ear.

Pushing down the fizz in my stomach, I leaned back and looked up at him as seriously as I could. 'I hope you're prepared for all the dance-offs.'

'Of course! But first . . .' He swung me back round to face him. 'More champagne.'

As we clinked our glasses of fresh champagne, a deep voice from behind startled me into almost spilling mine. I spun to find myself nose to chest with an impossibly tall man in, of all things, a cloak. Craning up introduced me to a goatee, dark eyes and an honest-to-God top hat.

'Good evening, madam, sir.' He nodded to me then Fraser in turn. There was an unnerving amount of 'madam-ing' going on this evening. A flick of his hand produced a small red flower from apparently nowhere and he presented it to me.

A magician. *Amazing*. And unbelievably well-cast. The man could be in jeans and a T-shirt at a bus stop and you'd tag him as one.

'Thank you!' I beamed at him, inexplicably pressing the obviously plastic flower to my nose to smell. He gave a small bow, turned to Fraser and pulled a coin out from behind his ear. Flourishing it in front of us, he made a show of passing it from hand to hand and having it disappear again. In the midst of his chatter, he asked if we'd ever seen someone bend metal with their mind. He quickly rubbed the coin and held it aloft in all its now-bent glory. I let out a cheer, before mentally reminding myself that this was a fancy ball – albeit a magicianed one – and that cheering and whistling would probably be frowned upon.

Mr Magician seemed to appreciate my appreciation, though. He smiled and bowed again, lower than before, and thanked us before moving onto a group nearby. The faint smell of aftershave alerted me to the fact that Fraser was leaning in to me again.

'Shame you didn't get to keep your bent coin.'

'Aw, man, you're right!' He looked ruefully over to the new recipients of the coin trick. 'Bastard.'

'He let me keep my flower,' I bragged. As I spoke, a woman walked past me holding an identical one in her hand. 'Well, damn.'

Fraser plucked the flower out of my hand. Before I could protest his thievery, he was tucking it into a tendril of hair behind my ear. 'It looks better on you.'

Were his eyes actually twinkling? No, of course not. It was just the fairy lights getting carried away. I suddenly realised his hand was still cradling the flower. Which felt very similar to cradling my face.

Out of nowhere, an electric guitar was strummed too close to a microphone, the mewling whine startling us apart. A voice announced the band that were about to take the stage.

Fraser turned back to me, and held out his hand. 'Ready to show them how it's done?'

I drained the rest of my champagne glass and took his hand as he led me to the edge of the dance floor. There was something so casual about how he looped his fingers loosely through mine as he walked that made the whole thing more intimate.

I mentally shook myself, feeling the room haze and wobble around me and let out a giggle. He looked back at me, dance-floor lights haloing around him.

'You OK?' He looked amused.

I attempted to make my thumb and finger into an O shape. It didn't go so well so I turned it into a finger gun.

He did one back, then turned and drew me into him to start dancing again. We attempted a box step and I accidentally trod on his toes. 'Shit – sorry!' I cried.

He wrapped an arm around my waist to stop me stumbling. 'I think you might have too many feet.'

'Excuse you, I have two feet. Three, tops.'

'I think I can see more.'

I looked down and then leaned up to his ear. 'I think they might be yours,' I whispered loudly.

He let out a laugh. 'So they are! Thank God for that, eh?'

At least I wasn't the only one feeling the champagne. I took his hand and we started attempting a box step again but we kept losing our rhythm and restarting.

'This isn't working, I think we might need to make it simpler,' Fraser said. 'Let's try this.' He took my arm and laid it round his neck, swiftly followed by my other arm.

Pulling me close, he wrapped his arms around my waist. We were nose to nose now and there wasn't a millimetre of space separating us. His cheeks were flushed and his hair had broken ranks, dropping a curl onto the side of his forehead. He looked hot and dishevelled and I could feel every inch of him on me. All of a sudden all I wanted to do was lose the layers and close any remaining gap between us.

The thought zipped through me. I could do it. Lean forward an inch and I'd be there. I found myself staring at his mouth.

One more inch.

'Champagne?' A waiter had appeared out of the ether.

Never in my life had I been less happy to see a free drink.

Fraser took a step back, looking a tiny bit shell-shocked. 'Uh, sure, yeah – thanks.' He lifted two glasses, handing one to me.

We each took a sip and then another and another. The heat had made me thirsty. It had clearly done the same for Fraser because he was gulping it back as well. Before I knew it, we were once again down to the bottom of our glasses.

'That's going to hurt tomorrow,' he said cheerily. I nodded, feeling a fresh wave of fuzziness wash over me. It turned into a lightheaded giddiness and I let out a hiccup, swiftly followed by a giggle.

I looked over to find Fraser watching me. It was a bleary, open, half-smile gaze. I could still feel the imprint of him on my body and I was suddenly, overwhelmingly wanting to feel his skin on mine again.

'Want to dance some more?' I asked. The question hung suspended in the air for a moment.

He didn't reply, but stepped back into me again until he was close enough that I could practically feel his heart beat. Taking one of my hands in his, he wrapped his other arm around my waist as if it was the most natural thing in the world. I curled my free hand round his neck and he led me on a lazy trail across the dance floor. We didn't speak but I found that I couldn't take my eyes off him. The room felt as if it was moving around us at a slightly different pace to the circles we were turning and I felt my head start to spin.

'Sorry,' I murmured, pulling us to a stop, half cursing myself for breaking the spell.

'Are you OK?' he asked, concern pulling at the corners of his eyes.

'Yes, just a bit dizzy.' He led me back to where we'd half-hidden before.

'Do you need some water?'

'No, no, I'm fine.' I held up my hand, shaking my head. 'I only drink champagne now, anyway.'

He smiled and moved beside me, gently guiding my elbow. 'Want to sit? We could find an empty alcove.'

'I'm feeling OK now – it was just a moment.'

He was looking at me again with the same hazy gaze as before. Still standing so so close to me, until the heat from our bodies felt like it was crackling back and forth between us.

'Ada,' he murmured. But he wasn't looking at me. His heavy-lidded eyes were watching my lips, as he leaned slowly, slowly, slowly towards me.

Head still spinning, I let myself fall into him and felt his mouth meet mine, butterfly soft. He pulled away, for the briefest of moments, eyes a question mark. I reached up and pulled him back again, wrapping my arms around his neck. He closed the gap between us, his mouth suddenly hungry on mine. His hands slid around me, trailing along the bare skin of my back, sinking warm fingers under the buttery soft fabric of the dress. I felt it down to my core, like a thousand tiny corks popping all the way through me. His hands went lower as he somehow found a way to mould me closer. I could feel every line of him, taut and insistent and setting everything in me on fire.

Out of nowhere, a voice boomed across the room. The sound startled us apart as the lights went up. An announcement to say the band would be resetting and to take the opportunity to get another drink.

I stared up at Fraser, wearing half my lipstick, still feeling the scratch of his stubble on my face and the warm tingle of his hands on my skin. A part of me wanted to dive right back in but another, bigger part of me was surfacing, demanding to know what the fuck was I doing?

The champagne reared up in my stomach, but not in the fun way it had before. The brighter lights brought a seasick, clammy wave crashing down on me.

'I . . . I don't feel so good. I need some air.'

He looked worried. 'OK, yeah. Let's . . . let's go outside.'

We made our way to the door in silence. Wobbling my way to the cobbled pavement outside, I sucked in a deep breath of cool evening air, willing the nausea to go away.

'Are you OK?' Fraser was beside me, sounding concerned. His hand brushed my back and a shiver ran through me again.

I could feel my tongue start to thicken, saliva pooling in my mouth. 'I don't feel good. I-I think I need to go home.' It took all my self-control to push down the champagne that was threatening to leave the way it had gone in.

He didn't even question it, giving me a nod and looking down the road to see if there was a taxi to be had in the vicinity. 'I think we'll need to get to George IV and we should be able to flag one down.'

We made our way there in silence. Part of me wanted to reach out and take his arm but decided against it. We made it to the bridge and Fraser stuck out his hand.

'I'm so sorry for . . . I'm just—' I felt my stomach turn and had to stop talking.

'Don't be silly.' As he spoke, a taxi stopped beside us. 'Do you need me to take you home?'

I shook my head gently. 'No, I'll be fine.'

For a split second he looked almost crestfallen and my guilt trebled in size.

'Thanks for a really fun night,' he said.

'Yeah, it was great,' I managed, before it became too risky to keep talking. Before he could say anything else, I wedged myself into the taxi, shut the door and closed my eyes, trying to keep as still as humanly possible.

Chapter Twenty-Six

I woke up feeling as if my whole body was dry-heaving. My head was too heavy for my neck and filled to the absolute brim with molten lava. What monster suggested you couldn't get a hangover from good champagne? Although the whisky we'd sunk beforehand probably hadn't helped.

As I lay trying to bring my ceiling into focus, the night came roaring back to me.

I'd kissed Fraser.

Well, shit.

The guilt was instant and all-consuming. How had this happened? I mean, I knew that I'd grown to love hanging out with him but I loved hanging out with Amal – it didn't mean I automatically wanted to kiss her.

Oh no – Amal. I'd arranged to meet her to fill her in on the ball. Why on earth had I agreed to that when I knew I'd be most likely drinking my weight in free booze? It would appear my capacity for bad decision-making really knew no bounds these days.

I somehow managed to manoeuvre myself into a position to see the time on my phone – nearly twelve and I needed to get to hers for one.

No, I'd die if I left this bed. I needed to postpone.

And then I had a flashback to the ball. And the kissing. And realised that if I stayed in bed that was all I had to look forward to. Was that better or worse than hauling my carcass to Amal's to be surrounded by screaming, hyper infants?

No. I couldn't move.

I closed my eyes and felt myself floating off into a doze. Suddenly I was back in the Signet Library, feeling Fraser's lips on mine.

Nope. Amal's it was.

I settled onto Amal's sofa, clutching the tea she'd handed me for dear life. She sat down opposite me with a tired sigh.

'Benji, love, don't hit the table.'

Benji, sprawled on the floor surrounded by toys, continued hitting the table with his little rattle hammer thing. 'Mama!' he yelled gleefully and giggled, hitting some more. On any other day I'd have thoroughly enjoyed that infectious little laugh but today it, and the hammering, went right through me. I took a sip of my tea and willed the painkillers to start their work.

'Where's Mo?' I asked.

'Aiden took him out to give me a break,' she said wearily. She looked almost as rough as I did. Well, no. Nobody looked *that* rough. But she was looking a little frazzled.

'Is he still not sleeping?'

She shook her head. 'Nope. I can only assume it's because I'm being punished for doing terrible things in a previous life.' She gave a weak laugh.

'Maybe you were, like, Genghis Khan or something?' I suggested.

'At this rate, I'm starting to think that might be it.'

I patted her arm. 'Sorry, pal. Anything I can do to help?'

'Figure out why my child hates me and never wants to sleep?'

'Of course he doesn't hate you – I'm sure it's just a phase he'll grow out of soon.' I remembered the almost sentence about date nights or the lack of them from her friend Catherine and had a brainwave, albeit a small one. 'I could babysit if you like? Give you guys a night out? Some time away?'

'That's very sweet.' She glanced over at Benji, who had called out to show her his toy. 'That's lovely, darling.'

'I could also potentially get my hands on some horse tranquilisers. I know a guy.'

She smiled. 'For me or Mo?'

'Why not both?'

She barked a small laugh and took a sip of her tea. 'So fill me in. How did last night go? You look suitably dishevelled, which means it either went very well or very badly.'

I groaned. I couldn't help it. I'd debated whether I should tell her what had happened, swinging back and forth. But I knew the second I saw her that there was no way I would be able to keep it in. It was ticking away inside me and if I didn't let it out, I'd literally explode. 'Let me take a wild swing here,' Amal interrupted my thought. 'You slept with Fraser.'

'What? No!'

'Shame. Aiden's won a tenner.'

'You bet on me sleeping with Fraser?' I howled, immediately regretting raising my voice as the hangover jangled its jailor keys in my head.

She shrugged. 'We take our thrills where we can find them these days.'

The idea that they'd discussed it, and that Amal had been so sure I would, stung a bit. I couldn't quite put my finger on why.

'I didn't,' was all I could manage.

Benji's banging resumed and Amal asked him to stop again. I felt her eyes return to me. 'I didn't mean to upset you.'

'I'm not upset,' I said, meaning it more now she'd apologised. I was being over-sensitive. I gave her a smile.

'So what happened?' she pressed.

I found myself picking at the handle of the mug. 'We kissed.'

I sensed rather than saw her nod. 'OK.'

I covered my eyes with my free hand. 'I don't know what happened. We were dancing and drinking and having fun and then . . . we were kissing.'

'That's what happened. You were dancing and drinking and having fun, it's not exactly rocket science.'

Was her voice sharper than usual? Another flash of irritation blew through me. I pushed it down. It was just

the hangover and general sense of doom and guilt talking. 'I know you don't believe me but I really didn't see it
coming. We're friends. There's nothing else to it.'

'Love, don't take this the wrong way, but you've never
been the best at reading these things,' Amal said gently.

'That's not true.'

She shook her head. 'I'm not going to argue with you
about this because I know you're feeling fragile at the
moment but it might be worth considering that both
Aiden and I saw this coming. You're into him.'

'I'm not into him!' I insisted. 'He has a girlfriend.'

'And yet, the kissing.' I moved to interject again and
she held up her hand. 'I'm not trying to stress you out.
I'm just suggesting there might be merit in you setting the
girlfriend aside for a minute and seeing if that's what's
stopping you acknowledging that you like him. It would
certainly go a ways to explaining why you're so against
meeting anyone else.'

'I am not against it!'

'I've literally set you up with a nigh-on-perfect man
and you aren't interested.'

I *knew* the Neil thing was bothering her more than
she'd been letting on. Fuck.

The front door opened and a wailing cry reverberated
down the hall. Benji dropped his toys and went dive-
bombing out the door to greet his dad and brother.

'The cavalry's returned,' I said, trying not to visibly
cringe at the sound. I had to hand it to Mo, it couldn't
have been better timed, but it was like nails on the black-
board of my hangover.

269

'Walk didn't work then.' She set her mug down wearily and stood up with a slow sigh.

The wail entered the living room, swiftly followed by its owner, carried by Aiden with Benji right behind. Aiden greeted us, looking fairly exhausted himself.

'No joy?' Amal asked, as quietly as the noise would allow.

'He dozed for a bit,' Aiden replied with a shrug.

'Better than nothing, I suppose.' Amal held out her arms and took Mo, giving him a kiss on the head and starting a shoogly motion. He quietened a bit, but continued grizzling.

'How was the ball?' Aiden asked.

'Great, yeah. Bit fragile today, mind.'

He cringed. 'Sorry, Mo probably isn't helping that at the moment.'

I waved him away. 'Don't be silly.'

'I got us a quiche and some salad for lunch while I was out – Ada, want to stay for some?'

The thought of egg and pastry made my mouth water in a bad way. 'No, I'm good, thanks. I just popped round to drop Amal's stuff back.' I nodded to the bag I'd set by the sofa.

Another wail echoed through the room. Mo's grizzling had escalated. It was my time to bounce.

'I'll get out of your way if you're having lunch.' I nodded to Amal. 'Thanks for lending me the dress and stuff, hon.'

She sighed. 'Sorry, Ada. Let's catch up later in the week? Are you still OK to help me prep for the interview?'

'Of course!' I pulled her into a hug. 'Love you, pal. And love you, Mo Mo.' I planted a kiss on Mo's screaming head before grabbing Benji for a hug. 'And you too, of course, Aiden.'

He gave me a tired smile. 'Do you need a lift home or anything?'

I would have sold my mother for a lift home. 'Nah, I'm grand.'

I made my way out the door and into the fresh air, escaping the sounds of a crying baby.

My phone buzzed as I put my key in my front door and I felt my stomach drop. Shucking off my shoes, I pulled it out of my pocket, unsure if I wanted it to be Fraser or not.

It wasn't Fraser. He hadn't messaged me since before the ball. Couldn't quite decide how I felt about that.

It was Dan. Yet again. Which I very much could. In my hungover state, I caught myself reading before I could swipe it away.

Hey, Ads, saw this and thought of the night we spent in that bubble tent, looking at the stars x

There was a picture attached. I didn't need to see it to know what it was. I remembered that night all too well – it had been the most romantic thing anyone had ever done for me. Now all it did was make me feel sad and sick. Although to be fair that could also be the hangover.

For the first time, I scrolled back through all the unread messages he'd sent to me over the months. Endless screeds of how terrible he felt; how much he missed me and his old life; how hard having the baby was. On and on and on it went.

And suddenly the penny dropped, so hard it almost made a sound. I'd thought that it would be a case of ignoring him and he'd disappear. That his new responsibilities in life might even make him feel some kind of remorse for what he'd done, understand the damage he'd caused. That given enough time, he'd become a lesson I would learn from – a warning I could heed for the future.

But no, it was the same shit, different day. He was still sending me plaintive messages and I was still, oh yeah, making out with men who were already in relationships.

The hangover mixed with the anger and the guilt was cutting right through me, sucking me back into utter misery.

Jesus fucking Christ. How had this happened again?

I needed to get some semblance of self-control back into my life. I needed to make better decisions. I needed to, knowingly or not, stop going for taken men. And above all, I needed Dan to leave me the fuck alone. I'd said it to him the day I left London, but I hadn't said it since. Well, that at least was something I could fix.

I started to text a reply.

Dan, stop contacting me – I don't want to hear from you. I'd assumed not having any kind of response would get the message across but apparently not so here's an actual message telling you to please just fuck off and leave me alone. Ada.

I hit send and then, for good measure, I actually, finally, blocked him.

It didn't cure my hangover or my Fraser-related concerns. Or my Amal-related concerns. Or my Neil-related concerns. If I was being totally honest, it didn't seem to do *anything* to make me feel better at all. But it did free up some space in my phone. So, there was that.

Chapter Twenty-Seven

I spent the rest of my weekend in bed, still trying to square away the ball and the kiss with Fraser. Everything that had happened had been because of the drinking and the great lighting and his fancy braces/jacket/kilt combo. The second I saw him again in his unabashedly hipster T-shirt and – admittedly well-fitting – jeans, I'd be right back in my comfort zone. Had I had a sex dream about him? Maybe. Was that a problem? Absolutely not. Because dreams weren't real and I had learned my lesson this time. I was going to see him in our same old place and he'd be right back in the handy little friendship box I'd whittled for him in my head. I would apologise for what happened, make it clear it would never happen again, and then we would move on. Or back, at the very least, to what we'd been before.

Except that I still couldn't shift the hangover or the wine fear. By the time Monday arrived I was still feeling pretty peaky. Making my way into the café, I found that Fraser hadn't arrived yet and I felt a tiny part of myself relax for a moment. It wasn't that I was worried about seeing him. It was just that I also wasn't *not* worried about seeing him. Unless he was avoiding me? Jesus, this was horrible.

I nodded hello to a few vaguely familiar faces and settled down into my usual seat, forcing my eyes not to flick to the entrance every time there was a movement as I set up my laptop.

Urgh, if he didn't arrive soon this was going to be an unbearably long day. Could he be avoiding me?

No, focus.

It was going to be a short day because I had shit to do – tonight was the night Myster-E and I were finally going to meet. The buzz of anxiety around seeing Fraser flipped into a slightly different kind of anxiety. In the jumbled haze of the last few days, meeting Myster-E had taken a back seat but it was well and truly back up front now and jostling for space with everything else. No, this would be fine. Better than fine actually. I'd meet him, it'd go great and I'd never have to worry about the Fraser thing again. I could apologise, and we could go back to being plain old pals.

And then there was my Indigo Dance presentation. The familiar flutter of fear I always got when I thought about it kicked up its heels. Normally I hated the squirrely seasick feeling this sort of thing gave me but today it was almost welcome. I hunkered down into it and let the fear force me into focus.

Two days and the pitch will be done, either way.

Half a day and you'll know about Myster-E.

You can do this.

I'd closed my emails on my laptop so I could concentrate but I'd forgotten to do it on my phone. Before I knew it, it was buzzing to alert me that something had come in and I realised an hour had passed. I decided to refill my coffee, and was irritated to find that I was once again back to checking the door. Still no sign of Fraser.

I could just send him a text and see where he was. I did it all the time. Nothing untoward about that.

Stirring in the milk, I returned to my seat and picked up my phone – no harm in a quick message. The flashing email reminded me I hadn't checked anything this morning. Clicking in, there was more than the usual. I skimmed through and realised they were all Steve and so naturally had no title or indeed indication of any kind of what he wanted from me.

Still, it was unusual to have quite so many from him in one go.

I got almost to the top of the inbox and spied an email that wasn't Steve – it was from Indigo Dance. My heart gave me a dizzy little shove. I pushed it aside – this would be more info about the pitch . . . hopefully not anything too big a change.

Dear Ms McKenzie,

I hope this email finds you well.

I am writing to inform you that we will not be proceeding with your pitch and presentation, due to take place on Wednesday at 3.00 p.m. While we were impressed with your work, Indigo Dance is in its infancy and in light of recent events we do not feel your connection with Steve Annick would be appropriate for the direction we would like to take the company in at this time.

Apologies for any inconvenience this may cause. We wish you all the best for the future.

Best wishes,

Joanna Markham

I stared blankly at the screen.

What the fuck? Why on earth would they cancel on me?

I flew my way back through the email in the hope of gleaning anything new but all it did was wash the shock off the words, leaving needles of panic in its wake.

Steve had done a lot of stupid shit in his time but he was known for it. Why would it all of a sudden be a problem? And then I remembered all the emails he'd sent me this morning.

Going back into my inbox I selected the most recent one.

All it said was, *I swear to God, Ada, I really didn't know.*

Jesus Christ. That was a statement I didn't need from Steve. Up there with hearing 'it was dark – I couldn't see what I hit'. Nothing good was coming next.

Scrolling down his emails confirmed I'd been right to worry that one story in particular would eventually come down the pipeline.

I forced myself to calm down. This was fine. It looked to be old footage from the nineties. Who hadn't been to an orgy in the nineties? Theoretically speaking, of course. I hadn't on account of not being old enough to buy matches. But still.

And then I remembered Steve's bread-and-butter demographic, who most certainly weren't the type to have been attending anything more risqué than a game of bridge at any point.

No.

This was fine.

First thing was damage control: find out exactly what everyone knew. Opening the search engine, I googled Steve's name. In big blaring black letters, the first headline screamed:

LEITH, LAUGH, LOVE STAR IN DRUG-FILLED FASCIST ORGY SHOCK!

Fascist? What the *fuck?*

I scanned through the article, which got worse with every passing sentence.

In what would presumably not be a surprise to anybody who'd ever met him, there were drug-filled orgies in Steve's past. Fine. Nobody gave a shit about sex parties. But he had entirely neglected to mention that said orgies took place in the mansion of a millionaire fascist currently under investigation for being the secret leader of a hate group that liked to burn down refugee centres.

Dermot Clemont. *Dermot fucking Clemont.*

And there was Steve in a million pictures, looking for all the world like one of his best pals. Jesus. No wonder Indigo Dance were distancing themselves.

I slammed my computer shut and fought the urge to put my head between my knees and scream.

Fighting through the panic, I picked up my mobile to call him. It rang for what felt like an eternity before being sent straight to answer machine. Because, of course, he was taking the coward's way out and not picking up.

I used the space between his message and the beep to try to get a handle on myself so that what came out of me wouldn't just be one elongated screech.

Beeeeep.

Deep breath.

'Steve, it's Ada. If you could call me back at your earliest convenience to explain why you were ever hanging out with a man like Dermot Clemont, it would be *greatly appreciated*.'

That about covered it. I hung up the phone and found myself completely at a loss for what to do next. For all Steve did stupid, sometimes dubious things, they'd never been actively harmful to other people. As far as I was aware, everything was above board and consensual – he'd certainly at no point given any kind of indication that he was secretly in league with a racist piece of shit. I'd taken him on as a client and put up with his occasionally rampant asshattery because, for all the ridiculousness, there was nothing truly . . . *bad*.

Until now, of course. This was pretty fucking bad.

I opened my emails again and scanned through his increasingly panicked missives. As was pretty much standard operating procedure for him, they didn't give any real information. Just plaintive calls for help and assurances like 'but it was the nineties – that was ages ago'; 'I barely remember it'; and my own personal favourite, 'it really wasn't as bad as it looked because I didn't actually know Dermot – he just invited me to his house once.'

Ah, yes, one casual invite to his fascist orgy.

I scrolled through yet more of the news articles carrying the story and found my day getting progressively worse. Nineties or not, there were *so* many pictures of Steve with Dermot. And there were other pictures too. Steve wasn't in these ones but they were the kind you didn't even want to be seen looking at in passing. Clemont hadn't always bothered attempting subtlety when it came to his affiliations but a lot of these pictures, albeit taken privately, were more than testament to the fact they'd always been there.

I felt my stomach roll at the sight of them. Had I been completely wrong in my judgement of Steve? Sucked in by the cavalier, fun-drunk-uncle energy he oozed, like so many other people had been? A part of me just couldn't believe he'd not have known about Clemont's leanings. I wasn't massively au fait with the floor plan of an orgy but was it really possible to miss a bunch of people Heil-Hitlering a swastika?

It was possible, I supposed, if it happened somewhere else.

But did that even matter? Even if it *had* happened in another room, even if he really didn't know, could I rep a man that unutterably myopic? There was no excuse for not noticing that this was going on right under his nose. Fuck.

How did the papers even get hold of this video? It was from twenty-five years ago so there were presumably not many copies of it floating around. Did anyone in the world still even own a video player?

And why on earth was Steve the main part of the headlines, given that Clemont was by far the bigger of the two fish?

Movement drew my attention to the doorway. I glanced up to find Fraser making his way through the door. He gave me a smile and a tiny wave, gesturing to tell me he was getting a coffee. For a split second all the anxiety that had been sloshing its way around my system before the Steve bomb dropped was back in full force. The memory of the dancing and the kiss and all the confusion it had kicked up. Clashing with my Steve panic, there was a genuine moment where I thought I might be sick.

Before I knew it, he was in front of me, smiling down with that not-a-dimple-but-kind-of grin, looking admittedly quite sheepish. 'Good morning.' He set down his bag. 'I wasn't sure if you already had a coffee so I brought you one. And biscuits, of course. They didn't have the nice ones but any port in a storm.' He put them on the table. I couldn't get my brain to work. There was too much swirling around. I managed a squeaky thank you and we fell into silence. I desperately wanted him to say something, anything, to sweep away the awkwardness. He was watching me and I was hundred per cent sure that he was thinking the same thing. Fuuuuck. Had we ruined this?

Suddenly, he cleared his throat. 'I forgot to tell you! Remember Skeleton Si? They're giving him an award and he's invited me to go to the ceremony with him and write an article about it. Maybe I could wangle you an invite? It's at City Chambers, which should be nice.'

An unexpected wave of . . . something . . . hit. He was doing what I couldn't. He was putting us back in our boxes. As if everything that had happened hadn't, with as much ease as breathing. Because apparently I was the only person feeling any kind of ambiguity about it all. Because I was a fucking idiot. Because I was doing what

I swore I'd never do again. I forced a small smile through the wave of misery that was engulfing me. 'I've never been into the Chambers.'

'I'll ask and see – they usually aren't too strict, so I'm sure it'll be fine.' He took a sip of his coffee and made a face. 'Needs more milk. Back in a sec.'

Through my misery fog, I watched him move to the coffee station and a ping drew my attention to my inbox. A fresh email from Steve. My current predicament came screaming back to me.

Fuck. Steve. What was I going to do?

And then something somewhere in my brain rattled and settled, like the moment you piece the letters together in a crossword.

Skeleton Si.

Only . . . no. Surely not.

I pulled my laptop back towards me and reopened my browser. Scanning through, it took me a second but I found what I was looking for fairly quickly.

The words in front of me felt as though they were burning into my retinas, setting nauseating sparks wheeling in the corners of my eyes.

The story originally broke in the *Edinburgh Courier*, and sure enough it was written by the same guy responsible for all those other sneaky little stories that had been breaking about Steve of late and giving me so much trouble. A man Fraser had openly told me he knew.

The linking factor between Steve and all the headlines was Fraser.

The link between Steve and Fraser was me.

The cogs started turning in earnest. Steve mentioning the orgy on the call to me the day we'd gone to see Skeleton Si. Fraser shaking with laughter. Hearing every word. God, I was such a fucking *idiot*. Of all the people I could have sat with, I'd chosen to set up shop beside a goddamn journalist. It was like a seal trying to brush a shark's teeth. He must have overheard so many of our conversations. Was that why he'd been so eager to help when Steve's other interview had fallen through?

I couldn't deal with this. I couldn't talk to him right now. I'd kill him. Or at the very least throw something at his head. I had to get out of here. Grabbing my bag, I dumped my laptop in it, piling all my other bits and pieces from the table haphazardly on top. I'd been in the process of pulling on my coat when I realised Fraser had already made it back to the table with his milky coffee.

Fuck fuck *fuck!*

He sat down and froze. 'Are you going somewhere?'

'I have to.' It was all I could manage.

'Is something wrong?' He sounded concerned, and God, it made me so much angrier at him.

'Don't pretend you don't know!' I burst out, only managing to bring the volume back down on the last word. A few of the people at nearby tables shot us curious glances.

He frowned, for a moment looking genuinely confused. And then I saw it, the slightest spark of recognition, confirming all of my fears.

He set his cup down on the table. 'Yeah, OK. Look, I'm really sorry about the ball. I know you're seeing someone and it crossed a line. We'd had so much to drink and—'

What? 'This isn't about the ball!' I hissed.

His confusion returned full-force. I could see him mentally flicking through his options and coming up blank.

Unbelievable.

I decided to enlighten him. 'It's about you telling your colleagues at the *Courier* about Steve's orgy.'

'I— *What*?'

'Don't, Fraser. Confidentiality was meant to be a given – it was part of the goddamn deal. I can't believe you did this to me.' I felt tears roll up the back of my throat and had to make a proper effort to swallow them down.

He threw his hands up. 'What stuff? I really don't know what you're talking about.'

'This,' I hauled out my phone and clicked back into the article. 'I know you leaked the story to your colleague!'

He took it from me and scanned through before handing me it back. 'I didn't do this,' he stated, matter-of-factly.

'Please! I know you heard Steve tell me about it. And now your colleague happens to magically stumble across it and find out the party was thrown by a fascist? I don't fucking think so.'

He shook his head, ruffling his hands through his hair. For the first time since he'd arrived he was looking stressed. 'I have no idea what this is and I certainly didn't have anything to do with it. I swear to God! Come on, Ada, you know me better than that.'

Did I? 'So it's a coincidence that all those other stories came out too?'

He froze. 'What exactly are you accusing me of here?'

'Sorry, was I not clear?' I snapped back. 'I'm accusing you of leaking stories I've mentioned to you about Steve.'

We both stood in ringing silence.

A part of me couldn't quite believe I'd said what I'd just said. I'd only half-formed the thought, really, but now it was out there between us and I couldn't take it back. I also wasn't sure I wanted to. There was a certainty in me that he'd done this. It burned right through and I was surprised at how much it hurt. He looked so alien all of a sudden. His face was radiating anger, making him all shadows and lines. It took him a moment to muster up words and I was expecting them to come out in a rush of rage. I'd forgotten who I was dealing with. When he finally spoke, it was with an iron-clad calm.

'Ada, I don't run stories based on idle gossip and, as you so rightly pointed out, *this isn't my story*. Even if, in some weird parallel universe, it had been me writing it, I wouldn't just base it off some passing comment from you without running it past you. How much of an arsehole do you think I am?'

I stared at him, wanting so much to believe him. But how else could this have happened? 'The only link here is the one between me and you, Fraser. How am I supposed to think otherwise?' I demanded.

The colour seemed to have drained from his face. 'Ada, this is bullshit and I'm not dignifying any of it with a response.'

'God, I knew it!' I hissed. My chest felt as though it was going to burst. I'd *trusted* him.

'Jesus, you know what? Think whatever you want – you're clearly going to.' He picked up one of the coffees he'd set on the table, obviously gearing up to leave.

'Do you even give a shit that this has tanked my career?' I replied, my stupid voice almost breaking. 'Indigo Dance cancelled our meeting and I've no doubt Contrast Creative will be following suit any minute now.'

Even as the words came out, I felt how pathetic they were. I was catapulted back to my last conversation with Dan, me crying, demanding to know why he'd not told me he was married, as if the question didn't answer itself. How had I ended up here again? Being lied to by someone I'd come to trust.

It hit some kind of mark. Fraser paused and turned back to me. 'I'm sorry – that's . . . shit. It's not your fault he did this.' His eyes had softened again. I'd noticed them when we'd first met, how kind they'd been. It felt like an extra slap in the face.

'Don't pretend you care.'

He shook his head, looking genuinely disgusted. 'Christ, Ada, I didn't leak those stories! You know who's the actual person to blame here? The idiot pissing about the place with his fascist best pal!' He let out a bitter, empty laugh. 'Look, I'm sorry it's fucked you over but you can't lay that at my feet. That's not fair.'

With that he grabbed his bag and left.

I stood and watched him go, head ringing with his final words.

Chapter Twenty-Eight

I genuinely didn't know what to do with myself. There were too many things going round my head, but screaming at the absolute front was humiliation. That I had somehow, once again, let myself trust someone and that I had, once again, been catastrophically let down.

There was a small voice piping up in the back, humbly suggesting that maybe it was also on me for opening my stupid flapping gums to a journalist. But I'd genuinely forgotten that Fraser was one. Well, maybe not forgotten. But it had been an aside, a non-issue because he'd become such a good friend. Such an important part of my routine. And now he was gone.

Nope. No space to deal with that just now. Because I had the mother of all publicity bin-fires to fight.

And meeting Myster-E. There was also that.

My stomach did another nauseating flip. With everything hitting the fan, there was a fair to middling chance I was going to roll into the bar a warbling, screaming mess. Which was not quite the impression I'd been hoping to make.

Should I postpone?

The thought had some appeal. Jesus, more than some. There was nothing I wanted to do more right now than get through this hellscape of a day and bury myself in my bed for . . . ever if I could somehow wangle it.

But no. That wasn't reasonable. I wanted to meet him and it would be deeply unfair to cancel at such short notice – not to mention a tricky thing to come back from, seeing as it'd been my idea to meet in the first place.

Plus what the hell else was I going to do with my evening? Sit and mope? No. I would meet Myster-E if it killed me.

I made my way home, hopped in the shower and forced myself to properly dry and style my hair and do my makeup. I always forgot that once I started doing it, it relaxed me in an almost hypnotic way. The ritual of it, how you could focus on it and not have to worry about anything else, how good it felt to look in the mirror and be a little bit happier with what you saw. Was that a slightly problematic window into my psyche? Sure was! Did I have time to dwell on that? I did not.

Sliding the green dress I'd informed Myster-E I'd be wearing out of my wardrobe, I pulled it over my head, enjoying the swish of the skirt as it fell to my knees. God, I loved this dress. I'd bought it in a fit of celebration when I'd got the book festival job in London and worn it a grand total of one time since. I finished the look with a spritz of perfume and made my way out of my room.

'Whit woo! Look at you!' My mum catcalled as I walked into the kitchen to say goodbye to her.

'Thank you,' I beamed, doing a twirl.

She stepped back from the concoction she'd been stirring on the hob. 'Neil's a lucky man!'

'I'm not meeting Neil. Just a pal.' I'd briefly debated telling Mum that I was meeting a total stranger from the internet whose name I didn't know and who I couldn't pick out of a line-up in a random bar. But only briefly. I'd left all the details with Amal. Should he turn out to be a crazy person, it was all on her to avenge me.

'Fraser?'

Oh. 'No. Different pal.'

She raised an eyebrow but somehow managed to keep her thoughts on that inside. 'Well, you look very nice.'

'Thanks, Mum.' I was so nervous, my palms were sweaty. There was a solid risk any drink I had tonight might slip clean out of my hands.

'How was your day?' Mum asked.

'Oh, horrendous. Absolutely the worst day ever.'

She stared at me for a moment. 'I can't tell if you're joking or not.'

'Nope. Very much not joking.'

Her eyes crinkled in concern. 'Why? What happened?'

'Turns out Steve has been hanging out with Dermot Clemont, and Fraser and I had a fight because he leaked it to his colleague at the paper. It's everywhere and now Steve is potentially ruined and I've no idea what to do about it.' I took a deep breath and tried not to freak out again.

'Dermot Clemont? Isn't he that Nazi guy with the fedora that I treated a while back?'

Really, was there a fedora in the world not attached to an arsehole? 'He is.'

'And Steve's been palling around with him?'

'Yep. I think it was back in the nineties but who even knows at this point?'

'Wow.'

'Wow indeed.'

'What makes you think it was Fraser who leaked it?'

I explained my theory.

'OK. I guess you never know, but it does sound like he's pretty adamant he didn't. Is it worth talking to him some more about it?'

'Not if I can help it,' I replied, barely managing to take the snap out of my tone – but only just. 'And to cap it all, Indigo Dance have cancelled my pitch because of my association with Steve, and Contrast Creative will never hire me now.' I felt heat prickle at the back of my eyes. Fucking Steve.

'Love, I'm so sorry.' Mum set the wooden spoon she'd been stirring with down and pulled me into a hug. For a second I almost let myself cry and then I remembered my makeup. I pulled away and dabbed at my eyes.

'It's fine.'

She took my face in her hands. 'It will be OK. You go out and meet your friend and have some fun. We can sit down and go over all your options when you're back in and figure out what to do next. We'll get it sorted.'

'Godammit, stop making me cry!' I pulled her into another hug.

'Love you. Now get out of my sight. You're ruining my bolognese.'

The chat with Mum had made me slightly late and I found myself almost jogging down North Charlotte Street and onto Queen's. By the time I reached the bar, my heart was clanging like I'd mainlined twenty espressos. God, I was so nervous. We'd chatted so easily online – that would surely translate to real life, right?

Right. It was just the stress of the day.

The bar was styled like an old speakeasy. I made my way down the stairs, through the fake library bookcase and into the dark, slightly cool room. It was all low ceilings, dark wood and twenties-style décor. Agatha would approve. I made myself take a moment to enjoy the sight and waited to be seated.

Looking around, I realised there were a number of men in tweed jackets – a fact I should really have seen coming. Shit. It was a Monday night – why was this place so full? And why so specifically full of tweed jacket wearers?

I smoothed down my dress – was the lighting good enough to show that it was green? I'd styled my hair swept up and pinned as I'd mentioned that I would to Myster-E. He'd said his hair would be sitting atop his head in a slightly curly equivocation of a short back and sides. Very helpful. Although I guess that did at least tell me he had hair.

I'd booked a table. As the waiter led me to it, I debated ordering a drink, remembering the awkwardness when I'd done that on my date with Connor. In the end, my nerves won out though and I ordered myself a glass of wine. I'd save the fancy cocktail until Myster-E got here but, in the meantime, a little social lubricant would go a long way. A quick glance around me didn't throw up any big indication that he was already here. Most of the men in tweed were here with people. There was one guy at the bar on his own. As he turned, my heart sank. He was mid-fifties if he was a day. I accidentally caught his eye and he gave me a smile. Was it a smile of recognition? No. He couldn't be. Myster-E had definitely said he was a nineties kid and the only way this guy was even tangentially linked would be if he'd had an actual kid in the nineties.

Oh God, but he was coming over. Before I could think of what to do, he'd arrived at my table.

'Hello,' he said. I had to admit, up close, he wasn't unattractive in his way.

'Hi,' I replied, stumbling up to greet him. 'You made it!'

He paused, confusion rippling across his face. 'Sorry?'

'You . . . ah, you're not – were you meeting someone here tonight?' I asked, incredibly vaguely.

He looked slightly cornered, as though he was the target of some kind of joke. 'Sorry, I didn't mean to be forward or anything – you just seemed like you might be on your own.'

Because he wasn't Myster-E. This day got better and better. 'I'm so sorry, I thought you were the person I was meant to be meeting,' I confessed.

His smile returned, warmer now. 'Ah, a blind date? That explains it. Sadly I don't believe I'm him. Although if he doesn't show, I'd be happy to buy you a drink?'

That was pretty smooth, I had to admit. I thanked him and he made his way back to the bar. Settling back into some alone time with my jumbled nerves, I greeted the waiter who'd appeared with my wine and looked at my watch.

He was fifteen minutes late. That was a reasonable amount of time – he could have missed the bus. I was, however, starting to wonder why I hadn't suggested we swap numbers. I'd be feeling a lot less gnarly if I'd had a phone I could text. I took a sip of my wine and tried not looking at the door when it opened. Failed every time.

Before I knew it, the wine was gone. I looked at my watch. Thirty minutes late. Less reasonable.

Fuck it, I was in a cocktail bar. I was going to drink a fancy cocktail, alone or not. The waiter walked past and I flagged him down. I picked one randomly and he left to get it. By the time he was back, another ten minutes had passed. I took a drink of the cocktail, biting back a cough. Jesus, they weren't messing about with their measures. I blinked away the alcohol fumes, deciding to log into the ACFF website in case there was a message.

Nope. Nothing. I took another gulp. It occurred to me that due to my train wreck of a day, I'd not eaten much. I could feel the drink swimming around my head a bit already.

How long should I give him? Maybe something terrible had happened. Maybe he was trapped under a car somewhere. Or being held hostage. Or rescuing a child from a burning building.

Or maybe he'd bottled it and decided he didn't want to meet me.

The thought wrapped around my chest and squeezed. I took another drink to try and loosen it. In all my imaginings of how this would go, I'd never seriously given thought to him not actually tipping up. It'd occurred to me, of course, but I hadn't really thought it was a risk – he'd seemed so keen, even if it had taken him a while to respond.

Yep. This man I'd never met, that I couldn't have even guessed at a name or description of, had really taken me by surprise by flaking on me. Because, apparently, I was clinically incapable of learning my goddamn lesson.

I was horrified to find my eyes were starting to burn – there was no way in hell I was crying alone in a bar today because some random bastard had stood me up. I had some pride left. Maybe.

My phone buzzed and for a heart-blinding second, I was sure it was somehow Myster-E. I picked it up. Neil's name popped up. I opened the message to find him asking how my week was going.

Ah, Neil.

I took another nip of cocktail.

Neil wouldn't leave me stranded in a cocktail bar or tell stories about my client to his newspaper behind my back. Sure, he made me climb and walk and be outdoors until I wanted to die. But he'd also brought me food when I was hungover and he was a generally good egg. Did my insides vibrate when he kissed me? Not so much, no. But that wasn't exactly a deal-breaker, was it? Insides vibrating hadn't done a huge amount of good for me so far.

Another gulp.

Fuck it. I reopened my messages and started typing.

Hey – I'm at a cocktail bar on Queen's Street, if you fancy a drink?

I hit send, flagged down the waiter and ordered another drink.

Chapter Twenty-Nine

Waking up was no easy feat. It took a minute to adjust and I realised I wasn't in my own bedroom. Turning over, I came face-to-back-of-head with Neil, who was out for the count. I carefully pulled myself up and looked around. I was at Neil's – of course. We'd come back here after the drinks. I was surprised to find I wasn't as hung–over as I really should have been, given the numerous cocktails we'd had.

Wait. No. That was bad. That meant this was the sneak-attack rolling kind of hangover, the type that lulls you into a false sense of security before swallowing you whole. I had a limited window to get home so I could die quietly in the comfort of my own surroundings. It had been too grim a few days to tolerate anything else. Not to mention the fact that I'd fallen asleep in my contacts and there was a solid chance my eyes would never fully open again. My eyeballs felt like marbles in my head.

Yes. My desire to get home was definitely all this, and in no way to do with the fact that a second sleepover with Neil had perhaps written a cheque I couldn't quite cash, emotionally speaking.

Careful not to wake him, I quietly dressed and sneaked out, sending him a message from the bus to say I'd had to get home and that I'd see him later.

I was halfway home when an alarm popped up on my phone reminding me that I had to go and help Amal prep for her interview for *Lawyer Monthly*. Fuckity-fuck-fuck, it had completely gone out of my head. How was that today already?

All I wanted to do was go home, take my bloody contacts out and get into my own bed. I mean, what I really should have been doing was figuring out a way to fire-fight the Steve catastrophe. As it stood, I hadn't even checked my email since I'd left the café yesterday.

God, was that only yesterday? It felt a week ago at least.

I got off the bus and started making my way to Amal's. I'd tick her off my list and hopefully get home before the hangover really put the boot in. Steve would have to wait. The bastard had yet to return a single call any way. Plus, maybe the cold shoulder would start to teach him that you can't party with fascist fuckheads without facing the consequences.

'Hungover yet again, are we? You look terrible,' Amal said, as I followed her into the toy-strewn kitchen. Aiden and the boys were out and about and the place looked like they'd left mid-hurricane. 'Did you sleep in that dress?'

'Erm, sort of,' I replied. No need for more details just then. I had to admit, though, my fragile ego could have done with a slightly less turbulent re-entry into orbit.

'I'm assuming this means things went well with your Myster-E man? Was he all you'd hoped?' Was her tone sharp or was it the wine-fear casting its shadow?

'No, he didn't show.'

Amal paused, mid-kettle filling. 'What?'

I shrugged. I had little else to add. 'He didn't turn up. I messaged him on the site but so far no reply.'

'Did you call him?'

'We didn't swap numbers.' Saying it out loud compounded my absolute misery. How could I have been so stupid about all this? What a staggeringly dumb thing to do and expect anything good to come out of it.

Amal watched me for a moment. 'So you didn't swap names or descriptions or numbers or any identifying features at all before the meeting?'

I sighed. 'Yes, I know, it was stupid and it won't happen again. Can we start on this interview prep? I've quite a lot to get through today.'

'I'm sorry, am I getting in the way of that busy hangover schedule?'

Jeez, ouch. 'I'm in the middle of an absolute shitshow with Steve.'

'Sorry. It's been a long day,' she sighed. 'I heard about Steve – is it true? The pictures seem incontrovertible but I guess pictures can be faked?'

'Who in their right mind would be arsed faking something like this over Steve Annick? No, they're real.'

Her tone softened. 'Sorry, pet. That's shit.'

'I just ... God, I can't get my head around how he could have missed it. Like, he's a bit of an idiot sometimes but he's not as dumb as he lets on. He swears he didn't know about Clemont's affiliations but you'll have seen the pictures that Steve wasn't in. Even if he's being honest and genuinely didn't know, does it really absolve him? They're Heil-Hitlering in front of a swastika in one of the pictures, for Christ's sake. How could he not notice?' I felt my rage crank up again. 'It's unacceptable that he didn't pay attention to what was happening there – that he didn't ask more questions.' I sighed. 'I don't know if I can bring myself to defend him at all. I know he's technically a victim of the story being leaked, but you know how you avoid having your picture taken with fascists? By not hanging out with them.'

'Has he ever done anything else to suggest he might be in with them generally?' Amal asked, making her way over and handing me a tea.

'Not that I can think of.' I slung my head into my hands. 'Oh God, am I doing the things I just bitched him out for? Was he a horrible racist this whole time and I just didn't see it?'

'If he is, you're not the only one to not see it. On balance, I'd say it's more like he just didn't know.'

'Probably,' I sighed. 'But still. He keeps doing this. It's like he never learns and everyone else has to pick up the pieces.'

Amal shrugged but didn't reply.

'Are you OK?' I asked. 'You look tired.'

'Gee, thanks.'

I couldn't help but wonder why it was OK for her to say it to me but not the other way round. No. That was just my bad mood talking. '*Are* you OK?' I pressed.

Amal took a swig of her tea. 'Fine.'

'Sorry to bitch about work but the Steve thing led to a blow out with Fraser because I kind of accused him of leaking the story. And then with Myster-E not replying and Neil kind of floating around in the background, it's just been a rough week. And then, of all things, I got a message from Dan.' I should have seen it for the goddamn omen it was.

'So you're still seeing Neil? Does he know about the others?'

I frowned at the unexpected emphasis on Neil. 'What others? I told you, Fraser's a pal and it's not like Myster-E showed up.' Oh God, saying it out loud sounded . . . not great. But Neil and I hadn't set any parameters. We hadn't said anything about being exclusive. So why did I feel that I couldn't say that to Amal?

'Fraser leaked the story?'

Well, that was an about-turn. I glanced up from my tea. 'Huh? Oh, yeah. He's denying it but it couldn't have come from anywhere else. So suffice it to say we're not currently on speaking terms.'

'Has it ever occurred to you that you might be too hard on people?'

She was speaking blandly but there was an edge to her voice that I was definitely not imagining now. 'Huh?'

'Even if Fraser did leak the story – and if he's denying it, and you don't have proof, then there's at least a chance he didn't – I doubt it was done maliciously. You've made mistakes yourself that could have been avoided if you'd been paying more attention. I don't think you're quite being honest with yourself about that – and about why you weren't paying attention in the first place.'

I stared at her, feeling as if my head was full of loose change, thoughts jangling all over the place. I couldn't pin one down long enough to think of anything to reply. Amal took another sip of her tea. She was suddenly uncannily unfamiliar, like when you have a dream about your bedroom but everything's been moved around.

'What are you saying?' I could barely push my voice out of my throat.

She didn't look up at me and I knew something bad was coming.

'You know what I'm saying. You're doing a version of it with Neil. And look at Dan. You're not a stupid person, Ada. You knew you were fucking a married man or you would have told me about it when you found out.'

Her words hit like whiplash, a short, sharp shock that left me reeling. How long had she been holding onto that thought? 'Amal? What the fuck?'

And now she did catch my eye. She was wearing a look I'd seen before but never directed my way: face taut, eyes carefully blank. 'You've been back how many months now? And in all that time you barely mentioned Dan to me – you only told me how it ended because I basically made you. You wouldn't have kept that a secret from everyone you know, unless you suspected there was more to it than what he was saying.'

Was she serious? 'That's in *no way* true! Is that what you think of me?' I could feel a kick of adrenaline and anger, but it was muted by shock. The woman sitting in front of me wasn't Amal. Amal wouldn't make such an awful suggestion.

She shook her head. 'God, you just don't—' She shook her head, took a swig of her drink. 'You know what? Nothing, it doesn't matter. Let's move on.'

I almost laughed. The bark of it barrelled up my throat and I barely managed to keep it in. As if we were just moving on from this. 'Amal, what's going on? Have I done something to upset you?'

She turned back to me and I was shocked by the sudden transformation. Gone was the Amal I knew; in her place a tired, worn, furious-looking stranger. If I'd been standing up, I think I would have taken a step back. 'Jesus, Ada, I already have two children, I don't need a third!'

What the *fuck*? 'That's a horrible thing to say!' All I could do was stare at her, feeling the shock of her words seep into me.

'Do you know I got postnatal depression when Mo was born?' Amal continued, voice completely toneless now. 'There were days I could barely get out of bed.'

Postnatal depression? *What?* 'Jesus, Amal! Why on earth didn't you tell me?' Was this what Catherine had been talking about?

'Because you were miles away and busy. It's not really the kind of conversation you can have on the phone, is it?'

Oh, hell no, I wasn't having that. '*Of course you can!* And you said yourself, I've been back for months – you could have told me at any point.'

'Because you should have noticed!'

And there it was. The horrible heart of it. The injustice burned through me.

'I should have noticed? *How*? How could I have noticed when you deliberately kept it from me, Amal? Just me, though, not your other pals. Not all your mum friends with your meet-ups and classes and heart-to-hearts. Maybe I should ask Catherine to explain all this to me – you clearly had no problem telling her. No need to hide it from good old Catherine! But no. Keep on telling me that it's all my fault and that I'm a terrible person. Please! I can't get enough of that this week.' I stood up, anger drilling through me. 'Dan broke my heart. I was so ashamed of it when I found out, even though it was *me* he lied to.' My voice caught and I knew I wasn't going to be able to stop myself crying this time and it only made me madder. 'I get that our lives are different now and I know it's hard for you but you don't get to tell me that I'm a bad person because my priorities are different and you don't get to keep stuff from me and then be mad at me for not knowing and call me out for doing it to you! That's not fair.'

'Ada, I have never said a single thing like that in my life to you! You know I don't think that! Yes, maybe I do tell Catherine things I don't tell you. You did it to me, too! God, you walk around so judgemental of other people without any self-awareness.'

'What's that supposed to mean?'

She threw up her arms, growing more agitated by the second. 'Look at Fraser. You like him but he has a girlfriend. But you still kiss him at a party and now you're basically not speaking to him? Why? Don't give me that bullshit about him leaking the story – that story would have come out regardless. No, you're doing what you always do, burying the problem. Burying your own complicity in it. Why invite a man with a girlfriend to do all the things you've been doing and then be surprised when it gets complicated? Why string Neil along – a lovely man and a friend of Aiden's, remember? – when you don't have feelings for him? Don't pretend that's not what's going on there – I know what it is. And don't *even* get me started on this random online guy. Meanwhile, I couldn't even get you to notice when I'm on my fucking knees!'

Her words rang round the room, burrowing into me. I had to force myself to suck in a breath and pull out words from the black mass swirling round my brain. 'How can you say that to me? I've always been there! I'd do anything for you – I *do*. Jesus, I'm here now, aren't I? Have I ever said no to you? You not asking isn't the same as me not doing, Amal. That is – that is so unfair!' I felt a tear rope its way down my cheek and I pushed it angrily away. She stared back at me, the anger on her face drying up and flaking away, leaving a kind of exhausted resignation behind. Silence expanded around us and I realised in a moment of horrifying clarity that I couldn't be around her right now.

Without another word I got up and left.

Chapter Thirty

My chest hurt. It was a physical pain, a weight pressing down that made it feel like my heart was constantly missing a beat. What the fuck was happening? Amal and I had been friends for two-thirds of our lives. We'd argued but we'd never fought. I'd never seen her like that.

Her words kept whipping around me, the anger in them. It wasn't the kind of thing that came from nowhere. Did she properly hate me?

My heart gave a pained sort of thud at the thought. And oh God – the things I'd said back.

All I wanted to do was rewind. To go back and change the direction of the conversation. React differently. Ask her something – *anything* – else. Because I had the awful fear that something had been broken today. I didn't know how or why but it felt . . . big.

Fuck.

Before I knew it, I was home with no memory of getting there. One minute I was in Amal's driveway and the next I was shipwrecked in my hall. Absolutely paralysed. I couldn't get to the next thought – like there was a physical barrier stopping anything getting in or out.

How had this happened? How had I gone from feeling that I was somewhere to being absolutely nowhere? Amal. Fraser. Myster-E. Steve. All the building blocks that had been holding up my new life had somehow disintegrated and I couldn't fix it. I didn't know how – there didn't seem to be any way to. It was all absolutely out of my control.

Mum must have been on night shift because her bedroom door was closed. Without even thinking, I found myself knocking on it. I just desperately needed to see her. To hear her voice.

'Mum?' It was only when I heard myself speak that I realised I was properly crying now.

'Ada?' Her voice filtered out through the door.

I opened the door. She was sitting up, blinking in the light coming through from the hallway.

'What is it? Has something happened?' She'd gone from sounding sleepy to alarmed.

Fuck. What was I doing? She'd been on yet another night shift and I'd just barged in and woken her without any thought for how knackered she must be. How much this would worry her. Jesus, Amal was right: I really was the fucking worst. I started backing out and closing the door. 'I'm so sorry – it's fine,' I sputtered out. 'Sorry I-I w-woke you.' I could barely get the words out of my throat. I made to crash into my bedroom but her voice rang out in the hallway.

'Ada, no, come back. Come in and tell me what's wrong?'

I made my way over to her and before I knew it, she'd folded me up in her arms and I collapsed into them like a tent in a tornado.

'I'm so, so sorry I woke you . . .' I couldn't stop the tears.

She lulled me, stroking my hair like she used to do when I was little. 'It's OK, love, you're OK,' she whispered.

I had no idea how long we sat like that but eventually it started to work; I could feel the hysteria dying down. Eventually, when she deemed it safe enough, Mum sat me up, brushing my damp hair off my face. Leaning to her bedside table, she pulled a tissue from a box by her bed and wiped my face, telling me to blow my nose. I let out a laugh. Even under the circumstances, that was too ridiculous.

'Glad to see a smile – you had me worried there,' she said, pulling out a fresh tissue.

'S-sorry . . .' I breathed out slowly to steady myself.

'What's going on, love?' Her eyes were full of concern and I felt all the guilt crash down on me again.

'God, I'm sorry – I shouldn't have woken you, it's stupid.' I could feel the tears leaking down my face again.

'Hey, hey, it's not stupid. What's going on?'

Jesus, where did I even begin? 'I . . . I had a fight with Amal.'

And I dissolved again. Mum pulled me into another hug. 'It's not like you two to fight – what happened?'

Somehow, I managed to cobble together what happened. She listened in silence, still stroking my hair. The repetitive motion calmed me down and by the end I was almost able to speak without my voice going.

'Sounds like she's been having a tough time.'

'I know, but she never said. I should have seen it b-but I didn't and now she hates me.'

'She doesn't hate you.'

I pulled myself up so I could look at her. My head felt as though it was full of syrup. God, I really needed to take my bloody contacts out. 'I think she might, Mum. You didn't see her. She was soooo angry.'

'No, but she's clearly going through some stuff. You're one of her closest friends – it makes sense that you would be a lightning rod for that.'

'I don't know what to do. She said some really horrible things.' I felt the tears crawl their way back up my throat again. 'It was just that I was away and there was all this stuff happening and she seemed fine and—' I took a breath. 'Our lives are so different and I feel like she's angry about that but I can't help that she chose to have kids and I haven't.' The words had fallen out of me before I'd realised and, as I heard them out loud, I felt the spiral start again. What was *wrong* with me? When had I become such a self-centred person?

'It's tough when the people you love go in different directions to you. And having kids is the hardest thing anyone can ever do. If you don't have them, it's not possible to understand what that's like and I'll be honest, it's something not enough people really know going into it. It can be incredibly isolating.'

I wiped my eyes. 'But I do try! I mean, I obviously fucked it up but I really didn't know. She didn't tell me but she didn't have a problem telling other people! And the old Amal would have been the first person in the line to say that it's not fair to blame somebody for not understanding something they've never experienced themselves.'

'True. I'm not saying you're wrong about this. I'm just saying the old Amal would also have had more than two hours sleep a night to live on.'

'I just don't know what to do.' I put my head in my hands and groaned. 'I don't think this is fixable.'

Mum sat forward. 'OK, now you're just being melodramatic.'

Stung, I found myself looking up to an expression I hadn't seen in years. I braced myself.

'Fights are horrible and I know you're having a stressful time but this isn't the end of the world. You need to take what you know now and try to see it from Amal's perspective. That might seem tough, but postnatal depression is a really hard fight and she's going to need all the love and support she can get. She's your best friend and she needs you now more than ever.'

I dragged a ratty tissue across my still-leaking eyes. 'She said some really horrible things, Mum. And I did too.'

'I'm sure you both did. I know you're hurt and I know this isn't all on you, but just for now you have to be the bigger person and take the hit because Amal isn't in a position to. You mean too much to each other to allow this to fester. Don't look at it as a fight. Look at it as an opportunity to check in and mend your fences.'

'That's so easy to say!'

'Did I say it would be easy?' She shook her head. 'This is something that happens more than you realise. Me and your Aunt Jen had a massive falling-out after you were born.'

I peeked out from behind my hands. 'You did?'

'Yeah. We didn't speak for a couple of months, I think.'

'What happened?'

She pulled me back into a hug. 'Pretty much this. It was hard for both of us to wrap our heads around such a huge change. It caused some friction.'

'I didn't know that.'

Mum shrugged. 'In the end, it didn't matter. We made up and it was water under the bridge.'

I let her words sink in, feeling them sooth the panic a bit. 'It's so strange to think she's been gone five whole years.'

Mum looked down. 'Feels like five hundred years sometimes.'

I took her hand and she squeezed it.

'I know this is tough, but you can't let it wreck your friendship. You have to talk to her. Believe me, you'd regret it if you ever lost the chance.'

I shook my head. 'I don't think she'd have me anywhere near her right now.'

'Look, you're clearly exhausted. Have a nap, get some food in you and in a couple of days when you're feeling a bit more solid, send her a message and tell her you want to talk.' She wiped my face one last time. 'You'll iron it out, I promise.'

I lay down beside her on the bed and she tucked me in.

'Wait,' I sat bolt upright and pulled myself out of the bed.

'Pet—'

'No, no, it's not anything. I just need to take my contacts out.'

I'd been right about the hangover being a creeper; by the time evening rolled around, I felt as though it was trying to turn me inside out. I'd made a vow not to leave my pit but there was something chewing at me more than my colossal headache and I knew if I didn't deal with it, I'd feel worse. Pulling open my laptop, I logged into ACFF. As I'd suspected, no reply from Myster-E. I'd been well and truly ghosted.

Whether it was the hangover, or the fact that there didn't seem to be an area of my life not causing me heart palpitations at this particular moment in time, I decided that I wasn't keen on beating about the bush.

So, you've not replied to my messages or tried to explain why you didn't show up for drinks last night. I hope you're OK and that it's not that something terrible happened. But, statistically speaking, I'm going to go out on a limb and say you've ghosted me. I'll be honest, I don't get it – I suggested meeting, yes, but if you didn't want to come, you didn't have to. I really would have understood. What I can't understand is why you think

*it'd be OK to leave somebody sitting alone in a bar
and not even bother to explain afterwards? After all this
time chatting?*

*Anyway, I wanted to say that I've really enjoyed
getting to know you and . . . best of luck for the future,
I guess.*

I hit send and shut the laptop, feeling numb. Back to
bed for me.

Chapter Thirty-One

For some reason my last payment to the café hadn't come out of my account. I couldn't bear the idea of them somehow thinking I was trying to cadge them out of money. Ninety-nine per cent of the people in my life were mad at me right now – the idea of the café owners, or worse, Barista Bertie hating me would only compound my misery. And I didn't want to give Clive the satisfaction.

After our night together, Neil was becoming a bit more of a fixture in my life and I found myself wondering if maybe it wasn't the worst thing in the world. Amal was right, he was kind and sweet and they'd gone out of their way to set me up with someone who was, in many ways, fairly perfect, even if my head didn't spin when I was with him. He'd texted to arrange a walk and when I'd said I had some admin in town, he'd chummed me along to pay my bill. The thought of him in the café bothered me, though, and the fact that it bothered me only bothered me more. So when we reached its doors I found myself involuntarily pausing.

'Listen, this'll be fast so how about you wait here and I'll nip in quickly,' I suggested. 'Then we can go into Mountain Warehouse and you can ask them about your . . . things.' What had he called them?

'Crampons,' he replied.

'Gesundheit.'

His face creased in confusion and then he let out an unbelievably loud laugh. 'Very good. Gesundheit. Like I'd sneezed.'

I smiled up at him. 'See you in a sec.' I pushed open the door and he called me back.

'I actually fancy a coffee. Shall we sit in? It's always nice to sit in and have a coffee somewhere, isn't it?' Before I could protest, he was inside and striding to the counter. A faint sense of panic overtook my higher functions. I swept the room to see if Fraser was about anywhere. Not that it would matter if he was, of course, and even if he'd been there, he'd be through in the back. But I'd not been in since our fight and I wasn't sure I was ready to deal with him yet. Particularly not in present company.

There didn't appear to be any sign of him, though, so I made my way to the counter and joined Neil. We ordered our coffees and I paid what I'd owed for the office space. Taking a seat in the corner by the door, I found myself feeling inexpressibly sad. I hadn't realised how much I'd enjoyed being here. The place was so familiar to me now – the décor, the friendly faces, the feeling of belonging somewhere again. It was insane to think how excited and nervous I'd been when I first started coming. God, that felt like a different person. Steve had just signed me up and my naivety, in hindsight, was genuinely hard to credit. Good to see I was consistent in something at least.

I realised that Neil had been talking. Shit. I tuned back into the conversation.

'. . . but when I rolled back my own version because of the incompatible API, it broke seven dependencies. Seven! Can you believe that? And I warned everybody about using it but would they listen? No! I don't know why I bother.'

'Seven, wow. That's . . . that's a lot of dependencies.'

He nodded enthusiastically. 'I know. Unreal.'

Our coffees arrived and we sipped.

'So,' Neil leaned forward and took my hand, 'I've been thinking.'

I glanced over at him and my heart hit the floor. Why was he looking at me like that? For a second I was afraid he was going to do something eye-wateringly insane, like suggest we get married. No, that was ludicrous. I chided myself for such a ridiculous assumption.

The door to the café swung open and a blast of cold air stopped his chat. We awkwardly smiled hello to the incomer. For a mad moment I imagined snatching my hand back and making a dash out that door. A few short steps to freedom and not having to hear whatever it was Neil was about to suggest.

'I have a pal with a house in Switzerland,' he continued, once the door was closed and the coast was clear. 'He said he'd lend it to me and I thought we could go on a walking holiday there. It's so beautiful this time of year. We could use his place as a base and then camp out along the way. I was thinking we could go for maybe six or seven days? Get a proper break.'

315

He was stroking my hand now and looking at me with such eagerness. I think I'd have preferred the proposal. Was he serious? We'd only been on like six dates. How on earth was a week-long holiday together a wise idea?

'Um, I don't know if I can commit to something like that at the moment,' I replied awkwardly. He deflated as though I'd stuck an actual pin in him. I scrabbled around to try and explain, say anything that might make my refusal less personal. 'With the whole Steve thing and F— inding new work probably needs to be my priority just now.' Jesus. Had I really almost said Fraser's name out loud? I picked up my mug and took another sip. This was fine. It was just being back in the café that made me think of him.

'It would be cheap, though,' Neil persevered. 'I could pay for most of it. And you need a break – you've been so busy and stressed. You were saying how tired you were.'

Yes, a week of walking was a known cure for exhaustion. I batted the thought down. *He's only trying to do something nice for you.* 'I just . . . I just think it would stress me more to plan something like that right now. Plus, I wouldn't want you to pay for me. That's too much.'

He let go of my hand and sat back. I wracked my brains for how to make all of this less horrendous.

Maybe . . . maybe that didn't matter so much. They say opposites attract. And let's face it, my own romantic history was positively *littered* with fuckwits I'd had endless things in common with. The definition of insanity is to do the same thing over and over again expecting a different result. What if this was the moment to try something new?

Maybe in time we would find things in common. Preferably something a smidge more sedentary. And perhaps spending a little more time together somewhere else might be a good gauge. 'We could go away for a night or something though, maybe? You could . . . bag another Munro? I could wave at you from the bottom.' I reached over and took his hand. 'What do you think? There's some nice places up in the Highlands.' He was silent, but I could see a bit of him softening at the fact that it wasn't a hard no.

He took my hand. 'I guess a weekend away could be fun.'

'Maybe we could spend a night in a spa?' I hazarded. It was as good a time as any to send out feelers for other things in common.

He shuddered an honest-to-God shudder. I felt it rattle down his arm and into mine. 'I hate spas. Saunas are so gross and claustrophobic. And I can't fathom why anyone would want a stranger's hands all over them. Nah, give me the open road any day.'

I felt my good intentions towards our future dealings shrivel. No. There would be other things we'd have in common. Maybe I could learn . . . software engineering?

The door swung open. Glancing up, I found myself staring slap bang right at Fraser.

The unexpected sight of him filled my head with a low-level buzzing. The bees were back and they'd busted out the party hats. Without even thinking, I sat back, breaking the link with Neil.

I couldn't get my brain to figure out the next step. Should I say hello like we were still speaking? Pretend I hadn't seen him? Climb under the table and hide?

317

Pretending I hadn't seen him would be a tough sell given that, for a frozen, endless second he was staring back with a presumably very similar expression to mine on his face. He looked like an alien abductee caught in a tractor beam.

And then someone was coming in behind him. He apologised to them and continued into the café without stopping.

The sound of his voice squeezed something in my chest and out of nowhere my heart felt as if it was trying to pump jet fuel. I couldn't help myself – my eyes followed him over to where he was queuing. Did I imagine how tired he looked? He glanced over, his eyes caught mine, darted away automatically.

The horribleness of it all prickled through me. I needed to get out of here.

'Wait, was that not Fraser?'

It took me a moment to register that Neil was speaking to me, and even longer to figure out a response. 'Oh, uh, yeah, I guess so,' I replied. Yeah. That was convincing.

'You guess so?' he prodded, looking over at what was obviously Fraser. 'What's going on?'

'Nothing,' I insisted.

'OK then. It's just – why didn't he stop and chat? He clearly saw us.'

Excellent question that I was not in any way inclined to answer. I gave Neil a stretched-out smile. We needed to get off this topic. 'It's nothing. He insulted my coffee-making skills so I murdered everyone he loved.'

Neil gave out a loud laugh that drew glances to us. I felt myself cringe at the timing. There was no way Fraser wouldn't know that it was connected to seeing him. I glued my eyes to Neil to avoid catching Fraser's again. It took every ounce of willpower I had not to peek across at him.

Neil took a gulp of his coffee and I realised that if we kept going at this rate, and if Fraser was getting a takeaway, we'd end up with a repeat of the awkwardness that had just happened.

No thank you, universe. I picked up my coffee and downed it in one. It burned the whole way.

Worth it.

'Shall we go?'

Neil looked at me, then down at his cup, and quickly, briefly, over to Fraser, pursing his lips with a tight nod. It was the tiniest of gestures but it filled me up to the brim with guilt.

'We can stay if you've not finished,' I replied lamely. As if there was any way to salvage this shit heap of a situation.

'No, it's fine. Wasn't really enjoying it anyway.'

Amen, brother. 'Let's go get your crampons.' I was so eager to try and make up for the last five minutes that I didn't even make a rubbish tampon joke.

As we left the café, I managed to only glance back once. Fraser had disappeared into the back.

We spent what felt like a year and a half looking for the crampons in the end. It also turned out they were not in any way what I'd expected them to be. I informed Neil.

'What did you think they were?' he asked.

'I dunno. Some kind of thermal underwear, maybe?'

His laugh bounced off the walls. 'I have so much to teach you,' he chortled.

In a road to Damascus flash of revelation, that should not have in any way surprised me, I realised that I didn't want to learn. Which was deeply unfortunate given I'd just resolved to give us a go.

But as I looked at him in front of me, still smiling, I knew Neil and I were never ever going to work on any level, and not solely because I was an ongoing arsehole. I just didn't care about this stuff in the same way he didn't care to piss about finding rubbish things to see and do. There really was no world in which we matched. Watching him wander round this place with his fellow outdoor folk, something clicked. This was a huge part of his life and it coloured everything about him. He was strong and fit and full to the brim with all the goodness that fresh air and exercise brought. He deserved to be with someone who felt the same, who wanted to share in that life with him. Who would get excited about yomping through the Swiss Alps on a walking tour and want to haul ass up every hill in sight when the opportunity presented itself.

I didn't want that. And if I continued seeing him on the off-chance I'd change my mind, if I continued because we'd been introduced by friends and because he was decent and because the thinking side of my brain kept insisting that he and all of this should be what I wanted, then I was doing a disservice to both of us. Keeping us both from being with someone who would actually make us happy. And I needed to clarify that with him before this turned into something that could actually hurt him.

'What's up?' he asked.

'Oh, uh, nothing.' Jeez, I really needed to work on my poker face. 'Listen, do you fancy a wander in Prince's Street Gardens after this?'

His face brightened. 'Great idea. I love it there.'

Oh no. Here was I hoping he took this well – I'd hate to think I'd ruined a local landmark for him.

'Was it something I did?' he asked, looking more confused than anything else.

I pulled myself away from the hypnotic splash of the Ross Fountain as it gleamed in the afternoon light. There were dozens of people out and about, enjoying this strip of grassy splendour in the heart of the city. Perhaps, in hindsight, not the best place for a private chat. 'No! God, no. You've been amazing. You really have.'

'Clearly not if you're breaking up with me,' he quite reasonably pointed out.

I shook my head. 'It's really not about you.'

'Please don't do the whole "it's not you, it's me" thing.'

A small child skidded past on a scooter, narrowly avoiding smashing into the side of our bench. Yep. Great place for a break-up chat. Nice work, Ada.

I shook my head and forced myself to focus on Neil, desperately needing him to understand that sometimes the clichés really were true. That was, after all, how they became clichés. 'But that's the thing, it is. It really, really is.' I put my hand on his arm and made him look at me. 'Neil, you're great, genuinely. One of the sweetest people I've ever dated.' I felt a little well of sadness open up in me. Because it was true. He was. And yet somehow I just couldn't make it work. 'And if it helps, honestly, like, the hottest. You are an unbelievably attractive man.'

He finally met my eye, not looking totally unamused. 'If that's all true then why not just hang out with me some more? See where it goes?'

Fair question. Luckily I had the answer to that now. 'Because we don't match. I want to sit in my pants and eat crisps and shout abuse at random TV shows. You need someone who's active and fit and loves hills and trees and spending every minute they can outdoors and . . . and GitHubs. Am I using that right? Can you love a GitHub?'

He let out a laugh. 'No.'

I smiled back. 'But you know I'm right. I'm the worst person for you!'

He was silent.

'I'm so sorry for how I've treated you. I-I strung you on a bit more than I should have and you didn't deserve it – but it really is only because you're a catch and it's hard to let go of a catch, you know?'

He shook his head. 'Maybe I wanted to be strung on.'

'We've all been there.' Wasn't that the truth?

He sighed, looking suddenly sad. 'I just . . . I thought when I moved here that it'd be a bit easier, you know? To meet people and make friends and stuff. It just seems so much harder when you get older. And I really liked hanging out with you.' He put a hand on top of mine. 'But you're right, I know you are. On balance, we probably aren't the world's greatest match. Thank you for being honest. I appreciate it.'

We sat in silence for a moment.

'Can I ask one thing?'

I felt a part of me freeze. There was nothing worse than thinking you were out of the woods only to look up and find more trees. 'Sure.'

'This isn't about Fraser, is it?'

'What? No!'

'It's really fine if it is. I just thought I'd ask. There seemed to be . . . something going on today, is all.'

I shook my head. 'No, we just had a row. About a work thing, actually. We're kind of not really speaking at the moment.'

'Ah, fair enough.' He looked as though he wanted to say something else, but decided against it. We sat in silence for a moment, gazing into the shadow the castle was casting.

Neil broke the silence. 'So, I'm probably going to head off.'

I wanted to say I was sorry again. Sorry for how I'd treated him. Sorry for how lonely he'd been here. How very confident I was that he'd have no trouble finding someone to fill those gaps. Instead, I nodded and said, 'Of course, yes. Those crampons aren't going to test themselves.'

He laughed and stood to leave.

No. He deserved better than a half-arsed quip. 'And . . . sorry again, Neil. It's been really lovely getting to know you. I hope I haven't upset you.'

He waved me away. 'Nothing a little countryside jaunt won't sort. I had a lovely time with you, Ada. You can't ask for more than that in life.'

I smiled and thanked him. Even let myself wade through a spot of jealousy, wondering what it must be like to live in a mind as upbeat as his.

Chapter Thirty-Two

It had been two days since Amal and I had had our row. There was still no word from her and I hadn't yet been able to gather the courage to send a message either. The band of awfulness that had wrapped itself around me during the argument somehow managed to pull even tighter – a feat I hadn't thought possible.

We'd had arguments before, obviously, but I'd never seen her look at me with such . . . disgust. And how was this the first time I was hearing that she'd had postnatal depression? I tried to think back. Sure, she'd been a bit frazzled but she'd just had a baby, nothing had seemed out of the ordinary. How hadn't I seen it?

I'd assumed that because Amal had always been the together one of the two of us that she always would be. That because she and Aiden were such a strong unit, they automatically had everything under control. Always with the knack of making things look easy – something I'd envied about her since the day and hour we'd met. She'd hit all her beats in life. Degree, great job, fell in love, got married, had kids – and all before she was thirty. It was what she'd wanted, what she'd planned for. And I was starting to realise that, because of that, all I'd done was buy into the image of what I thought her life was. Which was ridiculous, of course – as if anyone could plan their way around their mental health. I'd let her keep projecting the image she'd wanted the world to see, instead of looking behind it. She was my best friend and I should have known to look behind.

But *why hadn't I noticed*? Why hadn't I asked?

The thought unfurled in my head like the world's worst banner: I hadn't noticed because I hadn't wanted to.

Amal and Aiden were what I needed them to be in my head and I'd pushed out anything that didn't match that narrative. Amal had been struggling all this time and I hadn't helped her.

I curled myself into a ball on the sofa at the thought of it. It felt like the top three layers of every emotional nerve I had had been torn off, leaving the underneath gasping at the elements.

Because, as she'd so rightly pointed out, it wasn't only with Amal. It'd been with Steve too. I'd allowed myself to buy into his devil-may-care, harmless-cad act, without really considering the consequences. He was selfish, short-sighted and childish. His actions had actively hurt people and I'd enabled him to do it. And, on a lesser scale, with Mum and her surprisingly prolific dating history. Despite how close we were, I'd done the thing I swore I wouldn't do – reduced her to the role of 'parent' and then had the gall to be amazed when I learned she had a life outside that.

But nowhere was it more evident than with Dan.

When everything had fallen apart with him, I'd deliberately never allowed myself to think about it. Just kept telling myself it was something I would take out and unpack and learn from later, when it didn't hurt so much. Except that time hadn't come and a part of me hadn't really understood why.

Goddamn, I understood now.

Did I know he was still with his wife? No. I'd asked him and he'd sworn blind that they were separated.

But did I *know*? Deep down?

Amal's words spun round and round and round.

You knew you were fucking a married man or you would have told me about him.

The secret meetings, the long absences, the phone calls he'd take from her and say it was sorting some kind of life admin? Somewhere, under all the bullshit, I'd known he was a liar. I didn't dig because I didn't want to. Because I'd fallen in love with him like the total fucking idiot that I was and his version of life was what I'd wanted for myself.

The hot, restless shame of it tangled up in me until it felt like all of it might burst out of my skin.

I'd been the one to let him have his cake and eat it – a wife and a child and me on the side. I'd basically baked said cake and fucking spoon-fed it right into him.

A memory of asking him – more than once – *why me? How did I get so lucky?*

How much of a kick he must have got from it. How very, very easy he'd had it all.

And then I'd left. No comeuppance. No reckoning. And yet months of texts from him, despite the single reply he'd had from me, telling him to leave me be.

Christ, how had I ever wondered why I'd not told Amal when it happened? Who could ever bear to say something so pathetic out loud?

The dull pounding of a headache was slowly cutting a swathe behind my eyes and into my forehead. I found the will to pull myself up off my chair and went in search of some paracetamol. Chucking two down with some water, I decided the best way to distract myself was to properly distract myself. Time to get back to work and at least try to put out one of the bin fires in my life. And while I was at it, figure out how the fuck I was going to fix what had happened with Amal.

But it turned out I was at a total loss for what to do for work. Steve wasn't taking my calls and appeared to have disappeared off the face of the planet so I spent my days trying to figure out how to answer the screaming emails from *Leith, Laugh, Love* and the barrage of press requests and the panicked missives from Steve's publishers, without actually having anything to put in them. I also stepped up what was becoming an increasingly desperate search for new clients – an exercise in futility if ever there was one just at that moment. No one wanted to touch me with a barge pole, thanks to Steve.

And, to really add insult to injury, I'd also managed to once again burn my toast – the smoke had set off the fire alarm for the third time in as many days. God, I missed the café, Fraser or no. Their fire alarm never went off.

I was on a stool midway through the tea-towel flag manoeuvre when the door buzzer went. Because of course it did. Why did the postie always ring our door to get in? There was literally never anything for us.

The wailing siren mercifully stopped as I hopped off the stool and made a dash for the buzzer. Pushing it down long enough to let them into the building, I dashed back to remove the toast before anything else could anger the fire gods. Eyeing the slices, I wondered how many layers of blackened husk had to occur before it became inedible. Then I remembered the only bread left in the bag was the heels.

Burnt husk it was.

A knock at the flat door interrupted my attempts at drowning the toast, and with any luck myself, in butter. It would appear we did have post for once. Throwing the toast down, I clapped the crumbs from my hands and went to answer, my very friendliest smile at the ready, because there was no need to make an enemy of such a handy public servant.

'Hi, there!' I sing-songed. The words died in my throat.

Because it wasn't a postman at my door.

It was Dan.

The recoil was automatic. The whole world took on that awful heart-bursting wobble you get when you think you've missed a step. Was I hallucinating? Had the

329

smoke from the toaster accidentally brought on some kind of episode?

'Hey, Ads,' he said, with a sheepish smile. As if there was any universe in which he'd have a reason to be on the other side of this door, calling me Ads.

My brain wouldn't process it. I literally couldn't think of a thing to say.

'Can – can I come in?' he asked, looking behind me, as if to check I was alone.

Without thinking, I stepped away from the door and he followed me in.

I stopped moving and turned back to find he was standing much closer than I'd anticipated. Close enough to feel the warmth from his body, and catch the faint aftershave and coffee scent of him. For a split second I was catapulted right back into that world. *Our* world. Could practically feel his hands on my skin. How achingly familiar he was. His hair was longer, there was more stubble. But the same smell. Same eyes. Same crooked smile.

You're not a stupid person.

He stood in front of me, hands in pockets. 'How have you been?'

Amal's words were like a bucket of water over my head.

This. This was why I'd cut him off. Refused to even read his messages. Not because I didn't want to see him. If anything it had been the opposite of that. Because I knew that if I had, I would break. I would let him apologise. Let him draw me back in.

The truth of the realisation horrified me. That if he'd arrived at my door six months ago, I might have let him in. Christ! I just *did* let him in.

Clarity arrived, bringing with it its helpful pal: calm-rage – a phenomenon I'd only ever heard about from other people. But Jesus, did I know it now.

'It feels like such a long time since I've seen you,' he continued, giving me that crooked smile again.

In an instant the man in front of me became a stranger. He wasn't Dan, the handsome, funny catch I'd found myself falling in love with. He was Dan, a worn-down, lost man-child with no idea of what he wanted from life. And he'd dragged his wife and his baby and me along with him.

Despite our row and everything that had happened between us, I couldn't help but compare him to Fraser. I'd originally thought they'd shared a clear confidence in their own abilities but that wasn't actually true – Fraser wore the world so differently. Dan had seemed like an open book when I first met him but I could see so clearly now that every part of him was locked down. Fraser, meanwhile, was honest almost to a fault.

The thought ricocheted through me. I'd been so mad at him, felt so much like all the shit around Steve's story had been a betrayal of our friendship. But watching Dan watch me with that smile and those eyes I could barely read now – if I ever really had been able to read them – made me catch on to something I'd not fully understood until this moment. I tried to think back to my time with him, but my memories felt muddled now. This new recognition of my own complicity in where I'd found myself had cast shadows over everything. I couldn't tell real from realisation anymore. But Fraser's integrity extended through every aspect of his life; it was one of the things I liked most about him. Had he been telling me the truth? That he hadn't leaked the stories about Steve? The idea of it felt like a slap – had I been completely wrong? But no! I'd run through it a million times in my head – there was nowhere else the stories could have come from. Just because I wanted so badly for it not to be true didn't mean it wasn't. This was clearly me, once again talking myself into believing something I wanted to believe, just so I could have the old Fraser back. Which was extra-ridiculous, given I was currently standing in front of my last foray into that kind of epic self-delusion, being reminded of exactly where that had got me.

Dan was staring at me and I realised he was expecting some kind of response. I reflexively made to apologise for my absent-mindedness, or to ask him to repeat himself. Then caught myself in the nick of time.

'No, actually. No.' The words flew out of me, sounding raspy and broken, moving to clear. 'You have to leave. I don't want you here.'

He reached out and put a hand on my arm. 'Ada, I—'

'*Don't touch me*!' I hissed.

He took a step back, shock pulling colour to his cheeks. 'Don't be like that! I came all the way here—'

The calm-rage disappeared, to be replaced with plain old rage-rage. 'Why?' I found myself shouting. 'Why did you come here, Dan? What *possible reason* could you have to think I would ever want to see you? How do you even know where I live?'

He looked genuinely crestfallen. 'I-I brought you the stuff you left in the office. I thought you might like it back.'

I noted his lack of answer on my address, the bastard. For the first time I tracked that he did, in fact, have a bag on his shoulder though. 'Oh, have Royal Mail collapsed without me knowing?' I snapped.

He ignored me, continuing blindly along whatever track he'd clearly decided on taking. 'It's so different since you left,' he babbled. 'Veronica's gone. Set up her own freelance event company. And Cora had her baby.'

'Yeah, I know,' I snapped. I actually hadn't known about Veronica leaving. But he didn't need to know that. Cora had kept in touch though, sending me baby updates, so it wasn't all a lie.

His eyes were boring into me but there was no part of me that wanted to look at him. I held out my hand. 'Well, you've delivered on your errand.'

He took the bag from his shoulder and placed the handle in my hand, grasping hold of it. 'I needed to see you – I've missed you so much.' His voice cracked. 'I just want to talk to you. To explain—'

Was this man for real? I ripped my hand from his. 'Dan, I told you not to contact me again so you, what, travel 400 miles to do the thing I expressly asked you not to do? What part of that seems acceptable to you?'

He shook his head, scrambling around for words. 'Please, please let me explain – let me apologise. Talk to me, please!'

'How's your wife?'

He froze, looking like I'd pulled a pin out of a grenade.

'Did she have a boy or a girl in the end?'

He held up his hands in supplication. 'Look, Ada, it's complicated, OK? I swear to God we'd split up when I met you. But then she came back and things happened and I didn't know what to do and I . . . I fucked up. I know that.'

'Are you still with her?' I asked.

There was no more trying to meet my eyes.

Disgust rolled through me. I didn't bother to hide it. 'Do you want to know the thing I hate the most about what happened with us? It's that you made me real-ise that what I'd thought were core values in my life were . . . negotiable.' I held up my hand to stop his inevitable attempt at interruption. 'That's on me. And I should thank you, really, because at least it's something I know I have to fix now. But you know what *you'll* never be able to fix? The fact that you're a coward and a lying piece of shit. I hope your wife finds out the kind of man she's married to. I hope she burns your life to the fucking ground. Because she deserves better too.'

Well . . . wow! Even I hadn't expected that.

And nor, by the look on his face, had Dan. He was staring down at me like, well, like I'd just told him I hoped his wife found out he was a cheater and burned his life to the ground. He was blinking very fast, mouth opening with the beginning of several aborted sentences.

'This might be news to you, but you can't have it all ways. You can't. The fact that you're here – that you've ignored every line I drew . . . God!' I paused, feeling a light switch on in my brain. 'It really couldn't have come at a better time.'

His panicked blinking turned into a confused frown.

'If you'd have arrived at my door six months ago, if you'd told me you left her and all that . . . shit, I don't know that I can say I wouldn't have taken you up on it. I was so in love with you.'

He went to speak and I held up my hand again.

'*Do not interrupt me.*'

He froze.

'That was ludicrous, I know that now. I knew there was more to what was going on and I didn't ask because I knew I probably wouldn't like the answer. I heard what I wanted to. Because I was a coward too. But we're done, Dan. I wasn't kidding or playing some kind of game with you when I said that in my message. You showing up here isn't some kind of romantic gesture, it's a dick move and I don't want it.' I pulled the bag he'd handed me onto my shoulder. 'You should leave.'

'Ada, please. I wanted to apologise.'

'Yeah, you've done that now. So, bye.'

He stared at me for a moment but he must have been able to see there was no point in trying to push me further. He left without another word.

Chapter Thirty-Three

I was on fire. My skin was too warm, as if my blood was radiating heat from barrelling through my system at the speed of light. It felt like an exorcism. After all the fear that I might break if I ever saw him again, I'd faced Dan and said the exact things I'd hoped to say. For the first time in my life, everything had come out exactly as I wanted it to. Was this how hotshot lawyers felt? Jesus, it was heady stuff.

I was brimming over with adrenaline and if I didn't use it on something right now, my skeleton would walk out of my body.

I knew what I needed to do.

In what felt like no time at all, I was at Amal's door and there was a better than even chance I might puke. It was so strange – I'd had this feeling many times in my life, but never at Amal's. It also occurred to me that I'd never tipped up at her house unannounced. We'd been friends for nearly twenty years but there was something untoward about not warning someone you were coming. The window of opportunity to make sure your toilet was clean and your dishes were at least stacked neatly was golden.

And yet here I was.

Suddenly the adrenaline vanished, just in time for me to have pushed the doorbell. In its place was a sudden tsunami of anxiety. All of her words came crashing down on me; in that moment the anger in her voice was practically an external sound. And here I was. Arriving at her door unannounced.

I jammed my feet to the floor to stop them walking me back up her driveway. No. I was here now. The bell couldn't be unrung. The best I could hope for was that she wasn't in. Their car was gone, so that was a bit of a possibility. And normally you could hear Benji and Mo long before you saw them.

And then I heard footsteps.

My stomach felt as though it was trying to scale my oesophagus. The door swung open as it reached the summit and I had to force it back down.

Amal froze when she clocked who it was. Long enough for me to be genuinely shocked – she looked terrible. Her normally lustrous hair hung limp around her shoulders, her eyes somehow sunk deep into their sockets. It was as if she'd aged overnight and she'd clearly been crying recently. For a strange, uncanny moment, I almost didn't recognise her.

'Hey,' I blurted out. 'Sorry, I-I probably should have called first.'

She burst into tears.

I stepped forward and she practically fell into my arms. She's always been quite slight but she felt frail as a bird now. Answering tears pricked my eyes as she clung to me.

'I'm so sorry,' she wailed.

'*I'm* so sorry!'

We stood hugging for what felt like forever until I realised her shaking might be from cold and I walked us both inside the house.

She couldn't stop crying. I settled her onto her sofa and went and poured her some water, grabbing tissues on my way back. Setting them on the coffee table, I kneeled in front of her. She was still shaking, borderline hysterical now. Jesus, this was really bad. Where were Aiden and the kids? Had something happened?

I asked her but her only reply was a shake of the head. I wiped her cheeks with a tissue. 'Pet, why are you here by yourself? Where are Aiden and the kids?' I repeated.

It was enough to bring her back ever so slightly from what looked horrifyingly close to the brink.

She took another proffered tissue and blew her nose, sucking in a stuttered breath and letting it slowly go. Finally she was able to speak. 'He took the kids to the park to give me a couple of hours.'

Thank God.

She dissolved again.

I told her to let it out and I would make us tea. I made my way to the kitchen and boiled the kettle, willing it to go faster. Never had water boiling felt so slow. I threw together the drinks and brought them back out, by which point, Amal had managed to calm down enough to speak.

'I'm so sorry,' she said in a quiet voice. She looked other-side-of-tired done-in.

'Don't be silly. You've nothing to be sorry for,' I said gently.

'No, I do. Oh Ada, I said such terrible things to you . . .' Her voice cracked again.

'No, *I'm* sorry.' She made to interrupt me. 'No, let me finish. You were right. I didn't know he was married but I didn't know he *wasn't* either and I was happy to believe the lie because I didn't want to hear the truth.' She tried to interrupt again but I pushed on because I needed her to know this. 'And you were right about me being selfish. I've been ambling about, doing everything on my own terms, and I know that's a luxury that so many people don't get – that *you* don't get. You're the centre of my fucking world, Amal. You and Aiden and the kids. I'd be nowhere without you. And you've been struggling and I haven't helped. I assumed you were fine because you've always seemed fine – but that's not friendship. You needed me and I wasn't there and I'm so, so sorry.' It was my voice's turn to break. I cleared it out. 'But I'm here now, OK? Anything you need from me, anything you want to say or do or scream, I'm here for it. So . . . go.'

She let out a small hiccup-y laugh that turned back into a sob. It took her another few moments to try and compose herself. 'I feel so shit all the time,' she wept. But it was more controlled now, she was able to speak in full sentences. 'Everybody says your second child is easier but it's just . . . endless! He never sleeps. Never!

339

He cries all night unless he's held. And God help me, there are days I wish—' She stopped herself mid-sentence, completely powering down, as if suddenly in the eye of whatever storm was swallowing her up. 'I'm the worst mum in the world.' The eye disappeared and she was beside herself again.

I couldn't hide my shock. Not at her words, but at the idea she would ever think she was a bad mum.

'The doctor says it's postnatal depression,' she continued. 'Gives me pills and they help but . . .' She wiped roughly at her eyes. 'I feel like I've lost this time in his life. And I can never get that back. I'll spend my whole life knowing that. Benji got the real me and Mo got . . . this. I'm scared he'll somehow know that.'

Well. That at least I could help her with.

I leaned forward and took both her hands in mine, forced her to look at me. 'Amal, your boys are the luckiest goddamn kids in the world – no, listen to me. I know you don't feel that way. I'm not trying to diminish what's going on in your head and I can't imagine what that feeling is doing to you. That's real to you. But I need you to hear this. From someone who isn't in the middle of the hell you're in: you're an incredible parent. Better even, because even though every part of you is fucked right now, you've kept it going. You have two happy, healthy babies. So even if there was a way for Mo to somehow absorb how you feel right now – which there isn't – he'll still have a mum who would do literally anything for him, even without the hormones. That's an *incredible* thing.' I wiped some more stray tears from her face. She was clinging to my other hand like I was a life raft, looking utterly bereft. 'Need I remind you of all the children who have literally not got a single person to give two shits about them? Your kids are the luckiest bastards in the world. They have you. It doesn't feel like that now to you, I know. But I am absolutely sure that one day it will. And I swear to God, I will do whatever you need me to do to get you to that point.' I thought of my mum and what she had said to me. 'I'll fight this bear for you.'

Amal let out a snort. 'What?'

'Bad analogy.' I waved it away. 'But I'm serious. Whatever you need. I know I've said that already but I mean it. I didn't understand before but I do now.' I pulled her into a hug and we sat there for what felt like days. Finally she broke away.

'I really didn't mean anything I said to you, though. You do know that, right? And I'm sorry I pushed Neil so hard. I knew you weren't really into him but it just felt like the only thing I was able to be any kind of . . . use for.' She wiped her eyes, searched my face and then looked down at her hands. 'Sometimes I have these thoughts and I say them and they don't even feel like they're mine.'

I shook my head. 'I'm sorry about Neil – I know I didn't necessarily do right by him. And I do know you didn't mean the things you said, but you weren't wrong. They were things I needed to hear. I know I've been drifting for a while now. It brought me back and I needed that. So please, please don't be sorry.' I leaned forward and picked up my tea. My throat felt as if it had recently traversed a desert and was glad of the liquid.

'How are things with Fraser?' she asked. The question surprised me. For an all too brief period, I had entirely forgotten all about Fraser and Dan and Steve and even Myster-E. There was a lesson there somewhere.

'That's is a story for another day. Today we talk about you.'

And we did. I hadn't even realised we'd been there for as long as we had until I heard a car come up the driveway and Benji came bursting into the house, swiftly followed by Aiden holding Mo. Benji was carrying flowers he'd picked from somewhere. They were bent and had huge clumps of petals missing. He handed them over proudly to Amal, who took them with all the ceremony of a crown. Despite still looking exhausted, her entire demeanour had changed the moment they came into the house. She swept Benji up in a hug, moving across to kiss Aiden hello, before following up with a kiss and hug for Mo. Aiden pulled her in for a longer hug and I could see him checking up on her, with barely supressed worry. And Jesus, did I ever understand why now. No one should be that good at dissembling and reassembling. For the first time I fully appreciated the sheer strength of will it must have taken for her to continually don this mask. Now to figure out the trick of getting her to find a way to take it off . . .

Chapter Thirty-Four

Steve's name showed up in my caller ID. The bastard was finally returning my millions of calls. I set my mug down on my dining table and answered.

'Steve!' I cried, without any ado. 'Where the hell have you been? I've been trying to get you for days!'

'Hi, Ada.' His voice sounded smaller than I'd ever heard it. 'How are you doing?'

How was I doing? Was he serious? 'Not great, Steve. What the fuck were you thinking, hanging out with the likes of Dermot Clemont?'

'I really didn't know what he was into! I know you don't believe me – but, seriously, he was just a rich guy having some fun parties. I swear I didn't see any of that other stuff happening. You know I don't agree with his views. They're horrible. And it was such a long time ago – things were different then!'

'No. Absolutely not. That is not an acceptable apology. And even if it was, why the fuck has it taken you so long to return my calls?'

'I was scared – I knew you were mad.'

It dawned on me, perhaps not strictly for the first time, that I wasn't Steve's publicist, I was his surrogate mother.

'Not nearly good enough. You're not a child, Steve, you're a middle-aged man in the public eye and you have an obligation to people to not be such a massive idiot. We've wasted days we could have used getting in front of this because I couldn't find you. You know that *Leith, Laugh, Love* want to fire you, right? The only thing standing in the way of that is me repeatedly begging them not to until I can get to the bottom of the leak!'

'I know, I saw the emails. I really am sorry.'

I sighed. There wasn't much else to say under the circumstances, I supposed. And it wasn't as if I didn't share blame for flapping my gums in the general vicinity of a a journalist. 'Right. OK, then. Next steps.' I took a deep breath. 'I'm pretty sure I know where the leaks are coming from and they should have stopped now.' It'd be hard for Fraser to leak stuff if I wasn't speaking to him. 'So we need to think about the best way forward. The first thing is for you to release a full, caveat-free apology. I've written a couple of different versions that I'll send over and you can pick one. Add anything else you want to say in it but don't – and I really can't stress this enough, Steve – *do not* release it yourself. I'll arrange all of that. You have to run any public statements you make past me now, do you understand? This is non-negotiable.'

There was silence at the other end of the line.

'Steve? Are you there?'

'Yeah, I'm here,' he replied.

'And do you promise you'll do what I asked?'

'Yeah – yes, of course. Anything for you, dear Ada.'

'None of this is actually for me, Steve,' I pointed out.

He was silent again. It was cumulatively the quietest he'd been in all the time I'd known him.

'OK,' I persevered. 'So once the apology is out—'

'Did you say you knew who'd leaked the stories?' he interrupted.

Awkward. I'd been kind of hoping we'd blow right past that. 'Yeah. I, uh, I think so. A journalist I . . . kind of knew.' I paused, waiting for him to realise it was my fault and start shouting, but he didn't say anything. 'But I've sorted it now.' I continued. 'It won't be happening again.'

'OK. It's just . . . nothing.'

I felt my spidey senses tingle. 'What is it? Has something else happened?' I tried to wrack my brains – there'd been nothing new breaking in any of the local news feeds and I'd been keeping an extra-close ear to the ground.

'No, no, it's not that. It's—' He fell into silence again.

'Look, Steve, I may be wrong but I'm pretty sure the worst of it is out now. You might as well get whatever it is you want to say off your chest.' I mean, the odds were it wasn't worse than 'fascist bestie', right? Oh God . . . right?

He took a deep breath. 'OK, but you have to promise you won't get mad?'

I sighed. Pretty sure I'd run out of rage at this point. 'Sure. Fire away.'

'It's just that . . . *I* leaked the stories.'

There was a beat of silence as I absorbed his words. 'Sorry, what?'

He repeated the sentence.

No. That couldn't be right. And stories? Plural? 'What do you mean?' I asked carefully.

He paused. 'I . . . I don't know how else to say it. The articles that have been showing up about me recently in the papers? The one about telling the schoolkids that story? And the car thing? And the soap? Oh, and . . . the orgy, obviously? They came from me. I thought that it might help boost my profile but I knew you wouldn't like it so I didn't tell you.' His words sped up. 'And really, if anything it proves my innocence more – that I couldn't possibly have known the Dermot fascist stuff. I'd never have leaked the video if I'd known there was all that other nonsense going on in it. I never watched it the whole way through – just the bits I was in. If I'd thought for a second it would backfire the way it did, I'd never have done it. You have to believe me, Ada.'

I couldn't get my brain to engage with what he was saying. 'No! It can't have been you. Fraser, he said . . .' What had he said? Oh yeah, that he *didn't do it*.

But there'd been no reason to think it would have come from anywhere else. And yet . . . of course it was fucking Steve! Now that he'd said it, a part of me couldn't quite believe the thought hadn't crossed my mind. Not that he'd done this kind of thing before but it made perfect sense in a very Steve kind of way. And in a very Steve kind of way it had sort of been working, playing perfectly into his benign drunk-uncle image. Until the fascism part had opened up the fact that it wasn't all benign.

'You believe me, right? You know I wouldn't have leaked it if I'd known how damaging it would be?'

Fuck my actual life. I sighed. 'Yeah, Steve. I know.'

'Phew. OK. Just had to get that off my chest. God, I thought you'd be way angrier about it. You were so mad about the leaks.'

I wasn't mad. If anything, the revelation had come as a kind of relief, really. It had brought clarity to a situation that I hadn't realised needed it.

'I'm not angry,' I replied. 'But I do quit.'

There was silence at the other end of the phone. 'Wait – what? No! You said you weren't angry!' he cried.

'And I meant it. But I can't work with you, Steve. I'm a publicist, not a babysitter and all I've done is clean up after you. I can't do it anymore – I don't want to and, to be honest, I don't think it's good for you either. I'm grateful for you taking me on but consider this as me formally terminating our contract.'

'Ada, wai—'

I hung up the phone, feeling like a weight had been lifted.

For approximately ten seconds. And then the panic set in. I had just got rid of my only source of income. Jesus Christ.

I picked up my mug and made my way through to the kitchen. Boiling the kettle I tried to get my ducks in a row. Maybe I could email Indigo Dance back? Tell them I'd parted ways with Steve? It was a possibility, I supposed. But I hadn't even pitched to them so there was a chance they wouldn't have gone with me either way and the process alone would take too long. Could I try Contrast Creative again? Urgh, no. They'd been clear they wouldn't have anything for at least the next few months.

Fuck fuck *fuck*. What had I done?

I poured more hot water into my mug and wracked my brains. When I'd been going through the list of people, there had been a few other potentials. I could dig them out, maybe, see if they had anything going.

And I supposed it didn't strictly have to be in Edinburgh – I'd only really moved back to start the business. But a part of me was sad at the thought of leaving. Somewhere along the way I'd kind of fallen in love with being in Edinburgh again. It was funny, I hadn't noticed it happening but here we were. Being near Mum and Amal and getting to see Benji and Mo grow up. My little café-office, my coffice, and being able to walk everywhere and have such beautiful places within such easy reach. And then there'd been Fraser . . . no, I wasn't quite ready to dwell on Fraser just yet. There was a grovelling apology in my future and I wasn't sure it was going to cut the mustard.

All in all, this place felt like a lot to give up just now.

But the practical side of my brain wouldn't let it sit. London was a bigger pool to fish in, there was no getting away from that. Maybe I could set up initially there and relocate if it worked out? No, that wasn't the spirit. *When* it worked out. I could at least put out some feelers there. See if any of my old contacts might have anything of interest going on. A part of me worried about being away from Amal. But she had Aiden and her parents and her NCT group nearby. I could be the person she could run away and visit. The phone calls at four in the morning and the parcels in the post. I'd promised I'd get her through this and I'd make good on that promise.

Suddenly I remembered something. Dan had mentioned that Veronica had left to start her own business. For all she scared the shit out of me, I'd loved working with her. And when I'd left, she'd seemed genuinely quite upset.

What did I have to lose? She was a direct person and I knew she appreciated directness from other people.

I made my way back into the living room, settled down at the table and opened my email.

Chapter Thirty-Five

I hit send on the email to Veronica and then spent the rest of the day moving restlessly from the dining table to my sofa, trying to drum up ideas and new possible contacts. But I couldn't get myself to properly focus. I found a brief respite organising a flower delivery subscription for Amal – bright, bold, beautiful colours were something she loved. Maybe they'd help make her feel a little bit better. A small token, but it was a start and would be one of many.

And then it was right back to the fidgeting.

A whole day had passed since Steve had dropped his bombshell and I still hadn't figured out how I was going to go about apologising to Fraser. It'd been a while since I'd falsely accused someone of straight-up sabotaging my life – did Hallmark do a card for this sort of thing?

In hindsight I couldn't quite believe I'd so blindly accused him of it. What an awful thing to tell someone you thought they'd done. I'd not only called him a liar, I'd also called into question his ethics as both a friend and a journalist. I could feel the embarrassment and shame of it curdling up in me. I mean, I'd always known what an absolute clown Steve was. If anything, my first thought should have been 'this is clearly Steve's doing because he's a fucking idiot and it's exactly the kind of stunt he'd pull.'

But here we were. The apology tour that was my life continued apace. I wracked my brains for how to do it. Every time I tried to think of what to say, I remembered Fraser's face when I saw him at the café with Neil. He hadn't even looked angry, now that I thought about it . . . just sad.

And I missed him. God, it annoyed me how much I missed him. It hadn't been something I'd noticed before. I'd come across a house with a window inexplicably full of clown puppets on a walk yesterday. There had been not one but two leaflets put through my door for 'mediums in your local area'. Worst of the worst, I couldn't even look at a chocolate Hobnob these days. Seeing him every day, telling him all these things and getting stories back had become a part of my life that I appeared to have become reliant on. Which was ridiculous because I'd known him less than three months – nobody should become that important in that time. Had I learned nothing from Dan?

But it had been like putting a frog in cold water and slowly turning up the heat. I hadn't noticed how – well, hot I'd got, for want of a better way of phrasing it. Not until he was gone.

Myster-E had been rough too. Him disappearing felt like a bruise – tender to the touch and sore if I let myself lean on it, but when push came to shove, it had always been a risk. It was a bruise I could hide away and

351

give time to heal. But Fraser . . . Fraser felt more like an open wound that was constantly shouting for my attention now. Out of nowhere, the memory of his lips on mine would drop into my head, like the world's worst unannounced house guest. The heat of him. The taste of him. The spark in my stomach when his skin touched mine. If I was being completely honest with myself – and that was something I was trying to do as much as possible these days – I'd always known I'd been attracted to him. But that was something you could have with anyone. The number of times I'd been into someone and then kissed them, only to discover we had all the chemistry of a dead car battery, was more than I could count at this point.

But then Fraser and I had kissed and it'd felt like my spine had fused and it had never really unglued since.

It was an endless, vicious cycle. I'd remember how shitty I'd been. Then how hot it'd been to kiss him. Then how he had a girlfriend. Then boom! Right back to guilt.

But I also understood that that was all irrelevant because I'd tanked our friendship. I owed him an apology, even if it was the last conversation we would have.

I made a decision. I would message him to ask if he would meet me so I could say sorry unequivocally for what I'd said. I'd maybe even apologise for the kiss. I'd suggest that we have a bit of a break but that we could maybe circle back to being friends again, if he'd have me. Albeit, once I'd had a bit of time to get him out of my system.

Right. Now to send the message.

I stared at the blank screen. Tried a couple of different versions. All too long. Too silly. Too strange. Eventually, I lost the will to live and typed the most honest thing I could:

Hi, Fraser. I don't think I can ever actually tell you how sorry I am. I was an absolute prick and there's no excuse for why I could ever have thought you'd do what I accused you of doing. I don't deserve it, and you don't have to do it, but if you're free and willing, fancy a coffee so I can apologise some more?

I sent it out into the universe then switched off my mobile. For a whole five minutes. Then I switched it on again and off again for the next twenty minutes. It was looking as if it was going to be a punishing old stretch for my phone. Flashbacks to Myster-E were emphatically not a welcome addition to my day.

And then it beeped. A message from Fraser. My heart rate hit the ceiling.

'I'm busy just now – could maybe meet in a couple of hours?'

The relief was embarrassing. It flooded my system and for a moment I was worried I might up and float away. Was his message short and a bit sharp? Maybe. Was my anxiety going to carve me up into tiny little pieces waiting to see him? Damn right it was. But he had replied and he would meet me. It was a start.

I replied a time and hit send. A minute passed and then he replied, agreeing we'd meet at four.

Now to force myself not to try on every piece of clothing in my wardrobe. I glanced down at my ratty hoody, bestrewn with strands of straggled tatty hair. Maybe a small change and a brush wouldn't hurt? I didn't want to scare the general public.

I made my way into the café. I couldn't decide if I wanted to be the first or the second to arrive. It took a second to spot Fraser and then I had my answer. Definitely had wanted to be first, if for no other reason than I'd have had the time to be completely sure I wouldn't barf on him. Despite having had zero coffee, it felt like I'd been mainlining rocket fuel. Were my hands actually shaking?

He spotted me and gave me a small wave – if I didn't know any better, I'd say he looked nervous. But maybe I was projecting. I took a deep breath, double-checked to make sure I definitely wasn't going to be sick – still 50/50 – and over I went.

'Hey,' he said, with a smile. Goddammit, those eyes. I'd missed those eyes. Spilling over with all that kindness. And something else, though I couldn't quite put my finger on it.

'Hi,' I replied, returning his with a smile of my own.

'I got you a coffee,' he said.

Christ, coffee. My heart was going to literally explode. 'Thanks.'

'Decaff, of course – I know you'll die if you drink caffeine after midday.'

My heart squeezed, the pitter-patter scattering like marbles on a kitchen floor. Still very much at risk of exploding, it would seem. I smiled again, unable to help myself. 'Ah, you know me well.'

He caught my eye and there was a definite something new that I couldn't read. Different to before. Something had shifted or changed. A part of me wondered if it was the girlfriend.

No, shut that shit right down. The apology tour was a purely platonic affair.

Sliding in the chair opposite, I pulled the coffee towards me and took a sip, not ready yet to look him in those eyes again. I decided the best way forward was to rip off the plaster. 'Fraser—'

'Ada—'

We both stopped, laughed. 'You first,' we both said. More gales of laughter. God, actual sitcoms had less cringe than this.

But it did help me realise I had to go first – I'd shrivel up and die if I didn't. So in I went before he could stop me. 'I just wanted to say that I'm so sorry, Fraser. I can't believe what I said to you. Steve confessed that it was him leaking the stories. God, what an arsehole!' I set the mug down on the table. 'I should have known you wouldn't have done that. I should have trusted you. You gave me no reason not to. And . . . and you're right. He's a grown man who's spent his whole life making messes and expecting everyone else to clean them up for him. He deserves what he gets. Hopefully, he might learn something from this one.' I took a deep breath and let it slowly out. I could feel him watching me but I still couldn't bring myself to look him in the eye.

'Thank you.' He paused a moment. 'You do know that, though, right? That I would never do that to you?' His voice sounded surprisingly tight. 'I'd never intentionally hurt you or . . . or lie to you.'

I looked up. I was surprised to find he looked quite tired close up, but his eyes were like live wires now, a bright, sparking intensity I didn't think I'd ever seen in him before.

'I . . . yeah, I do.' I was surprised to find I genuinely meant it. Wasn't that a turn-up for the books?

'OK, I just . . . I need you to remember that, OK? For what I'm about to tell you.'

He was practically vibrating with tension. How had I missed that before? A nameless fear bloomed in my brain.

Except it wasn't nameless. It was very much named. I was shot right back to finding out about Dan's whole other life; suddenly, utterly sure that Fraser was about to tell me the same thing all over again. That his girlfriend wasn't his girlfriend – she was his wife and they had ten kids and that I'd somehow managed to do all of this again. Nausea barrelled through me.

No.

Breathe.

Even if it was true, all we'd done was kiss. And if it was the same thing again, it was all on him.

Wasn't it?

I couldn't look at him. Christ, if he did tell me that, I'd never look at another man ever again. Get me to a nunnery and be fucking done with all of them.

356

He leaned down and picked up a canvas bag from beside his feet, setting it gently on the table between us.

'OK, promise me that you'll remember that you believe I'd never hurt you or lie to you?'

I made myself look up. What on earth was this bag going to produce? 'O . . . K.'

'Because it's going to take some explaining and I need you to just . . . remember that. I don't want to fuck this up, OK?'

Jesus, the suspense was killing me. This felt very much like one of those 'before and after' moments. Fuck. Those were rarely good.

'Yeah, I promise,' I assured him. Hard to say if I'd be able to keep it but sure, we'd know in a minute.

He opened the bag and pulled out . . . the mugs we'd made at our impromptu erottery session.

'Oh my God, I'd totally forgotten about those! Shit, sorry! I'll not interrupt.' But I genuinely had clean forgotten them.

He picked them both up. Though his hands were covering most of each mug, I could see they were glazed. He'd gone back and glazed them without me? A part of me was a bit miffed that I hadn't been able to finish mine with him. But another part was unreasonably pleased. He'd gone back to a place he'd been unbelievably uncomfortable in by himself and finished our mugs, despite me effectively telling him he was a monster and to fuck off?

The knot in my chest loosened slightly.

'Right.' He took a deep breath. 'You're going to have some questions, but remember. You promised to trust me.'

'Right. Yes, yes, I promised,' I crossed my heart.

He set a mug in front of me and removed his hand. There was something written on it. I picked it up and the words made every thought in my brain disintegrate.

In bright, colourful letters around the centre of the mug read:

Myster-E ♡ Captain Marple

I stared at the mug for what could have been days, for all I knew. Time was too complicated a concept for my head to wrap itself around. Everything was. I couldn't get it to connect dots.

'Um . . . can you blink or something so I know you haven't had a stroke?'

I pulled my eyes off the mug and stared at him. 'I-I don't . . . I don't – h-how do you know these names?'

'Because I'm him. I'm Myster-E.'

My brain scattered again but I forced myself to piece enough of it back together to speak.

'You can't be. You . . . no, it's not possible.'

'I know, it's insane but I'm him.'

'No. No, that makes no sense! The odds of meeting you here? Of all of the stuff we did – all our conversations? It doesn't . . . you can't be him!' I tried to get my brain to go back, to connect, to try and take the round peg of what he was saying and fit it into the square hole of my memory of it all. Nothing could make it fit.

'The thing is that I am, though.'

Was I on TV? Was that it? Some kind of horrible reality show? Were cameras about to burst out of nowhere and a waiter bring me a large glass of wine with a wink and sassy comment?

Oh God, I'd lost my mind.

'Ada, are you OK?'

Fraser's words somehow managed to chisel their way through the fog. I put both my hands on the table and forced myself to focus on the coolness of the wood, let it run up my arms and into my brain, settling the chaos a bit. 'Explain this, Fraser. I don't understand. Have you been lying to me this whole time?' My voice cracked as I hit the end of the sentence.

'No, Christ, no, I swear, I didn't know.'

'But you did, you literally wrote it on the mugs!' I cried.

'OK. So, you know how we met on . . . on the fanfic site? I nominated you for that award and we got chatting, yes?'

The ringing in my ears started up again. It felt like I was one step removed from my body. 'Of course I remember that.'

'Well, she – you – mentioned this café and I'd been wanting a new place to work to get out of my flat. I'd enjoyed chatting to you and I saw your picture and thought you were pretty so I decided I'd take a wander there one day and check it out and maybe see if I could spot you? I know – I know, that sounds so creepy in hindsight but I really didn't mean it that way, I swear!'

Wait, but that didn't make sense. 'I don't understand. How did you see a picture of me? I didn't even give my name.'

He stared at me like I'd produced a dead goldfish from my pocket. 'From your profile picture.'

I let out a laugh that bounced off the walls, drawing eyes to us. Slapping my hand over my mouth, I tried to stop but I couldn't. Maybe it was shock or straight-up hysteria but I thought I might actually hyperventilate I was laughing so hard. It took a solid minute to stop. 'That . . . that was,' I tried to suck in air, 'that was Captain Marvel! From the film *Captain Marvel*! That was Brie Larson!' I dissolved again. 'Like . . . Captain Marple instead of Marvel?'

'Yeah, well, I know that now, don't I?' he deadpanned.

'How did you not know that *then*? She's a famous actress!' I could barely keep my laughter below hysterical. A new thought occurred to me. 'But she . . . she was in that outfit and . . . oh my God, you thought that was *me*?'

'I dunno, I assumed it must be some kind of Halloween costume or something – it was a tiny picture. I've never seen the film!' He looked fairly scundered.

'She's a famous Hollywood actress!' I repeated. 'And you're a *journalist!*' I just couldn't wrap my head around him not knowing it.

'I told you – I don't watch Marvel movies! I kind of roughly know who she is but I honestly didn't recognise her from what you used. You have to admit, your picture was really low-quality!' He was smiling now too, clearly embarrassed.

He wasn't totally wrong – it had been a very low-res choice.

'Anyway, I came here looking for a blonde woman and didn't see anybody who might fit the description. And then I met you and we got chatting and we started hanging out and . . . you know the rest.'

I most certainly did not. 'Did you not wonder why you never met her . . . me . . . if you were coming here every day?'

He shrugged. 'You never mentioned the place again in your emails so I kind of assumed you'd stopped coming.'

Now that he'd mentioned it, he wasn't wrong about that either. I had stopped talking about work. About anything at all that involved Fraser. I'd told myself it was because we'd moved beyond day-to-day things. Myster-E and I had dived right into the big stuff so the little stuff didn't matter.

God, I really hadn't been paying attention to anything at all in my life, had I? I hadn't wanted to mention the time I was spending with Fraser.

Goddamn, wasn't that awkward now?

'Jesus, I must have been a colossal disappointment if you came here looking for the woman in my picture, low-res or otherwise.'

'You were never a disappointment.' He said it quietly, and I felt the laughter leaving me. I forced myself to hold his gaze despite every single atom in my being scream-ing to look at the floor or anywhere else that wasn't the searching spotlight of those eyes. They lit up every part

361

of me and I wasn't ready for what that might reveal. I found my voice again.

'I still don't understand. If you didn't know then, how did you find out?'

He leaned forward and took hold of his coffee. He picked it up as if to take a sip and then thought better, setting it back down. Clearly nervous. This wasn't good. 'So. This is the bit I need to apologise for. I know it's going to sound terrible but I really didn't know what else to do. Please don't be mad. Because I really am sorry I did this.'

Oh God. 'Go on.'

'I came to meet you . . . well, Captain Marple. And that's when I realised it was *you* you.'

My stomach shrivelled. Jesus, how had I forgotten? The fucker had stood me up. I'd wondered why and now I knew. He'd arrived, seen it was me and not some blonde stunner and ran away. Fucking hell. I could *feel* the colour draining from my face.

'No, no, no, it wasn't like that!' he said. 'This is why I said you have to hear me out.'

'What was it like, then? You left me there, sitting on my own. Why?' I could practically hear the words he didn't have the balls to say out loud. *Because I wasn't what he'd wanted*. Fuck, that was going to be a horrific sentence to hear out loud.

'But you weren't on your own!'

'What?'

'I was running late and when I got there, you were there with Neil.'

Anger made its way into the melee. 'Because I'd been left there by myself for over an hour!'

'No, no, I'm not having a go about it!' He shook his head. 'No, look. Let me start again with what I wanted to actually say. I was late because ... I was upset about our argument. And it coming off the back of the ball and ... the kiss. And then I lost my keys and had to get my flatmate to come back and let me in. By the time I got there and realised you were Captain Marple, I think I had some kind of panic attack or something. I couldn't make sense of anything. And you were so angry at me. I honestly thought, even without Neil being there, if I'd gone in and told you that I was Myster-E, you'd think it was some kind of weird catfish thing and not give me a chance to explain. I couldn't think of how to tell you. It's taken me all week to work through it.' He rubbed the back of his neck awkwardly, cheeks flushed. I felt the anger disappear as quickly as it had arrived. 'I know this is insane, but I swear I was going to tell you and I swear I never lied. I never would. Especially not with the stuff you told me about trust and everything that happened with your prick ex.'

He fell silent and we looked at each other across the table.

'You didn't reply to any of my messages. You just left me on my own in a bar.' I couldn't help it, it still stung too much not to say it to him.

'I know. I'm so sorry – it was a dick move.' He shook his head. 'I . . . panicked. I didn't know what to do so I ignored it until I could figure out a way to tell you.' He gestured to the mugs.

As I watched him, kind eyes full of worry, waiting for whatever my judgement might be, I felt a flicker of something bolt through the miasma of emotions swirling through me. I couldn't put my finger on what it was – excitement? Joy? Unadulterated relief? Maybe a mix of all those things. Myster-E was Fraser. Fraser was Myster-E. Two of my favourite people were the same person. How the fuck had the universe managed to pull that one out of the bag?

As we sat, Barista Bertie came through from the main café and approached our table. I hadn't realised he was in and I was ridiculously pleased to see him. 'Hey, Ada, hey, Fraser. Just letting you know that we're closing in five.'

I thanked him and turned back to Fraser, looking no less cornered than before. 'I think I need a drink. Want to come back to mine and talk?'

We walked in silence. I used the time to try to sew the information I had about Myster-E into the fabric of what I knew about Fraser. A part of me itched to take out my phone and read through all the messages to remind myself, but even I knew that'd probably be a step too far.

But I knew the big things. Losing his parents so young. Losing his uncle so recently. How much the grief had taken him by surprise. I glanced over at him. He had his hands in his pockets, watching the ground as he walked, letting me work my way through this. Fraser was so familiar and yet I hadn't known these huge things about him – not in real life. How had that happened? I'd known he lost his parents and that he was close to his aunt. He'd mentioned his uncle had been unwell a few years ago. But I hadn't known anything else about the rest of it. All I could think was how much I would have missed out on if we'd never connected the dots.

I was so busy trying to work through it all that it only occurred to me halfway back home that I wasn't sure of Mum's shift pattern that week. On balance, odds were she wouldn't be in but I still found myself holding my breath as I let us in the front door.

'Hello?' I called out. No reply. Phew. I wouldn't have to explain my mother or her *Heartbeat* obsession yet. Not when we had so much else to talk about.

'This is nice,' Fraser said, gazing around him. 'You live with your mum, right?'

'I do, yes. Like all the cool kids.' I felt so lame saying it and then immediately guilty. Emphatically *not* cool chatting shit about my home life when Mum was constantly going out of her way to help me.

He shrugged. 'You're hardly the first person to have to move back in with a parent.'

He really didn't seem to mind. But then I guess he'd known my situation longer than I'd realised.

'Want some wine?' I asked. Before he'd even answered, I'd barrelled my way to the kitchen and poured two glasses. Bringing them back to the living room, I handed him one.

We settled in on either ends of the sofa, facing each other with a cushion as the DMZ.

'Why Myster-E?' I asked, the thought suddenly popping into my head.

'As in why the username?'

I nodded.

'That's easy. I like mystery novels and my surname is Evans.'

Hah – I'd known his surname! How had none of this ever occurred to me? 'Like, as in *Why Didn't They Ask Evans?* Evans? You lucked-out there' I laughed. 'That's one *mystery* solved, I suppose. How did it never come up with us that we were both such huge Aggie fans?'

He shrugged. 'It's not really something I talk about to anyone. I used to with my uncle but the whole fanfic thing – it's . . . I'll be honest, it's something I've always been a bit embarrassed about.'

I couldn't blame him. I hadn't exactly gone out of my way to bring it up either. 'Your stories are really good. I know I've said that to you as Myster-E but yeah, I like them.'

'Yours too, obviously – even if you never did win that award I nominated you for,' he replied. 'And I promise: I'll take your Poirot sex dream confession to the grave with me.'

I felt the heat roll into my cheeks. 'Shut up!' I squealed. 'I wish I'd never told you that!'

He gave a chuckle. 'I'm glad you did.'

We fell into silence.

'I'll put some music on.' I grabbed my phone and picked the blandest lift music the internet had to offer.

We needed sound, not distraction. Anything to feel less gapingly exposed.

'Wow, that's an eclectic taste you have. What is that, free jazz?' It appeared Fraser was getting some of his own jazz back.

'Shut up!'

Sitting forward, his face took on an earnest look. 'But seriously. I don't find it . . . easy to open up about stuff. About how I feel and the things that have happened in my life. Talking to you online and the – I don't know, the anonymity of it all, I guess – it gave me a space to do it. *You* gave me a space to do it. And when I found out I knew you in real life, and not just knew you but was pretty much really into you by that point . . . well, it threw me. I felt so weird about it. And then I realised that it actually couldn't have been a better outcome. That I didn't want Captain Marpel to be anyone else but you.' My heart was taking up too much room in my chest when the thought that should have been first in line of any discussion came to me.

'Hang on a minute, you have a girlfriend!'

Fraser looked shocked at the sudden about-turn in the conversation. Then his brow crinkled in confusion. 'What?'

'In your emails, you said you were single. That you'd been engaged and broke it off last year!'

The confusion continued. 'Yeah?'

'But you're not. You have a girlfriend – I spoke to her on the phone! Lara?'

A few beats past and then realisation dawned. 'Lana?'

'Lana! Yes!'

'Lana isn't my girlfriend.'

Nah. Absolutely wasn't having that. 'Yes. Yes, she was. You were seeing her – she called your phone that day I answered it.'

'Lana and I were just . . . friends with benefits. We'd hang out sometimes, occasionally hook up. But I haven't seen her in ages. I think she's back in London now.'

I blinked at him, trying to wrap my head around what he was saying. A saxophone blared suddenly out of the blur of lift music. 'Don't sit here and pretend that you not mentioning she wasn't your girlfriend wasn't deliberate. You could have cleared that up at any point and you actively didn't! Even after we kissed!'

He shifted a bit in his seat and took a gulp of wine, looking slightly cornered. 'OK, OK, I'll confess – I didn't correct immediately in the first instance when you called her my girlfriend. But it was because we'd only just met and I knew you had Neil so I figured you thinking I had someone would let you know that I wasn't just trying to hit on you or make a move or something. Plus . . . there was Captain Marple. I was finding myself increasingly . . . stuck. I was loving my online thing with her but then I'd see you and hang out with you and . . . yeah. It caused me some issues, I will admit.' He was turning pink again.

He wasn't the only one. I pressed my fingers to my flushed cheeks, enjoying the coolness of them from holding my wine.

'How's Neil doing anyway?' he asked, in a not totally casual way.

I suddenly found it hard to meet his eye. 'He's fine, I think.'

'You think? Did you guys break up?'

I *really* didn't want to talk about Neil. 'I mean, we weren't really together. It was more of a friends with benefits thing too.'

'Ah, I see.' I heard rather than saw him set his glass down on the coffee table. 'Did he know that?'

'Fuck off!' I cried, stung. OK, so he wasn't totally wrong. Didn't mean he needed to be a dick about it. There was a chance I might have still been feeling a bit tender on that one.

'Sorry. That was out of line,' he conceded.

I took another sip of my drink. 'Either way, we're not together.'

'How did he take it?'

'He's fine. We both agreed we weren't well matched.'

'I wouldn't be so sure he's fine. You're a lot to lose.' He said it so quietly that I almost didn't catch it. Almost.

My throat was getting prickly. 'That might be the nicest thing anyone's ever said to me.'

'I don't believe that for a second.'

And there were those eyes again. Suddenly the pillow between us felt like a mountain. Why was I sitting so far away from him?

'Want some more wine?' I asked, wondering if I could somehow wangle it so that when I sat back down, I could magically disappear under the bloody cushion.

'Um, sure?'

I stood and went to lift his glass, not realising till I had that it was still half-full. 'Sorry,' I turned to find that he had stood up. There was maybe an inch of space between us. He took the wine from my hand and set it back down on the coffee table, never taking his eyes off me. Watching me with an intensity I hadn't seen in him before. It fizzed all the way through me.

'Hey,' I smiled up at him.

'Hey, yourself,' he returned.

And then he was leaning in, cupping my face with his hands and I found that I no longer gave a shit about more wine.

I wrapped my arms around his neck and pulled him to me, revelling in the feel of his lips, as his tongue found mine. Jesus, it felt amazing. How had I managed to walk away from this at the ball?

Then his hands were winding through my hair and down my back, pulling me closer and closer until I could feel every line, every muscle, every hard part of him.

And then he was fumbling with the bottom of my top, pulling it over my head and I was returning the favour until we were both in only our underwear and his lips were on my neck and lower and . . .

'No, shit, wait,' I gasped out.

He froze. 'What? Are you OK?'

'Yeah, no fine. It's just, we're in my living room and . . . well, I don't live alone.'

It took him a second to connect the dots and then I thought his eyes might roll out of his head. 'Fuck!' He dived down and grabbed his T-shirt and jeans, holding them to himself as if it would have in any way covered him, had my mother chosen that moment to amble in the door.

I couldn't help but laugh. 'She's not here now, Casanova. I meant we should take this somewhere more private.'

For a second he looked absolutely scundered. 'Right, yeah.'

'Come on, then.' I leaned forward, took his hand and led him to my bedroom, closing the door firmly behind me. He was looking around again.

'Nice,' he said, as if he wasn't standing there in only his underwear.

I felt a bubble of pure adoration pop, sending little flecks of happiness showering over me. Reaching forward, I pulled him towards me as we tumbled backwards onto the bed.

I came to to find the sun peaking in through a gap in my bedroom curtains. Why did I never fully close those?

Fraser was curled around me and I could feel his breath on the back of my neck. I lay for a moment, revelling in the feel of his nearness and the memory of the night of unbelievable sex we'd had.

He stirred beside me, somehow pulling me closer.

'Good morning,' he murmured against the back of my neck.

I felt a shiver run through me. Goddamn was I into him. 'Hey,' I replied. My phone buzzed and I leaned away from him to grab it.

'No,' he groaned. 'I was comfortable.'

I twisted around and kissed him.

'Ah, that's better.'

We watched each other for a moment in silence.

'So, what's the plan?' he asked.

'For today?'

'Sure.'

'Well, I was thinking we could get some breakfast, maybe go for a walk?'

'All good options.'

I swiped into my phone and felt everything freeze.

There was a reply from Veronica.

'Sorry, one sec.' I pulled myself up and opened the email. Sure enough, she was telling me she'd happily work with me again. I felt my stomach fold up like a lawn chair.

Fraser followed my lead and sat up. 'What's wrong?'

Oh God. When I'd sent that email, London had seemed like such a good idea.

His arm snaked around me and he planted a butterfly-light kiss on my shoulder. 'Everything OK?'

I moved to face him. It was best to do this fast. 'OK, so, after I dumped Steve as a client, I sent an email to my old boss, Veronica. She's started up a new freelance event company so I asked if she wanted to bring me on board.'

'That's a great idea!' he beamed.

'Yeah, it is . . . but she's based in London.'

The beam dimmed. 'Wait – what? You want to move back to London?'

'No! I mean, not really, it's just there's so much more opportunity for me there.' I sighed. 'But now? Urgh, I don't know what to do. I need work.'

Fraser frowned. 'But Edinburgh is full of events. Jesus, you can't move for them three quarters of the year.'

'Yeah, but it's not London.' And then it hit me. Of course! It didn't need to be. I sat up fully. 'What if I suggest to Veronica that I work with her from here? I could go to London when I'm needed there. In this day and age – and in my industry – there's no real reason why I can't just commute, right?' The more I thought about it, the more I thought it was a genuinely good idea. If anything, it might even be of use to Veronica – after all, she knew me and how I worked and she already trusted me to get stuff done. Plus I had more contacts in Edinburgh than she did and that was surely not to be sniffed at? 'Yes. I'll run it past her. It's worth a go, at any rate. And who knows? Maybe she'll appreciate the gumption.'

'I bet she will. I know I do.' He planted a kiss on my neck.

'You do, do you?'

'Oh yeah, gumption really gets me going ...' he purred dramatically.

I felt a giddy wave of joy run through me at the thought of getting to hang out with this one some more.

I dropped my phone back onto the bedside cabinet and pulled him into a deep kiss.

Epilogue

'Why are there dinosaurs in our catering space?' Veronica strode into the conference hall I was in the middle of setting up for our Contrast Creative Productions launch.

I paused laying out some of our event brochures onto seats. 'Um, pass?' As I spoke, sure enough what looked like three – I wanted to say velociraptors – came tearing past the tent. As a child of *Jurassic Park*, this was a very unnerving sight. 'Oh wait, I know what that is. There's a showing of that new kids' dinosaur film. You know, with the singing pterodactyls and . . .' Veronica gave me a look. She did not care for the details. 'Fair enough. I'll tell the stewards to try and keep them to their bit.'

'They almost knocked over a whole table of prosecco.' She shuddered. 'Honestly, not a day goes by I'm not glad I don't have kids.'

As yet more screaming tiny dinosaurs marauded past, I couldn't argue her point.

'Did you manage to sort the AV mix-up?' I asked. 'Cos I can ask that John guy at the front desk – he said he could search out a spare projector if we needed it.'

Veronica gave me side-eye and a grin. 'I bet he did.'

'Oh, ha ha.' It was so unnerving having *Veronica* joke about that kind of thing. Fraser would also be thrilled to hear it, no doubt.

'Hey, Ada!'

I glanced up to see Amal sailing towards me, looking very snazzy in a yellow cashmere jumper. I, meanwhile, looked extra suave in my leggings and *Contrast Creative* hoodie. 'Twas ever thus. 'Hey, love!' I set down my remaining brochures and gathered her into a big hug. 'Let me just finish setting these up and we can nip upstairs and get lunch.'

Amal laid her sandwich and cup of tea on the table and settled into the chair opposite me. Aiden had taken Benji and Mo to a 'forest school' in the Meadows – which felt as though it was missing a fairly key ingredient, if I was being honest – to give her some Saturday free time.

I curled my hand around my own steaming mug of coffee and took a sip. 'How was your weekend away?'

'It was lovely! So great to get away. The kids *loved* their inflatable neon wings, by the way. Couldn't get them off Mo. Pretty sure they've fused to his skin now.'

I beamed. 'I do have excellent taste.'

Amal pulled out her phone to show me a picture. She was in a pool being dive-bombed by Benji as Mo planted a huge kiss on her cheek. She was laughing and the neon pink of Mo's wings were highlighting how glowy she was – she looked better than I'd seen her in months and, sitting in front of me now, it hadn't worn off. I was *thrilled*.

'Aww, oh my God, I love it! Send me it, will you?' I cooed. 'Can't wait for Benji to regale me on Monday when I get back to the babysitting.'

'Be warned, he's still not nailed the whole "pacing" part of a story so you're in for a bit of a slog.'

'Consider me warned,' I grinned. 'What's on the agenda for this particular date night? Not sure you'll be able to top that snazzy hotel.'

Amal raised an eyebrow. 'You have no idea.'

I let out a cheer. 'Glad to hear that I can still hook a sister up, even after all these years.'

My phone bleeped to let me know I had an email. I glanced at the subject line and then opened the email. 'Yesss!' I set the phone back down on the table. 'Indigo Dance have *finally* agreed to meet with me again after the whole Steve fiasco thing. God, that's taken so much work just to get my foot back in the door.' Bloody Steve.

'That's great news! God, I still can't believe his book went to number one, though. I saw he's being his usual self on that celebrity dating thing as well. You've dodged a hail of bullets there, I reckon.'

I laughed. 'Jesus, I know – not nearly enough synonyms for sorry in the world. Pity the publicist who has to wrangle that basket of nightmares.'

'He did make a good apology, though – and he seemed to really mean it. He's mostly harmless.'

'Aye, in the same way reheating three-day-old rice is mostly harmless: fine, until bam. Diarrhoea till you're dead. Mum still hasn't forgiven me for dropping him, mind.'

'What a delightful image.' She took a drink of her tea. 'Have you told her you're flat-hunting yet?'

'I did. She's thrilled to be getting her love nest back. Planning a *lot* of raves.'

'Well, good because as luck would have it . . .' Amal leaned over and pulled her laptop out of her bag, 'I may have done a little bit of research and found a few potentials for you.'

She opened it and swung it over to me. There was a document full of links and information on rental options, local information, council tax bands and an address for the Police Scotland website with crime reports on the areas.

'Amal, this is insane! You've done everything bar put down a deposit!'

For a split second, she looked slightly worried. 'Shit, I'm doing it again, aren't I? Sorry, it's not that I don't think you can do it – I just thought it would be helpful.'

'It's fine,' I laughed. Leaning forward, I put my hand over hers. 'You know you don't have to do this for me though, right? I will love you regardless.'

She squeezed my hand back. 'I'm sorry. I'll stop.'

I leaned back again. 'I mean, I wouldn't say no to a *little* help.'

'Fantastic! Because I lied. I'm definitely not going to stop.' She took another bite of her sandwich. 'How's the launch shaping up? I have to say, there are more dinosaurs involved than I was expecting.'

'Oh God, *don't*. Veronica's one step away from engineering an asteroid.' I shook my head. 'Are you guys still coming tonight?'

'Yep. The babysitter is locked in, some wine is chilling in the fridge and Aiden has *almost* managed to negotiate a slightly earlier bedtime for Benji so we might get a slight chance at actually drinking the wine before we leave.'

'Give that man a biscuit.'

My phone buzzed a message from Fraser. I clicked it open to find a picture of a sign that read THE LIBRARY OF CRIMINAL ENTERPRISE, with an arrow pointing down a creepy side street. Underneath was a text: *Came across this random inexplicable sign on my walk just now. Ready for another weird adventure, Captain?*

I replied a quick affirmative with many thumbs up and a smattering of kisses.

He replied almost instantly. *Good luck for the launch prep – see you tonight. I'll be the guy with the bowler hat and weird moustache xx*

I let out a snort. Jeez, you have one sex dream about Poirot and just never live it down. That was the last time I was ever telling secrets to a random stranger on the internet.

Acknowledgements

I'm going to level with you, if I were to list every single person I needed to thank in life, we'd be here 'til we're all dead, which doesn't seem like an overly good use of time, so I'll keep this brief and mostly book-related.

A huge thank you to my magnificent agent Florence Rees – without you taking me on board and believing I could pull this off, I wouldn't be fulfilling what is kind of a life-long dream so thank you for that (here's hoping this is the first of many!).

To Sarah Bauer, Katie Meegan and the Bonnier Zaffre team, thank you for working with me, trusting me and giving me the opportunity of shoving this bad boy into the world.

To Anthea Middleton and Alex Cammack, who have possibly read this book more times than I have. I wouldn't have got through this without your help, patience, frankly astronomical eye for detail and endless capacity for bouncing ideas off. I bet you're hoping this isn't the first of many.

To the Skriva Writing School and the writing friends I made there. Sophie Cooke, Lyndsey Croal, Jo Cole-Hamilton, Erica Stewart-Jones and Emma Steele (plus

Anthea, of course!) – our wee group and everything it taught me got me here and I'm so grateful for our time in that cosy little room in the attic of the Arthur Conan Doyle Centre.

To Mum and Dad (Pauline and Paul – actual names, would you believe), my sister Vicky, my brothers Ryan and Steven and all my family. You're a bunch of mad bastards – you make my life infinitely more interesting and I love you millions and billions and trillions. I don't know what I'd be without you.

To my friends, who I won't list for fear of missing anyone but you know who you are – I friggin' love you people. You help me live my absolute best life, put up with my ridiculousness and even tolerate me starting my Christmas prep in July (well . . . tolerate might be a strong word). You keep me afloat and I'd be lost without you so thank you – I love you a frankly embarrassing amount.